At the Crossroads

At the Crossroads

Global Security Unlimited 2

Sharon Michalove

Coffee and Eclair Books

Editor: Mackenzie Walton

Book Cover: Stefanie Fontecha, Beetiful Book Covers

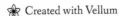 Created with Vellum

I create stories full of romance, suspense, and mystery. Seasoned romance where love has no age limit. Stories that prove second chances can happen, enemies can become friends, and friends can become lovers. Stories that show no two happy endings are the same. And at the core of every story is love.

I know there is no straight road. No straight road in this world. Only a giant labyrinth of intersecting crossroads.

Frederico Garcia Lorca

When at a crossroads, my father was fond of saying, "Go with your gut."

"Intuition," he said, "always has our best interests at heart. It is a voice that can tell us who is friend and who is foe... Which ones to hold at arm's length... And which ones to keep close. But too often, we become distracted by fear, doubt, our own stubborn hopes, and refuse to listen."

Emily Thorne

To the many great tour guides, particularly Fiona Lukas of London Walks, who has a cameo in this book. They have all enriched my life and inspired my writing, both in person and virtually.

Chapter One

November 2003
Grant House, near Grantown-on-Spey

Brian Grant sat on the sofa in one of the five reception rooms in the family's seventeenth-century Grade II listed house and sipped from a bottle of Belhaven Best ale, washing down a mouthful of cheese and onion crisps. The wood-paneled walls and rustic stone fireplace gave it a cozy feel, unexpected in such a big house. A television sat on a table, angled to make viewing convenient from anywhere in the large, rectangular room.

Now the days were colder, and the nights drawing in earlier, he spent less time in the hangar, tinkering with his granddad's World War I–era planes, and more time indoors, watching the box. Documentaries and sport for the most part. All five of kids had played rugby at school. Only their middle son, Max, continued to play, scoring the winning goal for Oxford in the Varsity Match against Cambridge in his senior year.

Today was a much-anticipated documentary on RAF prisoners in the Second World War. As a retired pilot, anything about the service drew his interest, especially programs about World War II. His dad, a flying ace, was shot down over Germany in 1942, and spent the rest of his war in a German Stalag. His grandfather had been one of the few in the Royal Flying Corps in the First War to come home.

A message flashed on the screen. "We interrupt this program for breaking news."

Brian groaned. What bloody disaster had happened now?

The scene shifted to a newsroom desk with a screen behind it trumpeting New Terrorist Attack in Turkey. Brian glared at the seemingly impassive news announcer, who had laced his fingers together, the tips turning white.

"Today, in the aftermath of the 15th and 20th of November Istanbul terrorist bombings, several smaller attacks have taken place."

A map of a portion of Istanbul came up on the screen, a red arrow pointing to the site. Max, Brian thought. He's in Istanbul. Brian's ragged breath and racing heart had him groping for his pills.

"In a narrow alley in the Fatih district, terrorists set an ambush for a Turkish counterterrorism unit. On the scene, Alisa Brand has this report."

A picture of a bomb-shattered Istanbul alley appeared, newly opened space surrounded by stubs of buildings, small craters, bricks, and twisted metal. Flames flared and danced in narrow rings around pools of oil, wisps of smoke hanging in the air. A woman dressed in khaki slacks, black polo neck sweater, and flak jacket held a microphone so close to her mouth she might have been licking an ice cream cone. Her short blond hair was pushed back.

"At one end of the alley are the remains of a rusted red compact car." The camera panned to the right, where a deconstructed metal skeleton glinted with hints of reddish paint. She took in a noticeable gulp of air. "Reports were received that a terrorist cell connected to Al-Qaeda in Turkey was operating in the vicinity. A Turkish antiterrorism unit was dispatched to this location"

Brian's eyes widened, and his hand shook. He put down his beer and called out to his wife. "Viktoria!" No response. Bloody hell. Where in the enormous expanse of Grant House was she? After a second, louder bellow went unanswered, he picked up his mobile to text her, never taking his eyes off the television screen.

Viktoria. Come to the sitting room. Fast as you can.

Brian refocused on the reporter's words. He detected an underlying tremor as she continued.

"Several hours ago, three Turkish security jeeps crowded into the narrow space when the booby-trapped car exploded. A fourth vehicle was starting the turn and was out of range of the explosion. According to witnesses, a deafening roar was followed by a moment of eerie silence. Then there was the blare of returning noise—loud booms interspersed with the tinkling of glass and brick, and sharp reports of metal hitting metal as a hail of nails, screws, and other sharp objects blew out of the IED. Vehicle gas tanks exploded, and the walls of abandoned factory buildings collapsed."

As Brian perched on the edge of sofa, his body reached

3

forward as if to run toward the correspondent. He heard, rather than saw, Viktoria Grant stalk into the room. Her thick silver mane swung around her shoulders.

"What is it, Brian?" Her voice was sharp with the ghost of a Russian accent.

Silently, he gestured toward the scene. Viktoria turned. Her mouth opened, but no sound came out.

"One terrorist is dead, and two others apprehended while fleeing the scene. Of the eight members of the counterterrorism unit, only the two in the last vehicle survived, including Turkish driver Ahmet Iskander and a British citizen consulting with Turkish security services." A camera swung to show a stretcher being loaded into an ambulance.

The reporter's voice continued as the camera swung to a tall, hawk-faced Turk standing next to her. "This is Burak Hazan, a representative of the Turkish Security Forces." She gave a slight pause. "Burak, could you explain what happened here?"

Hazan's voice, British intonation overlaying his Turkish accent, poured out like honey. But the camera had shifted again and the man staring out at the viewers was not the clean-shaven Turk in his olive drab uniform.

A different man was being walked toward an ambulance by paramedics. Brian gasped, squeezing his wife's hand, as the camera zoomed in for a close-up of a shockingly familiar face, blackened with soot, blood oozing from the tiny cuts that scored his skin. Dust and debris powdered his black hair, giving him the air of an eighteenth-century gentleman battered by time travel.

Sound faded away as they stood in front of the screen, transfixed by the image of the stumbling figure with sunken steel-gray eyes, clouded with pain and shock.

Brian hazarded a glance at his wife. Viktoria pulled her

hand back, then crossed herself. Her cry was breathy with horror and despair. "Oh my god. It's Max. At least he's alive."

Brian stepped forward, tears of relief running down his furrowed cheeks, and caught her as she crumpled toward the floor.

Chapter Two

C hicago, Illinois
    March 2014
    Max

Maria Alvarez stands in front of the antique oak desk that takes up half the space in my corner office and shifts from foot to foot. Petite, with dark, shoulder-length brown hair, she resembles Little Red Riding Hood confronting the Big Bad Wolf. Amused, I give her my best wolfish expression. I've suggested twice that the new PR director at Global Security Unlimited sit down, but she insists on standing, hands clasped in front of her, gnawing bright red lipstick off her lower lip. Although just shy of thirty, she appears younger. Anyone passing my office would think I'm the headmaster, and she an errant student.

When I glance up from the media release she wants me to approve, her face is scrunched with tension. I recheck the draft and pencil in the changes. The announcement of the roll out for our banking software is fine but a little wordy.

I catch her eye, lean over, and hand the sheet back to her. "Here you go, Maria. I made a few changes but nothing major. Just make sure the division name, CyberSec, is spelled correctly. The three mentions are all different."

She flushes to the roots of her hair. "I'm so sorry."

Waving off the apology, I tell her, "Just fix the few things I've marked and you can shoot it off to the distribution list."

She skims the sheet, frown lines on her forehead, her lips pinched. When she finishes, the corners of her mouth lift into a small smile.

I smile back. "You're doing a great job."

"Thanks, Mr. Grant. Oh, sorry, Dr. Grant." Her face is bright red.

"Max. Just Max." I throw her a farewell wave as she turns toward the open doorway.

After she leaves, I peek out the window of my fourth-floor office in the Rookery, tapping my fingers on the arm of my chair as rain streams down the side of the building. The deluge sounds like a waterfall against the imitation Romanesque stone façade and drowns out the usual honking of taxis and the scream of sirens from the street.

A stab of disappointment makes me wince. Cress sent me an email earlier to tell me it was too wet, so she wasn't going to write at Toni's Patisserie today. Instead of a tête-à-tête with *la mia stellina* I'll have to make do with another cuppa from the company lounge.

My favorite picture of the two of us sits front and center on the wide sill of the window. I run my finger down her face as if I could touch her. It was taken last year at a British consulate reception at Chicago's legendary Palmer House, before the evening turned violent. Cress is gorgeous in the black lace gown that was ruined when she was shot outside the hotel by a vengeful sociopath. The David Yurman earrings and necklace I bought her for that evening are the only pieces that survived.

I shake my head, turn back to the computer sitting on a credenza perpendicular to my desk and pull up my diary. The April drop date for our roll out, marked in red, pulses out from one of the multiple screens crowded on the surface. I rub my thumb across my chin.

Don't worry, Max. We'll be ready. Jarvis' assurance echoes over and over. I want to believe him. It's his baby, after all, but my gut hurts on the regular. Another screen is nothing but emails updating projects and requests.

Turning away, I cast my eye over the in and out boxes, printouts, and half-empty teacups littering the desktop. I clatter together the crockery, pouring all the bits of scummy, cold liquid into one large cup. I really need to take these back to the kitchen instead of letting them pile up. Not really fair on my assistant to assume she'll clear up the mess.

Kyril, our mail room courier comes in and dumps a dirty white hotel envelope with the name of a hotel in Konya, Turkey, on my desk. No sender's name, covered with foreign stamps, all taped up, handwritten address with just my last name, and Rookery Building Chicago with no street address. The postmark, Istanbul, is already a month old. My heart sinks as I think about the last time I was in Istanbul. Ten years ago. Right away I can tell its trouble.

"Wash your fucking hands, Kyril! And tell Elena to call 911." His frightened eyes regard me like a stoat caught in headlamps. "Go, Kyril. Hands, then the call. Now."

He slowly backs away from my desk toward the doorway. When he reaches the opening, he gives me a panicked glance, then turns and runs.

I pull my leather driving gloves out of my overcoat pocket, slide the envelope onto a piece of printer paper, and walk down to our small conference room, placing it carefully on the table.

Almost immediately a brisk Anglo-Turkish voice calls out from the doorway. "Hey, Max. Got a minute?"

Metin Hazan leans against the doorframe, a manila folder in one hand. I wave her in. At six-foot-two, she's tall enough to look me in the eye. Even at fifty-four, her athletic physique is stunning since she runs every day. I know a little about Turkish culture, and after years of burning curiosity, I asked her a few years ago why her parents gave her a masculine name.

"They wanted a son." Her voice was flat, and remnants of resentment marred her face. "Unfulfilled desire. They had three daughters and gave us all male names."

Now I summon a smile. "What brings the Senior Operations VP to our little corner, Metin? You hardly ever slum around over here."

She focuses on the envelope but is careful not to touch it. "What do we have here?"

"Good question. Suspicious envelope. I was just planning to lock this room until the police get here."

We leave the envelope and walk back to my office to wait.

Once we sit down, her smile shifts to a frown. "I know you and Cress are leaving for Europe soon."

"We have that meeting with the bankers in London about adopting our software. They insisted they wanted to meet in person. Then Cress and I have a week in Scotland for my dad's birthday, Cress' awards dinner in Paris, and her historical fiction conference in Venice." I smile thinly.

Metin leans back in the oversized armchair and repositions the folder. One arm drapes down, long fingers tapping against the leather. "Busy, busy."

She pauses and throws me a tiny smile, but the way her fingers weave together, so tight her knuckles are white, undermines her try at nonchalance. "The NSA picked up some chatter. Maybe it's connected to this mysterious delivery." She taps the folder and nudges it closer to me.

"Hacking alerts?" Hacking threats are so common that I can't imagine why they'd bother to pass anything on unless it's a major security alert. CyberSec has two security analysts who work on nothing but threats. We're bombarded with at least a thousand hacking attempts a day.

"No." She shakes her head slightly. "Nothing to do with GSU directly."

I slip my fingers onto the smooth paper cover and pull it closer and flip it open. Inside are some papers clipped together. I glance over the flimsy onionskin paper. The first is a half sheet with text messages.

> SKYWATCHER: *the breeze is blowing*
> DEMETER: *the holy grail?*
> SKYWATCHER: ...
> DEMETER: *This is bad*
> DEMETER: *and...*
> SKYWATCHER: *Smiley*
> DEMETER: *Okay*

I wince inwardly at the Smiley reference, but don't bite. I'm still not sure how I ended up with the nickname but John Le Carré is everywhere in the spy world. Even though I know the answer, I still ask the question. "Who are these from?"

"Texts between me and the NSA."

I nod at the confirmation, then move on. The other sheet, marked *Top Secret*, has today's date, an update from a communique released a month ago. I scan it quickly, noting the important names—mine and Nasim Faez.

My scalp prickles. Faez has been in prison for the last ten years. My testimony helped put him there after the bombing of an alley in Istanbul that killed most of Turkish security team I was working with. I skim the rest of the document.

I put the papers back and toss the folder on top of the bumf already there, trying to control my shaking fingers. "Shit. I can't believe this..." I can hardly get the words out. "The man was in a high-security prison. How the fuck did he escape?"

Metin's lips twist into a frown. "They moved him to a medium-security prison last year. No one seems to know why. Payoffs? Perhaps as part of a plan to let him escape."

"Why are we only hearing now, a month after the fact?"

She shifts uncomfortably, crossing and uncrossing her legs. "Sorting out the identification of the bodies has been tricky, but now the Turkish police believe Faez was not in the fuel refinery when it exploded. After the fiasco of allowing him to be moved to a lower-security prison, the Turks are giving out very little information."

I run my tongue over my lips. My mouth tastes of salt, and I realize sweat droplets are running down my face. I swipe them away with the back of my hand. Deep breaths help bring my heart rate closer to normal, but my voice is still full of gravel. "Bloody Nasim Faez."

We're both silent for far too long before I go on. "Thought he'd die in prison." I take off my glasses and rub my eyes, feeling phantom debris. A souvenir of the ambush. My hand trembles as I squeeze in some prescription eye drops, which run down my face, mixing with the remnants of the sweat. Damn.

Metin sits back, arms folded, and waits for me to go on.

"I'm not surprised I've heard nothing official from MI6." Hacking as if I had swallowed sandpaper, I wipe my eyes. "Allan Mason is in charge of Turkish operations now, and let's say there's no love lost."

"I heard there were some tensions." Her tone is dry, but the widening of her eyes betrays curiosity.

I choke, then take another sip of water. "Allan felt I was in the way of his advancement." Our acrimonious history goes back to our schooldays, but I don't bother to explain. I lean the chair onto its back wheels, then rock forward. "I was a highflier until the cock-up in Istanbul."

The police take pictures, put the envelope into a special container, and tell us they will let us know when they have the test results. Two detectives arrive a few minutes later and question us about the sequence of events. As they leave, I wonder if Faez sent this as a warning.

Now our CEO Clay Brandon, Metin, and the head of our security division, JL Martin, and I sit around the same conference table examining photos of the original. Addressed to me in block capitals, stamps festoon the outside of the envelope along with a printed drawing depicting a dervish. The smeared postmark and crumpled appearance makes me fancy the sender used a carrier pigeon, or at least on a cargo ship, rather than airmail. A slight rip in the paper reveals a shiny sliver, which the police told us is a small glassine envelope inside.

"Konya!" Metin stares at the photo. Dirty, creased, and crisscrossed with tape, the return address of a hotel in Konya is clearly visible. "Faez was imprisoned near there." She taps her finger against the photo. "I think that's a confirmation." Her eyes narrow as she stares at me, willing me to say something. I fold my arms across my chest, lips pressed in a thin line, and say nothing.

Metin's rubs her foot against the bottom crossbar of the oak conference table as the silence lengthens. Finally, with a sigh of exasperation, she barks at me, "But why was he hanging around there?"

"No idea." I shrug. "Maybe he has confederates in Konya, and they hid him there. He could have picked up an envelope."

"Unlikely, unless the hotel serves as a safe house. The papers splashed his photo everywhere when he was convicted." Her voice is shaky, going up and down the scale like a marimba player. She shifts back and forth in her chair, searching for a more comfortable position. Then she rubs a finger around the rim of her personal Turkish tea glass. Watching her fidget, I remember she still has family members living somewhere around there.

I put my hand on her wrist and examine her expression. "That was ten years ago. Anyway, I have no idea why he would have stayed in Konya." I remember my real connection with Konya, and swipe the back of my hand along my damp hairline. "It's possible he hasn't left the country and was hiding out there."

"If he was there, he obviously moved on to Istanbul before he sent this." Clay flicks the picture with his forefinger.

"Not necessarily. He could have given the envelope to a confederate to mail from Istanbul."

Clay scratches his cheek. "So we're all speculating with practically no data."

"What do you think is in it?" JL's brow furrows.

"Ricin, anthrax, talc." Metin's voice is matter of fact. "Any number of things are possible."

"Talc?" Clay sounds confounded. "Surely talc isn't dangerous."

"It's used to mimic other white powders, when you want to send a warning rather than kill someone." I rub my temples with my forefingers, attempting to stave off an imminent headache.

"Tabernak!" JL's voice explodes into the silence. "Who wants to kill you, Max?"

"Probably lots of people. I'm sure sometimes Cress would love to wring my neck." No one laughs.

"Is this a credible threat, Max?" Clay's voice is dangerously quiet.

Metin's voice smothers mine. "You saw the notice, Clay. I think this is a confirmation of a credible threat."

I massage my neck to relax my vocal cords. "We can't be sure he would target me after all this time." I'm still trying to downplay the situation.

Metin picks up the photo. "Stop playing the ostrich, Max."

"Why send a warning?" JL makes a growling noise. "Why not blow up your car, shoot you, whatever?"

"I don't know why unless he wants to watch me die. If he can't come to the US, this might be a lure to bring me to Istanbul." A familiar, gritty sensation irritates my eyes. I take off my glasses and put in more drops, wiping at the errant liquid that escapes down my cheeks.

Clay frowns and runs fingers over his scalp, leaving his blond hair in spikes. "You're flying out on Sunday?"

JL rubs his chin. "Why do you think Faez will have better luck getting into the UK?"

"If he travels on a fake EU passport, he can probably catch the Eurostar in Paris. Easy-peasy." I take a sip of the now-cold brew Elena, Clay's PA, had brought in at the beginning of the meeting.

"So, is there something we need to know about Konya, something connected to you rather than to Faez being in jail there?" Metin's voice rises with each word.

"My visit to Konya has nothing to do with Faez." My words echo in the quiet room.

"There is a Konya story?" Metin is persistent and I cave.

"Konya has nothing to do with Faez." I stare at the at the table top, trying to get my thoughts in order. "Faez is all about Istanbul." I pause. "And the ambush."

The three faces around the table are bemused.

"Faez wouldn't know about my one trip to Konya." I pick up my mug. The dregs, filmed over with scummy milk, are disgusting. Pushing back my chair, I stand and stretch. I should tell them the envelope is from the hotel I stayed at in '03. "I need a refill."

Clay motions me to sit back down. Picking up his phone, he hits some numbers. "Elena, would you bring another mug for Max, please?" Metin holds up her empty glass. "In fact, bring a few clean mugs, milk, and carafes of both drinks. Thanks."

Once the refills arrive, Metin leans over and picks up the tea carafe. "Let me be mother." Clay and JL look bemused while I shoot her a small smile. The expression reminds me her parents sent her to England to be educated at Badminton, one of the premier girls' schools.

I pick up my fresh drink and add a bit of milk and a sprinkling of sugar to the fresh, hot tea. Then I take a sip, put down the mug, tip my chair back and forth a few times, and finally lean into the table, my elbows and fists making a platform for my chin.

"MI6 sent me to Istanbul in late September 2003 to

work with Turkish security on credible terrorist threats to Britain. They teamed me up with a group of six Turkish security agents, including Yavuz and Zehra Arslan."

I squirm in my seat, wanting to stand, but—etiquette. I shift slightly, trying to stretch my legs under the table, but I end up kicking both Metin and Clay.

"Sorry," I murmur. "I expected a lot of suspicion when I came onboard, but everyone was very welcoming." I grimace at the memory. "And here I was, turning up like a bad penny."

Confusion clouds every face. "Seven is a lucky number, eight is not, but no one grumbled. We called our temporary team Octave," I explain.

JL gives a grunt of astonishment at the musical reference. "Who thought up that name? I assume not you with your well-known philistinism when it comes to music."

My smile is a brief upturn to the corners of my mouth. "Probably didn't hurt that I speak Turkish reasonably well."

"Did you have special training before they sent you there?" Clay asks.

I quirk an eyebrow. "Good at languages."

Clay growls. "I know about your language skills. I meant special counterterrorism training."

I snort. "Field operatives have that training, with updates as needed."

Eyes lifted toward the ceiling, Metin's clouded face resembles the Greek goddess Hera when she discovers Zeus has been unfaithful again. "Konya."

Not sure where to start with this utterly pointless story, I stay silent.

Seconds creep by. Each one is like hours. Chairs creak. My skin heats from glares emanating from the tribunal.

I crack. "Two weeks into the assignment, we had a little

time off. Yavuz and Zehra proposed a trip to Konya to take in the Rumi sights and take in a performance by the dervishes." Mouth dry, I take a swallow of tea, choking slightly as a muscle in my cheek twitches with nerves.

Back under control, I continue. "I was having difficulty with the posting because I had found out my cousin was dying, and my masters had refused compassionate leave had."

The lack of reaction clues me in. All of this must be in my fucking personnel file. I push on.

"I was very vulnerable and Zehra was exquisite." I sigh. Her long, red hair, willowy body, and the seductive curve of her calves. Yeah, I was susceptible. I was angry and my life was shit. I grabbed her with both hands. "Anyway, we started an affair, and I moved out of my hotel and into her flat."

I stop. Three expressionless faces. "Her brother wasn't best pleased. But we rubbed along. And the three of us took the trip to Konya a week before the bombings."

"Brother's name?" Metin picks up her mobile, ready to text.

"Yavuz Arslan. Why?"

"Always best to cross the Ts and dot the Is."

I lean over the table to grab one of the bottles of water sitting in the center, my breath ragged, chest heaving as if I had run a marathon.

"If you'd asked, I would have tossed you one." JL mimes throwing one at my head.

I gulp down a few swallows, coughing as the water catches in my windpipe. A few deep breaths later, I squeeze out a few words. "That's it. That's the story. No connection to Nasim Faez."

Clay's phone rings. He nods his head a few times,

making some indeterminate noises. He turns to us. "That was the lab."

One advantage we have as a company is Clay's network of connections, which in this case fast tracks the analysis of the envelope contents. "Talc."

We all breathe a sigh of relief.

"And a message." He pauses for dramatic effect. "Istanbul."

A beep alerts has us all focusing on Metin, who has a response to her text. "Yavuz appears clean. Except..."

"Except, what?" I press.

"He disappeared during the last year or so."

"Suspicious," Clay comments.

She shrugs. "May not mean anything. It was a quick search and they'll do more digging."

I cough. "Uh, Yavuz hasn't really disappeared. I got a message from him a couple of days ago. He heard I was going to be in London and suggested we meet up. He'll be there on business too."

Three pairs of eyes glare at me.

Finally, Metin says, "You probably need to talk to Cress. Convince her to stay home."

I consider how I can do that without letting her know about the threat to me.

"Don't do it, Max." Metin's voice is harsh. "You need to let Cress know what's going on."

I'm feel like my eyes are bugging out. How the fuck does she know what I'm thinking?

"Don't let the screen come down. Don't keep this a secret from her."

JL breaks in. "Max likes his secrets."

My mind shifts to the past, to Istanbul and Nasim Faez. Metin and JL's voices fade out, then filter back in and I wrench myself back to the conversation. "What makes you think..."

"Take it from an old married woman. Keeping secrets is not a good way to build a strong relationship. I think you're at a crossroads with Cress. Make sure you take the right path." Metin's eyes are cold with warning as we all depart.

Chapter Three

Cress

I love rainy days. They feed my writer soul. Usually. But not today. Rivulets of water run down the tall windows onto the deck as I contemplate the outline not taking shape on my iPad. Even though the thrumming sound of the downpour creates a soothing backdrop to my disordered thoughts, it doesn't help.

For the forty-thousandth time today, I berate myself. Why? Why did I think this book project was a good idea? Maybe I should put on my coat and walk in the rain to clear my head. Then a rumble of thunder and a flash of lightning dissuade me. I run a hand through my long, tangled curls, shaping them into ringlets with my restless fingers. I should probably have a trim before we leave for London.

I pace up and down the library, thoroughly disgusted with my lack of progress. My gym shoes make no sound on the parquet floor. I've been staying in Max's mansion on Chicago's Gold Coast since early December and I appreciate the spacious rooms, even though I'm still not used to the austere luxury. This room may be the coziest with its corner fireplace, mahogany bookcases crammed with an eclectic collection of over-loved books, and a plethora of Grant tartan lap rugs piled high on one end of the brown leather sofa. Floor pillows, scattered carelessly around the room, are in the same tartan. A large, highly polished teak desk faces the wall of windows and comfortably accommodates my computer with its large monitor and the iPad that sits in front of it.

Moving from a two-bedroom condo to this mansion has been an adjustment. My carefully curated space has given way to vast rooms, most minimally furnished with a few elegant antiques.

When I moved in, Max put in a few touches for me—a small armchair and a lovely chaise perfect for my size, both upholstered in a rich silk damask. The gilded emerald fabric glows in the soft light, throwing beautiful shadows on the wall, especially when Max lights a fire. He chose the leaf-and-floral Lionheart pattern, knowing how it would appeal to me as a medieval historian.

Instead of turning my thoughts back to my work, I continue to procrastinate. I picture his oversized, four-poster bed, so comfortable, even if we use very little of the space. Waking up in his arms every morning is the perfect start to the day. Then delightful goose bumps turn into a chill and I rub my arms, feeling sweatshirt fabric caress my skin as a sense of future loss washes over me. I still feel like a guest rather than an inhabitant, wondering if, at the stroke of midnight, all this will evaporate.

Max has burrowed into my life, and I don't know what I'll do if I lose him. The remodeling of my vandalized condo is taking forever, so I can't move back soon. We're only a few months in and that realization makes my heart plummet. Nowhere to run if life goes pear-shaped. Ever since he opened up about Istanbul, things have been so much easier between us. And yet, a small, nagging fear persists. *Everybody leaves*, a small voice whispers. I know it's not true, but somewhere within me, doubt persists.

Not one of my better days. Instead of making my packing list for our European adventure, I'm fretting over my new writing project. I've shelved the planned book about two rival painters, based on Turner and Constable. Instead, I've shifted to research to a little-known member of the Bletchley Park team, Munro Innes. I'm not sure whether writing a book with him as the main character is a good idea or not. The idea is seductive, starting with spying in the Middle East in the 1930s, then moving onto Bletchley Park.

The hitch is he's Max's great-uncle. When he dropped that little nugget, I was both gob-smacked and distraught. I still wonder if pursuing this project will damage any relationship with his family. Max is enthusiastic, assuring me that everyone will be thrilled about the project. I'm skeptical, but Innes had an interesting life and I think it will make a great story.

Usually, I don't use a real person for my main character, but his obscurity made the idea attractive, and the romantic possibilities are intriguing. Still, the fact that he was married to Max's grandfather's sister is a complication and I don't want to upset anyone.

Fitting in with Max's family is still a work in progress for me. My mother's death when I was eight, my father's abandonment and betrayal, and my grandparents' indifference left scars exacerbated by bullying in school and the feeling that I am a perpetual outsider. That's one reason I was thrilled to be nominated for the historical novel award, both in my category and the overall novel of the year.

When I suffered attacks from an envious rival that year, old wounds reopened and reminded me why I don't trust people. Max has helped me heal, and one goal of this trip is to forge a stronger bond with his family. To make myself believe that I can have a family, even if it's not the one I was born into.

Rubbing my eyes, I turn on quiet music that reflects my mood and consider my problem with Munro. Maybe he should be a strong secondary character. Or I could change his name. I'll have to broach the subject with Max's father when we're in Scotland, and I'm nervous about his reaction since he knew Munro well.

At least another hour goes by before the front door slams. The rain has redoubled, crashing against the windows. Max calls out from the foyer. "Hi. I'm soaking. Won't be a mo'. Going to change." His footsteps pound up the staircase.

His minute is more like half an hour. Beautiful hardwood floors in the living room are highlighted by rich Persian rugs with a gigantic, cream-colored couch taking pride of place. It is long enough to accommodate Max's height and deep enough that we can sleep on it together without having to remove the cushion.

The walls are painted in historical hues chosen to complement the carpets, creating a jewel-like quality. Almost all the furniture is oversized to fit Max's tall body, not my much shorter frame. Fortunately, his favorite armchair fits both of us, so we spend a lot of time with me nestled in his lap, much like my cats curl up in mine. I plop into the chair, throw my legs over the arm, and prop the laptop on my knees.

Max walks in carrying a tray with two cups, a plate of cookies, and a pot of tea. Lines crinkle around his cloudy gray eyes and the ghost of a smile hovers around lips, begging to be kissed. He's changed into black sweatpants and a T-shirt sporting the GSU logo with multicolored lines of satellite stars shooting through their slogan.

Global Security Unlimited

All the security you need wherever you are.

Thick, blue-black hair is damp and unruly, with silver strands popping out everywhere. He needs a trim. As if my thoughts have broadcast themselves, he runs his free hand through it, tiny spikes forming as he pulls at the wet strands. "Think I'm due for a trim."

"Me too. Maybe we should go together."

"Hmm." He puts down his cup and rubs his chin, before he kneels in front of the fireplace, and starts piling kindling and newspaper under the grate. Once he has the fire going, he grabs a couple of logs from the holder and throws them in. He swivels and a shiver runs through me at the frown marring the lips so good for kissing.

His next words astonish me. "Cress, you need to stay in Chicago instead of traveling with me to Europe. I've been getting notifications about possible terrorist activity whilst we're traveling. Probably no problems in the Highlands, but substantial alerts for London, Paris, and Venice."

I let out a breath of irritation. Terror alerts are a way of life these days.

The cats, who have been lying on top of me, jump down, jostling my cup. A few drops slosh into the saucer. Instead of looking at him, I glance through the arched doorway into the hall. Max's messenger bag rests on the black-and-white tiles.

From his grim expression, I wonder if he knows more than he is saying. He hasn't completely mastered his controlling, secretive side. Of course, I haven't managed complete toleration either. Then momentary calmness fades and my face flushes. Heat rises from my neck to my cheeks as I struggle to control my flash of temper.

He knows me too well. I ignore him and go back to the question of the trip, my voice reaching an abnormally high register. "Excuse me. You propose to go to London, have your business meetings, and see your family. In meantime, I cower here, missing the awards ceremony and the conference in Venice."

"Exactly. I don't want you to risk traveling. It's too dangerous."

I force my voice lower. "Chicago had fifty-two threats between 9-11 and 2012. Remember the eighteen-year-old who tried to detonate a thousand-pound car bomb outside a crowded bar in the Loop in 2012? The FBI had already disarmed it, but what if they hadn't? Either of us could have been in that bar or walking down the street."

My chest aches to think we might never have reconnected. I gulp and, with my pointer fingers, lift the corners of my mouth into a smile.

Max doesn't smile back. A grimace mars his gorgeous jaw. Steely gray eyes appear sunken, dark circles like bruises underneath. "Fuck, Cress. I bloody well know it's dangerous everywhere." His voice is hoarse with emotion. "But the high alerts in London and Paris have me concerned." Max's hands stretch out toward me.

"Are you proposing we move? Out to the wilderness? Where the survivalists live?" I narrow my eyes and glare. "Terrorists are everywhere, Max. Everywhere." I pointedly focus on the book.

Unmoved, Max looms over me, trying to intimidate me with his size. His height affords him an unfair advantage. "You. Should. Stay. Home." He taps me on the head with a finger to emphasize each word. His deep baritone grates, harsh and commanding. My skin prickles.

I stand to face him. It doesn't take away the height advantage. He'd have to sit for that, but at least I'm not in a submissive position. My back is rigid, and my tense muscles twitch. The impulse to slap his face tempts me, but I can barely reach that high.

I want to say, *"Who the hell do you think you are?"* Or maybe leave it at *"Fuck you"* before I storm out of the room. But I don't. Instead, I rub the goose bumps on my arms and try to be reasonable. The effort to rein in my inner hurt child makes my chest ache. I keep my voice soft as I answer. "No."

My hand flat against his chest, I push him to sit down. When a sudden chill leaves me shaking, move toward the warmth of the fireplace. "If we give in, the terrorists win. I was in London in 2003 when the Tube attacks took place, but I was lucky." He frowns and I roll my eyes. "I could be hit by a bus tomorrow." Picking up his half-full teacup, I walk out of the room and turnout of foyer toward the kitchen. As far as I'm concerned, this conversation is over.

"Wait. Don't just walk out." When I turn, Max's jaw is hard, his pupils dark. "I'm concerned for you. I don't know what I would do if something happened to you." He's back on his feet, pacing toward me.

"Please, Cress." Max's voice is low and soft, the tone pleading. "You don't have to go to the awards ceremony. If you win, they will send you the trophy. And maybe you could send your paper for the conference, and they could find someone to read it for you."

My fingers twist. "Is your meeting with the bankers canceled? You don't need to go to London after all?"

His answer is curt, snappish. "Of course I still need to

go to London. Besides, I want to be in Scotland for Dad's birthday."

"Without me," I say, ice in my voice. "What kind of relationship is this? What makes travel less risky for you?"

He swallows. I gnaw at my lower lip, riveted to the sight of his Adam's apple bobbing up and down. Can't tear my eyes away from the sexy movement. My anger drains away as the silence goes on and on.

Unable to formulate a response, his head drops to his hands. I put down the cup and touch his hair, tangling my fingers into the short black and silver strands.

"What are you thinking, Cress?" Max's voice is a soft rumble in my ear as he sits down and pulls me back into his lap.

"Adam's apples," I whisper into his chest.

He laughs. "I'm not going to dissuade you, am I?"

"No." My answer is loud and decisive.

The carriage clock on the mantel chimes six p.m. I yawn and stretch, mimicking the cats. "We need to think about dinner."

"Let's go upstairs and have a starter." The sly smile disarms me. "Then we can go out for dinner." Max puts his arm around me, kisses my temple, and murmurs, "Are we good?"

I nod, and he guides me up the stairs. Truce—for now.

Max

JL perches on the edge of the armchair and tosses me a wary glance while he sips a cappuccino. His frown creates deep furrows in his forehead. Either he doesn't like the coffee or he's wondering whether I will tell Cress about Nasim Faez. I give my head a minute shake. He called while we were at dinner and asked if he could drop by. He's been seeing Micki, Cress' best friend. She's working late, and he's at loose ends.

I move into the room and stand next to where Cress stretches out on her chaise, dropping a kiss on the top of her head. The scent of her hair, rain and citrus, reminds me of foreign markets. Rainy days, orange rinds littering the ground as vendors squeeze fresh juice for lines of customers. I nuzzle her neck, murmuring, "Here's your coffee. With a good slug of Bailey's."

She takes the cup and sniffs. "Yum, I love after-dinner coffees." Her gaze turns feral as she appraises my tight T-shirt and loose tracksuit bottoms. The corners of her mouth quirk upward and my neck muscles loosen.

She takes a sip, then sighs. "I sense a romance novelist moment coming on."

I grin.

JL shifts in the armchair, an exaggerated grimace spreading across his face. "J'ai les shakes. Please. Don't do this, Cress."

"T'affoles pas!" When I throw the phrase out, JL shakes his head. Amused, I translate for a puzzled Cress. "Means don't get your knickers in a twist."

She takes that as permission to go on, sensuality dripping with every word. "If I were describing you to my readers, I would wax rhapsodic about how your shirt hugs your biceps. And that your sleek runner's physique makes my heart flutter." She runs a finger down from the base of my neck to my waistband.

"Hey!" JL shouts, shielding his eyes. "Save it for the bedroom."

"Jealous?" I tease. "You invited yourself over, so suck it up."

Scowling, he sips the excellent single malt we're drinking. Cress swallows the last of her coffee.

Plopping onto my made-to-measure sofa, I bask in the lust radiating in my direction. Heat fills me and my fingers itch to strip off my shirt. But not to cool down. I swallow my drink and lean toward Cress. "More? Or some whisky?" She shakes her head no.

I fix on her extraordinary hazel eyes. Eyes that captured me the first time I saw her, over twenty years ago. when she crashed her bicycle into me. Looking up from the floor on that street in Oxford, into her flashing eyes. The same tingle of electricity runs through me now.

Then, with an inward chuckle, I throw out the joke. "Why is England the wettest country?"

Face morphing from adoration to displeasure, she puts down the cup, closes her eyes, and puts her fingers in her ears, humming some slightly familiar ditty.

"Because the queen has reigned there for years!" I chortle.

"Oh my God, they get worse every time." Cress groans while JL laughs in the background.

"By the way, what was the music you were humming to drown me out?" I don't really care, but it should be a safe topic.

"Bizet, 'The Toreador Song' from *Carmen*. Why?"

"Thought it sounded familiar."

"It should sound familiar. You've heard it about a million times." Cress' long-suffering tone ends with the heavy sigh of a music lover exasperated with the obtuse friend. Then she gets up, cooing at the cats. "Come on, Dorothy, Thorfinn. Let's leave the philistine alone."

They raise their heads, stretch, and sidle up to her, expecting treats. "I couldn't do much work today. I'm going to do a little research." She flounces out, the cats stalking after her.

JL eyes me warily. As soon as Cress' footsteps disappear up the stairs, he asks, "Are you going to tell her?"

I raise an eyebrow. He pushes out his lips.

"About Faez?" I can barely say his name.

He nods.

I shake my head. "It may be nothing, so no point in worrying her now."

"What if there is something to worry about? Cress deserves to know."

The darts from my eyes should be lethal. The more he pushes, the more I resist.

"Not now. Maybe not ever."

He gets up, walks into the foyer, and grabs his coat. "Tired of this, Max. Get out of your cave and into the sunlight." He leaves, letting the door slam from the wind.

He's fed up with me. I'm fed up to the back teeth with myself. Major arsehole. I need to figure how to climb out of the grave I've dug without telling her all of the truth.

Chapter Four

Max

M In the early morning gloom, I sit on the lounge sofa, glaring at the iPad set up on the cocktail table. This early morning video call knocks me for six.

Boxes filled with faces stare back at me. Kind of like the old game show, *Celebrity Squares*. Now the 1970s have invaded in the twenty-first century internet disguised as Zoom. Usually we Skype, but we are trying this out.

"Pardon. Did you say you have moved the party venue?" I put on my most ferocious scowl, which only causes general laughter.

Dad leans forward, eclipsing mum as he nods his big, close-cropped head. "RAF Club, London." Mum glares around him, and he subsides to give her equal space in their screen box.

Thumbs-up appear in every square but mine. Watching yourself on a screen is so weird. Emotions scroll over my face—confusion, anger, resignation. I settle on the scowl.

"Vedi sebya khorosho. Ty delayesh' slona iz mukhi." My siblings chuckle.

Cress clatters down the stairs and staggers into the lounge. "What did your mom say?"

"Mum is telling me to behave myself."

"Listen to your mom, Max." She laughs.

Even with her hair piled on top of her head, a stretched-out turquoise pullover hanging down to her knees, and sleeves brushing her knuckles, she makes my heart pound. A squirming Dorothy is cradled in her arms. When the restive cat nips her wrist, Cress drops her to floor. "I've told you not to bite, Dorothy." The cat stalks off, unrepentant. Then she focuses on my family and scrunches her face in apology.

"Don't make an elephant out of a fly," Mum says.

Puzzlement spreads over Cress' face as I breathe into her ear, so she can hear me through the wave of hilarity that erupts. "It's a Russian saying. We'd say don't make a mountain out of a molehill."

"What molehill?"

Meggy takes it upon herself to explain. "A change of plans. We're going to celebrate Dad's birthday in London."

Instead of looking at the screen, Cress turns to me. "Does that mean we aren't going to Scotland?"

"Of course you're coming to Scotland." Dad's voice is full of consternation. "Party in London, then a week in the Highlands. We can't wait to see you, lass."

"But...but...but..." My face heats and I brush hair back from my sweaty forehead.

"No buts." Ian grins from another box. He lounges on a sofa in his Homewood Suites extended stay flat, legs dangling off the end. As the temporary British consul in

Chicago, it's his home away from home. "Change your London arrangements."

My glare should turn him to stone, but the smirk remains. He knows about my plans, which include romancing Cress whenever I can. None of it is compatible with an all-family extravaganza. I planned to introduce Cress to the glories of the Milestone Hotel. I booked the Harlequin Room especially for her. I clamp my mouth shut.

"You already have her, Max. Why bother with romance?" Ian's knowing gaze rubs at my already raw feelings.

I stare at him through the screen. "This is why you are still a lonely bachelor at fifty."

He gives me a two-finger salute. "Bollocks."

"RAF Club. We've booked the rooms," Mum says, repressively.

"When do you arrive?" Cress breaks into the babble of family voices.

I turn my face away from the beaming family faces on the screen. My eyes focus on the woman before me. Disheveled, sleepy eyed, flushed, she is a vision of perfection.

Cress slips a hand around my forearm.

I move over so she can sit next to me. Now I'm mesmerized by the vision of our faces on the screen, practically cheek to cheek. Ignoring my family, I give her a kiss and murmur against her lips, "Why are you up?"

Cress presses her lips against my ear. "Missed you. Wish we could have stayed in bed longer and cuddled a bit."

In response, I thrust two fingers toward the screen. "Ruined my morning. Thanks so much."

"Max, really." All four women, in various on-screen cells, protest at once.

I go for maximum shock value. As I sweep an arm around Cress, I make a loud proclamation. "I could be in bed, having morning sex."

Wolf whistles erupt from the speaker. I give a mock glare. "Bloody hell. Do you think you're sixth-formers?"

"You're as young as you feel." Dad gives another whistle. Ian, Frank, and Les hoot in appreciation. Mum shakes her head, and the girls roll around laughing.

Sean's head pops into Diana and Les' box, his mouth hanging open. "Is that Granddad?"

"Yes. And I don't expect you to emulate him." Diana tries for a severe parental tone, but the twinkle in her eye undercuts the lesson.

"TMI." Meggy's shudder is over-the-top theatrical.

Mum grimaces. Voice stern, she says, "You should be ashamed of yourself, Max. Cress, I'm sure you're mortified."

I paste on a shit-eating grin. Not sorry. Not at all.

Cress' lips pinch and her eyes fill with suppressed laughter. She throws a mock punch. "Max can't always restrain his baser instincts."

Dad raps on the table in front of him to focus our attention in another direction. "In answer to your question, we will be in London on April 2nd. Around nine p.m. Do you want to meet us at the train or the club?"

Ian and I speak at the same time.

"Train."

"Club."

"Cress, love, you decide."

I stroke her cheek and mouth a response to her. "Club."

Cress wags her head no. "We'll meet you at the station."

36

Her fingers move to my mouth and push the corners up, forcing me to give a sliver of a smile.

"Good girl." Ian's crow can be heard around the world.

A groan erupts from my chest. Hazel eyes sparkling, Cress laughs. "That's the fun part. A train station is a perfect place."

A pang strikes my heart as I think of how Cress is estranged from her father and brother. My family have embraced her and she's trying hard to reciprocate. Pure selfishness trying to keep her all for myself. I pull her close and rub my check against her hair. The messy topknot comes undone and her curly locks flow down her back. "Of course, we'll meet them at the train." The glow that suffuses her face makes the gesture worthwhile.

Mum gives us our marching orders. "We know you arrive on April 1st, so that's when your reservation starts. We assume JL will stay elsewhere."

"I'll find out his arrangements. I think he is planning to stay at the Atheneum."

Meggy looks confused. "I thought you were all staying at the Milestone."

"No," I snap. "JL understands about privacy."

Frank cracks his knuckles. "That's convenient. Right round the corner from the Club."

"We're done here," Dad says. "See you London."

One by one, family faces blink off.

"Well, that was interesting," Cress says. "I need coffee. Want anything?"

Just you, I think, as she sashays out.

Chapter Five

M^{ax}

M^{ax} I bolt upright when the phone rings. That puts paid the dream I just had about ravishing Cress—something I planned to implement once we were both awake.

I check the time display on my screen. "It's six a.m., Erik. Did a warning come in of an attempted breach?"

My security admin clears his throat. "Nyet. It's tonight, Max." Erik's thick Russian accent pulses in the damp air.

"What about tonight?" We're having colleagues over for dinner. Bloody stupid if he's calling about that at this time on a Saturday morning.

He blurts, "Can I bring date?"

The mobile screen winks at me as if it knows some secret that I need to decipher. I grab the device and shut myself in the bath, trying to keep Cress from waking up. "A date?"

"Is okay?"

"You could have called at a more reasonable hour." The

growl that accompanies that statement should put the fear of God into him. "I hope you haven't woken Cress."

He lowers his rumbly voice. "Sorry, Max."

"I can hardly hear you."

"Trying to keep noise down like you asked."

"I've moved elsewhere, so we won't disturb her."

He increases the volume slightly. "Sorry." I'm sure he's staring at the floor.

"Let's forget it," I tell him.

"Thanks. Hope isn't too much trouble."

"Is your date someone I know?"

After a long pause, he lets out a guilty sigh. "Amy Shelby."

Bloody hell. Is this a budding office romance? I scratch my jaw and try to think about shaving rather than the implications of this relationship. When I don't immediately respond, the nervous tension from the other end is palpable. From the background noise, Erik seems to be pacing, occasionally rapping his knuckles against something wooden. I wrench my thoughts back to the Erik-Amy conundrum and come up with an inane response. "I didn't know you were together."

"Not together—yet. We try this out."

Amy is probably the biggest pain in my arse of all the CyberSec employees. I'm gobsmacked that Erik is interested. At least he's not her direct supervisor. All personnel issues come to me, unfortunately. She's smart and good at her job, but always dissatisfied. Her degree is from Stanford and somehow that inflates her self-importance. My Oxford degree is at least as prestigious as hers, which is the only reason she treats me with any respect. Her dismissive attitude toward her colleagues as stupid, slow, clueless means she has no friends.

Her complaints range from demands for raises in pay that are out of the industry standard to not having enough responsibility to being passed over for promotion. The prospect of her supervising anyone else is a nightmare I don't want to face. Once a month at least, I toy with firing her, but her contributions are valuable enough that Jarvis always convinces me to overlook her faults.

I wipe a hand over my face and struggle to keep frustration out of my voice. "There's no company policy." But I can imagine the havoc if this goes tits up.

"Okay, Max." He sighs. "We have understanding."

A heaviness settles in my chest as I push the mobile back in my pocket. I can't help wondering what Amy's angle might be. She's made no secret of her ambition and I'm sure she's hunting for another job. Her coding skills are excellent, but her abrasive personality makes her crap at dealing with others.

Cress glides in with a kimono robe over her T-shirt and sleep shorts, a cup in her hand. Her eyes are partly closed, hair a tangle of curls, face creased from sleep. Beautiful. She coughs slightly. Her voice is raspy. "Why are you skulking in the bathroom on your phone?"

"I was trying not to wake you."

"Heard the ring. Was it important?"

I shake my head.

"Morning tea." She holds out the mug.

I grab it and gulp some of the milky liquid.

A big yawn and then Cress squints tiredly. "Tell me again why we're having this dinner party."

"I just want to do something as a thank you to Jarvis for agreeing to stay here with the cats. And we don't leave until late in the day tomorrow, so we can sleep late after our blowout evening."

Cress' eyes narrow. "Is something wrong? Do you have to go into the office?"

I pinch the bridge of my nose, then adjust my glasses. "Nothing that serious. We have an extra guest this evening."

"Is that a problem?"

"No. Plenty of food. She's annoying."

"It's someone you know, then."

"She's part of our team. High dissatisfaction level, but she's good at her job. Feels overlooked, overworked, and underpaid." I take a deep breath. "Our manager, Erik, is dating her."

She lifts an eyebrow.

"We don't have any rules about it but he's not her direct supervisor, I am. Fingers crossed that it doesn't blow up in our faces."

"Oh, Max. Yes, fingers crossed."

My stomach gives a warning growl that has nothing to do with office complications.

"Was that you?" Cress pats my stomach, a cheeky grin lighting up her face.

"Bacon and eggs?"

"Sounds great." She yawns, then her mouth snaps shut. "I think there is some bacon left from the last order."

When I get down to the kitchen, there's no luck with the fridge, so I turn to the freezer, grab the slab, and push the drawer closed.

I glare at the brick on the counter, then put it back and call up the stairs. "We can have cereal this morning. And tomorrow."

The words *toast and marmalade* drift down the stairs. I cut some bread and put it under the grill. The jars of marmalade and almond butter sit next to a plate, ready to receive the golden slices when they issue from the mini oven. Then I slide a capsule into the coffeemaker and soon the aromatic scent of her favorite blend permeates the kitchen. I fill her mug just as she re-emerges swathed in a gray hoodie that proclaims *Writer at Work* with a graphic of a laptop and a pile of books.

"I'm going to spend the day doing research on the book and printing the final manuscript for Ivan. Ainsley must be one of the last editors in the world to demand a paper copy." Then she snaps her fingers. "Or do you need me to help you with the cooking?"

I shake my head and hand her a plate of toast spread with chunky almond butter and thick-cut vintage marmalade. "I'm planning to spend the day on the dinner. Shopping this morning, prep this afternoon, then the real cooking late in the day." I pick up my cereal bowl and cup and move toward the table. "You can check with me in the hour or so before our guests arrive, but I can handle all the early prep. Are you going out to work?"

"No, I'll just hole up in the library."

The gigantic, bright red mug of Cress' morning brew is already at her place at the kitchen table. She puts her plate down, then plops into the chair, pulling the coffee close and inhales.

"Pure bliss," she exclaims. "Oh my God, Max. Not just a pretty face." She inhales again. "You're a lifesaver."

Frozen in place, I can't take my eyes off her. Her head is bent over the cup, some of her salt-and-pepper hair up in a bun, with the rest of the curls streaming down her shoulders. Last year, she only had a little gray. All the stress changed the balance and the silver now equals the brown. She was dismayed but I think it's beautiful, so I've encouraged her to keep it natural.

Cress pushes up the sleeves of her hoodie. "What's the world's saddest cheese?"

"Are you telling a joke?" I put my palm against my chest.

"Uh." She rubs a finger against her bottom lip. "Y-ye-yeah."

The quavers are so cute. I lean forward and press a kiss to her temple. " Well, let's have the punchline then."

She grimaces. "Blue cheese." Her voice is low and so quiet it barely registers.

I let out a guffaw. "Good one."

I'm the joke teller. Cress is the totally unappreciative audience. She's turned tables and I want to encourage her.

Now that she's over the hump, she stands back, feet planted, hand on hips. She purses her lips. "Thanks. Getting prepared for the Scottish joke festival."

I love her feisty stance and lighthearted tone after her up-and-down moods during the last couple of weeks. "Dad will be pleased. Mum, not so much. I think she counts you as her ally in the fight against bad Grant jokes."

"If you can't beat 'em, join 'em."

"I can expect more jokes, then?"

She giggles. "A veritable assault. I downloaded dozens from the internet."

"Keep them short and memorize one at a time." She smiles gamely at my advice.

At Christmas, my family assaulted Cress with puerile jokes, a Grant family specialty. Smirking at the thought and her plan for fighting back,

Her tongue darts out and dips into the steaming liquid to gauge whether she should chance a sip or a gulp. A minute shake of her head tells me that the coffee is still too hot.

She picks up a slice of bread and thickly slathers it with butter, topping it with a layer of marmalade. When she takes a bite, sheer lust floods into me. My hand and some of the milk slops onto the floor. Before I can put it down and fetch a cloth, pink tongues snake out from two furry faces. Dorothy and Thorfinn make quick work of the spilled milk. I mumble a curse under my breath. "I'll mop later."

"Um-hum." Cress pops the last bite of toast into her mouth and washes it down with her coffee. "Is Jarvis moving in tonight?"

"I thought that would be easier. But I can tell him to wait until we've left for the airport tomorrow, if you'd rather."

"It's fine." She brushes a stray curl out of her face. "I am so excited about the trip. Tell me about the RAF Club."

An icicle forms down my back, heightening the fears that have haunted me for the last week. Fears about keeping things from her overlaid with fears for her safety. Until the packet of white powder showed up, we hadn't received any new rumbles about Faez. No one from MI6 has contacted me. Metin's source at the Company told her the police haven't found him and there is no more chatter. It's as if he's disappeared from the face of the earth. I wish.

"Hmmm. RAF Club. It's in Mayfair. Opened in 1918. Formal dress for the Cowdray Lounge and Dining Room."

"Formal dress?"

"We can go informal for almost everything but formal, in your case, that means a dress, with appropriate shoes. Informal includes jeans, and trainers are fine. Other than the party, I think about everything will be informal."

"And..."

"The decoration is beautiful, although you can guess the theme. Bedrooms are on the small side. I'm guessing that

45

we will have the mini suites. Not as luxurious as the hotel I planned. Maybe we can work in a short London layover on our way back from Venice and spend a couple of days at the Milestone."

I feast my eyes on this amazing, brilliant, prickly woman who has agreed to live with me. Praying that we might make this relationship work and find our happy ending. Thinking about the surprise I have planned for our time in Scotland and the threat from Nasim Faez that I can't bring myself to reveal, a frisson of nerves runs through me. Hope I've judged this right.

Fire lights up her eyes as she moves closer, and puts her hands on my shoulders. Balancing on tiptoe, her tongue caresses my lips. With a sigh of pleasure, I pull her closer, and move my tongue against hers, deepening the kiss. And time disappears.

Chapter Six

ax

When the bell rings, I saunter to the door. Cress is taking a shower after the kitchen cleanup. Through the glass doors, I spy JL. He leans against a column.

I glance at my wrist to check the Codebreaker watch Cress gave me for Christmas. The stainless-steel case glints, highlighting the white stitching on the rich blue band made from the same leather used for the seats in Jaguars. This watch is the very embodiment of me—spy and racecar enthusiast—as well as the family connection through my great uncle, Munro Innes. "Aren't you a bit early?"

He raises an eyebrow. "I assumed you would want me to be here before the lovely Amy arrives." His French-Canadian accent is strong tonight.

I grimace, then gesture JL inside and take his coat. "What about Amy?"

He shrugs. "Elle est parfois difficile a supporter."

I nod. "True. She can be a bit bolshie. Not sure what Erik sees in her."

A wide smile creases his face. "Sex." He rubs his hands together. "I thought I could be a buffer tonight. I hope this doesn't blow up in our faces."

"Where's Micki?"

"She'll be here in..." He pulls out his cellphone. No fancy watches for him. "Half an hour. She had to go into work for a bit."

"She's been working late all week. Her firm has a big court case coming up." Cress' comment rings out from the kitchen.

"It's unfortunate. Many times, I have to feed her at midnight." He yawns ostentatiously.

I clap him on the shoulder and move into the lounge where Cress waits, holding out two flutes filled with prosecco. A smile makes her hazel eyes sparkle. She rolls her R's like Piaf as she hands him a flute. "Bon soir, mon cher, JL. Cette une belle soirée."

"Bien sûr." JL kisses his fingers and wafts the kiss over to her.

"None of that. Save your romantic gestures for your own woman and leave mine alone." I take my glass and slump into the armchair.

"Are you two an item?"

"An item? Like in a newspaper?" He grabs his flute and gulps down half, sputtering a bit from the bubbles.

"I'll grab my glass." Cress slides around JL and runs off to the kitchen. I appreciate the view of her arse until she turns the corner.

JL hasn't looked up from his drink. "Not yet, but maybe soon? She's definitely not ready to commit. And Sam..." He bares his teeth and growls.

"Sam is still in the picture?" After the incident last

December, I can't imagine she'd have anything to do with him. "Cress hasn't mentioned anything."

"He keeps himself in the picture. Filthy text messages. Showing up at her place. I've asked her to stay with me so I can protect her, but of course she refuses."

"We both love independent women."

"Love? I don't know if I'd take it that far."

"After that Valentine's Day karaoke fest?" I drain my glass and fold my arms across my chest. "Keep telling yourself that."

The cats stalk in and sniff at JL's shoes. "Did you step in something?" I ask.

JL ignores me.

"Who are you talking about?" Cress stands in the doorway, sipping her wine.

"Micki. Did you know that Sam is harassing her?"

"Kind of." Cress bites her lip. "She won't really talk about it."

The bell rings again and I carry my glass as I open the door. Speak of the devil. Micki stands on the steps with Erik and Amy. I usher them in, noticing that in the half hour since JL arrived, the temperature has fallen and ice films the pavement.

One thing I've learned about living in Chicago is that March can produce the worst winter weather. I take Micki's orange quilted coat, Erik's army surplus parka, and Amy's motorcycle jacket. "Go through while I hang these up."

As I finish, the bell rings again. Jarvis and Metin walk in.

"You came together?" I ask.

Metin hands me her coat. "No. Burak is parking the car. I ran into Jarvis on the sidewalk."

Jarvis pushes past me, strips off his trench coat. He isn't carrying anything.

"Where's your stuff?"

"My duffle is in the trunk." He moves toward the lounge. "I need to say hi to the cats."

A chorus of voices greet him as he rushes forward, calling to the felines, who stare unwaveringly from under the console table.

I take Metin's coat, and we stand by the door, watching Burak limp up the icy steps, holding onto the metal railing, itself coated with ice. He was shot in the ankle a few years ago during an op and it never healed properly. Metin's intake of breath turns into a sigh of relief when he crosses the threshold, none the worse for wear.

Metin is stylish in a calf-length dress, swirled in black and gray. She toes off her boots and pulls out black flats from the plastic grocery bag dangling from her arm. Then she balls up the bag and slips it into the top of one boot. Burak pulls off the rubber overshoes encasing his black loafers.

Burak is about my height with thick gray hair, cut short. Clean shaven, he is unlike most Turkish men, who tend to have mustaches or the newly popular hipster beard. A blue Oxford shirt matches his eyes and the subtle stripe in his Harris tweed sport coat. Gray gabardine slacks complete his ensemble, while all the rest of us dressed in jeans. His bearing screams retired military.

Metin casts an eye around the lounge. "Aren't Clay and Kath coming?"

"They're on their way to Wisconsin to visit her family," I say. By my reckoning, the grandparents should drive down here.

"Should be a fun four-hour drive with three little kids," Jarvis says.

A thoughtful expression crosses Cress' face. "I'm sure they love getting away from the city. The Wisconsin woods give them a chance to unwind and the kids a place to run around."

JL breaks in. "C'est dommage, ça. C'est la meilleure partie de parler en français."

We all crack up. Twitting Clay with foreign languages is always good value.

Cress brings in the charcuterie platter and small plates and flutes are juggled. Jarvis sits on the floor, with Dorothy and Thorfinn, more interested in the cats than the food. He truly is an animal whisperer. I hide my grin, popping a piece of bruschetta into my mouth. Jarvis needs a pet of his own.

Cress narrows her eyes as she gazes at him. "Are you sure this will be okay? You don't mind staying here for at least a month?"

Jarvis glances at her, then turns his attention back to the cats as Thorfinn assaults him with head butts. "It will be fine. I can mostly work from here. And if something comes up where I have to be away for a day or two, my sister agreed to help." Jarvis pulls Dorothy close and rubs his face against her soft fur. She purrs so loudly that we can feel the vibrations all over the room. Jarvis croons. "I loooove animals."

"We've noticed." I sip my drink.

Micki is usually Cress' cat sitter, but she will join us in Paris for the award ceremony. "Why is Jarvis cat sitting?" she asks. "What about Arlette?"

I remember my housekeeper's expression when Cress and her tiny menagerie moved in. "Nothing will change.

51

She doesn't have to do anything differently. In fact, she has become quite fond of them in the last few months." At least she hasn't quit.

Cress purses her lips but says nothing. She's still not convinced that Arlette really likes the cats.

We've moved several chairs into the room, including a second oversized armchair that Amy and Erik have been sharing. They barely fit. Erik is a bear, his long reddish hair pulled into a man bun. He sports one of his trademark lumberjack shirts, his way of proclaiming that he grew up in Siberia.

JL chirps at him. "Planning to move to Oregon?"

As always, Erik rises to the taunt. "Why do you ask that? I love Chicago."

Crammed in next to Erik's bulk, Amy, like Cress, is angular. She shed her black motorcycle jacket when they arrived and her tank top shows off toned arms and sloping shoulders.

Washing down bruschetta with a mouthful of fizzy wine, Amy gurgles, swallowing hastily. "This is an amazing house, Max. Your home office setup must be state-of-the-art. What do you do with all this space?" She sounds breathless with anticipation.

I stiffen. Her avid curiosity unsettles me. "We'll give you the shilling tour after dinner." No one goes into my office. Not Arlette. Not even Cress. Not because it's state-of-the-art but because that's where I wired in the ethernet connection. Even though VPN is usually secure enough, occasionally I need a more secure connection.

"Tell us about trip." Erik sounds wistful. "I know you go to London, Max. But why is so important you go for whole month when we have big rollout coming up?"

Micki breaks in, waving her hand like she's waiting to be called on. "Cress is nominated for a writing award."

"You don't need me in Chicago for that." I wave away Erik's doubtful expression. "I haven't had a holiday in years. My family is having a seventy-eighth birthday bash for my dad and I want to be with Cress for the award ceremony and her conference in Venice. It's not like I'm going to Timbuktu. I'll be reachable. Besides, the upgrade is Jarvis' baby."

"Yeah, you're totally expendable." Jarvis winks. "So far, everything is right on target for the release."

I walk into the kitchen, pick up the bowl of mousse and the toast points, then call into the lounge. "Dinner is served. Bring in your glasses if you haven't finished."

Chapter Seven

Cress

C I look around the table. Except for Micki, everyone else is one of Max's work colleagues. People I don't know well, but need to know better if Max and I stay together. With a sigh, I spread some mousse on a piece of toast.

"We heard your building went condo, Amy." JL pointedly moves the conversation in a new direction. "What are you doing with your stuff when you move out? Or have you already found something else?"

Amy's lips pucker like she's been sucking a lemon. She waves her fork around with a dismissive flip. "I don't have much and I rented the furniture, anyway. Footloose and fancy free." Tossing her head, she goes on proudly. "I passed the hundred things minimalist challenge. I only have about fifty."

My eyebrows shoot up incredulously. "Seriously? How do you do that?"

Amy shrugs. "I mostly don't eat at home and don't need

a lot of clothes. And, I'm a digital girl and access movies, music, and all that crap on my laptop. I work a lot too."

"Perfect that Erik has offered to let you stay with him." A mischievous smile plays around Jarvis' lips. Then he goes back to shoveling in Yorkshire pudding and roasted vegetables.

Max frowns at Erik. "You didn't volunteer that information when we spoke."

The big Russian smirks and runs his fingers through his beard. "Nice for me."

After he clears away the mousse, Max brings in the wine. He has decanted two bottles. Now he pours a small amount into his wineglass, sniffs and swirls, tastes it, then moves around the table, pouring a taste for each of us. There is just enough to go around.

I admire the way the deep ruby color reflects on the white tablecloth. Brunello is my favorite wine and Max tells me this vintage is extraordinary. Cinnamon and licorice flavors blend with herb notes of rosemary and thyme, among others. Black and red fruit tastes explode in my mouth with my first sip. Leather, tobacco, and chocolate linger on my tongue.

"It's a Soldera Brunello di Montalcino Riserva 1990." Max sniffs, swirls, sniffs again, then tastes. "Lovely, silky tannins, layered fruit flavors of currents and cherry, hints of spice and chocolate." He has a bit more. "Fortunately, you can cellar a Brunello for decades—sometimes as long as a century."

JL whistles. We all take a taste and appreciative murmurs rise around the table.

Max removes the now-empty decanter and brings in the roast. Then he displays the Regency silver carving set his parents gave him as a housewarming present when he moved to Chicago in its beautiful mahogany presentation case. Green felt at the bottom, with white silk on the top. Max loves it. The handles have Paul Storr hallmarks and a lovely shell pattern on the ends. He flourishes the carving knife and fork.

"Wow. That set is impressive." Micki has a gleam in her eye. "Spill the story, Max."

He shrugs. "One of my ancestors, Frederick Grant, bought it in London in 1822 as a wedding present for his future bride. Storr was the premier silversmith in London in the first half of the nineteenth century. His pieces were popular with the royal family and the aristocracy. That Frederick bought this set and had a special box made shows Storr's reputation spread outside London. Unfortunately, his intended died before their wedding, but the set stayed in the family."

"Why are you using if is unlucky?" Erik frowns.

"My dad said Frederick thought of selling it, but thrifty Scot that he was, he decided it would be too expensive to replace. We're not superstitious, and the bride dying before the wedding was the only incident. When Frederick finally married in 1824, he presented the set to his new bride and nothing bad happened." He takes out the sharpening steel and expertly runs the blade back and forth. "Traditionally, it goes to the first son married. That would be my younger brother, Frank. But my parents bestowed it on me for my twenty-fifth birthday, maybe as a hint that I should find someone and marry. I will present it to my nephew on his wedding day."

He stabs the fork into the perfectly cooked meat, proceeding to carve beautiful uniform slices, which cascade to the platter in a neat overlapping pattern. The carving takes everyone's attention as we pass the plates up and down the table. Once the meat is served, the side dishes start around, and the only sound is chewing and slurping, with an occasional piece of silverware clinking against a plate.

~

After a quick tour of the house, we're back in the living room, Max pulls out a bottle of Glen Grant and pours drams for everyone. I sit on the edge of my chaise longue and leaning forward to take a sip of scotch. Metin slides in next to me and lays her fingers on my forearm.

"I'm stunned that you're still going on the trip, Cress." She frowns.

Irritation swamps me. "Not you too. As I keep telling Max, we can't stop our lives because terrorists are everywhere."

"I agree with general threats." Her words are slow and barely above a whisper, as if she doesn't want to be over-heard. "But these threats are specific to Max."

I scan her face. She looks back, her eyes shadowed, lids partly lowered.

A chill runs through me. Damn Max. What the hell is he playing at? "Let's talk in the kitchen."

Metin expels a breath, sounding relieved, as I pick up my coffee and walk out of the living room. No one seems to notice. When I glance back, Max is in deep conversation with Burak. Metin trails behind me. The leather soles of her shoes susurrate as we move from carpet to wood to tile.

My cup and whisky glass clatter against the counter as I turn around, eyes narrowed and hands on hips. "What are you talking about?"

Her voice hardens. "I knew he hadn't told you, but I think you need to know."

"He keeps harping on high-level threats in the places we're going." I squinch my eyes.

"You know about Istanbul. In 2003?" Metin levels are hard stare at me and I nod. "The terrorist who set up the ambush escaped from prison, and some of the chatter from the NSA sounds like he may want revenge. Two days ago, Max got a suspicious letter that contained white powder. While the powder turned out to be talc, the attached note said 'Istanbul,' so the NSA chatter seems to be verified."

I cross my arms. "Damn him anyway. He promised not to keep secrets."

Metin's lips twist into a wry smile. "Spies learn early to keep secrets and letting go of that training is difficult."

Even though I know this, I'm having trouble accepting it. " What about you and Burak? Do you still keep secrets?"

"It's different for us." Metin pats her French twist. "Burak was Turkish military intelligence, and I was CIA. We knew what we could share and what we couldn't. And we have the same training. We both understand the rules." Her smile is smug, and I flinch.

"Max retired from the spy game years ago. I'm not asking him to reveal official secrets. Besides, this development affects both of us."

"I know." She holds my hand in hers. "It's instinctual. He will probably struggle against the impulse forever."

I don't want to hear this. My chest feels as if someone plunged a knife into it. I squeeze Metin's hand so hard she gasps.

Max and Burak walk into the kitchen. I turn away.

Burak calls to Metin, "Time to go, my dear."

"Yes, I think you should." My voice is cold and

controlled when I call out loudly. "Thanks, everyone, for a wonderful evening and have a safe trip home."

Max's expression would strike me as comical, eyebrows raised and lips rounded into an O, if I weren't so furious.

Then, as he connects the dots, Max's voice explodes. "Bugger. What the fuck did you say to her, Metin?"

"I told her what you should have already told her." Her voice is cool and distant.

"Bloody hell. You had no right to do that." He hits the counter with the flat of his palm.

"You had no right to keep it a secret."

"Not. Your. Bloody. Decision."

Glares at fifty paces. I visualize antique pistols at dawn as Burak steps between them, hands held up. "Don't speak to my wife that way, Max. Friendship only stretches so far." He puts his arm around his wife and turns her toward the doorway. "Let's go home, Metin."

Rooted to the spot, Metin doesn't budge, and he can't persuade her to move. "Wait, Burak. I'm not ready to leave." She folds her arms.

"Please go. Max and I need to have a conversation, in private."

Max's jaw goes slack as he rubs a hand through his hair. Then his mouth snaps shut like a rattrap. He swallows. When he finally manages to get any words out, his voice sounds strangled. "Yes. Time for everyone to leave."

Jarvis' eyes are wide. "Do I need to leave and come back?"

"No, of course not. Go sit in the lounge." The tremolo in Max's voice is painful to hear.

Then, his voice switches gears like a car engine at maximum revs. "Everyone else go home. Your coats are in the hall closet. Thanks for coming. Sorry to break things up this way."

He moves forward, herding them like a sheepdog; his hand on Erik's back, pushing him forward. Amy hurries alongside.

Micki comes over and offers me her hand. I grab it and she squeezes so hard I think she'll break my fingers. Then she lets go and kisses my cheek. "Call me in the morning before you leave for the airport."

"What makes you think I'll go to the airport?"

She hugs me. "I just know."

JL grabs her arm and they are gone.

When everyone but Jarvis has left, I stand by the sink, staring at piles of dirty dishes, my arms crossed in a self-hug. Max walks back to the kitchen and starts toward me, but when he sees my lips drawn into a narrow line, he turns around and goes back to get Jarvis settled.

The door slams as they walk out to retrieve Jarvis' stuff. Then, heavy footsteps stamp up to the second floor. Muffled voices sift through the air. Then silence.

Fighting through the tremors, I put away the food and start the dishwasher. Holding a wet paper towel to my inflamed eyes, my discarded glasses teeter precariously on the edge of the sink. Footsteps strike the tiled floor as Max comes back into the kitchen. He stands behind me, chest pressed into my back, arms imprisoning me. A hoarse murmur vibrates against my neck. "I'm an arse, again."

I pull away. With a sigh, I explore his handsome face, now marred by deep lines bracketing his mouth. "What did you do with Jarvis?"

"He's in the Piccadilly guest room. He loved the idea of all that British kitsch and wants to know where you found the phone box."

When I moved in, Max asked me if I wanted to decorate two of the empty rooms. I thought it would be fun, so I did an English room and one for the south of France. Sighing, I say, "I'll give him my list of suppliers."

"Good," he says. "Now come into the lounge and we'll talk."

By this time, I'm over the initial shock, but I'm not sure what the next move should be. We face each other. His hangdog expression should soften me, but I've seen it once too often and right now the effect is to stiffen my resolve.

"I haven't forgiven you." My voice grates.

"I know."

"Promises to be better won't cut it. There have been too many of those."

"What about your promise to try to be more understanding?" he throws back at me.

That was a hit to the solar plexus. I know he's right, but I'm not going to admit it. At least not yet.

My voice is shaky as I say, "I'll fly to Paris and go to the awards ceremony with Micki, then travel on to Venice for my conference. You can go to your meetings in London and visit your parents. Come back to Chicago on your own."

"No. That's not acceptable. We need to resolve this tonight. And, if we're traveling, it's together."

Suddenly my knees start to give way but I manage to sit down on a kitchen stool. I cry out, "Why didn't you tell me that the threats were against you?"

"Would that have changed your mind about staying home?"

"No. But that's not a good reason to keep it secret. We're supposed to be partners in this relationship."

"I can't help believing that the less you know, the safer you'll be."

"That's false logic, Max."

He opens his hands and spreads out his fingers in supplication. "I wanted to tell you, but I just couldn't bring myself to do it. Metin and JL have been chivvying me to 'fess up."

"So everyone knows except me? Micki and your family too?"

He winces at the steel in my voice. "As far as I know, JL hasn't said anything to Micki. And my family doesn't know anything either. Navigating all this has been so hard. Maybe I need to go for more counseling."

He's been moving closer and closer and now pulls my hand up to his lips and kisses my wrist, palm, and each finger. I pull back. He watches me move, his eyes clouded. "Were you serious about going alone?"

My hand moves up to my mouth and I pull on my lower lip before answering. "Probably not. Let's sleep on it and talk in the morning." I move toward the stairs, hating the weak, whiny note.

"No. I told you, we have to settle things tonight."

He takes my elbow and steers me into the living room. I perch on the edge of the big armchair. Thorfinn climbs up and puts his head in my lap. Max settles on the couch.

The ensuing silence grows heavier and heavier.

Finally, I can't stand just watching him watch me. "How do you know I'm not in as much danger here?" I ask him. "Your terrorist could target me to net you."

His head snaps back. Then he stares at his shoes.

But he doesn't answer.

I push on. "How do you think your parents will feel when they find out?"

"I expect a stern telling off," he mutters, his head turned

63

away like a small boy who knows he's wrong but doesn't know what to do about it.

A voice comes out of the darkness. "Hey, Max, can I heat up some milk? I'm having a hard time getting to sleep."

Max groans. *Jarvis*, he mouths, as if he thinks I've forgotten that we have a houseguest.

"Jarvis," I call out. "Go ahead and have your milk. If you can't find a pan, let me know and I'll get one out for you."

Max catches my eye and smiles. "Can we agree that we'll take the trip together?" Then his gaze drifts back to the floor, as if he's bracing for bad news.

"I made a commitment to you. A commitment not to run away. And even if you still haven't learned not to keep secrets from me, I'm honoring my part of the deal."

I stare at him until he glances up, then give him a thin smile. "Anything else you're hiding?"

"No. What Metin told you is all of it. Well, not the little details. I can tell you those." Circles show black under his puffy eyes as he pulls off his glasses. The only sound is the scrape of his nails against the scruff on his chin.

"Too tired." I yawn, pushing up from the chair.

"You still haven't forgiven me." Each word lands like rain dripping from the roof.

"Not yet." The promise of eventual forgiveness hangs in the air. "Your nose is cold," I tell him as he nuzzles my neck. Then I say, "Amy's kind of scary."

His laugh wobbles. "Scary? Maybe, but mostly annoying. She's good at her job. I don't socialize with her."

My snarky side comes out. "I was unconvinced when she told us she grew up with pets. Gerbils! You could tell she was grasping at straws before she thought of that."

"And the fish." I can't suppress a gurgle of amusement.

"Assuming she really had any, I wonder how long it took before she overfed and killed them."

I'm giggling helplessly, visualizing fish stuffing themselves, the water murky with fish food. Finally, I spit out, "She seemed awfully interested in seeing your office. I wonder why."

"Tech envy, maybe. She probably thinks I have a room stuffed with advanced equipment." He laughs. "If she only knew it's a graveyard of crap."

"Really?" I've never been in Max's office.

"Do you want to see it?"

I feel as if we've reached a crossroad in our relationship, and taking this step commits us to a path. I think of Robert Frost's poem and hope it's the right one. "Uh, yeah."

He takes my hand and leads me upstairs. "Turn out the lights when you come back up," he yells to Jarvis.

"Will do."

When we reach the third floor, Max keys numbers into a pad on the door and the sound of a lock disengaging sounds loudly. He pushes the door open and waves me in with a flourish.

A dozen monitors sit on a couple of long tables. Underneath are a variety of CPUs. Keyboards and cables spill out of boxes. It's the most organized junk room I've ever seen.

"This is where equipment goes to die. Every computer I've ever owned is here."

"Why?"

He raised one shoulder in a half shrug. "Can't seem to part with them. Maybe I'll open a tech museum some day."

I start to say something, but a huge yawn comes out instead. "I'm really tired."

"A good night's sleep wouldn't hurt." He looks a question at me.

"I'll sleep in one of the guest rooms tonight."

His hurt expression almost convinces me to change my mind, but sleeping apart for one night is probably a good move.

He puts his interlaced fingers behind his neck, then stretches. "I'll spend a couple of hours at the office getting all the London bumf finished, but I'll be home in time for lunch. We don't need to be at the airport until five."

He gives me a squeeze and I rub the top of my head against the soft cashmere of his sweater briefly.

"Night," I say.

"Call me if you find monsters under the bed." He kisses my cheek and we go to our separate rooms.

Chapter Eight

Cress

Monsters under the bed. My childhood nightmares were more about being alone. Left in a forest, thrown out of a car, coming home to an empty house where all the locks had been changed. Being chased by monsters would have been a relief from all that aloneness.

When I was older, the dreams changed from my being isolated to being ridiculed. When I dreamed of walking down the halls of my high school, having just discovered I was still in my pajamas, or had forgotten to put on a blouse, mocking laughter would follow me.

Dreams of forgetting an exam and getting to the room only to find it was barred, was accompanied by my grandparents' scolding voices. "Worthless. Sorry we ever took you in. Just like your mother."

I swallow down my memories, disappointments, bad decisions. I'm alone and it's my own choice. Cutting off my nose to spite my face. I drop said face to my hands as feelings of worthlessness sweep over me.

Pointless, I tell myself. Time to move forward. Maybe

after a night apart, we can figure out how to move on in the morning. We started with glib promises, but the reality is that changing decades of behavior is a constant struggle. He needs to be more open and I need to be more tolerant, less judgmental. Wanting Max so much, I have to believe we can make it. And I have to trust that he wants the same.

The newly decorated guest room should be inviting, with its soothing Provençal theme. Purples, blues and yellows wash the walls and remind me of the ocean, fields of sunflowers and lavender, and the glow of sun-washed stone houses perched in the shadows of the Alps. The furniture is country French with light woods and upholstery in cream linen.

Instead, the air is cold and lonely, "stale, flat, and unprofitable" in Hamlet's words. I climb onto the tall, king-sized bed, its vast expanse reminding me of the empty Antarctic plain. The new mattress should feel wonderful—it's called a Wonder mattress—but I'm as trapped as the princess and the pea, tossing and turning, no comfort here.

I've been discounting the danger that Max has been pounding on for the last few weeks. Years of warnings and threat levels since nine-eleven have tended to blunt fears. You can only live with high-levels of anxiety for so long before everything fades into the background. Even reports of terrorist attacks are just fleeting blips in the radar.

Now, the idea of danger seeps into every pore. Metin's words haunt me.

These threats are specific to Max...a suspicious letter that contained white powder...the terrorist who set up the ambush escaped from prison...he may want revenge...

I miss the comfort of Max's arms around me. The feather-light kisses on my neck. The murmured endearments.

The feel of his skin against mine. The feeling of safety. I almost get up to go to him. Almost.

Instead, I pummel the pile of pillows into submission, throw myself back against the mound, and try to adjust my neck, my arms across my chest, close my eyes, and will myself to sleep.

My mind churns, imagination running away with me. Although I have no idea what this terrorist looks like, I envision a tall figure, swathed in white robes, looking like Anthony Quinn in *Lawrence of Arabia*. Faceless minions range behind him, each holding a cartoon bomb. The ones that are round with a sparking fuse, and the word *bomb* written across the front. Ridiculous stereotype, but the image seems burned into my thoughts. He shakes his fist, mouthing words I can't hear.

Should I stay home? Let Max face this on his own? I stiffen. No way. My arguments about being a target even if we are separated still make sense. And, foolish though it may be, I would stand with Max than be the little woman pacing the widow's walk while her man faces danger.

Exhaustion overcomes me as I slump back against the pillows. My mind quiets. My eyelids flutter...

In the middle of a web, I see an enormous spider. Max is caught in the sticky, silken threads. He struggles but can't escape. A voice says, *"I've got you now. You'll never get away."*

I wake up screaming.

∿

Max

I bolt upright. The screaming isn't a dream. Cress. Running out into the corridor, the guest room is improbably far away and I smack into Jarvis, who stands outside her door, fist raised to knock.

"Is that Cress?" His comment strikes me as inane.

I put my hands against his chest and push him out of the way. Getting to Cress is the priority.

My voice is a low growl. "Just move, Jarvis. Go back to bed. I'll see to this." He glares, then turns back to his room.

I fling open the door to Cress' temporary space. Trip over the doorsill. Bugger. My arms windmill as I teeter. She's stopped screaming and sits up against the pillows, rubbing her arms, trembling uncontrollably.

I pull her against me, stroking her hair, trying to warm impossibly cold, pebbled skin. I tip up her chin for a kiss. Her lips are blue.

"Monsters under the bed after all?"

"I-I-I dreamed there was a huge spider, kind of like the one in *Harry Potter* or Shelob from *The Lord of the Rings.*"

I stay silent, but hold her tighter.

"It was in the middle of its web. And you were caught in the web, struggling to get free. And then, the spider said, 'I've got you now. You'll never get away.' And I screamed." She pulls away and peers at me. "This threat..."

"Nasim Faez is a dangerous man. And after ten years in prison, he's patient."

"That's his name?"

I nod.

"And he wants revenge because you put him in prison?"

I make sure she is looking at me. "Because I killed his brother."

Folding her back into my arms, her tight grasp around my waist is comforting. We stay silent for a long time, arms around each other, rocking gently.

Chapter Nine

M^{ax} Bright sunlight pours through the uncurtained window, striking my face. My bleary eyes remind me that I am in the guest bedroom with Cress. The door is slightly ajar, a cat slinking out. Disoriented, I reach for my glasses, but they aren't on the bedside table. A quick recce doesn't turn up anything.

With a groan, I slide down to the floor, stretching out to snake an arm under the bed. My hand finds the frame and the tightness in my chest loosens. I've given up contacts completely. At one time the ophthalmologist told me that the lenses would protect against more deterioration, but now that everything has stabilized, contacts irritate rather than protect. I glance around and remember why I'm in the Provencal room, with Cress.

My thoughts return to the dream. I was on one knee, begging Cress to forgive me for being an arse again. I woke up before she answered. Glasses firmly affixed, I sit down next to her, bouncing slightly on the oh-so-new mattress. She makes enchanting whimpers as she wakes up, stretches and scoots her back against the headboard. "What time is it?"

I grab her phone. "Uh, half-past seven. Sorry I woke you. Go back to sleep." I get up and move toward the door.

She raises her arms above her head, hands clasped. "I'm awake now. And I still have packing to do."

"Our flight isn't until seven p.m. Plenty of time."

"Why do I keep thinking we have an earlier flight?"

I open my arms, elbows bent, palms up, and shrug. "No idea. Maybe you're just anxious to get there." I sit back down, my thigh pressed against hers.

She picks a piece of lint off my shoulder. "Where did this come from?"

"One of the cats knocked my glasses on the floor last night. Took a bit to retrieve them this morning. We need to keep them locked out of the bedroom."

Cress scratches her scalp, then looks at me through partly lowered lashes, her luminous eyes piercing me. "They'll just keep us awake with loud protests. Put your glasses in the nightstand drawer when you go to bed. That's what I do. Otherwise, Dorothy decides they're a toy." Her chest heaves with a heavy breath. "And maybe Arlette needs to vacuum more carefully."

I ignore her comment about Arlette and make a grumbling noise. "Dogs are easier."

"They chew up your shoes." She pushes hair back from her eyes as she squints in my direction. "And if we had a dog, you'd be outside right now, walking it."

True enough. Not that I'd mind. Having grown up with dogs, I'm used to all that. Not that I've had a one for years. When I'm home, I enjoy the family dogs. I nip at her ear, then nuzzle her neck. She smells like orange and ginger.

Stretching, I swing my feet onto the floor. "I'll make some coffee and bring it up."

"You spoil me."

"That's the idea."

When I get back, a mug in each fist, I lean against the doorframe. Cress has gone back to sleep so I walk over and put the coffee on the nightstand. "You look beautiful when you're all sleepy and disheveled."

Cress glows, as she props herself up against the pillows, curls disordered as they hang past her shoulders, eyes filmy with sleep. She yawns, pressing a palm against her mouth partway through.

"Yeah, right."

I move back and hop onto the bed again, setting our drinks on the night table. Then I lean against the headboard and pull her into my chest, and press my lips against the top of her head. "Makes me want to ravish you."

Ribbons of curls blow as my breath caresses her. She pulls away slightly. "Let me brush my teeth."

I pull her back against me, kissing her deeply. "Later."

When I get back, Cress is taking a shower in the guest bathroom so I go back to our room, strip out of my T-shirt and flannel sleep pants, and take my shower too. She walks in just as I'm buttoning my shirt. "Nice. Could you go shirtless all day?"

A chuckle rumbles from my chest. "Don't think 2 Sparrows will let me in without a shirt."

"Forgot we are going there. But once they see that chest, they'll drag you in the door and put you on display."

I give her a cheeky grin and a little bow.

"Is Jarvis going too?"

"Yeah." I continue, buttoning my shirt. "By the way, I have something for you."

Her eyes narrow as she searches for a physical object. "You know I hate surprises, Max."

With an insouciant air, I slide my tie under the collar. "I arranged for a fire-eater to perform in the hotel courtyard while we're in Paris."

She throws her arms around me. "Oh, Max. I can't wait. I've been hoping ever since I missed the one you arranged for my birthday." She falls on me and starts kissing my neck. I join with enthusiasm. After a few minutes, she pulls away.

"Thought you hated surprises."

"Guess it depends."

"So, are there any other surprises that would be acceptable?"

Cute lines furrow her forehead. "Any surprises I wouldn't mind. Hmmm. Chocolate. Tickets to a play or concert. A hockey game. But not something that actually changes our lives."

"How about weekend breaks, that sort of thing?"

"Yeah, that would be okay." She nibbles her bottom lip. "Not long trips, though. Two days in northern Michigan, sure. A month abroad would need to be discussed."

"Got it. I have to learn to open up about the big scary stuff." I swallow. Not going to come easily. "Somehow, I have to trust that you can cope with anything I tell you. Then my protective side kicks in and convinces me you are better off not knowing."

"You need to talk yourself out of that, Max. When the voice in your head tells you, 'Keep her safe and in the dark,' just say 'hell no.' I'd rather know what's facing us. I know you think this guy may be targeting you. Tell me how serious this revenge threat is."

I frown. My first thought is—how much can I keep back? NO, NO, NO. Wrong thinking. I have to come clean.

She strokes my cheek. "Hey, you don't have to tell me every detail. Use the Homeland Security levels if that helps."

Her casual use of Homeland Security levels makes me realize how embedded the mindset after 9-11 has permeated public consciousness. "Uh, between yellow and orange, I guess. We don't have absolute confirmation that Nasim Faez is targeting me directly. We're not sure whether the white powder sent from Istanbul is a threat or a warning. It might be from him, but we have no real proof. And if I am the target, why the cat-and-mouse game? He could have sent something that would kill me. Or he could activate a latent cell in Chicago and blow up the house." I put my head in my hands.

"I guess I should take this seriously. In fact, I toyed with the idea of staying home."

An unreasoning bubble of hope rises up, followed by a wave of desolation when I think about being without her. *Get a grip, Max. You can't have it both ways.* I give my shoulders a shake.

I must look unfocused, because Cress taps my chest. "I decided against that. I still believe I could be in just as much danger alone. Besides, I would miss you far too much."

"I can't bear the thought of anything happening to you."

She laces her fingers with mine, pulling me close for a kiss. "Same. That's why I'm going. We have to take care of each other as best we can."

Chapter Ten

London
    Cress
    We land at Heathrow at the same private terminal where heads of state arrive. The posh lounge is inviting and I want to drink in the experience. Pretend I'm the first female President of the United States, arriving to visit the Queen.

Thick blue carpeting, decorated with colored lines that remind me of the Tube map, muffles sound, making the room much quieter than most airport lounges. Plush, dark gray upholstery tones beautifully with light gray walls, the effect soothing. Great for anxious travelers. Small, round granite-topped tables dot the room, mostly for the drinks that are available at the corner bar, although they are big enough to accommodate a laptop in a pinch.

My stomach burbles and I would kill for a bottomless pot of coffee and a full English breakfast. But there is no time to hang around absorbing the atmosphere. Max tells me that GSU arranged a limo service that takes us straight to the RAF Club. JL is staying around the corner at the Athenaeum Hotel, so it's a one-stop trip.

Ian pulls me aside. "I didn't think to mention it on the flight, but knowing Max, I'm sure he didn't tell you that he and dad have the same birthday."

"No. In fact he sidesteps every time I ask when it is."

"He doesn't like to celebrate it for some reason. Especially this time, when we are have a big party for Dad coming up. He walks to the curb, where a traditional black cab idles, and calls out, "Tomorrow at Rules."

I yell back, "Aren't you staying at the Club?"

"Of course, but that doesn't guarantee I'll catch you tonight or tomorrow morning." He waves, then ducks into the backseat.

Traffic is heavy making the trip a bit slower than the half hour it normally takes to drive into central London. After the eight-hour flight, we are tired of sitting and gladly tumble out of the car when it pulls up the curb. A few deep breaths in the mild London sun, wonderful. Then I stand on the sidewalk, looking up at the enormous white pile of a Victorian building.

"It's a Grade II-listed building that originally housed the Ladies Lyceum Club, with stables behind. Lord Cowdray, the founder of the club, financed the leasehold of the building and architect Maurice Webb handled the reconstruction between 1919 and 1922." Max waves a hand toward the large white Victorian mansion that looms up from the sidewalk. "After the renovations were complete at the end of December 1921, it opened to members in January 1922. The Duke of York attended the official opening in February 1922."

I grin, watching Max take on the role of tour guide.

Max puts his arm around me, and I snuggle into his

warmth. "I haven't stayed here in years, but Mum and Dad use it as their London base."

I flush as my stomach gurgles.

Max smirks and gives me a pat. "Let's check in. JL, do you want to walk 'round to the Athenaeum and drop your bag, then come back here for breakfast?"

"I'll leave it with your stuff and eat first. I've heard the club offers an amazing breakfast."

Max checks his watch. "After that message from Cress' stomach, probably a good idea. They only serve until ten, and it's already past nine." He sweeps me into the elegant hall and up to the desk.

The receptionist raises his head up as we walk in. "Good morning. May I help you?"

"Good morning. I'm Max Grant and I believe my father made a reservation for me until the fifth."

He runs his finger down a ledger. "Yes, Dr. Maxim Grant and Dr. Cressida Taylor." He glances up at me and nods. "Two single rooms."

Max pales, his fingers digging into my arm. "Sorry? That can't be right."

The man turns the ledger around so Max can view the booking. He runs his finger under each of the two lines. "Your parents reserved and paid for these rooms. I took the booking myself and your mother was quite clear about the arrangements." The man sounds apologetic as he turns the ledger back.

Max's mouth twists into a rictus of anger. He snarls, his voice vibrating with pure gravel. "Oh, was she? Well, I won't have it." His face has gone from stark white to a deep red. If he weren't so healthy, I'd worry that he's having an apoplectic fit. Bringing his voice under control, he asks, "Have you any other rooms available?"

The man runs a finger around the inside of his collar. "I can check, sir." But he stares at Max, rather than looking at the reservations screen on his computer.

Max growls into my ear. "I don't know what my parents are playing at. They aren't particularly prudish." He glances toward the frozen desk clerk and growls, "Other. Rooms. Available." His glare could incinerate a Cotswold village.

A sinking feeling moves up from my stomach. My sense of hunger disappears, replaced by something that might be abandonment. My past rises to taunt me. Did I misjudge his parents' feelings about me? Did I mistake tolerance for affection, kindness for acceptance? Do they disapprove of our relationship? My body trembles with the betrayal I feel.

Max, tired of waiting, loosens his collar. "Come on, Cress. We're leaving."

I had turned my back to the desk, transfixed by the stained glass set in the door. Now I swing around, my mouth open in shock as I stare at Max. His gray eyes are almost black, a vein pulses in his neck, and his fist hovers above the counter.

The clerk squeaks. "Surely we can resolve this problem." He taps the screen.

Slowly, Max opens his fingers and puts his palm onto the wooden surface and takes a deep breath. "I don't care what the reservation says. I would like a mini-suite, if possible. If none are available, a superior double will do. If those options aren't possible, cancel the reservation, and we will find accommodation elsewhere." His tone is stiffly reasonable, but a deep rumble emanates from his chest like an awakening volcano.

I gasp. Making a scene is not Max's style. Essaying a smile, I add, "If you can find us another room, we can close the matter."

The clerk opens his mouth, but Max holds up a hand

"We can't refund the payment." Another man has appeared as if by magic.

"Not a problem." The harsh tone tells me that Max will be fine if his parents pay for rooms that we won't be using. "Well, do you have a room?" Impatience oozes out of every pore as Max taps his foot against the desk.

The clerk wipes his forehead and seems relieved at the appearance of the new arrival, presumably his supervisor. Max's steady stare seems to have left him tongue-tied.

"What is the issue?" The second man's tone is icy.

The clerk and his supervisor step back from the desk, the posture of both men rigid, as they whisper. JL puts a hand on Max's shoulder. Max shakes it off and steps back, arms crossed. "What, JL?"

"Max, calm down. Even if there is no better room here, I'm sure the Athenaeum would find you a room. You will be so close that your parents will hardly notice." He elbows Max in the ribs. "More private, too."

"Oh, they'll notice." Max's lips draw into a narrow line that promises an early confrontation with Brian and Viktoria.

"Mr. Grant?" The desk clerk speaks so softly that we barely hear him call Max's name. The man is tapping the ledger. His supervisor stands behind him, his eyes darting back and forth between Max and the back of his employee's head.

As he steps back to the desk, Max uncrosses his arms. "Any joy?"

The man nods. "Fortunately, we have a mini-suite available next to the room your parents will be using. Is that acceptable?"

"Perfect." The blinding smile that suffuses Max's face is

the sun coming out after a thunderstorm. I drink in his gorgeous face and my heart lifts with love and joy. I want him to smile like this every day.

The supervisor regards our two small bags and my computer case. "We'll have your luggage taken up."

"Thank you." Max takes the proffered key, then checks his watch again. "Too late for breakfast here. Check in at the Athenaeum, JL, and meet us at the Wolseley. It's straight down Piccadilly." His eyes twinkle. "I guarantee you'll love this place, Cress. Fabulous building, amazing food."

I force words out around the lump at the base of my throat. "Not hungry."

He scrutinizes my face and makes some decision. "That's your standard answer. But it's a lie. Of course you're starving."

With a wave, JL cruises out the door. Then, tenderly, Max offers me reassurance. "You have to believe that, what ever is going on, my parents are not rejecting you, Cress. I have no idea what is in my mother's head, but my parents love you."

I shake my head. His words should make things better, but I can't believe them. He wraps me in a hug, peppering my face with kisses. "We'll straighten out this tangle. But we need to assuage the raging appetite you are ignoring."

Max evades my glare and puts an arm around me. "I need you to myself for a minute," he croons as he steers me down the sidewalk. He matches his long stride to my shorter steps and never removes his arm from around my waist.

JL hasn't arrived yet, but Max gets a table. Once I'm ensconced on the banquette, he gestures to the menu. "Check out the offerings. I need to make a call." He gestures toward an empty spot in the busy dining room. "I'll be right over there." As soon as he has a connection, he walks away, whisper-yelling into the phone.

By the time he comes back, JL has joined me. Max drops into a chair and grabs the menu out of my hand, slapping it down on the table.

"I don't know what my mother was thinking." Max scratches his neck. "That's not true. She told me exactly what she was thinking. Mum remembered you were always looking for a space to write when they visited at Christmas, and she had the idea that you might want to have a space of your own to retreat to. Her heart was in the right place."

Relief floods me. His parents aren't rejecting me. Tears pour down my face and I can't stop shaking. Max pulls me up from my chair and hugs me fiercely. "Go clean up and I'll order you the biggest breakfast they offer." He points out the sign indicating the toilets.

My lips tremble. "Coffee, but no beans." I race off to the loo.

Chapter Eleven

Max

After breakfast, we walk Cress back to the RAF Club. Once she's settled in the suite, she can crash. The events of the morning have exhausted her. Then JL and I take off to the GSU offices in Leicester Square. He has meetings with the security staff about new procedures WatchDog is implementing.

I put in a few solid hours of work on tomorrow's presentation to the heads of three private banks before we adjourn for lunch at the Garrick Arms. Their steak-and-ale pie is outstanding. A pint of Old Speckled Hen ale, first brewed for the fiftieth anniversary of the opening of the MG factory in Abington near Oxford, is the perfect accompaniment.

The fruity smell rising from the pint glass takes me back to my college days. I take a sip of the familiar malty flavor and wipe the foam from my lips, basking in the intermittent sunbeams bombarding the windows through the partly cloudy skies. JL is wiping grease off his fingers from the fish and chips.

When my mobile rings, I assume Cress is calling. But

Clay's voice booms out of the speaker. "We have a problem. I need you on a video call, stat."

I look at the time on my mobile. It's only seven a.m. in Chicago. "Finishing lunch. We can be back in the office in ten minutes."

"Fine." He hangs up.

"Calisse. Not looking forward to finding out about this." JL's forehead creases in a frown.

I nod my agreement. "Clay is more than pissed off."

Clay's assistant's voice sounds over the speaker system as we reach the conference room. "Max and JL have arrived, Mr. Brandon."

Clay's flushed scowl fills the screen as a door slams behind him.

My stomach rumbles. I'm already regretting the beer. "What's going on?"

"We have a problem with the update." A chair scrapes against the floor. Clay shifts and growls "where the hell were you?" as Jarvis lowers himself to a seat.

I talk over him. "What the hell, Jarvis? Everything was fine when we left."

The small conference table in our London office is placed optimally to view the oversized screen. Elena is sitting at the end of the long table, originally used by Burnham and Root to plan the 1893 World's Fair, poised to take notes.

All occupants of the Rookery Building can use the historic conference room and library on the eleventh floor with its collection mementos of the fair. Access is a cool perk, but today, even through a screen almost four thousand miles away, the venue feels somehow ominous. We normally only use it for client meetings, but it's the logical place for a conversation about the security breach. It is well away from our offices on the fifth floor and no one goes up there except to use this room. Clay sits at one end of the long antique rectangle. Jarvis is between Metin and Erik.

Metin's lopsided grin is slightly feral, with one sharp eyetooth visible. "Hi guys. Heard anything new, Max? Any incidents we should know about?"

"No. Have you?"

"Nothing."

I scowl. "Moving on." We're not here for my issues.

Erik's red hair stands up, like he put his finger in a socket. He shifts, the chair creaking under his bulk. He takes his glasses off, cleans them, puts them back on, over and over.

"Erik?" My voice is accusing. The tremor in his left hand is more noticeable than usual.

Jarvis waves a sheaf of papers. "Hold on, Max. Let me lay it all out for you." If we were in the same room, he would have thrown it across the table at me. Then he taps his pen against his teeth and stares out of the screen. We watch his chest inflate, collapse, inflate, collapse. "Okay, short and dirty. Troy Diamond found spaghetti code in the upgrade and reported it to Erik, who came to me."

Troy came to us from Cal Tech via the Navy a little over a year ago and looks to be a new star on the horizon. "Spaghetti code? That's not possible," I yelp in disbelief. "We checked for that at the beginning of the project."

"Tell me about it." I blink at Jarvis' flat tone. The confidence he had when I left on this trip has evaporated like raindrops on hot pavement. "It's there now."

I drum my fingers against the brown, wood-grained tabletop. My face, pale with red spots on my cheeks, reflects from the glass of the screen. Erik fidgets.

"How long have you known?" My voice catches as Clay glares around accusingly.

"I found out this morning." Jarvis sounds evasive. "But..." He glowers at Erik, who seems even more unhappy as he twists his glasses between his fingers. The thin wire frames snap. He drops them on the table, twisted metal glinting in the artificial light.

With an overgrown goatee and his scruffy band T-shirt decorated with smears of egg, Erik resembles the caricature of the bloke who lives in his mother's basement. He studies his clenched hands. Finally, he peers at the screen.

"Troy told me two weeks ago," he mumbles into his beard, his thick Russian accent difficult to understand.

"What did you say?" Clay's deep voice reverberates, echoing from the transmission.

A rush of adrenaline overwhelms me, and I push to my feet.

Clay glares at me through the screen and slams his hand on the table. "Sit the fuck down, Max."

I compose my face and glare at Erik on the monitor. "Why didn't you say something to me or Jarvis?"

Erik squirms and turns his eyes toward the floor. "Group has had issues for couple of weeks, but team thought they could figure out glitching, so seemed pointless to say. But keeps getting worse, not better. Now, delays are massive, so had to tell Jarvis."

Clay's eyes are icebergs. "You should have told Max or Jarvis when this started. The delay could cost us contracts and good will besides damaging our reputation. I'll discuss your decision-making with Max and Jarvis later." He pauses. "We need to figure out a fix."

"Was only this morning we knew things were out of control." Lips moving frantically, Eric's panic makes his words almost indecipherable. "Troy and I came early to run test." He shakes his head and his shaggy red hair flies around. "No improvement." His voice wobbles, harsh with fear.

"Pull it together," Jarvis snarls at Eric. "Can you tell how much spaghetti code is in there? Are there other issues as well?"

Playing with his ruined frames, Erik squeezes his eyes shut, then pops them open and frowns. "Glitches started two weeks ago. Found few problems and fixed them. That was good for couple days. Then glitches start again and keep getting worse. Now we recheck all code. We think it is spaghetti code in there, gumming things up. Hard for us to figure out where problem is. Can't tell if is one person or several programmers at fault."

"Now that you've found it, can you remove it and write new code quickly?" I ask.

Erik shrugs. "Not sure. Depends on how widespread. We're not sure we've found all."

Clay examines his fingernails. When he responds, his voice chills like frost forming on a windowpane. "Thank you, Erik. You can go back to your office. I'm sure Jarvis will speak to you later."

With a shaky wave of assent, Erik sweeps up his broken glasses and wobbles off our screen.

Clay runs his fingers through his crew-cut. "Where do we go from here? And the more important question—is this incompetence, or sabotage?"

Around both tables, we cast uneasy glances. Hack attacks are an occupational hazard. But no one wants to think that someone in the company is intentionally trying to destroy the system. Still, now that it's out there, we have to take it seriously.

Metin chimes in. "There's been an escalation of Russian activity on banks."

"Anything from the services?" I ask.

She shakes her head. "Not so far, but if word gets out about our problems, they'll come sniffing around." Bank security software is always subject to governmental interest.

"Should we contact them before they barge in?"

"No." Clay's bark is decisive. "For now, we will treat this as an internal matter."

"I think we need to explore all the possibilities. We may uncover sloppy coding." Jarvis tries to sound optimistic.

I jot down notes. "Who can start looking through the personnel files and the coding logs?"

"I'll put Marlene on it. She hasn't been involved with the project and I know we can trust her. I'll check her work every night, too." Marlene is the assistant Jarvis and I share. For an admin, she's a demon.

I nod and go on. "In the meantime, we need to crack on with trying to repair the damage. Erik should have told us sooner. But I think we should let him assess whether we can fix the upgrade. If it can, great. If not, we need to put together a small team, re-vetted, to rewrite the whole thing. Unfortunately, we can't continue to use the complete team if this is sabotage—and rewriting will take time."

Metin chimes in. "Clay, we need to contact the clients about the delay. Something about unforeseen problems, but that still makes the company sound good. And you need a new timeline for the upgrade release. Max and Jarvis need to figure that out ASAP."

"We'll give Erik a deadline to assess. If he can't meet that, I'll check it out myself. If we need to rewrite, I'll lead the team." Jarvis' lips turn up in a small smile, as if making a plan allows him to hope.

"Elena, contact the clients on my behalf. Once that's done, have PR do a press release." Clay is a hands-on owner for a reason. His take-charge personality comes to the fore in clutch situations.

I add my tuppence to the mix. "We need to hire a malware analyst as a consultant. Give Elizabeth Talbot a bell, Jarvis, and find out if she's available."

Jarvis winces like I punched him in the face. "Come on, Max. I don't need her."

"She's the best, with no formal connection to the company. We need fresh eyes, and someone we can trust."

Clay swings his gaze to JL. "Once you're back, you'll have to deal with the day-to-day, not with WatchDog, but putting out fires while I cope with the fallout."

"I can put Case in charge of day-to-day stuff for the next few weeks while I go on to Scotland and Paris with Max and then to Vancouver to visit my mom in two weeks. Dealing with my asshole uncle again. He's really proven himself and I'm planning to promote him to second in command." JL holds Clay's gaze. "None of this software crap is in my purview anyway. WatchDog is ticking along fine."

"Far be it from me to put the company before your personal lives." The acid in Clay's voice could dissolve bones, presumably from our dead bodies.

My heart pounds and heat rises up my neck. "The choice isn't that simple."

His teeth clenched, Clay sweeps my comment aside with his hands. "Are we actively monitoring the team's email and text messaging?"

Jarvis nods. "All employees sign an agreement to allow us to monitor email and text. I'll pull what we have on the team for the past few months and have a copy of everything in the future routed directly to me. Of course, if they have burner phones or use public access terminals with anonymous email accounts, we can't monitor those."

Clay's eyes bore into me. "Are you still planning to stay in Europe for the month, Max?" His tone is less than friendly.

"Of course we are. I'll try to stay in contact, but Jarvis is the point person. He'll deal with the day-to-day issues. And, if it turns out to be sabotage, Metin has the contacts to help us out."

Jarvis' face melts like ice cream on a warm day. "Are you kidding?"

"You designed the software and helped build it. You are the perfect person to see it through."

"I don't know how to deal with saboteurs."

"That's why you need Elizabeth for the malware consulting," I tell him. "Depending on how long the process takes you, I may be back before you get everything resolved."

Clay leans toward focuses on the trio sitting around him. "Jarvis, make sure you have your team together in two hours to meet with Max. Elena, we need a follow-up meeting for Wednesday afternoon at three p.m. Chicago time for Jarvis, Erik, and me to follow up with Max." He shuts down the connection.

Picking up my now cold mug, I decamp to the small office I use when I'm in London.

JL follows me. "Where do we go from here?"

"Damned if I know."

Chapter Twelve

Max
As I settle in front of my computer, my mobile goes off. A glance at the screen shows me that Allan Mason is calling. Arrogant prick. My response swings from "fuck you, Allan" to my eventual "about time, mate."

"Hullo to you too, Max." The dry tone of Allan's greeting grates, even though it's not unexpected. "Meet me at the National Gallery. I'll be in Room 51." A royal command, not a request. I'm tempted to blow him off. Of course, I don't.

"Ten minutes." I don't ask why. Faez, of course. The Wilton Diptych as the meet site seems random, but maybe he wants to pretend he's Richard II and I'm a lowly vassal. Be careful what you wish for, Allan. Remember Shakespeare's line—"For God's sake let us sit upon the ground And tell sad stories of the death of kings." Oh, right. Maybe he sees *me* as Richard II.

The National Gallery is only a two-minute walk from our office. And I can't afford to snub him. Too bad Cress

93

can't be with us. She would probably have some great insights into the late fourteenth-century painting. I chuckle, thinking about how my perfect girl would irritate the hell out of him.

I pull on my jacket and call out to the receptionist as I rush out the door, "Have a meeting. Tell JL I'll be back in an hour or less."

Bloody bad timing, considering the bombshell that hit us. I need to prepare to video conference with my team. Meeting Allan was not on my agenda for today. Our tensions go all the way back to school. He was with me when I found my roommate, Preston St. John Matthews, had hanged himself after some boys spread the word that his father was a famous swindler.

I race across Trafalgar Square with barely a nod at Nelson's Column, run up the main staircase. My shoes click along the floor, announcing my presence. Allan sits on a long wooden bench near the altarpiece, facing away from the entryway. As I walk up to him, he stands and holds out his hand. Our shake is perfunctory, not much more than a touch of fingers.

His receding hairline accentuates the prominence of his sloping forehead and his thin, gray hair. He seems older than forty. Hard to believe this was the fresh-faced, angular youth I went to school with. Collar-length brown hair that curled at the ends and guileless blue eyes, now enlarged by contact lenses, once gave him a cherubic, chorister mien that has decayed into a disappointed, dissatisfied air.

A flash from the past hits me like a tidal wave. When, as a sixth former, I came back from rugby practice to find Preston, my roommate, hanging from the rafters, Allan had been the one to fetch the prefect and the housemaster while my sixteen-year-old-self stood immobilized. I imagine he despised me for my inaction. That moment of cowardice can still shame me all these years later.

MI6 recruited us together, but my career seemed to be fast-tracked. The first time I received an assignment he coveted, autumn coolness became early winter frost. As they rewarded my successes, they pushed him to the middle of the pack. And he was the obvious choice for promotion when the sidelong looks and mumbled conversations after my breakdown took their toll, convincing me that my days as a field operative were over.

I might have come back to a job in cybersecurity after I took my doctoral degree, but the few times I went to MI6 headquarters were like stepping into a polar vortex. Clay's offer of the CISO position at GSU was a lifeline I was eager to grab. Signing on with GSU is one of the best choices I've ever made.

As we stand next to the painting, his eyes shoot flames. He'd incinerate me if he could. His lips are so compressed that they are a barely visible chalk-white line. A tic in his cheek signals his desire to be elsewhere.

"Welcome back to London, Max." His laser gaze assesses me, checking for the weakness he saw when I was released from the clinic. Sending him to assess me had been one of many cuts the service inflicted before I finally took very early retirement. "You look a lot better these days." His jaw is so tight he can barely speak.

"Thanks." I plant my feet, arms folded, as I stare back at him.

"I'm sure you've heard all the news from the Americans."

"Roundabout, but yes. The NSA is a bit more forthcoming than my old mates."

He huffs. "We gave them the goods to pass on."

A portable altarpiece, the Wilton Diptych, as the name shows, is two panels, connected by hinges that allow it to be closed. We're standing behind the panels, which are on a stand so that the viewer can see both sides—the White Hart, neck encircled by a chained crown, and Richard II's coat of arms. Created before the spread of oil paints, the unknown artist prepared Baltic oak panels with a gold background and created the painting in egg tempera and glazes.

"Do you understand all the symbolism?" Allan leans forward and peers at the shield.

"Only what's in the description. My partner would probably know more."

Allan steps back from the display. He rubs his pointed chin and regards me speculatively. "Cressida Taylor...the author?" I incline my head slightly. "Have to say that was a turn up. Didn't think you'd go for the brainy type. I seem to remember that the service used you as a honeytrap on occasion. Saw the inner fuckboy, perhaps?" His leer stings like falling into a patch of nettles.

I blink at the verbal slap, force my shoulders down from my ears, and unclench my fists.

"You wanted to talk about Faez?"

We move from the diptych to "The Man of Sorrows." This room reminds me of a chapel, filled with thirteenth- and fourteenth-century Italian altarpieces and crosses, beautiful but uncomfortable for someone with little religious sensibility. The painting, highlighting the gore of Christ's wounds in a way that is both stylized and graphic, makes me scratch my neck.

"Let's move to Room 38." I stride away, sure that Allan will follow. Heat from his glare hits my back like arrows as he rushes to catch me up.

He hisses, "The crowds around the Canaletto paintings

will be much bigger." With a twist of his lips, he pulls out his mobile and taps a few words on the screen.

I stop, turn, and lift a shoulder. "Too bad. All those altarpieces suck the air right out of the room. When did you become a Catholic?"

"I'm not, but I can appreciate the beauty in suffering."

Suppressing a shudder, I remark, "I don't consider suffering beautiful."

His face is sour. "I knew you were still wet."

Even though the room is practically empty, I pitch my voice to barely above a whisper. "Berk."

Our footsteps echo on the hardwood floor as we reach the haven of Canaletto's Venice and my chest loosens as I glimpse another empty gallery. "Guess Canaletto isn't popular today."

Allan grabs my arm and gestures to a bench. His gaze sweeps around the room. "I took care of it." Then he shifts on the bench. We're so close, our noses are practically touching, as he hisses into my face. "Lots of speculation on terror attacks here, but I'm not convinced that any of them are targeting you specifically. No signs of Faez or his group."

I'd love to believe him, but I don't. He's standing uncomfortably close. Close enough that I can smell the fish and chips he had for lunch.

I force a smile, I start to edge away toward Canaletto's painting of the Piazza San Marco. Keeping my tone casual, I ignore his remark. " This is the ultimate onlooker painting. Canaletto makes you feel as if you are standing in the arch-way, rubbernecking and eavesdropping on the variety of people walking through the square."

Allan shrugs. "I prefer religious art. It gives me hope. Canaletto produced paintings for tourists, not for the soul."

"Superior tourist paintings. Every Brit on the Grand

Tour wanted one." I move to the two Turners. "Turner is one of Cress' favorite artists." The corners of my mouth turn up at the thought of her. "I really should take her to the Tate."

"I can understand the appeal. Certainly, the light is more engaging." His tone is grudgingly conciliatory.

"He's known for it."

I stare at "The Dogano, San Giorgio, Citella, from the Steps of the Europa," on loan from Tate Britain. Venice with Cress in a few weeks is a sweet promise of relief from all this stress. Gondolas and cafés. I can almost smell frito misto and risotto al nero di sepia, taste the bitter tang of Spritz with Campari, and smell the salt air waft in from the Adriatic.

"Turner said, 'It is necessary to mark the greater from the lesser truth: namely the larger and more liberal idea of nature from the comparatively narrow and confined; namely that which addresses itself to the imagination from that which is solely addressed to the eye.' Inspirational, don't you think?"

"Pure drivel," Allan replies.

Baiting him reminds me of our schooldays, and the way his face darkens is all the satisfaction I need to move back to his point. "If there is no evidence that Faez is in London, why are we meeting?"

Allan's snakelike hiss carries over to me. "Time waster."

Arms crossed, I turn and roll my eyes. "You're the one who chose this venue and started us chatting about art."

Allan makes a face like he's sucking on a lemon. "Believe it or not, my assignment is to liaise with you."

I chuckle. "Liaise? About what?"

A huff blows into my ear as Allan nudges up next to me. "This meeting is rather hole in the corner."

I scoff. "Hole in corner? The National Gallery? You're joking."

"True. We arranged for it to be cleared out. Next time, we'll meet in a pub or a wine bar for a drink. Put you on show. Set up the idea that you still work covertly for MI6. We want to use you as bait for the terrorists. They go after you, and we are Johnny-on-the-spot to catch them in the act."

What a crap idea. I repress a shiver, visualizing myself caught in a huge mousetrap. "Doesn't that depend on what they want to do? If it's a straight assassination attempt, that's one thing. But I doubt that's the plan. If it was, I'd already be dead."

"I heard about the white powder incident." Allan drops that nugget casually into the conversation. "Wondered if Faez sent it as a shot across the bows or by someone else to warn you to watch out. Seems like a warning, so I agree that an assassination isn't likely."

"If I had to guess, I think the goal would be collateral damage in a bombing attempt. We know Faez for that sort of attack rather than targeting an individual. Of course, if the plan is revenge for the death of his brother, he might want to kill me face to face. But you said there is no sign that he's in London."

"We haven't turned up anything so far, but he could have come in on a forged passport. MI5 and Special Branch have been looking into connections he has with several cells."

The ensuing silence makes my neck itch. I check my watch. Time to go.

~

"I want him fired." Clay's command carries a note of finality.

After my encounter, with Allan, I don't need this. JL and I sit in GSU's offices in London, before I meet virtually with the team. Through the screen, I watch Jarvis fiddle with his pen while I toy ideas about how to answer.

Before I can say anything, Jarvis tries to paper things over. "It was a lapse of judgment on his part."

Clay hits the table with his fist. "A lapse of judgment. Is that what you call it?" He can barely suppress his rage.

"I agree that he should have informed us when the problem cropped up. But ..." Clay turns from the screen to glare at me. I hold up my hand to forestall the next explosion.

"He is one of our most valuable team members." I hurry on before Clay can respond. "We have two priorities. One is to either fix or rewrite the software. The second is to find the culprit. Letting anyone go will not forward our second priority. My recommendation is to reprimand Erik, start working on a plan for the software, and figure out how Jarvis is going to flush out the culprit." I lean back in my chair, exhausted from a day full of confrontations.

Clay inclines his head slightly, a grudging nod of agreement. Jarvis lets out all the air he's been holding in for the last minute. "I'll leave you to it then. Keep me in the loop, Jarvis." Then he looks straight into the screen. "I'll see you on-screen tomorrow, Max, for the meeting with the banker." He walks out of the room.

Elena's voice is audible in the background. "You can have them come in now," she says to the admin on the other side of the door.

Out of his chair, like the Olympic sprinter he used to be, Jarvis waves. "See ya in a minute."

"I'm going to find a pub," JL tells me.

"There are a bunch of them all around here. Enjoy."

He gives a small wave and walks out of the room while I review my notes for the team meeting. The chatter from the group filing in is just background noise.

A PA slips a cup of tea onto the table. "Thought you might want this."

"Thanks. And do you have some biscuits?" I ask him.

He comes back with some cream crackers and bits of cheese. "I can bring you beer, if you'd rather."

"No thanks. You can go home. I'll shut everything down when I leave." I wave him off. It's the end of the day and I'd rather be alone while I meet with my group.

Jarvis comes back into the frame, noisily. I look up. "Sorry, needed the toilet. Back to back meetings are brutal."

The assembled staff in Chicago titter and gawk at me through their screen as I shift in my chair, feeling as if I'm a zoo exhibit. Sitting alone in London, while the rest of the team huddles in GSU's fifth floor conference room, is alienating.

I eyeball the monitor, trying to assess the mood of the team. Most of them act true to type. Jarvis sits at the head of the table, making notes and conferring with Marlene. Mary and Lorraine, who are a code and test team, whisper and cast worried glances at Jarvis. They should be worried. They should have found this problem.

Troy has his chair tipped back, arms crossed, scowling. Amy fights to maintain a neutral expression. Her face shifts back and forth from glaring at Troy to covert glances at me. Erik paces. He has replaced his broken glasses, but the way he is twisting them, they may end up broken too. His hair stands on end, his face so suffused with color that I worry that he will have an apoplectic fit.

101

Sharon Michalove

I raise my voice. "Guys, let's get this circus moving."

Erik's chair creaks as he plops down. All eyes are staring at me on the screen. Big Brother personified.

"I know it's only eleven a.m. there and you're all thinking about lunch, but over here it's five and I'd like to finish in the next hour. Jet lag." I put cheese on a cracker, hold it up to the camera, smile, then pop it into my mouth.

"I know we're all aware of the problems that have cropped up with the software update. Now is not the time to apportion blame. We need to come up with solutions. What's the timeline you'd recommend, Jarvis?"

Jarvis stares at each team member. "You all know that we have glitches in the new upgrade that we are planning to roll out in two weeks. That roll out will have to be delayed." He turns to Erik. "Clay is going to want an evaluation by our Thursday afternoon meeting. Do you think you can establish whether we can clean everything up or need to rewrite by tomorrow afternoon, Erik?"

The big Russian, who has been staring at the floor, raises his head. "Guess so."

"You sound uncertain," I say.

"Is already Tuesday afternoon. That allows twelve working hours for evaluation by tomorrow afternoon if I am to write a report for Thursday morning."

Jarvis is tapping a pencil against his teeth. "That doesn't mean having it cleaned up, just assessed."

Erik snorts, but then nods in agreement. "I will make it work."

"Everyone, be available in case Erik has questions while he does the evaluations." Jarvis glares around the table. "If any of you have planned time off tomorrow or Thursday, cancel it. On Friday, we will meet again and let everyone know where we stand." He raises his voice slightly. "At that point, you will all have a part to play, and we'll make assignments. In the meantime, you are not to discuss anything outside the team. Even though you all have company NDAs, we have new ones for you to sign for this project. If we hear the slightest murmur outside this group, we will fire anyone involved. Got it?"

Troy's chair clatters as the front legs hit the floor. Marlene passes around papers and pens.

"When you're back to your desks, you will find interim assignments. For the time being, only Erik and I will have access to the upgrade. Any questions?"

Lorraine raises her hand. "Are you looking at incompetence or sabotage?"

"We haven't made a determination. Once Erik has made his assessment, we may have a better idea of what happened."

Silence blankets the room.

"If there are no more questions, hand over the NDAs, and we'll all go back to work." Jarvis catches Erik's eye. "Please stay, Erik. Max and I want to run a few things past you."

Team members jostle as they rush to escape the room. The door snicks closed. Erik runs a finger around his collar.

Jarvis and I scrutinize each other through the screen. We need to trust Erik for the time being, but I can tell Jarvis is uncomfortable with the direction this conversation has to take. We need to narrow down our suspects, even if that means taking one of them into our confidence.

I take a mouthful of my now lukewarm brew, then stare fixedly at Erik. "Although sabotage is a possibility, we want everyone to think this is a more routine problem for the time being."

"Do you suspect me?" Erik strokes his beard and trains

his gaze on the huge decorative stone fireplace in the room used to plan the 1893 Columbian exposition.

"Until we know whether it's sabotage, we aren't actively suspecting anyone. If it is sabotage, we will scrutinize everyone. But we're trusting you for the moment, or we wouldn't ask you to do the assessment."

"Stavit' lovushku," he mutters.

"Don't assume we're setting a trap for you because you're Russian."

Erik shifts uncomfortably. "Sabotage..." He scratches at his beard. "Most of them probably aren't good enough on their own. And some of them, like the Davids, Lorraine, and Mary, have been here for years."

I swallow a choking laugh. As an escapee from the Russian system, he should know better. "Longevity means nothing. Countries embed spies and collaborators years, even decades, before they go into action." My mind shifts to the Cambridge spy ring. "Think of the FBI's Operation Ghost Stories."

"Who else is possible?" Jarvis prompts.

"Amy could do it." Erik's reluctance coats every word. The fact they are involved complicates everything. He tugs his beard. "I don't think she would, but she could. So could Jarod, Felix, or Tracy. No reason they should, though."

"Motives are easy. Money is probably the biggest. Or someone who feels that they haven't gotten ahead as quickly as they think they deserve. Blackmail. Lots of reasons." I prowl around the small office, ready for this meeting to finish.

Erik frowns. I can tell he is not happy with my assessment. Then he goes on. "I would rule out Michael. He's really marginal on this project. Biotech is his specialty, but we needed another coder and pulled him in. If he offered, might be suspicious, but we had to twist his arm."

Jarvis adds his agreement. "Under normal circumstances, Michael wouldn't have expected to be part of the team, so he's not a real possibility."

"Troy is relatively new, so maybe hacking group plant him." Erik smiles, displaying the full mouth of implants he got when he emigrated. He has his suspect tagged.

I keep my voice level. "Didn't he bring the problem to you?"

"Of course. But that does not make him innocent." Erik drags out his answer. He twirls his fingers in his beard, pulling. "Perhaps cover his tracks. Keep him from suspicion." He sits back with a small smile, but his face falls as he observes our skeptical expressions.

"He's been here for two years, so he's not really new." Jarvis breaks in, impatient. "Part of your job is to know the staff. When all this is over, you can expect a comprehensive review. I'm disappointed right now."

"You fire me?" Erik's voice breaks.

"Not at the moment." I think of Clay's demand. "But you have definitely pissed off Clay."

"We're done here." Jarvis makes his hands into a T and twists his face into a scowl. "Remember, Erik, you report to us. From now on, you need to tell us everything. And I mean everything." His grim expression doesn't bode well for Erik's future.

I sigh as Erik leaves. "So how are the kitties, Jarvis?"

His face morphs into a big smile. "You only left last night. My sister is there, keeping them company. But I can't wait to get home to play."

"You realize cats don't need that kind of attention?" I try to keep from laughing.

A stubborn expression comes over his face. "Of course they do. Even animals need love."

"I'll let Cress know her babies are fine."

I shut down the equipment, but instead of locking up, I sit in darkness. My mind drifts from cybersabotage to Cress. I check my watch. The car should pick her from the Club in three-quarters of an hour. She'll be at the restaurant in an hour. I could text JL and see if he's still in a pub nearby and still be waiting for her in Covent Garden.

I'm just starting my text when the sound of sirens fills the air. Someone starts banging on the office door. I'm alone, so I dart out to see what's going on. Through the glass I see two members of the fire brigade, one in his early twenties, the other near retirement age. They motion me forward.

The younger man says, "Gas main leak. You need to leave the building now."

I sniff the air and the smell of gas fills my nostrils. "Just let me get my coat."

"No time, sir. Just come with us."

"Is this a terrorist attack?"

They shake their heads. "No, just some road work gone wrong."

Maybe. As I walk out with them, locking the door behind me, I scan the area for possible threats. Only the fire service team. The bustling square looks desolate. As if a catastrophe had erased the population but left the buildings intact. I shiver. The evening air is already chilly and I'm sorry I had to leave my coat as my escort leads me past the lines of tape.

Finishing the message to JL, that I had started just before the interruption, I send it off.

My phone starts ringing. I don't bother with the formalities. "Hey, where are you?"

"Lamb and Flag."

"I'll join you for a drink. Just five minutes."

"Great. I'll order you a pint."

I'm there in no time, and true to his word, JL pushes a pint of Fuller's in my direction as I drop into a chair at the small wooden table he's snagged. "Finished the meeting early?"

"I had to evacuate the office."

His eyebrows raise. "Why?"

"Gas main break. They cleared the area." I rub my cold hands before picking up the pint and taking a good swallow.

"London Pride. That okay?"

"Perfect."

JL, his elbows on the table, chin resting between his palms, lean toward me. "Was it a terrorist attack?"

"They say not. But who knows?" An unwelcome realization hits me. If we can't get back into the office tomorrow, we'll need to meet somewhere else with the bankers. I hold up a finger to keep JL from saying anything and send a text to our chief PA in the London office. She gets back to me almost immediately.

Not to worry. Everything in hand. Contact you if meeting venue moved.

I exhale loudly and take another gulp.

Nasim Faez's snarling face rises to the surface, shreds of torn keffiyeh hanging around his neck, venom in his eyes as he spits at me in Turkish. All the while the Turkish police haul him out of the rubble. "I won't forget. You will pay."

I'm sure that hasn't changed. The question is, how sorry does he plan to make me?

Chapter Thirteen

Cress

RING. RING.

I wince. My head pounds as I reach for my cellphone. I hit the button, but the ringing doesn't stop. When I squint at the screen, it's blank.

RING. RING. RING. RING.

Crap. I try to focus, but everything is a blur. The sound seems to come from everywhere. With a groan, I roll off the bed and survey the small bedroom. Nothing. Then I move into the sitting room. A black rectangular block sits on a table/desk.

RING. RING. RING.

"Oh, shut up." I grab the receiver and the noise stops. "Hello?" My mouth is dry, making my voice sound scratchy.

"Dr. Taylor?" His Geordie accent is so pronounced even two words are enough for me to identify it. He sounds like Sgt. Lewis from the *Morse* television series. The staff must come from all over the country. I wonder if they all have an RAF connection.

"Y-e-e-s." I move to find my glasses, but the phone

attached to the wooden top restricts my movement. An involuntary growl of frustration rises from my chest.

"You have a visitor." The voice is emphatic, with an undertone of impatience.

A visitor? Then I realize what's happened. My mouth snaps shut, and I rub my eyes.

"Dr. Taylor? Are you there?"

"Uhhh, yes. Sorry. What time is it?"

"Fifteen hundred hours."

"What? Sorry. I..."

"Fifteen hundred hours." Fingers tap against keys. "Three p.m. for you."

Maybe it's my imagination, but condescension drips from those few words along with the subtext "stupid American." Right. Military time. We're staying at the RAF Club. Of course, they would use military time.

"I was asleep and I'm..."

He interrupts smoothly. "Not to worry, Dr. Taylor. Dr. Hillary Jones is here."

Tea with Hillary. I've been so looking forward to seeing her after all these years.

"Tell her I'll be down in ten minutes." I pause, wondering if it's enough time. Yeah. I can do this. "Thanks so much and sorry for the confusion."

Eight minutes later, breathless, I run into the lobby. Hillary leans on the counter, chatting with the desk clerk, who is grinning. Hillary's patter is unsurpassed.

Her matching black skirt, top, and asymmetrically zippered jacket in fleece are perfect for the cool April weather and showcase her interest in the latest fashions. Blue eyes twinkle behind the white-framed glasses. Her caramel-colored hair is in a sleek chignon adorned by her signature silver hair clips, crown-shaped, and covered with pavé diamonds. An oval enamel blue badge, framed in white, with an image of Tower Bridge at the top, is on a chain around her neck.

Hillary and I studied history together at Somerville College and became good friends. She was my only friend, really, after my Oxford boyfriend, Kev, left me. The only confidant I had outside my Chicago buddies, Michelle and Paul. And we weren't making a lot of expensive, long-distance phone calls in those days. These days she's a London Blue Badge guide.

"Hills."

"Cress. Darling." Her posh Kent accent carries across the acres of space.

"It's been far too long," we both cry.

"Snap." She laughs and rushes over to give me a hug and air kisses.

Far too long, indeed. The last time had been in Chicago five years ago, where I played tour guide.

She smirks and checks out the smart navy pantsuit Max made me buy before we left Chicago. "Not bad. Who's choosing your clothes these days?"

"Max is a clotheshorse. And he loves to shop for me as much as he enjoys buying stuff for himself."

"Miraculous. This is your sexy MI6 agent? I can't wait to meet him."

"Retired, Hills. And don't expect James Bond."

"Pity. I was hoping he was Sean Connery in his prime."

I choke. "Well, he *is* a Scot."

She fingers her badge, her forehead furrowed. "We have a reservation at Brown's. I imagine you're up for a slap-up spread."

I love having afternoon tea and I squeak, excited. "I've

never been, but I've heard their teas are wonderful. Didn't Queen Victoria have tea there?"

She nods. "They have Victoria sponge in her honor. Lots of famous guests like both Presidents Roosevelt. Alexander Graham Bell was at Brown's, making the first phone call. Cecil Rhodes was a frequent visitor."

I frown. Rhodes is not one of my favorite historical figures. Even though it would have been much more prestigious, I'm glad I didn't have a Rhodes scholarship. The Rotary was fine.

"The literary glitterati loved the place. Twain, Maugham, Oscar Wilde, Tolkien, Orwell. Agatha Christie, of course. And Rudyard Kipling wrote much of *The Jungle Book* there."

We walk down Piccadilly, enjoying the view of Green Park, and turn down Albemarle Street. Brown's Hotel is in a white building with a façade resembling the RAF Club.

A frisson of excitement shoots through me, as if I'm entering Agatha Christie's Bertram's Hotel. Will there be murder and intrigue? I can't help scanning the lobby for a glimpse of Miss Marple. But no one resembles Joan Hickson.

The English Tea Room is really three adjoining room. The walls are lined with banquettes, the upholstery alternating solid tan and red, with cream embroidered with large red and green flowers. The chairs are deep horseshoe shapes upholstered in red and comfortable armchairs, in the same flower pattern on the banquettes.

A piano sits in the corner of one room and a pianist plays show tunes, providing a lively backdrop, while the fireplaces make the high-ceilinged space appear extra cozy.

"You and Max?" Hills prompts.

"Uh, uh, uh," I stutter.

She spirals her fingers, urging me on.

"Remember my telling you about the guy I hit with the bicycle when I first got to Oxford?"

She giggles. "Mortifying for you, but hilarious in the retelling."

"Yeah, well, it was never particularly funny to me." I fidget with the extensive tea menu while Hillary watches the other patrons while she waits for me to decide.

"Cress, a guide pal of mine is over there. I'll be right back." She trots toward the entrance. "Fiona." Her voice is audible over the genteel murmur of the tea takers, even though she hasn't raised her voice.

"Hillary, fancy seeing you here. Are you doing a private tour?" Hillary murmurs something back, but it's just meaningless sound to me.

Lips pursed, I continue to contemplate the menu. I'm reluctant to order the full spread with the prospect of an elaborate dinner with Max coming up.

"Cress, this is my colleague, Fiona Lukas. She's a guide with London Walks." As I scramble to my feet, the chair falls silently on the thick carpet. "Fiona, this is my friend Cressida Taylor. We were grad students together at Oxford. She's in London for a few days, so I thought, why not Brown's?"

I hold out my hand. "Pleased to meet you. I've taken several walks with your company. Always excellent."

Fiona and I shake hands. "I'm so glad you enjoyed them, Cress."

I smile back and study Hills' friend. Fiona has longish blonde hair, broad cheekbones, and a winning smile. We're still all standing around the small table. Hills raises her eyebrows in a question and I nod.

"Would you like to join us, Fiona?" I ask.

"You're sure you don't mind? I only came in to check things out for a private tour I'm putting together. They're keen on Agatha Christie and want to end with tea. I thought Brown's would be perfect." She grins. "And I've never been here before, so I thought I could combine business with pleasure."

I wave over a hovering server. "No. It's fine."

"Thank you." Fiona shrugs off her orangey-red coat and drapes it over her arm while we figure out the seating. Underneath, she is wearing a bright blue blouse and her blue badge hangs on a chain. Between Fiona's bright colors and Hillary's fashion-plate outfit, I'm the drab country mouse.

"Fiona's been a guide for yonks and a great mentor when I was getting started. specializes in tours of the Underground. A real transport aficionado."

Fiona's face lights up with a grin. "Are you here on holiday, Cress?"

"Not exactly." I hesitate, as usual balking at the idea of calling Max my boyfriend. Sounds too jejune. Finally I hit on the right word and go on. "My partner is in London for a meeting and a seventy-eighth birthday bash for his father and I'm using the opportunity to get together with Hills and meet with my editor."

"Ah, an author. What sort of thing do you write?"

"Are you ready to order?" The server glances over at our now-expanded group.

"May we have a larger table? Or at least an extra chair." Hillary produces one of her irresistible smiles.

Once moved, we hastily check out the menu. The tea sommelier arrives, and we decide on the Silver Needle Supreme White. I push down my misgivings as Hillary and I plump for the Traditional. Sadly, the champagne version is only available on the weekends. Fiona, being a bit more prudent, opts for tea and a scone.

Returning to Fiona's question, I lean forward, hands clasped in my lap. "I write historical novels."

"Interesting. Any particular time and place?"

"My last book was about Caterina Cornaro, the last queen of Cyprus. The one coming out next is about the Merchant Adventurers Company and their outpost in Moscow. Cameos by Ivan the Terrible and Queen Elizabeth I."

"Cress is a nominee for some prestigious book award for her Caterina Cornaro book. London is a stopover before the awards ceremony in Paris." My heart squeezes with gratitude when Hills delivers this news. I may not have a vast circle of friends, but the few I have are stars.

"Congratulations. Write down the title for me and I'll check it out."

I pull a small notebook out of my bag and scrawl my name and the title, tear out the page and hand it to her. She tucks it into her wallet.

"Cress was telling me about her new man."

Fiona smiles. "Fine with me. I'm always up for a good story."

"Right. To catch you up, the first time I met Max was when we were both studying at Oxford University in the 1990s. I was a graduate student in history, and he was an undergraduate student finishing his last year in languages."

"Did you have a memorable meeting?" She takes a sip of water. Conversation halts while we survey the now loaded table with two silver-tiered servers filled with sandwiches, pastry, and scones with clotted cream and jam. The server sets a plate with one scone at Fiona's place. A silver pot with strainer and porcelain dishes decorated with berries and leaves complete the table.

"We can have seconds or even thirds." Hillary rubs her hands before diving in; her eyes glimmer with anticipation.

I groan. "Max is taking me to Clos Maggiore for dinner."

"How romantic." Fiona clasps her hands, enthusiastic. "The decor is fab. Lots of cherry blossom hanging everywhere."

Oh no. Flowers. How could Max not remember my allergy? Especially after the visit to the emergency room last year when the bouquet he sent me brought on an attack. My alarm must show as Hills breaks in. "Don't worry, Cress. All artificial."

Breathing again, I smile gratefully.

"But with this sumptuous repast and the amazing dinner to come, you'll need to run a few miles. Probably should have plumped for a scone, like my abstemious colleague." Hills laughs at me.

We fill our plates from the assortment of sandwiches. Fiona nibbles her scone. "Go on with your story. Please."

"I was new to Oxford and was late for my initial meeting with my supervisor. So, I borrowed a friend's bike, thinking I could make better time. Instead, I ran into Max and knocked him down."

"And you fell instantly in love. So romantic." She sighs.

I roll my eyes. "Love, no, although Max evidently felt an immediate attraction, or so he says. At twenty, it was probably insta-lust on his part. Not that I was anything special."

My younger self was too thin, with messy hair, nose a bit too long, and saggy clothes that made me feel bohemian but probably marked me as one step up from a vagrant. I was definitely no beauty queen, and awkward with it.

Today's smart outfit, courtesy of Max, makes me a well-dressed comic stick figure.

I pull my thoughts back and refocus on my audience. "I couldn't wait to escape from this gorgeous, pretentious upperclass twit. After that brief encounter, I saw him all over town that year. He stood out and who resists looking at eye candy. But we never really met. I tried to put the whole thing out of my mind."

I picture twenty-year-old Max, gangly, dressed in a tweed jacket and khaki slacks, his dark hair mussed from our encounter. "Our real meeting came last year after he saw me on television, being interviewed about the Cornaro book. It was after I heard about the award nomination. He still remembered me after twenty years."

My listeners are sitting forward, faces rapt. Hillary is holding an egg sandwich but seems to have forgotten it. I pick up a cucumber one and take a bite, rolling my eyes with delight. "Ernest Worthing and Algernon Moncrieff would scoff the lot."

Hillary chortles. "Poor Lady Bracknell, cheated again."

We move on to the scones, and Fiona plays mother, pouring the last of the pot into our cups. The sommelier appears immediately to remove the empty pot. "Would you like more?" I nod, then savor another bite of scone before continuing with my story.

"Max showed up at my book signing and convinced us to let him tag along for dinner afterwards."

"Sounds like he can talk the birds out of the trees, to use a tired cliché," Fiona teases.

"And then he was persistent. Like a fly who keeps buzzing around but evades the swats."

I think about our roller coaster of a relationship. How we come together and pull apart. It's still so new; only a few months. Not surprising Max is still fighting his reluctance to tell me about his past. And how difficult I find overcoming my dread of betrayal. Our story is not simple. Not simple at all. How to explain the attraction, desire, and fear. Do I want to explain my past, talk about my insecurities?

"Tell us more." Hills' expression is avid. Being pried open, like an oyster, makes me squirm.

"There's really nothing to tell. Even though I was reluctant, Max was wonderful about arranging protection for me when I was being threatened by a narcissistic sociopath." Fiona's eyes are wide. It was news at the time, especially because of the press hysteria over Tina's accusations of plagiarism, so Hillary knows the outline of Tina's persecution. At the moment, I don't want to re-live those events. I roll my shoulders.

"This is the woman who accused you of plagiarism, then shot you?" Hillary clarifies.

I nod. "Yeah. Anyway, let's talk about something else."

Fiona checks her watch, then stands. "I really enjoyed meeting you and I wish I could stay longer, but I really need to run." We stand with her and Hills gives her a big hug.

"See you soon. And let me know how the Christie tour and tea goes."

Before Fiona slopes off for another engagement, I press her hand. "So lovely to meet you."

"You too." Fiona gives a little wave and hurries out.

"She's lovely," I say.

"Yeah, she is. And a great guide and mentor." Hills pours more tea, leans back, and peers at me through the fringe obscuring her eyes. "So you're not sure how you feel about Max?"

Warmth spreads across my cheeks as I think of Max pulling me into his lap, nuzzling my hair. "I'm mad about him, but I'm not convinced Max really knows what he's getting into. This is his first relationship, and frankly, I'm not sure what he sees in me. At some point, he'll realize he can do better."

"There is no one better." My friend is staunchly in my corner. "I would say he knows he has the best."

"You've never met him," I protest.

"If you care for him, sit back and enjoy the trip of a lifetime."

Pent-up emotion forces an unexpected outpouring. "Max should be with someone glamorous. He could have anyone. Anyone. Actresses, heiresses, models. High-powered business executives. The crème de la crème. I'm a short, too-thin, dull, middle-aged novelist. Besides," I choke out, "Everyone leaves. Nothing ever lasts."

Open-mouthed, Hillary stares at me, then pointing a finger at her chest, she declares, "Stop projecting your dysfunctional family on the rest of us. I'm still here." Her voice is a mixture of pain and ice. Micki told me the same thing. Why can't I believe them?

I drop my head to my hands and groan. "God, I thought I had shed these insecurities." I crumble the remnants of my scone into finer and finer crumbs, then wipe my fingers with the linen napkin that matches the dishes.

"Hey, show me your Max photos?" Hillary's voice is full of fake cheer.

I pull out my phone, click on the photo app, and bring up the album labeled Max.

"My God." Hill's voice climbs toward the clouds. "You're sure this isn't a photo of some hot model?"

I point to myself. "Not...in...his...league."

She swipes through the rest of the album. "When he doesn't have stars in his eyes, he looks at you as if he's afraid

119

you'll vanish any second." Hillary's voice holds a note of envy.

At the end of our lovely tea, I'm worried I'll be too full to enjoy dinner. I push back my chair and place my palms against the table as I stand.

Hills is already at the entrance to the tearoom. She motions and calls out, "Get a move on, slowcoach."

I linger for a last appreciation of the lovely room, before moving slowly away from the table. As I weave through the room to join her, I mutter, "Don't get your knickers in a twist."

I remember Max warned me not to walk alone, so I grab Hillary's arm. "Walk me back to the club."

"Something wrong?" Her voice is a tightly wound string, her gaze assessing.

I survey the vicinity, making sure we aren't overheard. "I didn't want to say, but Max is getting some threats and I'm nervous something will happen while we're in London."

She nods, slips her arm through mine, and walks me back to the Club, where the doorman salutes us. Safety in numbers.

I give her a grateful hug. "You're a brick, Hills. Tomorrow at Rules."

"Think nothing of it. See ya tomorrow." With a queenly wave, she walks off.

As I enter the foyer, a memory returns like a wave.

I remember going to an amusement park with Micki and Paul when we were about ten. I hated the rides, but they begged me to go, calling me a spoilsport. When we go there, they dared me to go on the spinning teacup ride. I hated it even more than the Ferris wheel and the roller coaster. Once it started whirling, I panicked and screamed.

The operator brought the ride to a sudden halt, knocking everyone to the floor.

I remember stumbling out, crying and shaking, while the other riders and the operator berated me for spoiling everyone else's fun. Mick and Paul looked ashamed for pushing me. We never went back.

The sensation of rotating and revolving at high speed, wanting to stop but clinging on tightly, afraid the acceleration will fling me out, is nauseating. And now I've reached another crossroad. If I can't stop clinging to the deep belief that Max may never make good on his promise to shake his difficulty in sharing secrets, and I can't overcome my refusal to accept that reality, we may never make it.

Chapter Fourteen

Max

The walk from the Lamb & Flag to Clos Maggiore is only a minute but JL and I take an evasive path, down St. Martin's Lane, up Long Acre past the Covent Garden tube station to Bow Street. We dawdle a bit by the Royal Opera House before turning down Russell Street, where we duck in and quickly check out Benjamin Pollock's Toyshop before ending up on King Street in front of Clos Maggiore. No followers as far as either of us can tell.

Clos Maggiore is so much in demand I made our reservation in January, as soon as I knew when we would be in London. Even then, this was the only night they had available and nothing earlier than nine p.m. My long meeting with the Chicago work group means I'm still running it fine.

The problems at GSU might be the proverbial straw, even though I'm leaving everything in Jarvis' hands. The blow is like being hit in the back of the head with a cricket bat whilst the ball whacks me in the chest. I am aggrieved and desolate all in one fell swoop. For a moment I toy with rushing back to Chicago, but Jarvis is technically better able to deal with the coding issues and Clay has operatives well-placed to find the saboteurs. With Nasim Faez on the loose, I face bigger issues.

Maybe I need to put Cress on a plane for Chicago, whether she likes it or not. Damn, much as I want to, I can't treat her like the helpless heroine of a Victorian novel. She knows the risks, and I am grateful she stands with me, even though I want her to run away.

A black taxi pulls up at the red awning and Cress hops out just as we reach the entrance. I breathe a sigh of relief.

JL punches me in the arm. "I'm off now. Think I'll go somewhere for pizza."

I nod absently, unable to take my eyes off Cress as she crosses toward me. My breath catches as I take in her slender figure, wrapped in a black cashmere agnès b Swindon coat is an extravagant replacement for the red coat ripped by a bullet when Tina shot her last year. The stand-up collar frames her delicate oval face. She has it unbuttoned, and I notice flashes of green underneath as she comes toward me. I slip my hand into hers, dropping a kiss on her cheek, and lead her into paradise.

"Hello, you," she whispers.

"I feel like it's been forever, even though it's only been a few hours."

I check her coat, and when I turn to look at her, I'm transfixed. Even though I saw the dress when she bought it, the ivory V-neck bodice, lace design at the waist, and flared green silk skirt, sheer enough to hint at the satin underskirt in a slightly darker green, shows off her figure to perfection.

Her face lights up as I slip my hand onto the small of her back as we follow the maître d' through the elegant Georgian townhouse to a room festooned with a forest of branches, fairy lights, and cherry blossom hanging from the ceiling and running down the walls, to a cozy table for two, to the right of the fireplace. The mirrors surrounding it made the room appear twice the size.

When we first walk into Clos Maggiore, Cress sniffs the air and checks out the tiny flowers hanging everywhere. They are so lifelike, I can understand her reaction. When she's not assaulted by fragrance, her shoulders, which had been brushing her ear lobes, drop.

"Not to worry." I smirk. "Can you imagine the mess if all those blooms were real?"

She snorts. "I can imagine the floors covered with drifts of blossom, waiters in hip boots shoveling them into giant trash bags."

I try to hold in my laughter without much success as the other diners turn at the sound.

Cress drops into the rose-colored armchair the host had pulled out for her. She kicks at the fabric of the burgundy underskirt for the white tablecloth, trying to put her feet under the table. No time to chat as a waiter comes up asking for our drink order. After ordering cocktails, a Negroni for Cress and an old-fashioned for me, Cress leans her elbows on the table, chin resting on her entwined fingers, eyes pinched with worry.

"Did you have a bad day?" She pitches her voice so low even the soft jazz in the background makes it hard to make out her words. "You look tired, and sad."

I swallow more of my drink while I try to decide what to tell her. This meal is supposed to be a tangible expression of how much I love her. Why am I treating it as if it is the last meal of a condemned man? I finger the small box in my jacket pocket. Now is not the time.

To distract her, I lob a question. "How was Brown's?"

I expect Cress to give me the blow-by-blow. But she frowns at my attempt at a diversion.

The glass in my hand is empty, and I wave over a waiter. "Another, please." As he grabs the heavy crystal beaker, I glance at Cress' Negroni. She has only taken a sip.

We sit, barely moving, waiting for my fresh drink. I can't figure out to respond to her earlier statement. Right now, talking about my meeting with Allan Mason is off the table.

Instead I peruse the extensive wine menu. Whatever we order, Cress will want a red. For myself, a Montrachet Grand Cru will be perfect with seafood. I'm twenty-six pages in before the reds appear. The depth of their cellar is astonishing, and I give all the options careful consideration as a welcome diversion from terrorists and saboteurs and arsehole former colleagues. I toy with the idea of a Côte de Rhone or a Pomerol or even a Chianti Classico because I know she likes all of those, but in the end, after a serious conversation with the sommelier, I plump for a Brunello. They have an excellent selection, and it is Cress' favorite.

Once the sommelier moves on, she tries again. "Is it the terrorist, Faez? Have you heard of something else? Is he in London?"

The concern in her eyes overwhelms me. Her fingers brush against the crystal tumbler, and she regards as if she's forgotten that she ordered it. After a sip or two, she sets it carefully on the table and runs her finger around the rim. "Heavy base." Her eyes crinkle as her mouth turns up in a cheeky grin. "Less chance of knocking it over."

Relieved that she's decided to let things go, the knot in my chest loosens and I wish we weren't sitting in the most romantic restaurant in London. The siren song of our RAF Club bedroom calls as if inviting us to give up on dinner for another kind of feast. Cress flushes as if she can read my mind. I stare at the open fire and breathe in the calming atmosphere of a Provençal auberge.

"Nothing like that. Nasim Faez has gone to ground at the moment." Telling her about my meeting with Allan is pointless. "Work problems. Issues with the software update. Plenty to worry about, but I can't do anything."

"Do we need to go home?"

My head jerks up. She would do that for me? After all the arguments about this trip, I can't believe it. Pointless, though. If we're together, then the danger is still there. The only thing to do is to find Nasim and eliminate him once and for all.

"No." My voice shakes. "No. I'm on holiday. And I'm damned well taking it." Firmer. "Jarvis can deal with the software issues." I stroke the soft skin of her inner arm from wrist to elbow. "Once my meeting with the bankers finishes, we'll celebrate with my family and enjoy your triumphs." I gulp down half of my drink. "And to hell with terrorists."

Cress salutes me with her own glass. "To hell with them."

Cress

After the afternoon feast, hunger is not an issue. In fact, I am still so full I worry I won't be able to eat much. The lure of oysters with caviar and foie gras with duck confit from the starter menu makes my mouth water. I can't pass up a rack of lamb either. "Max," I wheedle. "Can we share some dishes? I want to taste everything, but I'm not sure how much I can manage."

"Order what you like, and I'll hoover up whatever you

don't eat."

"What are you going to have?"

He scratches his cheek with one long forefinger. "Seafood, I think. I'll start with the Cornish crab and then the lobster with the spinach salad. You can try it all if you like. And save room for pudding."

"Will you share it with me?"

"Knowing you, I won't have the chance. I'll take the cheese plate." He takes another small mouthful of his old-fashioned. "They have some excellent wine pairings with the desserts."

Now I lean back after my final scrape of a luscious peach and raspberry dessert and take another sip of the recommended Coteaux du Layon. Even though I have a sweet tooth, I'm not fond of sweet wines, but this dessert wine from the Loire Valley was the recommended accompaniment and complements the fruit flavors perfectly. True to his word, Max finishes with cheese, an assortment of savory biscuits, and port.

I suppress a yawn.

"Tired?" He picks up on my moods so scarily quick.

I nod and cover my mouth to hide another yawn. "Hard to believe we only arrived this morning."

I'm nonplussed when he stands and holds out a hand to help me up. "We should make a move."

"We haven't gotten the bill."

He waves a hand in dismissal. "Already taken care of. They have my card." We walk out and he points to the line of taxis queueing nearby. "I'll flag a taxi."

I cover another yawn. "It's a lovely evening. Can't we walk?" Ignoring Max's frown, I start toward the Piazza and stumble on the cobbles.

Max's arm snakes out and grabs me around the waist.

"Taxi." He guides me toward one of the black behemoths.

"Fresh air might be good," I mumble.

"We can take a stroll in Green Park later, if you're up for it. I don't think anyone followed either of us to the restaurant, but I'm taking no chances. Walking back to the club isn't a hop, skip, and a jump."

Grudgingly acknowledging his concern, I climb into the cab. A quick ride later, we roll out of the taxi at the gates of Green Park. I take a deep breath and the ground undulates. "Too much to drink, Max," I slur. I can see the doorway to the club. The doorman is helping a couple, one using a cane and the other in a wheelchair, through the entrance.

He rests his hand on the small of my back and guides me toward the entrance across the way, when a rowdy group, dressed in Arsenal gear, tries to push past us. "

"Hey, watch it." Max growls and pulls me to the side.

A stocky middle-aged man turns to confront us with a belligerent glare that turns into searching confusion. I eye him without a hint of recognition. His eyes widen and his mouth drops open as he chokes out, "Cress Taylor?"

"Ye-es." Who is this guy accosting me on a London street as if he knows me?

"Well, well, what do you know?" Weaving drunkenly, he grins at his pals. "This woman," he slurs. Then he peers at me again, gives an exaggerated double take, and waves his arms around, almost losing his balance. "Correction, this cold bitch was my girlfriend in Oxford. Three bloody boring years. Christ!"

Max's hand tightens, threatening to crush my fingers. I stare at the unfamiliar figure, realization slowly dawning. "Kev?"

My emotions swing from incredulity to embarrassment to anger. Bile floods my mouth and I swallow it back down with a shudder. I haven't seen this man for almost twenty years, but he had no problem weighing in on the accusations of plagiarism against me last winter.

As I step back, memories of Tina and her vendetta flood in. I always thought of myself as was an inoffensive, inconspicuous person, and yet there are at least two people with animosity so great that years later, they are still out to injure me.

Before I can say anything, he continues his taunt. "Fancy seeing you here. I thought you were still cowering in America after the hoo-ha last winter. But here you are, bold as brass, swanning around Mayfair."

He swaggers closer and flicks a finger against Max's lapel. "And who is this git?" He twists his lips into a grimace. "Paid escort?" He moves back and surveys us. "Or have you given up writing and plumped for being a rich man's plaything?" His short laugh is unamused. "Nah. You have to being paying him. No one would pay you."

Kev hasn't aged well, but he's still trying to make a youthful impression. His hair is shaved close on the sides, while the top stands up like a brush. His physique has morphed from muscular to paunchy. His light blue eyes, sunken and reddened from drink, squint in the bright shine from the street lamps. An Arsenal shirt strains across his belly, and he is wearing a beanie and scarf in the team colors.

Max still has his arm around me, and I feel his muscles bunch as he realizes who this jerk is. Releasing me, he shields me with his body while stepping forward, forcing Kev to retreat. I'd say he was up in Kev's face, but he towers over the shorter man, fists tight at his sides. His eyes narrow. "Piss off, you mingy bastard." He pushes Kev's shoulder.

Drunken bravado gives Kev false courage. "Try to make

me, you wanker," he says, moving closer. The sneer on his face is a dare. Then he focuses on me and licks his lips. "Mutton dressed as lamb."

Max stands his ground as I back off, struggling not to run away. Kev's friends grab hold of Max and pull him away. Even though he struggles, he can't break loose. But he's still taunting my ex-lover. "Can't face me on your own, wanker?"

Kev ignores him, laughing as I puddle down, my knees banging onto the sidewalk.

"Still hiding away, Cress? Afraid of your own shadow. Haven't changed much in all this time, although you dress smart now. Like trying to make a silk purse out of a sow's ear, though."

His friends crack up as if this is the funniest thing ever. Max takes the opportunity to break away. "You all right, Cress?" he calls out as he grabs at Kev's shirt.

Anger replaces fear. I manage to get back on my feet, my knees raw and stinging as I move. "Fine, Max," I call out.

Dancing out of Max's reach, Kev yells, "I bet you're still a rubbish screw. Don't know how I put up with you all that time." I gasp as if from a physical assault. Unbelievable that this is happening in a public place in a posh area of London. Where are all the people who should be milling around?

"You'll be sorry that you ever ran into me, c—," he starts, moving in my direction.

Before he can finish the taunt, Max reaches out a long arm and latches onto the back of Kev's soccer jersey, then throws him on the sidewalk. Kev scrambles to his feet, fists clenched in a caricature of a boxer's stance as he continues his taunts. "This ponce probably doesn't even notice you lying rigid, like a corpse."

That's the last thing he says before Max punches him in the stomach. Kev goes down with a cry. His friends pull him up. Kev struggles as if he wants to go for Max, who curls his lip like he stepped in a pile of shit.

"He hit me. Call the cops," Kev snarls as he backs away, rubbing his belly. Max moves forward and lands another hit to the solar plexus and Kev drops to the ground, groaning.

"Should have hit him in the jaw," Max says. "Probably the only way to shut him up."

Much as I hate violence, I can't suppress a chuckle. Kev was always a bully. Most of his abuse was verbal. He never hit me, but he would grab my arm so tightly he left bruises. He pushed me when I walked in front of him, and occasionally knocked me down, always apologizing as if it was an accident. I enjoy seeing him swallow a taste of his own medicine.

Kev struggles to his feet, balls his fists and comes at Max again. This time, Max punches him in the face. Kev's ensuing howl rends the air.

"He broke my bloody nose. Get the cops." He shakes his fist from a safe distance as Max lets out a derisive laugh. "I'll have you up for assault." His breathing sounds choked.

I peek around Max and see blood gushing from Kev's face.

A chorus of shouts come from his friends.

"Leave it, mate."

"Not worth it."

"Cops will side with the bint."

His gang pulls him away. As they leave, Kev levels some parting shots. "Good luck, pal. You'll find out what a cold, whiny bitch she is. Then again, a wanker like you probably deserves her." His yells continue, fouling the air until they are out of my now blurry sight.

By now, the doorman has popped out of the Club. "Everything all right, Mr. Grant? Sorry I wasn't here. Helping a party in to register. Should I call the police?"

Head down, arms wrapped tightly around my middle, I can't face anyone. I clamp my teeth on my lower lip. *Don't cry. Don't cry.*

"No, it's all right. Just a few drunken football louts."

The doorman a doubtful expression on his face, shrugs and walks back into the vestibule.

Max hugs me tightly, rubbing my back as I shiver.

He turns me around toward the doorway, then lowers his head and whispers, "Let's get you inside." Then he interlaces his fingers with mine and leads me through the doorway and up to our suite.

I move stiffly, my knees bruised. The chiffon on my dress is scraped and dirt speckles my coat. Max helps me undress and slips both pieces into a garment bag. Once he has me settled in an armchair wrapped up in an enormous white bathrobe sporting the RAF Club insignia, he calls down for ice, then roots through my stuff for an extra pair of glasses. When I fell, my favorite pair slipped off and broke. Now they lie on the dresser, irreclaimable.

Max puts down the house phone, which he had used to call the desk to pick up the dry cleaning and bring some ice. I notice that his knuckles are swollen from the fight and he had been flexing his fingers.

"What do you think caused him to go after you?" Max faces the bed, taking stuff out of my case and throwing it on the bed. "And why didn't you unpack?"

I shrug. My unpacking practices are none of his business. "When he came out with his statement last year about the plagiarism, I looked him up. I had always avoided any mention of him, but I was curious. Why come out of the woodwork then?"

"And?"

"He always expected to be a captain of industry. That's why he was working on a graduate business degree. But he never made it past middle management, and he changed jobs often—and not in a good way. I guess, because success eluded him, he somehow resented the woman he discarded having done so well. The award nomination might have been the last straw." I take in a sharp breath as the stinging from my knees starts in earnest. "A guess, but a plausible one."

He turns from the search, and I try to focus on his face. Brandishing my glasses, he puts them on the small table next to the chair. Then, fetching a tube of antiseptic cream and a damp cloth, he drops to his knees and carefully cleans off the debris, rubbing cream into the abrasions. I inhale sharply as the antiseptic stings in the wound. Max strokes my face with his fingertips, sending tingles everywhere to compete with the burn in my knees.

Electricity runs up my spine and I lean into him. Gently, he gathers me into his arms, repositions me on his lap, my legs dangling over the arm. Kisses rain down into my hair, onto my cheeks, against my neck. A knock on the door is an unwelcome interruption.

A male voice calls out. "Dr. Grant? I'm here with the ice."

Max lets out a low growl, then slips out from under me, making sure that I am still securely settled. "Half a 'mo," he calls out. After straightening his clothes, he grabs the garment bag and strides to the door, exchanging it for the container of ice. "Thanks, mate."

"Anything else, sir?"

"Think we're set. Have a good evening."

The man closes the door and we hear his footsteps as he retreats down the hall.

Coming back with the silver ice bucket, he sets it on the desk and fetches a towel, wraps up some cubes, and holds it against his swollen hand. Even though every muscle aches, I manage to get upright. "Sit down, Max.

He groans and lies down on the couch in the sitting room. I pull the desk chair over, and hold the ice against his hand. After a while, he pulls away and peeks at his hand. "Enough ice for the moment. The swelling is going down. I'll just get some Nurofen. I'm sure I'll be right as rain the morning." He pauses, then gives me a speculative look. "I plan to go swimming tomorrow morning with the Serpentine Club. Are you up for it?"

I roll my eyes. "No. I don't like to swim and the idea of getting into a cold lake in the middle of a park..."

"It would set you up for the day."

"Or make you a sitting duck for a sharpshooter."

"Unless a sniper is waiting outside the club, I don't really see that as a possibility. In any case, if that happened, I'd never get to the Serpentine in the first place."

Horrified at his matter-of-fact acceptance of the danger, I put my hands up to my mouth.

"Hey, it's all right. The theory right now is that Faez wants to be face to face when he kills me, so a sniper isn't really in the cards."

As if that makes me feel better. The idea that someone would kill him is overwhelming. For all my insecurities about our relationship, I am stupid in love and I can't imagine life without him.

Max moves my hands away from my face, caressing them with his now somewhat oversized thumbs.

Eventually, I ask, "How will you explain the swelling at your meeting?"

"Unlike Americans, these uptight bankers would never comment. So I won't have to address the issue."

My encounter with Kev has made me feel filthy. A Turkish bath is out of the question, Then, I announce, "I'm going to take a shower."

"Let me know if you want me to scrub your back at some point." Unfortunately the tub in this place isn't big enough for the two of us, so I don't invite him to join me.

The water from the showerhead is feeble, but I stand under it for a long time, scrubbing and scrubbing to wash away the feeling of being covered in slime. I can't bring myself to leave the safety of the water.

Max calls in to me. "Cress, need some help? Should I come and help you wash Kev away?"

I shudder. Kev's taunts spoil my thoughts about our romantic evening. They play on a loop and tears pour down my face.

Do I want him to come in? Yes. But I don't want him to find me in this pathetic state, so I lie. "No thanks. I can manage."

I hide there until Max walks and turns off the tap. He wraps me in a towel, and gently pushes me toward the door. I collapse onto the bed. He follows me into the bedroom, hands me a glass of water and a couple of ibuprofen, then slips into sleep pants and a worn T-shirt.

"Might mitigate the aches and pains from the fall and the hangover you'll have after the Negroni and all the wine at dinner," Max tells me, his face creased with worry.

I groan and choke down the pills and a second glass of water. Then I huddle under the covers and let him cradle me until I finally fall asleep.

Chapter Fifteen

Cress

Watery sunlight penetrates the blinds when I wake up. I reach out for Max, feeling a little empty when I realize his side of the bed is empty and cold. "Hey, Siri, what time is it?"

A computerized voice rises from my cellphone to announce, "It's seven thirty a.m."

My stomach clenches, and a whirling sensation fills my chest. Panic sets in. Max should be back from his swim by now. Where the hell is he? I lie there, fighting for control using deep breathing and muscle relaxation routines to calm my rapid heartbeat and give me space to think.

Still uneasy, I turn over and bury my face in Max's pillow. The faint scent of eucalyptus and menthol from my nightly application of Vick's overlays the delicious aroma from Max's pillow of lime from the shampoo he gets from Trumpers. Calmness flows over me from the familiar smell, and I slide up the headboard, don my glasses, and look around.

Footsteps clatter on tile. Max walks in from the bathroom wearing a long-sleeved T-shirt. *Danger! Dad jokes falling*, it warns. The graphic is a facepalm. I couldn't resist getting it for him when the ad popped up on Facebook. Max cracked up when I presented it to him. I bought one for his dad too.

His gray sweatpants have damp spots from splashing water. He rubs his chin, smooth from his morning shave, and takes in my unsexy long-sleeved tee with its faded Somerville crest. No provocative nightwear for me. Pajamas are where old T-shirts and threadbare sweatpants go to die. I run my hand through my hair, feeling the tangles.

When I move, twinges set up everywhere. I must have tweaked every muscle last night. Nausea and a headache from the hangover Max predicted make me wish, not for the first time, that I hadn't had so much to drink.

No matter how much I travel, the first few days are always an adjustment. This time is worse because I'm not alone and the multiple threats surrounding Max cast a pall over everything. Usually, it's just getting used to budget hotels with showers in hallway cabinets, cramped rooms with the only electrical outlet high above the TV fastened to the wall, and unfamiliar beds. Being in the lap of luxury hasn't mitigated my feeling of dread.

I stretch like a cat. I miss the weight of Dorothy sleeping on my stomach. Or Thorfinn poking his nose into my face. Next trip we need a place that supplies companion animals. I know I should get up, but wallowing is so seductive.

Max sits on the edge of the bed and examines my face. "Wakey-wakey."

I swallow so words don't catch in my throat. My just-got-up voice sounds clogged. "How was your swim?"

"Refreshing. Saw a few people I know."

I push myself out of bed and move toward the bathroom. "I need a shower and some coffee."

Max raises his arm and turns his wrist to expose his watch. "JL expects us at eight."

"Go without me. I'll just order something from room service."

"Not bloody likely. I don't want you out of my sight."

"I don't meet Ainsley until one at the Savoy Grill."

"And I have a favor to ask."

I raise a brow as if I'm not sure I am willing to grant a favor.

"I need you to pop in to Sheremetov Brothers Rare Books. They have some books I ordered for Dad's birthday."

I perk up. I'm all about rare books. "Sure. I haven't been to Cecil Court in quite some time." Then I realize Cecil Court is around the corner from the GSU offices in Leicester Square. "Why can't you go yourself?"

Max shakes his head. "The banker meetings will take all day. Make sure Serge or Alex wrap the books up as a gift."

"Don't you want to check the books first?"

"I'm sure they'll be fine. We've bought books from them since their father had the business. They're relatives."

I snort. Relatives. Of course they are. Max may have the biggest family in the world.

He stands up. "We're cutting it fine, sweetheart."

Bossy boots. I take a quick shower to scrub away lingering feelings, and pull my unruly curls into a scrunchie. I root through my tiny carry-on for the outfit I plan to wear. The wide-leg black wool twill pants and oversized gray polo-neck sweater are cozy and smart enough to make me appear pulled together but not overdressed.

In the sitting room, Max taps away on his laptop. When he turns his head in my direction, heat flows up my neck into my face. The spark in his eyes as he runs his tongue over his lips sends a frisson of desire through me.

He looks up. "Just checking if there have been any changes for today's meeting." Max's phone beeps. "JL is downstairs."

The Athenaeum Hotel is literally a one-minute walk from the RAF Club. As we walk out the door, I notice the spot where the confrontation with Kev took place last night. There are no signs anything occurred, not even a smear of blood from Kev's nose, but a shudder shakes my shoulders.

I've been to London at least a dozen times since I last saw Kev in Oxford, the day he walked out, and we never ran into each other. The shock of seeing him last night hit me like a bowling ball to the chest. Max's arm comes around my waist, and he squeezes me.

JL is waiting in the Athenaeum lobby when we arrive. "Mon Dieu. Two minutes late." He shakes an admonitory finger at us. "Let's repair to the restaurant."

A double macchiato and I'm human again. Max sips his usual morning beverage. True to form, JL has a cappuccino, the first of many. We all choose the full English, although no beans or black pudding on mine. I ask the waiter if I could have a dram of whisky for my oatmeal.

He winks at me. "The Scottish influence. Been to Pitlochry, have you? I know many restaurants there offer the option."

I point to the man smiling at me across the table. "My partner is Scottish."

The server eyes him thoughtfully. "Well, I hope you're a proper *Outlander* romance hero, although you don't have the right coloring to be Jamie. Pity. You really resemble David Tennant."

I snicker. Max is no Jamie Fraser, and I'm glad he's not.

I can understand Sam Heughan's appeal, but Max's dark hair and long, lean body are more to my taste. "David Tennant with dark hair and glasses. Not David Tennant as Doctor Who."

His gaze flicks back to Max. "Is the Proclaimers' 'I'm Gonna Be' your favorite song? After all, David Tennant is their biggest fan." He sings under his breath.

My mind drifts back to before Christmas last year. Max, his father, brothers, and brother-in-law, all in kilts, serenading me with that very song in Micki's apartment.

Once breakfast has arrived, JL asks, "Did you connect with the office this morning?"

Max splutters through a mouthful of oatmeal. "Checked to make sure the meeting place hadn't changed but I didn't check with Chicago. It's only two a.m. there. Although, with our meeting at ten a.m. GMT, Clay and Metin must be up and getting ready." He picks up JL's shot glass of whisky and downs it.

With an exaggerated scowl, JL summons the waiter back. "I need another glass. Your friend purloined mine." He puts special emphasis on *friend*. When Max doesn't follow up, I realize he is on his phone, texting. He must have gotten a message because he usually puts his phone away at meals. Then he slips his cell into his jacket pocket, scowling.

JL touches his arm. "Problem?"

"Yeah." The restaurant is empty, and no waiters are visible. "There was an attempted breach into the system last night." Max purses his lips. "Jarvis found a back door that shouldn't exist."

Shadows flit over JL's face. "Was there an actual breach?"

"The hacker wasn't able to break in, but it was a close-run thing." Max's ragged breathing echoes painfully around the room.

He slaps a palm on the table, his voice hard. "Jarvis has to handle it. We can't put off the meeting with the bankers and it will last all day." Pushing away from the table, his breakfast hardly touched, he shrugs on his jacket. "I'm going to the office. Jarvis is balking at bringing in Elizabeth Talbot, so we need to have another little talk. If he flat-out refuses, I'll call her myself."

"I'll come with you." JL's plate is still full, and he's only eaten a bite of the oatmeal.

Max waves away the comment. "Finish your breakfast. You can't help with any of this." He puts fifty pounds on the table. "Keep Cress company. First the Sheremetov Brothers on Cecil Court, then to the Savoy for her lunch appointment. Meet me at Simpson's with the bankers. Two of them are very interested in the physical security that we offer as well as the software."

After he leaves, JL sips his cappuccino, frowning I take a bite of toast. "Go catch him up. You don't need to babysit me."

He studies my face. "Yeah, I do."

Max

I grab a taxi. In less than ten minutes, I'm walking in the door of the GSU office. "We weren't expecting you for another hour, Mr. Grant," the receptionist says.

"Calls to make before the meeting." I pull off my overcoat and hang it in our tiny closet. The larger coat cupboard is in the conference room for clients. I peek into the room. The staff set the table with packets of papers and a trolley sits nearby with the makings for tea and a plate of sweet biscuits.

A team of interns occupies my borrowed space. Startled, they quickly pack up their project and log out of the computer. "Sorry," two of them mutter as they scurry past me.

The third stops at the open doorway. "We were told working in here would be okay." His tone is a mixture of apology, defensiveness, and belligerence.

"It's okay. No one expected me in this early. But I need to use the space." I turn and slip into the now vacant office chair. As if he can see straight into the office, Clay rings me at that precise moment. I knew he'd call as soon as he heard about the breach. And he would have been notified right away, no matter the time.

"You heard?" Clay barks in my ear.

"Yes. I've already been on the blower with Jarvis."

He snorts. "Is this Elizabeth Talbot chick worth all the tumult?"

"She. Is. The. Best." My fist hits the table with each word. "Jarvis is a bloody idiot. They have history. Tell him to get over himself and get on with the job."

"Got it."

"Thanks, Clay. I don't have time to deal with it today."

"You deal with the double-barreled bank presidents and sell the hell out of them. I'll be the closer."

"Thanks. Anyone else besides Metin and Charles?" Charles is our CFO. Always good to have the money bloke at a meeting with bankers.

"Just JL. He'll join after lunch, right?" Clay continues to focus on the logistics.

"He's coming to lunch. We're taking them to Simpson's."

"The place with the silver trolleys and carved roast beef?"

"The very same. Perfect for wining and dining old-school private bankers."

"Bit heavy for lunch." He stretches. "I'll join you later. We can talk about contracts and close the deal. Three your time? That should give me time to talk to Jarvis so he can bring this consultant on board."

"Great."

When the representatives of three small, prestigious private banks, Glister-James, Clothier Regent, and Rybrooke Marshal come in, it's like looking in a funhouse mirror. Did they coordinate in advance? I stifle a chortle and compose myself.

All three white-haired men wear navy pinstripe suits and white shirts with French cuffs and heavy gold cuff links. They are all tall, but while Glister-James is lanky, the other two are portly. They remind me of *Punch* caricatures of British clubmen. I focus on their ties. If clothes make the man, ties are an insight into their souls.

Glister-James sports an Old Harrovian tie, Clothier Regent is a member of the Worshipful Company of Drapers as a sign of the origins of the bank, and Rybrooke Marshal proclaims his Cambridge Blue in rowing. Interesting that they project themselves variously as a public school old boy, a businessman, and an athlete.

I could have presented myself in any of those guises, but I made a different choice. None of them went to Oxford, so my Balliol tie doesn't impress. Maybe I should have worn my Grant tartan. Full kilt kit would have made an impression. But maybe not the one I want.

First off they ask about Clay and I tell them that he will join us later in the day. This causes some disgruntlement since they all thought that the bulk of their dealing would be directly with him.

We have a long morning of presentations. Metin starts off with the big-picture presentation. Then I explain more about the cybersecurity side and what our software can do for them. They have with many pointed questions about the functionality of the software and the security protocols, which I assume were prepared by their staff computer person.

Charles is grilled about the costs because they all want more for less. I also explain how going cheap doesn't save money in the long run and how an integrated package provides much better protection than adds-on to an existing system. When they ask the cost of adding security people, the additional cost doesn't seem to sit well.

We finish the morning session and adjourn for lunch at Simpson's. After four grueling hours, we are all knacked, except for the bankers.

~

Cress

JL and I walk down to Cecil Court to visit the Sheremetov Brothers bookshop before lunch. My face itches a bit from the heavy application of makeup, but JL did a fabulous job to minimize the injuries. When I asked him where he learned how to do it, he was noncommittal. A mystery for another day.

Cecil Court is a London treasure. Neither JL nor I are inclined for chitchat, but our cabbie is more than willing to pick up the slack.

"Interesting place, Cecil Court. I expect you're going there for the shopping. Dead posh and all. Nicknamed

Bookseller's Row, even though it's a glorified alley. Chock-a-block with bookshops, antique stores, and map purveyors." He glances back at us through the rear-view mirror to gauge whether he's boring us. "The Cecil family has owned it since the sixteenth century and I heard the name commemorates Robert Cecil, first Earl of Salisbury."

When we say nothing, he chuckles. "You might ask who he is when he's at home? Can't blame you. Even those of us who are from here might not know. He was a big fish in his time. Chief minister in the reigns of Good Queen Bess, and the first King James." He pulls up at the curb. "Five pounds, mate. No charge for the history lesson."

JL wrestles his wallet out of his back pocket and fishes out a ten pound note. "Keep the change."

While holding out his hand, the cabbie continues to talk. "The street itself is quite old, but the current buildings date from the late nineteenth century. Before the books moved in, the street was the home of the early British film industry." He pockets the cash. "Ta. Hope you find a few bits and bobs for your new home."

JL and I share a laugh that turns to guffaws. Our cabbie must have thought we were newlyweds.

The Sheremetov's store has a blue-painted wooden front, and the name painted on double glass doors framed in rich dark oak. They've propped one open, inviting visitors to browse.

Inside, it smells of parchment and vellum, calfskin bindings, old paper, and furniture wax—beeswax overlaid with turpentine, linseed oil, and lavender. They crammed most of the floor space with tightly packed shelves. We edge our way toward a long library table pushed against a wall. Light-headed with desire, I could lose myself in here for days.

JL touches my arm. "I'll wait outside."

Astonished, I narrow my eyes. Who can resist the lure of old books? "You don't like books?"

"I like books." He's indignant. "But this? Too confining. Dark. Claustrophobic. I like modern, brightly lit bookstores with plenty of space."

"Where will you go?"

"I'll be right outside. Maybe try to find a bench."

A man stands at the table, paging through a folio volume that might be an atlas. He turns at the sound of our whispered conversation, and, oh my God. He's almost as tall as Max, with jet-black hair, oval face, pale complexion with a reddish undertone that reminds me of Russian figure skaters. His deepset eyes are a mix of dusty blue and gray framed by tortoiseshell glasses. Long thin fingers seem just right for a rare-book **connoisseur**.

"May I help you?" He focuses on JL and I frown. "I can put a chair out in front if you want to sit." His smooth tenor voice is standard London British, with a slight tinge of something I can't identify.

"Merci." JL accepts the offer with a nod.

"French-Canadian?"

"Oui. How did you know?"

"Sounds different from the French across the Channel. I have a cousin who is a whiz at languages, and I've learnt a lot from him." He drags a chair out from a corner of the room and sets it up in front of the shop window, then comes back to me.

"Are you looking for something in particular?" As he goes on, I realize his intonation has the same quality that colors Max's mother's speech—a slight hint of a Russian accent. He must be one of the Sheremetov brothers rather than a salesclerk.

Before I can respond, another man rushes in from the

back. He's slightly shorter and heavier. Brownish blond hair stands up in spikes. He comes forward, hand outstretched, moving between me and the other man. "Good morning." He shakes my hand. "Serge Sheremetov. This dolt is my brother, Alex." He gives a negligent nod toward the now-scowling man standing behind him, arms folded across his chest. "And you are?"

His grip is a little forceful. I disengage and move back a few steps. "Cress Taylor."

"American." Alex's voice is flat and not exactly welcoming. "I hope you realize this is not a regular bookshop. The only bestsellers here are at least a hundred years old."

My mouth drops open and I gape at him.

Serge takes over smoothly. "Not technically true, but we don't stock the newest things." He seems supremely oblivious of his brother's venomous glare. "I'm sure we can help you." As if we share some secret, he gives me a complicit wink.

"I'm here to pick up a book," I tell him, relieved to deal with someone rational.

"We aren't holding anything for a Cress Taylor." Alex continues his grump. Is this the good cop/bad cop bookstore?

"It's not for me, it's for Max Grant. He said it's a birthday gift for his father, Brian."

"How do you know Max?" Alex sounds incredulous.

"I. Uh. He. We're together..."

Serge turns to his brother. "Idiot. Max wrote to us about his girl. She writes historical novels." Alex's muscles go from bunched to relaxed as he lowers his shoulders and shakes out his arms.

I start to relax, although his snarky anti-American comments still needle me.

"Forgive my brother." Serge's eyes crinkle as he throws me a flirtatious grin. "We are frequently besieged by tourists who assume we're a full-service bookshop and ask for guidebooks, Harry Potter paperbacks, and the latest thrillers. They are not best pleased that we only offer rare books. A lot of Americans come to Cecil Court because they think it was J. K. Rowling's inspiration for Diagon Alley, although there are other candidates for the honor."

Alex growls. "Let them go visit the Shambles in York if they're offended we don't carry a complete line of Harry Potter books and knickknacks."

Serge's smile is merely a shadow. "Well, we have several first British editions of the first book—*Harry Potter and the Philosopher's Stone*. Good little moneymaker if you can find a copy. "

A gravelly bass voice booms into the room. "We have Max's book order." An older man limps slightly as he walks toward us with a thick stack of books. "Here they are."

Alex takes the books and sets them on the table, and the third man holds out a large hand with neatly manicured nails. He grips my hand lightly, the calloused palm scratching against my fingers. "Yevgeny Sheremetov, Viktoria Grant's cousin. "

I watch JL lean in at the door. "Everything bien in there?"

All three men look at him. I wave my now-freed hand. "Everything's fine, JL." I turn back to the Sheremetovs. "Max's colleague, JL Martin."

"A pleasure to meet you." They are a Greek chorus, perfectly sync'd. JL waves and goes back to his chair.

Yevgeny spreads the books out on the table where Alex has been working. "My father founded this bookshop when the family fled Russia in 1920. We were nobility in a world where nobility was hardly worth a kopek. Everyone scattered—Paris, London, the Far East, even America." He bestows a glower on his younger son. "We came to London and became shopkeepers." His Russian accent is much more pronounced than his sons.

Shorter than his sons, Yevgeny has a wrestler's physique. I would estimate him to be close to seventy, with thick gray hair and a neatly trimmed beard. In contrast, Serge and Alex are both clean-shaven.

He points to the four books, bound in well-preserved red leather stamped with gold crowns. "*The Rulers of Strathspey* by Archibald Kennedy, 1911. First edition, excellent condition. And all three volumes of *The Chiefs of Grant* by William Fraser, 1883. Privately printed, only 150 copies, so very rare. Also excellent condition."

"Max wouldn't accept anything less." Alex's comment is in a warmer tone.

Perhaps they're close, even though Max has never mentioned him. I suddenly realize when Alex mentioned the cousin who was good at languages, he meant Max.

"Do you want to check them before I wrap them up?"

"Sure." My fingers itch to fondle the beautifully bound volumes.

Alex lays the quarto-sized volumes out on the table. "Do I need to show you how best to handle them?"

I can't help the glare I send in his direction. "I have a DPhil in history from Oxford." My tone could cut glass.

"Of course you do." Alex sounds unconvinced.

I'm shocked at his continuing hostility. Guess my being with Max hasn't really softened his attitude. My temper gets the better of me. "Why would I lie?"

Serge puts a restraining hand on his brother's arm. "Alex, where are your manners? Apologize to Dr. Taylor."

Alex scowls, then mutters sorry with bad grace. His father shoots icicles in his direction.

"I'm so sorry.'"

" You don't need to apologize," I tell Yevgeny as I glare at Alex.

He lifts a shoulder. "I thought I had taught my sons better manners. Alex isn't usually front of shop." He shakes his head. "Even if Dr. Taylor weren't a scholar, you know better than to treat visitors to the shop like this."

Alex frowns and I hear, "Blasted Americans," as I move toward the promised treats. My bonafides don't make a dent in his disdain for U.S. Then he turns back to me with a charming smile. "I really am sorry. I've had some unfortunate news, and, well, it's rather thrown me. But I shouldn't have taken my bad mood out on you."

"You mean that manuscript I told you not to acquire?" Yevgeny's angry tone makes Alex flinch.

"Ah, well, yes, um." He runs a hand gently over one of the red leather covers, a finger tracing a gold crown. "They really are lovely books. I'm sure Brian will love them."

I gently touch the covers before carefully opening each one. The aroma of old wood-pulp paper rises from the yellowed pages of each volume, telling me these books are post-1843, when publishers abandoned cotton rag for wood-pulp paper. While book lovers salivate over the fragrance, most don't realize it's the acid in the paper creating the aroma along with the yellowing of the paper—both signs of deterioration.

But the books are beautiful, and I sigh with delight. I page through the nicely illustrated volumes and the Fraser books have a plethora of documents. They are part of a larger series on the histories of Scottish families. "You can wrap them up," I tell Alex. "Max asked if you could use gift wrap."

He grins, all signs of belligerence forgotten. I think we may still have a few sheets from the Queen's Jubilee celebration." He moves to the back of the shop, where there is a small office, and comes back with some sheets of blue-and-gold striped tissue paper stamped *Sheremetov*. "Handle them carefully. This paper is a little flimsy."

While he's wrapping everything up, I remember that I don't have a gift for Max's birthday. I turn to Yevgeny. "I'm also interested in getting a book for Max since it's his birthday, too. Do you have any classics about racing?"

"Serge is the expert." Yevgeny calls out to Serge, who has disappeared.

He pokes his head out from the back. "What do you need?"

"A classic on racing for Max."

Serge walks out, rubbing his chin. "He gave me a list of a few things he wants. Let me check." He walks over to a bulging section of books, scans them quickly, and pulls one off the shelf. "This would be perfect." He pauses, frowning. "But it's quite expensive."

My eyes narrow to slivers. "How expensive?"

"Maybe a couple hundred pounds?"

I imagine the joy on Max's face when he opens his gift. "Wrap it up for me, please. Brown paper is fine. Max won't care."

Serge takes the book to the worktable and deftly wraps it, just as Alex has finished wrapping the volumes for Brian. He carefully loads them into a shopping bag. Serge puts Max's book in a different bag.

Not knowing who to ask, I blurt out, "How much do I owe you?"

I watch as Serge rapidly calculates the total in his head. "One hundred and sixty-five pounds."

I wonder if he's giving me a discount as I pull out my credit card, and he rings up the sale.

They send their best wishes to Brian and assure me they will be at the party. I exit and find JL hunched over his phone. Tapping him on the shoulder, I say, "All done. Anything wrong?"

He slips his phone into his pocket and stands up. "Texting with Micki."

"Ready to walk me to the Savoy?"

"Bien sûr. I'll put the chair back."

Once he's delivered me to the restaurant, JL takes off for lunch with Max and the bankers down the way at Simpson's on the Strand.

Chapter Sixteen

Max

Back from Simpson's, we sit at the small boardroom table. As JL gives his presentation, more paper is handed out, along with teacups and a plate of biscuits. After an hour, we all get up to stretch and I notice that all that is left of the biscuits are crumbs. Surprising, really, after a huge lunch at Simpson's. We all ate rare beef from the domed silver trolley, served with gravy, cabbage, and Yorkshire pudding. Yet the bankers fall on the biscuits like ravenous wolves. By the state of the tray, Bourbon Creams outclass digestives with bankers.

I snap back to attention as one of the three clears emits a loud "ahem" before asking another question. "I understand you have delayed the introduction of your newest security update. Why?"

Crap. I slip my glasses back on, tent my fingers, and focus on a point above the heads of the three men across from me.

"We've bumped up against some unexpected coding issues." The excuse rolls smoothly off my tongue.

Clay, who has just appeared on-screen from Chicago, picks up the conversational ball. "Software security systems have very complicated structures and because of the massive increase in attacks, we've been adding some extra features to protect our clients from the newest hacking threats. That has meant some changes to the architecture of the system, which means modifications to the coding. We hope to roll out the upgrade soon. But don't worry, our current version is safe and stable."

Finally, after hours of presentation and negotiation, the bankers decamp with assurances contracts will follow.

What a horrible day. I stretch my neck and rub my fingers through my hair. The effort to present our cybersecurity services to the heads of three private London banks takes my mind off the sabotage issues and the terrorist threat. I roll my shoulders to loosen tense muscles. Then I drop my head into my hands and rub my temples to stave off an incipient headache.

JL groans and rubs his back. "Calisse. Glad that's over. Three pretentious jerks. Thank God the on-the-ground security they're contracting for will be minimal."

Clay and I share a look. These bankers were what we expected.

"Max." Clay's bark rolls out of the speakers. "I told Jarvis if he doesn't contact Elizabeth Talbot, I would."

"And...?" Jarvis can be one stubborn SOB.

"He was on the phone by the time I got out the door."

I squeeze my eyes shut. Jarvis is going to be a whiny asshole once Elizabeth shows up. But we need her if we are going to fix this mess. Fingers crossed she's willing to take on the project. "What about the investigation? Are you calling in anyone?"

"Not yet. I'm still trying to keep it internal. With the

latest hack attempt, we have some traces to follow. I'm convinced one of your team is working with Russian hackers. Jarvis has suggested a honeypot."

"Good idea. I can't wait to collar our traitor."

I watch as he pushes back from his desk. "Time for lunch here. I'm meeting Kath at Al's. She can eat their Italian beef every day." He disappears from our screen.

JL turns to me. "We're going to Rules Restaurant for dinner?"

I tear my thoughts away from visions of lines of code, twisting like models I've seen of damaged genomes. "Yes. Then Cress, Ian, and I will meet my parents at King's Cross."

"Should I come along?"

"No need. You can just go back to the Athenaeum and work off the huge meal."

He groans.

My face is deadpan as I tell him, "You can always order a salad."

He laughs and the mood lighten.

Rules, one of the oldest restaurants in London, is one of my favorites. With effort, I turn my mind's eye to visions of potted shrimps, braised shoulder of lamb, and sticky toffee pudding suddenly intertwine with scrolling zeroes and ones. At least terrorist bombs aren't exploding as well.

"The clientele has included famous writers from Charles Dickens to Evelyn Waugh and actors like Charlie Chaplin and Laurence Olivier," I tell him. "When King Edward VII was Prince of Wales, he had a private room upstairs where he could entertain Lillie Langtry. You can reserve to eat there now on certain days of the week."

JL raises an eyebrow. "So, you chose it because of it's reputation as a high-class bordello?"

"I don't think they would appreciate that description."

"Fortunately, we have a couple of hours before dinner to digest lunch." Then he punches me in arm, grinning like the Cheshire Cat. "Ah, a pub. Let's get a drink."

"I'm meeting someone."

He puts his hand on my arm and we come to a stop. "Who?" he demands.

"Yavuz Arslan, Zehra's brother. I told you that he contacted me about meeting in London."

A voice calls out. "Max?"

I take a deep breath. "Yavuz, I thought we were meeting at the Lamb & Flag."

"I was just on my way there when I saw you. We can walk there together." Yavuz gives me a critical once-over. "Ten years and you haven't changed, Max. Still an elegant bastard. A little gray, but otherwise the same."

I reach out and shake his hand. I can see that the last ten years have taken a toll. He's older, more mature, with evidence of a hard life. Yavuz, at thirty, has the air of being closer to fifty. At twenty, he was skinny. Now he's bulky with muscle. I notice ink on his wrists. Tattoos are becoming more common in Turkey, although the government frowns on them. No longer a bright, eager fighter for justice, he's beaten down like a boxer who's seen better days. He used to be a snappy dresser, but now he's dressed in jeans, an untucked Oxford shirt, and a worn cardigan that strains against the overdeveloped biceps and quads. I wonder if he works in a gym.

The deep grooves and gray cast to his skin give him the air of a man who has spent time indoors. Prison, maybe? Metin's sources still haven't found his missing time, but that doesn't mean he didn't spend it inside. Silver threads through his thick black hair. At five-seven, he's a little shorter than Zehra was. They never looked much alike, but then, not all siblings do.

"Introduce me to your copain, Max."

"Boyfriend?" Yavuz giggles.

"Une blague." JL's riposte is sharp.

"JL, this is Yavuz Arslan. Zehra was his sister."

JL holds out his hand, face sober. "Sorry, man. "

"Yavuz, this is my colleague, JL Martin."

"Enchanté de faire votre connaissance." Yavuz's formal greeting is stiff with politesse. I had forgotten he had gone to the lycée in Istanbul. Zehra had gone to a school that specialized in English, one reason Turkish security services attached me to her group even though my Turkish was perfectly serviceable.

"What are you doing in London?" I ask.

"I live here now. My younger brother works at the Turkish Embassy."

"Tanik? He must be, what, twenty-five, twenty-six now?"

"Twenty-six. Yes. Ten years is a long time. Everything is different now. Emre is studying in Paris, so there is no reason to live in Turkey any more." He rubs the back of his neck. You live in Chicago these days."

"Yes. I took a job there a few years ago."

"You are in London for work?"

"A combination of work and family. I'm traveling around, first to Scotland, then with my partner to Paris for a writing awards dinner. I am her plus one."

"You've done well. Moved on." Something in his tone is off. Jealousy, maybe, or sadness.

"The reason we're going to the Lamb &Flag is that Charles Dickens used to drink there," I explain to JL. "Yavuz is, or at least to be, a big fan of Dickens."

"Still am. Besides, it's my local. Very convenient."

JL looks surprised. Is it because Yavuz likes classic literature or that he lives close to Covent Garden?

"Yavuz had just finished studying literature at Koç University, when he joined the security services on Zehra's recommendation."

With a faraway look in his eye, Yavuz says, "Dickens really appealed to me. All that social injustice, the examination of the class system, and the spying, conniving, and mystery. I wrote a senior thesis on *Bleak House* because it embodied so many of those elements. Having a pint at the Lamb & Flag makes me feel as if Dickens might pop in for a chat at any moment."

By now we're just outside the pub. JL claims a table while I go up to the bar to get the first round. Yavuz comes with me as if I might disappear if he takes his eyes off me. Once back at the table, we pause any conversation to check out the draught beers on offer. JL and I go for Fuller's London Pride, while Yavuz picks Sticky Wicket.

"You like pale ale?" JL asks.

"I like the name." Yavuz gives a small smile, as if savoring a private joke.

I had thought of arranging a car to take Cress to Rules, but now I think I'll go collect her. I want to make sure she's all right, and, even though there haven't been any incidents since we arrived, I don't want her out on her own.

"Look, chaps," I say. "I need to get back to the club and pick up Cress for dinner."

Yavuz looks hurt, as if his best friend just kicked him in the teeth. "I thought we could spend a bit more time together," he protests.

"We're going to Rules for dinner. Why don't you come along?"

He looks down at his totally unsuitable wardrobe. "I'm not dressed for it." He drums his fingers on the table. "I suppose I could pop home and change."

"Great. Meet us there at 7:30 pm. If you get there earlier, just mention a reservation in the name of Ian Grant."

"Going by a new moniker, Max?"

"My brother. He's meeting us there, and a friend of Cress' too."

JL takes the pint glasses back to the bar and Yavuz leans over confidentially. "I heard that Nasim Faez is after you."

I start in surprise. "How do you know that?"

"I still have friends in Turkish security. And I may know where to find Faez, before he finds you."

Curiosity burns into me. "Why do you want to risk it?"

"I'm doing this in memory of my sister," he says.

"Thanks. I'm grateful." And I am.

JL comes back to the table and we go out to wave down a taxi back to Mayfair.

Cress grumbles that I'm babying her when I show up to escort her to the restaurant.

I wish I wasn't working while we're in London, so I could spend all my time with her. If I didn't have to work here, we wouldn't have come. Last night's jaunt to Clos Maggiore is still on my mind. There are more dangers than my elusive terrorist. And on these busy London streets, trying to spot a tail is difficult.

When we arrive, the tuxedoed maître d' greets us. He remembers me from earlier visits.

"Welcome, Mr. Grant. Your brother is in the Winter

Garden Bar. If you and your date would like to join him there, I will bring the other member of your party along when they arrive."

Ensconced on a red settee, a cocktail on the glass table in front of him, Ian is as relaxed as if he is in his own lounge. He stands up and holds a hand out, moving past us. "Content de te revoir, JL."

JL brushes past me.

"Content de te revoir, aussi." JL moves around the table and claims part of the small sofa, nudging Ian over. You would think he and Ian hadn't seen each other for months rather than yesterday.

Ian scratches his temple. "You look particularly lovely tonight, Cress."

"How kind of you, Ian," she says. For some reason, I want to sock him.

Yavuz has just arrived and hovers behind us, unsure of his welcome. His suit is off-the-peg but fits him well.

"Ian, this is Yavuz Arslan, an old friend from Istanbul. He happens to be in London on business so I invited him along for dinner.

"Enchanté," Yavuz says.

"Enchanté," Ian echoes.

We subside into chairs to wait for Cress' friend Hillary. JL contemplates Ian's greenish-tinged drink with suspicion. "Is that a witches' brew or some sort of froufrou drink?"

Ian huffs. "It's a Rules Royale. House drink, you know. Crémant, Chartreuse, Gin. Worth trying, old boy."

I wonder if he'll adjust an imaginary monocle. I answer him with a snort. "Poseur." Ian smiles as if I'm complimenting him.

I take a breath."Who do you think you are? Noel Coward? We aren't in a 1920s stage play. Old boy, indeed.

No one has said that in probably forever, except to refer to schoolmates."

"Let me have my bit of fun." Ian's tone is deceptively mild and, damn, if he doesn't adjust that imaginary monocle. "If I remember correctly, you and Cousin Guy went through a Brideshead phase at Oxford." JL laughs, while I push away a sense of loss. Guy was my best friend until he died at thirty.

Ian seems determined to needle me. Pasting on a smile, I try out the first joke of the evening. "What's the difference between a smart Englishman and a unicorn?"

Silence. "No takers? Okay then." I let the silence lengthen. Finally, when the tension has escalated satisfactorily, I grin. "Nothing, they're both fictional characters."

"Saying you're not smart?" JL says.

"I'm not English," I snap back.

Ian smirks. "My mannerisms are infinitely more amusing than your lame jokes. And by smart, are you referring to looks or intelligence?"

My studied shrug is perfection. This is only a minor skirmish, but neither of us likes to lose. "Your choice."

JL snorts, but I'm not sure whether it's the joke or the banter.

Ian runs his finger around the rim of his glass. I can tell he has something to say.

"Out with it, man." I give him the come-on hand signal. His lips twist into a frown.

"I heard you might be in a spot of bother."

I raise a brow. "Where did you pick up that titbit?"

"A pal at the FO."

"Why would the Foreign Office be interested in Max?" JL sounds flabbergasted, although I'm sure he's not. Of course, the FO is interested in Faez, and by extension, me.

I'm on everyone's radar. Not good. Not good at all. Right now, I'd love to be back in Chicago with nothing to worry about besides our software problems.

Cress has been chatting with Yavuz while Ian and I skirmish, and now she scoots closer. I pull her in, resting my chin on the top of her head, and nuzzling her hair. Wolf whistles break us apart. Somehow, PDA has become part of our relationship. Possessiveness, pride, ownership. No, not ownership. But the desire to show she's mine and I'm hers.

"Hello." A tall blonde dressed in black approaches our table.

A big smile spreads across Cress' face as she gets up and relinquishes her chair. "Guys, this is Hillary Jones, Blue Badge Guide extraordinaire and old friend from my Oxford days. Hills, these reprobates are Max, his brother, Ian, his friend Yavuz Arslan, and his colleague, JL Martin."

Hillary's smile twinkles at us as she sizes us up. Her gaze lingers longer on JL. Hmmm.

"Drinks?" The cocktail waiter has sneaked up. Cress startles but recovers quickly as she slides into the new chair the waiter has placed next to mine.

"I'll have what he's having." Cress points to Ian's green concoction.

"No, no. While this is a delightful drink, I have a better idea for you." Ian bows, then gestures toward Cress and Hillary. "They will have the Lucky Lady."

"You Grants are so bossy," Cress complains.

"What's in it?" Hillary wonders.

"Bombay Sapphire, Crémant, Champagne Nectar, Maraschino, Cointreau, and citrus garnish. You'll love it."

Cress purses her lips. "Sounds sweet. I'm not really a fan of sweet drinks." She's not kidding. Her usual tipples are a Spritz or a Negroni and both include Campari. A friend of mine once described Campari as tasting like the dregs of an ashtray.

"The gin will make it all right." Ian's bossier than I am and his too-suave response sets my teeth on edge, but Cress gives him a small smile of agreement. The waiter's approval seals the deal.

JL asks for a draft lager, and I decide on an old-fashioned. Even though we all had heavy lunches, we're all feeling peckish. We have at least a half hour wait for our table, so we add lots of oysters and crispy duck croquettes as.

Cress strokes my fingers. My hand tingles. She nudges her chair closer and puts her lips to my ear. "Thank you."

I grin, knowing she'll love the croquettes, but the oysters will excite her. She can eat her weight in oysters and still manage dinner. Would it be too OTT for me to feed them to her? Probably. I'll have to arrange a private oyster party, so I can hold the shells to her lips and watch her slurp the liquor before each luscious mollusk slides down her throat. Reminders of the mussel dinner at Hopleaf, where we reconnected last November, make heat rise to my neck. I loosen my collar and try to shift unobtrusively to readjust myself.

A tray appears in my peripheral vision. Once the drinks are handed round, the warning in Ian's eye tells me he plans to pursue our previous topic of conversation, so I head him off.

"How was lunch with Ainsley?" I ask Cress.

"Oh, you know. Mostly him trying to pry out the details for the new book and taking charge of the draft of Ivan. I asked him if he'd gotten the digital version and, as expected he just rolled his eyes."

"Anything else?"

"Ordering substantial quantities of yumminess."

"Is he happy with your new idea?"

"Bletchley Park and the Middle East are hot topics right now, so he's definitely happy. Everything really depends on how your dad feels about my digging into your family history and then fictionalizing it."

"Fictionalized Grants. Great idea." Ian is too enthusiastic. "And Munro's sons will be at the party, so you can sound them out."

The alarm on Cress' face would be comical if she wasn't quivering with anxiety. "How did you know I was planning to write about Munro Innes?"

"We all know. Max managed to let that little titbit slip out in one of our family chats."

If my eyes could emit death rays, he'd have vaporized.

"Dad will be thrilled. We all loved Munro." Ian points to his chest. "Let me know if I can help."

"Leave it." Fuck Ian, he can't stop pushing.

Cress throws me a look that might be relief, but might also be a little irritation as I snap at my importunate brother. When she hisses "loose lips sink ships," I know it's the latter.

"Trying to be helpful." Ian takes another sip of his green concoction as the waiter slides drinks and snacks onto the small table.

Cress smiles at him. Her hand is trembling, but she manages a sip without mishap. I gently remove the glass and set it on the table, holding her hand until she gets it under control.

"We are very lucky ladies to have you order these for us, Ian. The drink is delicious." Hillary fills the gap smoothly.

"Glad you like it." The corners of Ian's eyes crinkle as he smiles at her.

Cress inches her hand away to pick up a wedge of lemon. When she squeezes lemon juice over an oyster and picks it up, I feel a little tingle brush over me. She stares into my eyes and everything else disappears. As she maneuvers it to her mouth, I realize no matter how dark things may be, I'm happy. She makes me happy.

I lean toward her, ready to taste the tang of oyster and salt on her lips, but she's looking beyond me, amused. When I glance over the table, Hillary is flirting with Ian and JL.

Drinks and nibbles finished, we decamp for the dining room and what should be one of our best meals in London.

As we sit down, the maître 'd comes over to our table. "Sorry to intrude, but there is a gentleman here who says he is a member of your party. I have a larger table over there."

"What the effing...?" I stare at Allan Mason, who beams with bonhomie. Another thistle up my bum.

I swallow my ire, stand, all graciousness, and hold out my hand. "Hullo, Allan. Fancy seeing you here." I throw a conciliatory smile at the maître 'd, before turning to my gobsmacked dining companions. "I'm afraid we need to move. In the meantime, let me introduce you. Allan Mason is a former colleague." I pause, not sure what order to use.

"MI6?" Cress lowers her voice as she asks.

Allan nods.

"JL Martin, cofounder and director of our subsidiary, WatchDog, Inc. Hillary Jones, Blue Badge guide." I gesture at Ian. "I believe you know my brother, Ian."

Allan inclines his head. "My brother was at school with him."

"Alastair," Ian affirms. "Your brother, I mean. Big family, aren't you? Eight or nine of you? All of you have 'A' names."

"Yes, all eight of us."

I slog on with the introductions. "Yavuz Arslan, an old friend from Istanbul." Allan narrows his eyes but says nothing.

"And this is Dr. Cressida Taylor, my partner."

The maître d' returns just at that moment and indicates a large table in the corner. We pick up our glasses and troop over. Allan somehow inveigles himself on one side of Cress and Yavuz is on the other. She dips her head in apology.

"Delighted to meet you, Dr. Taylor. I very much admired your book on Caterina Cornaro. I understand that it has been nominated for an award." Allan is at his smarmiest.

Cress nods and gives me a sidelong glance. "Yes, we're going to Paris for the awards dinner in a couple of weeks."

After an infinitesimal pause, I ask, "What brings you to our table, Allan?"

His eyes flit from face to face, assessing our group. "When you mentioned dining here this evening, I took that as an open invitation." I wish my gaze were a dagger to his heart. But Allan has no discernible heart. "And, well, we don't encounter each other often, so I thought…"

Insincerity oozes out of him like sweat. Didn't mention Rules to him, so he's keeping tabs somehow. I'll try to find out, but I don't fancy my chances. So far, several sweeps haven't turned up any tracking or listening devices.

Can't figure out why he's popped up tonight. Either something has happened, or he's enjoying yanking my chain. I scowl, the corner of my mouth curled. Fuck him. Then I wipe the disgust off my face.

As I lean back, I wish I could change places with Allan or Yavuz. I fantasize teasing my fingers up and down her thigh. When Allan maneuvers his coat-hanger frame closer to her, the hair on the back of my neck bristles and I barely restrain a growl. Ian elbows me in warning.

Allan bumps Cress' arm, oyster liquor splashing down her front. She startles, then grimaces at the wet spot. Her muscles tighten as she looks around the table. She has nowhere to move with Yavuz on the other side.

"Sorry. Clumsy of me." Too bad he doesn't look sorry.

Ian gloats. "I knew something was up. What exactly is going on, Mason?"

I narrow my eyes. Ian's fishing for information about Faez. Nosy bugger.

I shake my head and open my mouth to remonstrate. Allan's interruption is abrupt. "Have you heard something?"

"Rumors." Ian's mouth turns down. "Not the hush-hush stuff."

This is patently untrue, and we all know it.

"Your appearance makes me wonder, though. It's not like you and Max were chums at school or MI6."

Allan swats the comment away as if flies are swarming the table. "Eating at Rules is a treat that doesn't come my way very often. Government drones aren't well paid." He chortles, snaps his napkin open, and places it precisely on his lap. The insincerity in his voice drips like acid. "I appreciate your hospitality, Max."

And there it is. He's making it clear that I'm paying for this meal in more ways that one. I swallow my retort. "My pleasure, Allan."

We busy ourselves with the menu. No one offers another topic of conversation. Finally, Cress comments on a dish. "I thought Pithiviers was a dessert?"

The waiter hurries over. "It's pastry, with a filling.

Usually almond, but in this case, savory. The mix of wild mushrooms and herbs is divine."

JL purses his lips. "And the venison? How gamey is the game?"

"The venison is excellent, sir. Well-seasoned and not overpowering. And the port au jus..." He makes a kissing gesture with his fingers. "It's perfectly balanced. The dish will make your tastebuds dance. The accompaniments really enhance the dish, especially the quince and chestnuts."

"Okay, the venison." JL leans back with a satisfied air as the rest of us order.

Cress passes on the pastry, but I order a slice to share with her and slide a sliver on her plate. She barely notices as she toys with her lamb and mashes the potatoes into the grilled fennel. Normally, she hoovers up her favorite meals. Lately, though, she has lost her appetite a lot. My chest hurts as I watch her push morsels around her plate, lost somewhere in her head.

"Something wrong, la mia stellina?"

She moves her chair a little farther from Allan. "After the huge lunch I had with Ainsley, and the oysters and croquettes, I'm not very hungry."

Hillary's appetite is unimpaired, and she enthusiastically shovels in lemon sole while still flirting with JL. He joins in with gusto between bites of venison, dripping with sauce and topped with the celeriac puree.

Cress puts down her fork. "You're such a tease, Hills." She looks across at JL, pointedly. "Have you heard from Micki, JL?"

"Not since our texts this morning." He swallows a bite of quince and chestnut. "We'll talk later. I told her I'd drink a glass of wine with her while she has dinner." He seems unconcerned about his interactions with Hillary.

Cress' lips tighten with concern for both Hillary and the absent Micki. JL is too charming for his own good.

She throws her friend a glance, freighted with meaning. Is she warning her off? The whole interaction is fleeting. Then Cress goes back to pretending to eat her food.

I wish she was sitting next to me. Then I could ask her what's wrong, stroke her hand. With Allan between us, I'm hobbled. I stab at my much-anticipated steak and kidney pie, now a congealed, unappetizing mess of pastry, meat, and gravy that has oozed into the rest of the Pithiviers.

"I thought this was one of your favorite restaurants." JL points his fork at me.

"It is." I try to muster some enthusiasm, but it's hard work. Maybe I should make a joke. I rummage in my memory bank for something apropos

During a lull in the conversation, I say, "Why doesn't England have a designated kidney bank?" I point my fork at a piece of kidney on my plate.

Ian smirks. "This is one of dad's favorites." He pauses, building up nonexistent anticipation, then delivers the punchline. "They have a Liverpool." A beat goes by and JL snickers. Allan's mouth twists in distaste. Not a humorous bone in his body. JL guffaws loudly. "Crisse. That was a good one."

"Typical Grant family joke." Ian and I speak as one.

Cress gives me a weak smile and puts a bit of pastry in her mouth. I watch her throat work as she forces it down. She smiles at me, apologetic. "The tart is very good, Max. Thanks for ordering it."

"I know how much you love mushrooms." I'm warmed

171

by the tiny glow in her hazel eyes. Eyes that captivated me from the first time I saw her.

Allan has thrown a wet blanket over the table, even though he never says a word throughout the meal. None of our conversation has any relevance to terrorism or to GSU's fucked up software.

As our party breaks up, I push past Allan to grab a taxi, but Ian beats me to it. He's Johnny-on-the-spot for everything tonight. I grit my teeth and help Cress into the back.

"What was all that about?" Cress turns to me, her face crunched up with curiosity.

"Allan? No idea. We talked about Faez yesterday."

"Oh." Her voice sounds pinched.

I slide an arm around her and pull her as close as I can, considering the seat belts. Sitting across on one of the jump seats, Ian has a sly, knowing look on his face. He calls out to the cabbie, "we're going to King's Cross."

Cress seems exhausted. "Sure you're still up for meeting my parents at the train?"

She nibbles at her lip, her eyes shadowed. "Yeah. I'm looking forward to seeing them."

"Are you still thinking about Kev?"

"This trip isn't turning out exactly as I hoped." She puts her head against my chest. "Sorry. I don't mean to whine."

"You're not whining. Anyway, I don't mind as long as you're whining to me."

Chapter Seventeen

ress

I snuggle up to Max for the short ride to King's Cross, ruminating on Allan and Yavuz. Allan seemed to make Yavus as uncomfortable as he made me, casting a pall over everything. I could hardly enjoy the historic surroundings in Rules. Even the food seemed to lose its savor. Ian and Max's banter couldn't lift the mood. Max and I will have to go back and have a more romantic dinner for two, maybe with a little historical role playing.

I'm not used to such constant socializing and I haven't had enough chance to recharge. Since we arrived yesterday morning I've gone out for tea, been involved in an altercation, met Max's cousins, had lunch with my editor, and been to a couple of fancy restaurants. Except for running into Kev, everything was good—or would be if spread out over a week instead of less than forty-eight hours. I yawn and snuggle closer, ignoring the fact the Ian is watching us.

"We should be good in time for the train from Edinburgh," Max says. I think back to Union Station in Chicago, when we said goodbye to his family after Christmas. This should be less frantic. I straighten as the taxi pulls up to the curb, combing my fingers through my hair and pulling it up in a loose twist.

We find the track on the board and walk to the barrier. The way Max keeps looking around is unsettling, and I start to worry that a man with a gun will jump out from behind some pillar or kiosk.

I jump and bump against Max when Ian asks, "What's the time?"

Max holds me steady and produces an irritable growl. "Aren't you wearing a watch?"

"Of course I am." Ian pushes up his cuff and shows off his antique Rolex Oyster Perpetual.

Max glances over. "Grandfather's watch. If you're wearing that, why did you ask me? Too lazy to push up your cuff?"

As usual, Ian smirks. "Wanted another glimpse of your fancy Bremont Bletchley watch."

"Jealous?"

Ian huffs. "As if."

The announcement comes over the tannoy. "Train now arriving on platform ten from Edinburgh."

Max slips his arm around me. "Maybe they'll have less luggage on this trip."

I turn into him, laughing. "Do you believe in magic too?"

"It's only Mum and Dad," Ian butts in. "Everyone else lives in London."

I'm confused. "Then who is staying at the RAF Club besides us and your parents?"

"All of us." Ian smiles smugly.

"But if you have your own places..."

"Easier if we're all together. I'm sure everyone else moved over sometime today."

"Ian! Max!" A stentorian yell in a distinctly Scottish accent rises over all the noise at the station. Max's father may be almost seventy-eight, but his lungs are in good order.

A tall, white-haired man in a Grant tartan kilt strides toward us, towing two huge roller bags. A slightly shorter, black-haired woman in a ruby-red, single-breasted pea coat totters behind on three-inch stiletto heels in matching red, as she struggles to keep up with her husband.

She collapses into the arms of her sons. They hug her, then make sure she's stable as they release her. Viktoria holds her arms out to me. "Cress. So good to embrace you again." I move toward her, readying myself for the hug, the kisses on both cheeks, the overwhelming scent of her Rose Desgranges perfume.

I try for an arm's length embrace, but she crushes me to her. My eyes begin to itch. I hope I can hold back any sneezes as the heavily floral fragrance envelopes me, but a warning tickle from my sinuses warns me a tissue emergency is coming.

Max gently pulls me out of her arms. "Mamoushka. You know Cress is allergic to your perfume."

"So sorry. I forgot." Viktoria's face falls. "Two taxis, Brian. We can go with Ian, and Max and Cress can have some time alone."

I move closer and squeeze her hand. "It's okay. You go with Max and Ian, and I'll ride with Brian. I know you want more time with Max."

"Come on," Brian yells, waving his arms madly. "I have two taxis waiting. The cabbies are restless."

We make our way to the exit, where two traditional black cabs sit by the curb, Brian standing between them and waving. Viktoria still has her arm through mine. "Hah. Max will spend the drive scolding me for all my faux pas."

"No, he won't." I call over to Max. "Max, you be nice to your mother."

He fakes a hurt expression. "When am I not ?"

Ian opens his mouth, but after Brian gives him the stink eye, he snaps it shut.

Viktoria whispers in my ear, "When we are out and about tomorrow, you and I will find a perfume I like and you can tolerate." She presses another kiss against my cheek. "Something without flowers. Now, let's go to the Club." With a frown, she cranes her neck, searching for Brian.

I point. He is in the cab, slumped down against the backseat.

Two major crashes when he was a pilot means Max's father finds travel difficult and flying impossible. Last year, the whole family came to Chicago for Christmas and took the *Queen Elizabeth II* and the train rather than fly.

I whisper to Max, "I'll go with your dad. You ride with Ian and your mom."

"You sure?"

Viktoria calls out, "Your father is tired. He spent so much of the trip pacing up and down the train." With a doubtful expression, Max climbs into the cab where Ian and Viktoria share a seat.

"RAF Club." Tired as he is, Brian's Scottish burr and military tone make him sound like the martinet he isn't.

"Yes, sir." The cabbie pulls the brim of his cap.

"In the service, were you?" Brian pats his shoulder.

"Royal Navy for twenty years."

"Good on you. I have a daughter in the navy. And a son in the RAF. Pilot, like me."

The cabbie, who must be close to Brian in age, glances back. "My folks met during the war. They were both wardens."

Brian lets out an admiring whistle. "That was a brave group of people."

"They were both at St. Paul's the night it was bombed. Guess all that danger brought them together. Never spent a day apart after they married, and Mum died only a few days after Dad. Couldn't live without each other."

The story touches my heart. Maybe I can find a place for it in the Bletchley book.

Our driver is chatty. "What brings you to the Smoke?"

My historian senses go on alert. I know I've heard the term before, but I can't place it. "Is that a reference to The Great Fire?"

"Nah, for the pollution. When we had coal fires. Don't have those pea soupers now, but the name stuck."

Of course. I should have remembered from all those Golden Age British mysteries I devoured as a kid.

"We're here for a party," Brian tells him.

"Sounds fun. What sort of party?"

Brian chortles. "My seventy-eighth birthday." As we pull up in front of the club, he goes on. "Bet you thought I was younger."

"Seventy-eight! I wouldn't put you a day past fifty."

Delighted, he ripostes. "Hardly likely when my eldest is fifty."

"No." I try for incredulous, but I'm laughing too hard. "I thought Ian was your twin."

"I'm seventy-two myself," the cabbie says. "Love the job too much to retire, although the wife is pushing for it."

Max is standing on the sidewalk, hands jammed into his pockets, head on a swivel. Now he stares, open-mouthed as, laughing like a loon, I wait for the cabbie to come around and open the door.

Brian reaches over the seat back and slips something into the hand of the driver, who then opens the door with a flourish, and offers me his hand to help me out. I wince as Brian struggles out after me.

Back in the driver's seat, the cabbie calls out, "Hope you enjoy your time in the city," waves, and drives off.

When we reach the lobby, the rest of the family has assembled near the desk. Even the kids are still up. Lots of hugs and kisses all around, although I stand a little way off, still not really used to this big family dynamic. Or any family dynamic, really.

Max's sister, Meggy, suddenly throws her arms around me. "Cress. It's been too long. You and Max need to spend more time on this side of the pond."

I try not to pull away. "Good to see all of you, too. We're hoping to buy something in London and spend some time here each year."

Meggy raises her eyebrows. "Max has a place here. He shares a house with Ian."

"I know. But he—"

"He what?" Max slips an arm around me.

"Cress was saying you're looking for a place to buy in London."

"Ian's going to buy my share of the house. I want to find a new place with Cress."

"Still in Clerkenwell?"

"Doesn't have to be. Up to Cress, really. She has the final veto." Max leans down and kisses my cheek. We don't really have time to explore on this trip, so we'll come back in a few months, to go house hunting. I always thought I'd like to be in Bloomsbury or Fitzrovia, but lately I've been more open to possibilities and Islington has always intrigued me, so Clerkenwell may perfect.

"We're tired." Viktoria makes the announcement loudly. "Going up now. À bientôt. I assume everyone has the schedule."

I turn to Max. "Schedule?"

"I have it." He pulls it out of his jacket pocket and hands it to me. "Mum gave it to me in the cab. Go on up and give it a shufti. Whatever she has planned, tomorrow will be a busy day."

"Aren't you coming up too?"

"In a few minutes. Frank wants a word." He wades back into the press of family, and I straggle over to the elevators. I stand by the doors, staring back at him, but he never turns toward me. Finally, the doors open, and I go up to bed.

~

Max

Frank leans on the reception desk. When I approach, he motions me toward the lounge. Ensconced in club chairs, we sip whisky and exchange a few bits of family gossip. Then I lean forward and pin my brother with a hard stare.

"It's late, Frank. Do you need a little brotherly bonding, or is it something more serious?"

He drops his eyes to his glass, swirls the liquid, then downs the whole thing, choking slightly as the peaty Laphroig catches.

I sit back and take a sip of the Balvenie Portwood on offer. A nutty dryness offsets slight sweetness from aging, making it much smoother than the smoke aggressiveness of my brother's drink. It brings back memories of Cress' book signing last year, when I first made contact, twenty years after our first encounter at Oxford.

Going to that bookstore was one of the best decisions of my life. The oysters at Rules this evening remind me we need to recreate the mussel dinner at Hopleaf we shared after the signing. But this time, the two of us instead of with her friends.

Frank taps his glass to attract my attention. "Max, I'm worried."

He can't be asking me about his kids. Even though I'm a fond uncle, I know fuck all about raising children. Is he having marital issues? Not much experience there either. Must be something about Mum and Dad. Cautiously, I ask, "What about?"

"You."

That's a bit of a beamer. "What for?"

"RAF intelligence has been hearing some chatter and your code name came up. I wanted to pass that along in case you didn't already know."

My face tightens and heat runs up my neck. This bloody news is everywhere. Doesn't say much about the terrorists having secure communications. Or the RAF.

"You're not in fucking intelligence, Frank. Who told you?"

"I have a mate—"

"Balls. It's a breach of security. Your mate had no business passing on anything."

Frank's face flames as his mouth tightens. "Fuck you, Max. He was trying to help a pal. Worrying a mate's brother might be a terrorist target. Wanting to make sure you know." He wipes his hand over his face. "It's no secret how things fell out with MI6, so he had every reason to believe they wouldn't warn you."

My mouth dries and I wish I had a glass of water, but the whisky will have to do. Shaky, I pick up my glass and swallow the dregs. "Another reason to keep quiet. The RAF could cashier your pal if his superiors find out."

"Yeah, I know." Frank regards me anxiously. "I owe him big time so, uh, don't..."

"I have no intention of tipping off RAF intelligence," I tell him drily. "I've heard from the NASA, the CIA, MI6, and even received a warning packet of white powder sent me from Turkey."

Frank's eyes grow wide. Guess he hadn't heard that tidbit.

"I'm big news in the intelligence world. Ian has been trying to weasel info out of me, so the Foreign Office has all the same intel."

"Now I'm even more worried."

"Everyone in the world is looking for this bloke. It's a matter of time." I don't tell him about the cat-and-mouse game MI6 want to play, with me as the cheese. Instead, I contemplate my empty glass. "More?"

Frank catches the eye of the barman, who takes our glasses. "Balvenie and Laphroig, right?" We nod.

"Don't spread it around the family. I don't want everyone worrying about me. Let's make dad's party a stellar event."

He gulps. "May have mentioned it to Liz."

My basilisk stare should make him quake in his boots. "Make sure she doesn't spill to Diana and Meggy. And definitely not to Mum."

"How do you know Ian will keep his gob shut? He loves to pass on info."

"We've had that conversation. Besides, he's still looking for information, not passing it on."

"What about Cress? She must know. How does she feel about it?"

I rub my eyes and fumble for my drops. After such a long day, my eyes are burning. I squeeze them in without having liquid running out. Then I keep my eyes shut for at least thirty seconds before I answer. "We don't talk much about it."

"You're joking."

I take a deep breath. "No joke. When she found out what was going on, she was, well, we had quite a knockdown, drag out."

Frank's eyes are on stalks.

"I told her I wanted her to stay in Chicago and be safe." I pause, then deliver the punchline. "It didn't go well."

"Evidently."

"She pointed out Faez could make her a target wherever she was. Couldn't disagree."

The barman comes back with our refilled glasses. Frank grabs his and swallows it down, then hands back the empty glass. "Another, sir?"

"No thanks. Two is enough for me." Frank smirks.

"I'd like a limoncello to take it to the room."

"Can't picture you drinking that muck." Frank grimaces as the waiter returns with a small bottle and a glass.

"It's for Cress, you berk."

"Cress drinks that muck?"

"She's a huge fan. From her trips to Italy."

He gives an exaggerated shudder. We fall silent, not sure where to go with this conversation.

I take a sip of whisky and regard my brother thoughtfully. "Frank," I start. He holds up his hand to stop me.

"I'll try for as much damage control as I can. Liz has

been pretty busy with the kids since we got here, so I doubt there has been much time for gossip."

I glance at my watch and finish my drink. "Time for bed. Maybe your pillow talk could be a warning to keep all this to herself."

"Fine." He shuts down and we go to our rooms without another word.

Chapter Eighteen

ax

M After my chat with Frank, I find Cress checking hockey scores on her iPad.

"Are the Blackhawks winning," I ask, knowing she's been unhappy that she can't get the broadcasts here.

"They're playing tomorrow night." She frowns. "They've lost their last three games. Fingers crossed they beat the Wild tomorrow."

"Are you sorry you aren't home to watch?"

"I'll survive." She grins wryly before suspicion mars her beautiful features. "Is this another attempt to send me home?"

I hold up my hands in protest. "Not a chance. I've learned that lesson at least."

We work through the schedule while Cress downs several small servings of limoncello, all the while bemoaning the fact I'm breakfasting at the Wolseley, and she's having spa day.

Then she pulls out a package. "It's after midnight, so happy birthday, darling."

185

I heft the neatly wrapped rectangle.

"Tear off the paper." Cress bounces up and down as if she's on springs.

I stare at the book cover, gobsmacked. *Mon Ami Mate: The Bright Brief Lives of Mike Hawthorn and Peter Collins* by Chris Nixon. A book I've wanted for years. I carefully place it on the floor and pull Cress into my chest, dropping kisses on her upturned face.

"How did you know?" I murmur.

"Serge told me you'd like it."

I send a brief, silent thank you to my cousin, who is as enamored of cars as he is of first editions. Then I kiss her again, heat rising between us. I have no more words as I take her to bed.

When the buzz of an alarm finally penetrates, I groan. Cress doesn't react to the annoying sound. Waking up next her is always a joy, but we don't have any time this morning to luxuriate. I touch her shoulder, but she doesn't respond. I lean over and drop a kiss on her neck. Still no reaction. I turn off the alarm and slip out of bed. I wish I could give her a little time, but I'm already running late.

After I scramble into my clothes, I go back and sit on the bed, shaking her shoulder gently. "Cress."

She startles. "What the..."

"Rise and shine. I let you sleep a little longer, but now you only have half an hour to get ready. And I need to leave."

She groans reaches for me. "Can't you stay?"

"Sorry. No choice." I pull her into a quick embrace.

After wishing me a happy birthday, she complains, "I'd tell you to bring me one of the Wolseley's green juice drinks, but I'll be out all day—at a spa." Her eyes glow, not with excitement, but with loathing.

"Isn't this your second spa visit in the last few weeks?"

She curls her lip., "Micki insisted on a spa day just before we left. It was okay." Her expression is grudging.

Then, as if realizing she's giving the wrong impression, her voice softens. "A day out with your mother, sisters, and sister-in-law." She pauses, her face scrunched into a frown. "Not that I don't enjoy being with them, but it's been nonstop socializing and ..."

"You're not comfortable with my family." Damn, I'd hoped we were past this now.

"They still make me kind of nervous. Everyone is really nice, but..."

I press her hand to my lips. "I know we're an overwhelming bunch. But they already love you." Her eyes tell me that she thinks my claim dubious, so I soldier on. "You just have to trust that everything will work out. And the spa should be amazing."

"Not really a fan," she tells me, a catch in her throat.

Puzzled, I press, "You told me you loved the hammam in Istanbul. What's the difference?"

"At the hammam, you lie on a hot slab of marble until your muscles relax. Then a woman comes over and starts pouring hot water over you, scrubs you with a loofah, then douses you with more water while she works you over. Not exactly a massage. Since she only speaks Turkish and I don't, her gestures are my orders. Eventually I go to the pools—hot, tepid, then cool. After an oil massage, I sit in a lounge and drink tea. All without conversation. When I leave, I'm relaxed and wonderfully clean. My skin glows for days."

I really don't understand the difference. "So, it's a spa without verbal interaction."

"It's a transaction. No one is chatting with me, trying to

upsell products or other services. Some of them offer things like facials, but I never bothered. Many women go as groups, and it is more of a spa experience for them. But personally, I enjoy the aloneness and the anonymity of the whole thing."

Her eyes are distant, as if she is reliving the experience. "And you are so clean. I never realized how inadequate we are at washing our own bodies until my first time at a hammam."

"Think of today as a chance to relax before the stresses of the party. Lots of people you don't know. I know how much you love crowds."

I drop light kisses on her face. My phone beeps and I check the screen.

YOU'RE LATE.

Damn. Ian's message galvanizes me.

"Gotta run." One last, longing gaze, and I'm out the door, gift in hand.

First up on my schedule is a bachelor brunch. Not all actual bachelors, of course, but no women allowed. They have their own thing going on. I survey the assembled Grant clan and, much as I love them all, I'd rather be with Cress, having breakfast in bed.

When I reach the lobby, everyone is milling around, except JL.

"Happy birthday, Dad." I give him a hug and hand him the shopping bag.

"This is heavy," he says, putting on the floor at his feet. Then he gives me a hug. "Happy birthday to you too," he says before hefting the bag and taking it to the reception desk so they can put it in his room.

Ian claps me on the back. "Did Cress give you something smashing?" He accompanies the comment with a leer.

"This is your day, Dad. Don't worry about me." I've never really cared about my birthday and I want him to garner all the attention. The family story is he was so chuffed to share his birthday with one of his children, so he wanted me named Brian. Mum put her stiletto heel down to burst his bubble. Dad insisted on naming Ian for a Grant forebear, and she wanted me named for her father, Maxim. And that was that.

The rest of the gang comes over to add to the congratulations. JL joins us in the lobby and adds to the birthday wishes, then pulls me aside. "Didn't catch sight of any lurkers on my way over."

He only walked a hundred yards, so the chance he'd notice anyone was minuscule, but I appreciate vigilance. "Good."

As we walk over, we both do discreet surveillance. No one comments as JL focuses quick glances on Green Park while I stare into hotel entryways, plate-glass windows, or turn my head slightly to check out passersby before crossing over at Dover Street to walk in the magnificent gilded wrought iron entrance on Piccadilly.

My shoulders loosen and my breathing becomes easier as we take our seats at a table where the six of us can spread out comfortably. We're tucked away in the parlor where prying ears can't overhear us.

Dad tells the waiter we want porridge all around as a starter. JL doesn't demur, even though I know he won't eat it. When it arrives, we lift our drams of whisky and shout, "Slàinte Mhath" before pouring the golden liquid into the steaming bowls, while JL downs his shot. A few curious patrons crane their necks to watch.

The shine from the chandeliers catches my eye. Their round, open shape and hanging lights remind me of the fixtures in the Hagia Sophia and the Blue Mosque. Everything brings back my Turkish experiences. I shake off my disquiet and appreciate the rest of the opulent setting. It's a far cry from the building's start as a car showroom and its later incarnation as a bank.

My dad plays the quintessential Scot, downing a plate of fried haggis and duck eggs with whisky sauce. Duck eggs are a signature ingredient at the Wolseley. Les, my English brother-in-law, plumps for fried duck's egg and Bubble & Squeak with wild mushrooms, after scoffing not only his porridge but JL's too. Stalwarts all, Ian, Frank, and I go for the full English breakfast with fried eggs.

Dad puts some egg and haggis on his fork, but instead of popping it in his mouth, he points the fork, egg yolk dripping onto the plate, at me. "What's this about terrorists targeting you?"

I glare at Frank, who shakes his head. Then I switch my gaze to Ian. He smirks. "You arse," I spit at him.

In the meantime, Dad has calmly eaten several forkfuls. Now he lays down the cutlery. "Well?" He raps it out as a command and a demand. Then he essays another bit of brekkie, waiting for my answer.

My brother-in-law, who works at Government Communications Headquarters, looks alarmed. "Max, is this classified information?"

I pause and scratch my cheek. "The whole family knows what happened in 2003, so not really."

With an air of relief, he goes back to his bubble and squeak.

Dad has turned completely white, as if a vampire has drained away all his blood. He sways slightly in his chair. JL sits next to him. "Mr. Grant, are you all right?"

"Fine," Dad chokes out. "Remembering the broadcast."

"Broadcast? What broadcast?" My voice sounds scratchy, and I guzzle more tea, my eggs and beans growing cold on my plate.

"Your mother and I saw the news the night you got blown up." His quaver is alarming and he takes a pill bottle out of his shirt pocket. After a quick swallow, he goes on. "We spent the next few days trying to find out if you were really all right and pestering the government to bring you home."

"I wondered why MI6 whisked me away so quickly after giving my statement to Turkish police. I sent a written statement when the court needed my testimony for the trial."

"I called in a few favors to get that done." Color has flooded back into his cheeks, thank God. "Where is this threat coming from?" Now he's recovered, Dad's like a dog with a bone.

"The man imprisoned for the bombing has escaped and there are some indications that he might seek revenge."

"After ten years?" Les sounds incredulous.

"Why are you astonished? People have long memories. Especially if they have been sitting in a maximum-security prison. Wouldn't you spend your time thinking of ways to strike back at the people who put you there?"

"Go on, Max. What indications?"

"Mentions of my code name, a suspicious package..."

"How worried do we need to be? Could the family be a target?"

I shrug. "Maybe... I don't know."

"Max is getting as much protection as is possible," JL tells him. "Any whispers of terrorist activity are being followed up." He shrugs. "It's all that can be done."

As we walk out of the Wolseley, a limo pulls up. The chauffeur opens the door with a flourish.

We all open our mouths to ask what's happening, but Frank gets in first. "Where are we going?"

Before Dad can reply, Ian breaks in. "Nowhere. At least I'm not. I have to go into the office."

Dad snaps, "Not today, boy. Check your messages. I think you'll find your boss has given you the day off so you can spend the day with your old dad." He reminds me of an aged fox. "And in answer to your question, Frank, Highgate Golf Club." Satisfaction oozes out of Dad as he makes this pronouncement. "Noel Green, an old pal of mine, is a member. We can easily play a round before the party."

I've never had much time for golf and don't play a lot, but the rest of the family does. Frank and Ian are scratch golfers, Dad's handicap is around eight, and Les and I are around twelve. If Adrian is a member, I'm guessing he is very good on this course or spends a lot of time in the bar with pals. Maybe both.

Sitting back in the luxury vehicle, I have another question. "We can rent clubs and shoes, yes?"

"Of course," Dad huffs. "Noel is treating us all as my birthday present. All mod cons."

I lean back against the butter-soft leather seat and breathe a sigh of relief. At least that will end the discussion on terrorist threats.

~

Cress

After breakfast at the Club, we walk up South Audley Street to the Connaught Hotel, home to the Aman Spa. I try to hang back with Diana, but Viktoria and Meggy surround me, each slipping an arm into mine.

"Did you celebrate Max's birthday already?" Viktoria quizzes me.

"Just after midnight. I knew he didn't want to move the focus from Brian." I wince as she squeezes my arm.

Meggy chuckles. "Max has always been sensitive about sharing a birthday with Dad. But we're going to surprise him this year."

I hope they aren't planning to make tonight a joint party. Max would be furious.

Viktoria must be able to read my mind. "Don't worry. Not a peep about his natal day tonight."

I relax fractionally. "Will there be gifts? I already gave Max his gift."

Diana calls from behind, "We're going to have a family party at Grant House."

"No overshadowing, stepping on toes, or anything," Liz adds.

"There has been a change of venue. But not to worry, Cress. There will be plenty of gifts for him to open when we are in Scotland." Viktoria's smile is mischievous.

I expect her to ask me what I gave him. But she doesn't. Then again, she probably figures he'll tell everyone, eventually.

A bow-fronted late nineteenth-century red-brick building looms up on the corner of Mount Street and Carlos Place. At the entrance is a white-columned portico with a small balcony that reminds me of a howdah on stilts rather than on the back of an elephant. The balcony sports the name in green, which stands out against the white paint.

The other is on a green-painted wrought iron structure within the columns, the name in gilt. Potted topiary grace the entrance on both sides. Two signs announce the name of the hotel, one near the top of the wooden portico, and as we step through, a doorman dressed in a dove-gray jacket, black slacks, and a top hat greets us and ushers us inside.

Before we start, Viktoria steers us to the Aman Store, where she tries out their various fragrances, asking me how I like them. She decides on Zuac, inspired by Marrakech. The combination of pink pepper, tangerine, clove, saffron, Frankincense, patchouli and vetiver make a wonderful combination that doesn't cause an allergic reaction. The girls are all enthusiastic too, so she buys a bottle for each of us. I appreciate her willingness to abandon her signature scent for the sake of my allergies.

The spa provides us with robes, some kind of herbal infusion, and foot baths to relax and prepare us for the rest of the day. We have access to the spa facilities for up to two hours before the treatments begin. We all decide to swim, although I plan to stay out of the water as much as possible. Then we'll use the steam room. Because Viktoria is a member, we have access to the gym, but none of us are interested.

"Lifting weights and running on a treadmill." Meggy's mouth twists in disgust. "Swimming is so much better."

Hah! I like the treadmill, but I know I need to hang around the pool with the ladies. After I shake off a few calls to take a plunge, chatting is minimal in the pool as everyone else does laps.

During the steam stage, I ignore the talk surrounding me as I think about Max and how, even after an hour or two, I miss him. This trip has shown me how much I crave his nearness. He has become an integral part of my life and I wonder how I lived without him all these years.

After the swim and steam, we go to the lounge.

"We have most of the spa to ourselves for the day." Viktoria explains as we wait to begin our various treatments.

"Are we all having the same things?" It's not really the spa that I can't stand, it's the group experience. I went a couple of times when volunteer groups I worked with won them as prizes and never enjoyed being in a big room with a bunch of women all obsessing over nail polish colors and facial treatments. Even the recent one with Micki had a fraught manicure session where both Micki and the nail technician both tried to talk me into weird varnishes.

"There are five treatment rooms for us. One double and the others single. You and I will share, Cress. I hope you don't mind. They asked to keep one free in case the club needs it for a hotel guest."

My stomach heaves as I imagine the questions she might ask. Why did I indulge in breakfast? A piece of toast and coffee would stay down better.

"Mamoushka, I hope you aren't planning an inquisition." Meggy scowls at Viktoria. "I can share with Mum if you'd rather have a private room, Cress."

"No one expects the Spanish Inquisition," Liz and Diana intone.

I picture sitting in a comfy chair, being poked with soft cushions. Monty Python invades so many facets of life.

"Certainly not," Viktoria retorts. "I am not Torquemada."

My skin prickles as the intensity rises. "I'm fine sharing." I'm not, but I swallow down my unease. Thinking of the different treatments and the fact that therapists will be in the room, I assume we won't have much opportunity for conversation, anyway.

"You and I will do the nourishing treatments, Cress, as will Meggy. Wonderful stress relief. Liz asked for the purifying journey. You probably don't know yet, but Diana is pregnant."

"Yeah, we were floored. Les and I didn't expect another baby at our age." Trepidation underlines Diana's comment.

We all offer enthusiastic congratulations, but I wonder how Sean is taking the news. The prospect of a new sibling could upend everything for him.

Viktoria goes on. "She will have the body nurturing treatment. It's shorter than the other two, but..."

Then we are called in for consultations before the ritual journeys begin. Viktoria and I settle on adjoining massage tables, towels discarded, light sheets covering us. A therapist comes in and lays hot stones on our backs.

"This will help relax the muscles. My colleague and I will be back in a few minutes to start the massage."

I hate lying on my stomach, but I try not to squirm. Having the stones slide off my back would be more embarrassment than I could stand. I turn my head to the side, contemplating the blurred, narrow slice of the room.

"Cress." Viktoria's murmur startles me.

I feel the stones shift. I try not to move as a squeak comes out. "Uh, yeah?"

She gets right to it. "How do you feel about Max?"

"Feel?" She's painted a large target on my forehead.

"I know you care for him, but do you love him? Is this for the long term, or just a fling?"

"Fling?" We've been together for months. And she worries it's a fling? "Not a fling," I mumble. "I don't do flings. Not a fling person." Now I'm rambling.

"Max doesn't let people in. Except family. And his friend, JL. He's very private. But I can tell you are special to him. And I don't want you to break his heart."

Where is this coming from? If anyone is likely to get their heart broken, it's me.

"Promise me, if you decide to end things, you will be gentle with him."

End things. I sit up and the stones crash to the floor. I try to push my fingers into my hair, forgetting it's all wrapped up in a turban. "End things? I-I-I..."

The door slams open and a therapist rushes in. She stares, openmouthed, at the flat rocks lying cracked on the floor. "What is happening here?"

She calls the other masseuse and they clean up the mess, make sure there is no damage to the floor, and resettle me with new heated stones. Meanwhile, Viktoria has been apologizing profusely, promising to pay for any damage.

Silence descends on the room. My mind is whirling and I don't have any idea of how to restart conversation with this woman.

"Cress?" Her soft call is barely audible.

"What is it, Viktoria?" I try to keep my voice level, even though I feel shattered.

"I shouldn't have questioned your feelings for Max."

No, I think. *You shouldn't have.* But now the damage is done.

"I just want you to know Brian and I already love you like a daughter, and Max isn't the only one who would be broken if things don't work out."

A wave of longing, mixed with sadness washes over me. "I love him," I tell her. "I love him so much. I just worry he will eventually decide he can do better."

She cackles. "Max sees you as the moon and the stars in the midnight sky. He doesn't give his heart lightly. You are his best and he won't be searching for better."

197

Sharon Michalove

Tightness in my chest gives way to relief, just as the therapists return to pummel our muscles into submission.

Once we are polished, wrapped, and rejuvenated, Viktoria draws me into a hug. "Welcome to the family."

"We aren't even engaged."

She disregards my protest. "Doesn't matter. Max adores you. Brian and I love you. All the kids think you are the best thing that has ever happened to their brother." She's grinning from ear to ear. "Maybe you marry, maybe just live together. But you are a couple in an enduring relationship. So you are family."

She hugs me again and, arm in arm, we rejoin the others in the lounge. Everyone is glowing and relaxed, as we're each handed a shopping bag filled with products used in our individual treatments.

"Are we going back to the club?" I can't remember if there was anything else on the agenda besides the party.

Meggy shakes her head. "Of course not. We still need mani-pedis and a slap-up tea. The party isn't until eight, so we need some nourishment to hold us over since we missed lunch."

Mani-pedis. I suppress a groan.

Like everything else at the Connaught, tea is as luxurious as we expect and, relaxed from three hours of spa treatments, we fall on the sandwiches, scones, and pastries like ravening vixens. As dinner is at least five hours from now, no one worries about being too full for later.

"Besides..." Meggy gestures with the scone in her hand. "We'll be so busy schmoozing with the guests that we probably won't have much chance to eat."

"Schmoozing!" Viktoria exclaims. "You didn't pick up it at home, or at the palace."

Dismissive, Meggy retorts, "I'm forty-five years old,

Mamoushka. I can use any words I like—as long as I'm not speaking to the royal family. Anyway, I picked it up from an American friend."

Viktoria glares at me. I hold up my hands, proclaiming my innocence. "Friends don't lead friends down the path of slang," I tell her while trying to keep a straight face.

Awash, Diana groans that she needs the toilet. She moves off decisively, and we all follow like lemmings, hoping enough stalls are available.

We are waiting in the lounge when Diana finally emerges, grumbling over the inconvenience of pregnancy. Donning our coats, we set off toward Green Park. "I have manicurists coming to the Club to do mani-pedis for us as the last stage. We shall all be the embodiment of shining perfection." Viktoria makes this pronouncement with a conspicuous air of satisfaction.

Liz sidles up next to me. "I've noticed you don't really wear makeup, Cress."

"Not very often," I tell her sotto voce. "Mostly it makes me itch, so I never really learned how to put it on. And Max doesn't care."

"I have some hypoallergenic stuff that should work." She studies my face carefully. Clever cosmetic work is what I will need for this evening. "I'd be happy to serve as your makeup artiste. I've been told that I'm quite good."

"Thank you."

She smiles at the relief in my voice, then nods enthusiastically. "I'll dress your hair too. Believe me, you will turn heads."

Not sure I want to be the cynosure of everyone's eye, but I doubt Liz will let me be a wallflower. With an inward sigh, I hurry after the rest of the group. Max's family is wonderful, but exhausting.

199

Chapter Nineteen

ax

MCress disappears into Frank and Liz's room while Frank, Mum, and I make a last check on the Churchill Bar, which is beautifully set up for the pre-dinner drinks where we decided on champagne only and a selection of canapés. The Club set the Ballroom up with tables of eight, Dad and Mum seated with his three best mates from RAF days and their wives. The rest of us are at a table nearby. Other than these two tables, and one for the kids, we've left the seating as a free-for-all.

Sean grumbles over sitting with the little ones instead of his grandparents, but we tell him he is being entrusted with ensuring the sprogs' good behavior. Now he knows he is a boss, his attitude has improved.

Dark blue chairs surround tables dressed in pristine white linen. We decided on a served meal rather than a buffet, featuring a choice of lamb or lemon sole. And there is enough room left for a four-piece band and dance floor.

As soon as we are sure everything is ready, Frank and I hustle into the lobby to greet guests as they come in. A few minutes later, Ian and Les join us. We entrust hotel security with keeping a tight rein on who enters, but JL is already in the ballroom along with a couple of GSU guys as backup, making sure the security stays tight.

When our girls—sorry, women—come down, loud intakes of breath swirl around our space. Meggy is smashing in a teal gown with a deep v in the back, her short, dark hair dusted with something that makes it silvery. Liz's dress is burgundy, a color that should clash with her red hair. Instead, they enhance each other. Diana's gold gown is also a cracker.

But when Cress comes in, my pulse goes up to stratospheric levels. Her emerald gown sets off her salt-and-pepper curls and the mesmerizing hazel eyes that drew me in from the first time I saw her.

All the Grant men are in formal kilts tonight, as are many of the others, who sport the RAF hundredth anniversary tartan in light and dark blue with white and red stripes.

I reach out to Cress and wrap her in my arms, heedless of messing up her makeup or hair, the scent of her intoxicating me. "La mia stellina," I breathe against her neck.

Cress nuzzles her nose against my chest.

"Don't destroy all my hard work, you two," Liz growls as she walks up to us.

A broad hand slaps my back. "Break it up," Les rumbles.

Startled, we move apart. Cress, horror washing over her face, touches my jacket. "Oh, Max. Your beautiful waistcoat."

I look down. Foundation and mascara are smeared onto the fabric, along with some lipstick. Brushing at it makes it worse.

Ian laughs. "I'd tell you to get a room, but you already have one." Then he whispers, "Go sponge yourself off, then mingle, and introduce Cress to Colin and Desmond. She can test how they feel about her plan to write about Uncle Munro."

I glance around the room and spot my cousins, identical twins, standing like sentries on either side of tiny Aunty Grace, Dad's younger sister. Somehow, she missed out on the Grant gene for height. At seventy-five, she's even shorter than Cress.

Cress is standing patiently while Liz puts her to rights, so I punch my brother's shoulder. "I told Cress they would be here. I'm sure she will be interested in talking to them. She was planning on asking Dad what he thought, but this will be even better."

Even as I say this, a tremor of concern prickles my scalp. Colin and Des rarely agree on anything. So if one of them likes Cress' idea, the other might take against it to be contrary.

I turn to Cress. "I need to go wipe off this muck," I call over, as I head for the toilets.

When I return, Liz is still fussing with her hair. I wonder if Cress showed her the picture from the night of the reception at the Palmer House. Her hairstyle is almost the same, most of it up in a twist with a pearl and crystal clip in the shape of a branch with leaves. A few curls hang down to her shoulder. "Enough, Liz. She's fine."

Liz's glare could melt Vatnajökull, the largest glacier in Europe. "We are not going for fine here."

Now I've pissed off my sister-in-law. I scan the room and wave to my Sheremetov relatives. I need to thank them for the books. Dad was so pleased with the gift.

I turn back to Liz. "Leave her alone now. I need to introduce her to someone."

Cress moves away from Liz, calling back over her shoulder. "Thanks so much. But I'm sure I'll be a mess again soon."

"We'll do a refresh later." Liz searches the room. Then she gives Frank a little wave. "A handsome gentleman has a glass of champagne waiting for me. See you at dinner." She glides off in her ridiculously high heels. I can't fathom how she keeps her balance. My arm resting on the small of Cress' back, I can't take my eyes off Liz until she reaches the safety of my brother's side.

As he reaches out to hand her a glass, the startling sound of a trumpet voluntary pierces the air. Then the kilted trumpeter bellows, shaking all the glassware.

"Please welcome Wing Commander Brian Grant and his beautiful consort, Viktoria."

Dad, dapper in his Grant kit with badges for the RAF displayed on the sash with Mum on his arm in a long silk dress with a Grant tartan sash, are the brightest stars in the firmament. They walk down the red carpet, then wait at the far end while a line stretches back to the doorway with guest eager to greet them.

When I move my arm to pull Cress into my side, she relaxes into my touch as I tell her in an undertone, "Dad's cousins, Colin and Desmond Innes, are here I know you want to talk to them about their dad."

Cress puts her hands over her mouth to muffle the soft squeal that comes out of her.

"Oh my God." She sways slightly and I slip my arm around her waist, gazing into her worried eyes. "What if they don't think this would be a good idea?"

"Why are you so concerned? The woman I know is confident about her work."

"My characters are fictional, or dead."

"Munro's dead," I point out.

"Well, his sons aren't. And it's your family," she ripostes.

With a little pinch of her waist, I try to remind her not to overthink. "I'll warn you that those two never agree on anything, but I'm guessing Colin will love it and Des won't. Don't let Des deter you."

"Where are they?" She quivers with a mixture of excitement and anxiety as she tries to swivel. Caught against my side, she has no room to maneuver.

"Relax." I release her and pick up a couple of champagne flutes. "They're chatting with my aunt Grace. We'll go through the receiving line and congratulate the parents, then find them."

We push toward the bar, and I pick up two flutes, handing her one. "It's pretty full, so take a couple of sips before we move on." Cress is famous for her ability to spill liquids everywhere. She obediently sips from her glass, then I take it and carry the two glasses as we move toward the receiving line, where I neatly intercept Colin as he moves on from kissing Mum's hand.

"Hello, Colin. It's been such a long time."

Colin holds out a hand, and we shake. "It has been a long time. Too long. Perhaps at my dad's funeral?" His keen gaze sums up both Cress and me.

"May I have a word?" I ask.

He nods. "Me, or me and the grouchy bastard over there?" He inclines his head toward his twin, who is now shaking hands with Dad.

"Both of you," I tell him. "Just give us a minute to greet the birthday boy."

We join the end of the queue as Colin moves back and pulls at Des' sleeve. A quick exchange takes place. Colin gestures in our direction, while Des replies with a frown and a shrug.

We finally reach my parents. Cress gets a big hug while Dad squeezes my shoulder. "Thanks for the books," he says. "Can't wait to get stuck in."

Once through the line, we walk toward the space where the lobby meets the Churchill Bar and I check out my cousins, who have changed since I saw them last. Roughly my dad's age, they have shrunk a bit, now a hair under six feet. Sandy hair has turned white and sparse. But both are lean as ever, verging on gaunt, noses sharper and cheekbones more prominent. The waxiness of Des' skin hints at underlying ill health.

Resuming the conversation, I say, "Fifteen years. Far too long." I hand Cress the glasses and turn to Des and hold out my hand. "Des. Glad you could come."

He shakes my hand and looks me up and down. "The Grant tartan looks good on you. Obviously not the worse for wear after your adventures. That scrape in Istanbul." He grimaces. "Something right out of Dad's own boy tales."

What a perfect opening. I gesture to Cress. "This is my, uh—"

Holding out her hand, Cress says, "Cress Taylor. Pleased to meet you, Drs. Innes."

Colin isn't drinking, so he takes her hand between both of his and holds it for a minute, staring like he wants to sketch her. "Nice to meet you too, Dr. Taylor."

Des briefly touches her hand. "Hello," His clipped tone is less than friendly.

Cress' mouth drops open as Colin goes on. "Viktoria was telling me all about you, in enthusiastic detail."

I jump into the flagging conversation. "Then you know Cress writes historical novels."

"Yes. Very impressive. I plan to read your first book, Dr. Taylor, as soon as I can. Brian raved about it, especially as he knows my fascination with polar exploration knows no bounds. And Viktoria says you recently finished a book about the Merchant Adventurers and the court of Ivan the Terrible."

Des, arms crossed, is silent. Still mute, Cress nods.

"When will it be available?"

When Cress still doesn't speak, I say, "June. It's already available for preorder, I think."

After a couple of tries, Cress manages a few words. "Yes. You can order it from your favorite bookseller." Determination settles around her eyes and mouth, and I watch her chest inflate as she takes a deep breath. "I've been thinking about a new project, and I was wondering if I could speak to you about it."

Colin glances over at his brother. "Us? Why would you care about our opinion?"

"I was... I was..." Again, she's tongue-tied. This isn't the Cress I'm used to.

I take her hand and start stroking the inside from her palm down to her wrist and back. After a pause, she begins again. "I'm thinking about writing a novel centering on your father and his time at Bletchley Park." Her voice is timid. She lowers her eyes, studying her feet.

Colin doesn't even pause. "Brilliant. I've always hoped someone would write about Dad. He's one of the unsung heroes of Bletchley."

Cress melts, in a good way. Her shoulders are no longer at her ears, and she is breathing normally, pulse slowing, and the slight tremors she hadn't been able to suppress have subsided. I hand her the champagne flute, and she manages a sip without choking.

207

Des straightens. "No."

Colin regards his brother with a resigned expression.

"Why?" Cress' voice is a barely murmur.

"I have no desire to have someone fictionalize my father's life. Perhaps I should say sensationalized, in print."

Colin presses Cress' hand. "He can't abide agreeing with me on anything. Don't worry about it." He presses her hand again. "I'll give you my contact information so we can stay in touch. I'm agog and I can't wait to discover what you're thinking."

A gong sounds and we are called for dinner. Colin takes Des' arm and drags him off toward their table.

With an uncertain smile, she hands the glass back to me. I grasp both stems in one hand.

As we troop in for the meal, I have my other hand on Cress' shoulder. "I'm so sorry. I warned you about Des, but I hoped he might be reasonable, for once." I press my lips together, frustrated.

"I guess that 's the end of it." Cress' voice is even but her hands are shaking.

"Don't give up yet. Let Colin try to work things out. And if he can't, maybe you can name the character something else and fictionalize him enough that it will still work."

"Maybe," she agrees uncertainly. "In the meantime, I'll go back to some other ideas I was playing around with."

By now we've reached our table and I set down the glasses and pull out her chair. "In all the excitement, don't forget you've promised me a dance."

Chapter Twenty

M^{ax}

M*ax*   I go for the Serpentine swim on my own again this morning. Swimming with a group seems safer than the runs I normally do at home. Cress is knackered and slightly hung over after the party. When I suggest she join me, all I hear is a groan as she puts a pillow over her face. I try to shake off the feeling of being watched as I check behind me on my quick walk to Hyde Park. No one. But if anyone is following me, they can hide in the early morning gloom.

When I reach Leicester Square, Clay, Jarvis, and Metin are in the Chicago conference room with Elena, who is taking notes. A PA brings me a full mug and a plate of biscuits, which should tide me over. JL is probably at the gym at the Athenaeum. He told me he plans to go to the Tower with Hillary. He's fascinated with the opportunity to observe the security around the crown jewels, and she told him she will introduce him to the Ravenmaster.

My legs ache and I shift farther from the table to stretch out as I stare at the screen. My knees are still sore from the fall two days ago, exacerbated by a night of standing too much and many dances. Not only the three I managed with Cress, but dances with my mum, Aunt Grace, Meggy, Diana, and Liz, as well as the wives of my father's three best friends, and several elderly cousins I hardly remember. I'm fagged and awash in tea, with the constant calls from my bladder.

After another trip to the loo, I slip back into the uncomfortable office chair, my back and thighs screaming. I haven't kept up my running for the last few months and my body is protesting the lack of exercise. Two days of swimming doesn't make up for daily ten milers.

My shoulder muscles bunch up as I try to find the best position to take the strain off my neck. I'd love to reposition the screen, but the installation isn't adjustable. Frustrated, I rub my neck, trying to work out the knots.

"Okay. Let's start." Clay's voice is gravelly and impatient. He has been tapping his pen against a portfolio as we wait to start. "Has Erik made his report? Any new ideas about who's sabotaging the software?" His voice turns deceptively soft.

"Looking at Erik's report, I doubt we can clean it up." I watch Jarvis clench and unclench his fists as he gives us the bad news. "I'm guessing a complete rewrite will be the only solution."

"How long will that take?" I'm edgy, as sharp as broken glass.

"Since the upgrade planning was done, and I designed the architecture, a small team might recreate a clean version in a few months, if we're lucky. In the meantime, I'm worried there may be a fresh attack on the current software. If that's compromised, we'll be at ground zero." We all wince at the reference.

Clay explodes. "A couple of months?"

"Sorry," Jarvis says apologetically. "I know it's bad news, but even if we worked 'round the clock, it would take more time than you want."

Holding up a hand, I put in, "We do have backups of the current software."

"We do." Jarvis verbally agrees, but shakes his head. "However, if the sabotage is internal, nothing may be safe."

I swallow a groan. "Cleaning up infected clients will be a nightmare."

"This only affects the upgrade—so far." Jarvis gives a thin smile.

"Since our suspicion is it's a Russian op, we need to find out whether it's government sanctioned or one of the independent hacker groups. I am convinced we have an insider at GSU, presumably working with this outside group." Metin's remark adds to the doom and gloom that pervades the meeting.

Russian hacker groups usually have some government connection, which complicates everything. I stretch, then start moving around the cramped conference room. What I really want to do is lie on the floor to ease my aching back. Maybe do some yoga.

Metin licks her lips. "I've been in touch with the CIA, FBI, and NSA." Her fingers are busy undoing and redoing her hair. "No luck so far in identifying who it is."

Jarvis scowls. "As you know, the server has been under unusually heavy attack for a couple of days. Last night, someone opened a backdoor into the mainframe but it hasn't been used yet. I left it alone so the hacker wouldn't realize we're onto him or her, but I put on an alarm, so I'll know when they go back in. My team can set a trap ASAP to catch the perp." Jarvis loves his TV cop lingo.

"Timeline?" Clay asks what we all want to know.

"I've been working on it all morning. Tonight I'll put in the trap, and close their backdoor. We can track them while the primary system is untouched. Of course, this will only work if whoever accesses it isn't internal. None of the team would mistake the decoy for the real thing."

I hold up my hand. "If the plan works, it should give us a bit of breathing room. Still, there are risks. If our saboteur is internal, he or she might be tipped off by the outside entity."

"Only if they realize it's a dummy with fake data. We hope that might take a while."

I shrug. "We have attacks on the server all the time."

"Someday, one will be successful." Jarvis' warning is grim. "A matter of time, really."

Metin nods. "Ransomware is a bigger and bigger threat worldwide. Whether they could blow up our server isn't clear. It's a possibility we need to take seriously."

"Looks like their aim is a combination of data mining and theft." Jarvis' comment breaks into my thoughts. "But if we lock the door to frustrate the perpetrator, they might do something more destructive, like trying to take out the server or installing ransomware. My trap will make them think they are getting data, but none of it is real; a data set I concocted to keep them busy. I also created some fake accounts they can 'pilfer.'"

"Are they that good?" Metin stares at me, but Clay answers.

"Probably not as good as Jarvis. But maybe they don't need to be." He frowns. "Working it through the security agencies takes a long time, and I'm never sure we can completely trust them. Anyway, we don't have that kind of time."

I lean back and put my clasped hands behind my head. "There's no way to hurry the process."

"Most companies can survive data leaks." Clay tents his hands. "We are in a unique position. Our job is to make sure data leaks can't happen. If they do, we lose our reputation, probably clients, and possibly the company."

"You're joking." JL walks into the conference room. He grabs a chair and stares at the screen. A traditional security bloke, JL knows this is serious, but not how serious.

I turn to ask him why he's here, but Clay's growl travels through the air like a slap.

"If you started having complaints that your security guys were sleeping on the job—or sleeping with the clients —what do you think the fallout would be?"

JL's mouth drops open, his fingers tugging at his hair. "Okay, I get it. I was kind of thinking about all these data leaks we hear about. You know, two million emails exposed, that kind of thing. Those companies are still in business."

"The difference is our clients are banks. The stakes are astronomical. And if I'm right and Sergei Ivanov is behind this, taking me down might be the driving force for his plan." Clay untents his fingers and rubs his palms over his head.

"Even if we find out the Russians, or rogue hackers, are behind this incursion, it doesn't mean we're any closer to finding out who the internal player is. No way to put pressure on anyone to tell us, either." Metin's hangdog expression at Clay's words says it all.

Jarvis continues. "It's not like we can grill the Russians. If they are government sanctioned, we end up in a huge diplomatic imbroglio. If they are rogue, it's like the Wild West. The hackers can operate from anywhere."

I sip my eighth or maybe eightieth cup of tea. "We have

a couple of other options. One is to bring in the FBI and let them interrogate the staff, assuming they can screw more out of them than we can. Another is to make some educated guesses and see if internal questioning brings us any answers."

Clay gives us a searchlight glare, his blue eyes icy. "Not a fan of bringing in the feds, so an internal investigation it is. If we are looking at people in your department, Max, who would you single out?"

I squint a bit, then slide the faxed report over to him. "Erik thinks it's Troy Diamond. First, he thought the problem was sloppy coding, but now he agrees we're looking at sabotage. He thinks the Russians puts Troy here as a mole."

"You're not convinced." Clay's voice is flat.

The bald statement startles me. "No-o-o-o." I run my finger along the faux wood grain of the table. "Decorated ex-Navy, Cal Tech. He appears to like the work and the company. And he brought the problem to Erik's attention. I wouldn't say definitively he isn't the perpetrator, but right now I'm not buying it."

"Double bluff?" Clay's voice is gruff. He glares around the table, then through the screen at JL and me. "I don't like finger pointing." He drinks some coffee. "Erik himself is another possibility."

"Because he's Russian?" JL's eyebrows raise toward his hairline. "He's been here almost since the beginning."

Metin taps on the table. "His story about leaving Moscow checks out, but that doesn't mean it's true. If he's a Russian agent, he'd have a convincing cover. I can ask some of my CIA contacts to recheck."

"Okay, do it. Anyone else?"

"Almost anyone in the department could be a suspect,

but that's doubtful." Jarvis chews on a pencil now. "We have two more reasonable possibilities. Amy Shelby has been very pushy about trying to work with me if there is a new build. That could be suspicious."

We've all been squirming in our chairs. No one in this meeting is comfortable.

"Maybe she's ambitious and looking for a promotion."

My MI6 Spidey sense says no, but my obligation to fairness kicks in. "Could be. She has a thing going with Erik. She also has a chip on her shoulder, whines about being overlooked and underappreciated." They can all tell I'm not convinced by my own argument. I soldier on. "And she complains we are a boy's club. Maybe dissatisfaction is all it is."

"Her dissatisfaction might make her more vulnerable to subversion. Perhaps it means she's our mole." Clay stands and spins his chair around. We watch, fascinated, as it makes three full rotations before slowing. He sits back down. "Worth checking her out, anyway."

"We have a few other possibles," I throw in. "Although I would leave out Michael Francis. He came in late when we realized we needed more help. He wasn't originally on the team."

"The Davids. Lorraine, Felix, Jarod, Tracy, Mary, and Bennett are also on the team." Jarvis adds more layers. "I don't think they have the skills, though. They are all competent, but I don't think they can function at this level of sophistication without leaving an obvious trail."

Metin rises and picks up her tablet. "We can put some guys on them for a few days. Watch where they go, who they meet, monitor their phones. Report back if any of them do something suspicious. We'll scan their emails, texts, and social media accounts, too. Do you want to let Case know, JL? Or should I tell him?"

"You go ahead, Metin. It will be faster, and you can explain exactly what you need."

She waves at the screen, pivots, and heads for the door, calling over her shoulder. "I have another meeting. Let me know if you need anything else."

Clay raps on the table to grab her attention before she makes it out the door. "Metin, start this afternoon. We'll do the internal interrogations on Monday. That will give us four days of surveillance. Elena set up the interviews—Erik, Amy, Troy. If we need to talk to others, we can set them up later. About an hour for each one, with discussion in between. If any of you have another commitment on Monday, reschedule it."

I jerk my head up. "I'll be in Scotland."

Clay frowns. "Can you join securely from there?"

"Yes. I can connect via VPN from my pa rents' house."

"Fine." He pushes back, the wheels of the chair scraping against the linoleum floor. "We're done here. Thanks, Elena, Jarvis." He turns off the screen.

I turn to JL, eyes narrowed. "I thought you were out sightseeing with Hillary."

He raises an eyebrow. "Does this bother you?"

"No," I tell him. "Curious."

"Well, going to the Tower was the plan. But she ended up having to pick up a tour group from another guide. I'm sorry I won't meet the Ravenmaster. Now we can go for a pint and a pie."

Chapter Twenty-One

Cress

 I spend some time this morning thinking about a possible new project if the Munro Innes book isn't going to work. Max's cousin Colin calls to invite me out to lunch and we meet a Pret-a-Manger not to far from City, one of the colleges of the University of London, where he taught and still has an office. He tries to assure me that everything will work out, but I'm noncommittal. Graciously, he walks me the short distance to the Guildhall Library.

The library is a treasure trove of London history and my mind whizzes with possible ideas related to crime and livery companies. Immersed in the riches on offer time gets away from me and now I'm going to be late. Max told me he wanted me to meet him at Heal's, a famous furniture store, at six p.m. I have no idea why he wants to look at furniture, but I'm game. Afterwards we will meet the family for dinner, even though I'd rather just have room service and a quiet night alone.

I walk out to Aldermanbury Street. Not a cab in sight.

In the end I walk to Bank Tube station to catch the Central Line to Tottenham Court Road. It takes longer than the usual six minutes because I keep glancing at the windows of the buildings lining the street, worrying that someone might be following me. With the bustle of pedestrians, I can't really tell, but I make sure my purse is slung securely cross-body with my hand on the top as I try to check out people around me. Pickpockets are not uncommon.

I take care to stand well back on the platform and when the train pulls in, quickly find a seat, scrutinizing the few people who push on behind me. My muscles are tight as adrenaline runs through me at each stop. At this time of day, the Tube is crowded with commuters and relief washes over me when I get off at Tottenham Court Road. As far as I can tell, no one follows me out of the station. I hurry down the busy shopping street, breathless by the time the blue-and-white awnings of *Heal and Son* come into view. When I'm a little closer, I glimpse Max, who loiters on the sidewalk, glancing between his cellphone and the crowded sidewalk. When he catches sight of me, which is much more difficult since I am short and frequently hidden by other pedestrians, he waves his arms like a semaphore.

I smile at the vision of a guy, six-foot-five, in sober city attire, making a spectacle of himself outside a furniture store on a busy London street. When I am close enough, he grabs my arm, pulls me out of the mass of humanity, and presses me against him.

"Sorry I'm late," I tell him, still gasping for air.

"Are you late?" He teases, the skin around his eyes crinkling in amusement.

I stand back and drink him in while he makes a show of checking his watch. "I don't think that six minutes really counts as late." Max hugs me again.

My skin tingles from the warmth of his body, grateful that he hasn't asked why I didn't take a cab. The buckle fastener from my purse digs into my abdomen. "Ouch."

Max moves back. "What's wrong?"

I adjust the bag to move the offending piece of hardware. "Let's try again." I move back into his arms, heedless of the shoppers milling around us.

"Ah, la mia stellina. I missed you the whole day."

I snuggle in a bit more, not caring we are cuddling in full view of gawkers and hecklers. "I missed you too."

"Did you write?"

"No. I had lunch with your cousin Colin to tell him I was dropping the project. He begged me not to give up and promised to set me with interviews and access to the family archive." I'm mumbling into his chest. "And he told me Des will come around—or at least won't make trouble. I hope he's right. But if not, I have another idea. I spent the afternoon at the Guildhall Library and I'm kind of excited."

"Colin's a good bloke. Des is an arsehole. But he usually comes right in the end. After he's had his fill of mischief-making." Max makes it a pronouncement.

Distantly, passersby emit the usual clichéd cries.

"Nice."

"Clear off the pavement."

"Disgusting."

"Damned Americans."

"Come on." Max releases me, then slips my arm through his, then leans over for another kiss. "You've never been to Heal's?"

I shake my head no. "I've passed it many times, but I've never gone in. Never needed to buy furniture when I was in London. Are you looking for something for the London house?"

"We're not here for the furniture."

"Then why are we here, Max?"

"I wanted a little time alone with you. And I wanted to give you a treat. Except for our dinner Clos Maggiore, we've been accountable to other people."

"I suppose we can't blow off dinner?

Max laughs but there is no joy in it. "Are you kidding?"

I turn toward the building. "If we aren't looking at furniture, why are we here."

"You'll see." He puts his hand against the small of my back, and steers me into the 200-year-old furniture emporium. We stop near the entrance to drink in the ambiance.

I crane my neck to see his face. His gray eyes have darkened, hunger rolling off him in waves as he deepens his already deep voice, the words rolling off his tongue like honey. "They're still known for their fine handmade mattresses. I have one on the bed here."

His feral expression makes me wonder. Is he thinking about the bed? Of us on that bed? Of pillows tossed in all directions and tangled, sweaty sheets? I try to picture the bed in his flat. Is it like the one in Chicago, which has a great mattress? His next statement brings me back to earth.

"Unfortunately, we're not here to test mattresses, even though that would be fun. We're here for the cat."

I can't help yelping. "A shop cat. Let's see. Let's see. Take me now."

"We need to climb Cecil Brewer's spiral staircase." He makes everything sound mysterious. Is there a gallery of cats? Is Heal's a purveyor of cats as part of the proper accouterments for a home? What a kick that would be.

After threading through many displays of home goods, we've reached the back of the store where an enormous staircase with amazing hanging lights rises up into the ether.

I stare at him in horror as it comes into view. He knows I hate heights. I'm barely been listening, focusing more on how high the top of the staircase is as I near the dizzying spiral. "Climb? That staircase?"

"You're not climbing Everest. I'll hang onto you." He leads me over. "I could have taken you to the O2 to climb over the arc."

I swallow, then put my foot on the first step and grasp the banister, my knuckles whitening immediately. As I slowly put one foot in front of the other, Max has one hand resting on the small of my back. He murmurs in my ear, "I've got you, la mia stellina."

Not willing to turn, I keep going. "What if I fall backwards? Won't you just tumble with me?"

He huffs. "I'll be your soft landing."

Puffing, I reach the landing that houses a large bronze cat sculpture. When I take a closer look, I realize it's a serval, an African wildcat, but most people would label it as a cat. The figure is sleek, and I want to stroke it. Instead, I wrap my arms around myself and lean against Max as if he's a retaining wall. "Tell me the story." I sound both shaky and demanding.

"In the 1920s, Dodie Smith, the author of *101 Dalmatians*, worked here. A failed actress, she ran the toy department until she had success as a playwright."

"Really? Dodie Smith?" I lift my chin and admire a sliver of his face. "*I Capture the Castle* is one of my favorite books."

"She was quite a character, our Dodie. She was one mistress of the owner, Ambrose Heal. He was quite the player. Married and had another mistress already when Dodie made her play for him." He pulls me against his

221

chest. Over his shoulder, I a his grin reflecting from the window.

"She went after what she wanted. Good for her. Not that I condone stealing another woman's husband. Although it sounds like Ambrose was an easy mark."

"He was. After all, he already had another mistress." His tone is nonjudgemental. "But the best-known Heal's story about her is that she sold this, the store mascot!"

I stare at the patina on the sleek figure. "I guess she preferred dogs. Maybe she wouldn't have sold it if this was a Dalmatian."

Instead of applauding my feeble attempt at a joke, Max groans. "It was for sale, so even though she saw it as embodying the spirit of the store, and told the staff that it granted magic wishes, when a customer wanted to purchase it, she really had no choice."

"Is this a replacement?"

"No. The staff protested to an appalled Ambrose. He contacted the buyer and canceled the sale. The customer didn't protest." He continues with a chuckle. "To make sure it never happened again, he had a sign made—Heal's Mascot: Not for sale."

There's nothing attached to the bottom of the plinth where the cat perches. "What happened to the sign?"

"Probably not needed now." Max shrugs and pulls an antique postcard out of his pocket. Grasping it between his thumb and forefinger, he presents it to me. It's dated 1933. On it is a picture of the cat with the caption *The Cat on the Stairs. Mascot of Heal's Shop.*

I clutch it against my chest, then reach up to give him a kiss. "What a great story. Thanks for bringing me." I grab his hand and hold it all the way down.

Chapter Twenty-Two

M^{ax} By the time we travel from Heal's to St. John, we are barely on time for our eight p.m. reservation. We walk in to find the place buzzing as usual.

JL jumps to his feet and waves. "Here they are," he shouts. Other diners turn at the sound. Mum winces as nine pairs of eyes watch our progress toward the table. I notice Ian and Meggy are missing. The kids ignore us, intent on a video game.

We make our way over. The rest of the party sits at one of the long wooden tables. This is a place for glorying in meat but definitely not in privacy. Fergus Henderson, known for using every part of the animal, is a genius. The restaurant's location, close to Smithfield Market is perfect. Cress wouldn't know it, but she wasn't too far from here earlier today.

When we cross the room, I do a double take. JL has brought Yavuz.

I pull out a chair for Cress, then slide the bag with my other trousers under my seat.

I move around the table to Yavuz and clap him on the shoulder. "Fancy meeting you here. I thought you would be at a family dinner." We shake, and I move back over to sit next to Cress.

"My brother is out with his mates. JL suggested that I join you and meet your family." Yavuz opens his arms as if encompassing all of us.

This is the first time that everyone has met this friend from my past. Frank and Les have been checking him out. Yavuz is wearing the same suit he wore the other night. "Sorry," he apologizes. "I only have two suits these days, and the other one is still at the dry cleaners."

Waving away his comment, I introduce him around. "For those of you who haven't met him, this is Yavuz. His sister was one of my teammates when I was in Istanbul in 2003. Zehra." I wait for that to sink in. "Yavuz lives in London now and we arranged to meet up. He had dinner with us at Rules the other night." I clap him on the shoulder. "This is my family. We're big and noisy, but friendly."

"You've been reminiscing?" Liz turns guileless blue eyes on our guest. Frank leans over and whispers in her ear. She flushes.

"Hardly," I say drily. Liz and Frank weren't married at the time and the family doesn't talk much about what happened. The details are still too painful.

"When did you move to London?" Dad asks.

"A few months ago. One of my brothers lives here and the other, Emre, is studying in Paris. The political climate at home isn't good, so moving here seemed like a good idea. I'm going to Paris soon to visit Emre."

Everyone goes back to general conversation, and Cress and I have our own little bubble. She looks troubled.

"I didn't pay much attention the other night but you said he's Zehra's younger brother. Was she older than you?"

"No. Why?"

"He looks older than I would have expected."

"Yeah, he definitely looks older than thirty."

She gasps. "He's only thirty?"

"I guess he's had a hard ten years."

"Don't you think it's suspicious that he shows up in London when we're here, and he's going to Paris—like us?" Cress' voice quavers.

I shrug. "The CIA says he's clean." But I do wonder about that gap in time. Maybe he fell afoul of the conservative government in Turkey. I give a mental shrug and scan the table. Everyone has a drink, so I motion to the waiter. "Two Rosales 75 cocktails."

There is a slight commotion at the entrance. We all crane our neck, wondering which celebrity is gracing us with their presence. Striding down the Art Deco room is my brother, Ian, with my sister Meggy.

A waiter follows behind with two chairs. No one says a word as we crunch together to make more room.

"Isn't this cozy?" Meggy's salutation appears forced.

Ian apologizes for their lateness—Tube delays—but stops short when he sees Yavuz. "Good to see you again, Arslan. Enjoying London."

"I always enjoy London," Yavuz says politely.

I stand up and hold my sister's chair. "Meggy, this is Yavuz Arslan, one of my colleagues from my posting in Istanbul. Yavuz, my older sister, Margaret." They exchange polite nods.

Meggy narrows her eyes, staring at Yavuz. "Gate crashing, are we?"

"Margaret," Mum says repressively. "Mr. Arslan is a guest."

"Sorry," Meggy mumbles with bad grace.

The waiter brings our drinks and takes orders from Meggy, who asks for whatever we are drinking, and Ian, who plumps for whisky.

I stand and push my chair out of the way so I can lean over and brush my lips against Cress' ear. "Be right back." She ignores me, deep in conversation with Meggy about what they want to eat.

As I move toward the toilets, I notice Allan and a small blonde at a small corner table. A plate of smoked salmon and a bottle of Cristal sit between them. On my way back, I stop. Their glasses are still full and the salmon remains untouched. I stand unnoticed, scuffing a toe against the floor. When I touch his shoulder, Allan starts.

"Hail, hail, the gang's all here. Is this a special occasion?" I wave my hand over their comestibles.

"Something like that." Allan leans back and crosses his arms, making no attempt to introduce me to his dinner guest. He's dressed in an off-the-peg black suit and white shirt and the red-and-gray tie from Fitzwilliam College, Cambridge.

The woman shifts in her chair and doesn't lift her eyes. Her straight, dishwater blonde hair is in a bob with a blue band that matches her plain blue dress in imitation of *Alice in Wonderland*. She fingers the short single strand of pearls at her neck, rubbing them against her teeth while she gives me quick sidelong glances.

""I see Arslan has joined you again this evening."

"He was at a loose end. What's one more body when you have a group as big as ours."

I take one more peek at the woman. She gulps her drink

and turns away, but a sparkle from the wedding band catches my eye. A colleague, or is she married to Allan? Or someone else? Not my business but I'm congenitally nosy.

A slight movement at our table catches my attention, and I notice Yavuz staring at Allan. An uneasy expression flits across his face before he pastes on a smile and gives a small wave.

I rub my the back of my neck. If walking out of the restaurant was an option, I'd grab Cress and be out of here in two seconds. Instead I take two deep breaths and square up my shoulders, getting back to our group just as Ian tells some off-color story. Three empty chairs make me quickly scan the room. Cress, Liz, and Meggy have disappeared.

My heart races. "Where the fuck are they?"

"Take it easy, Max." Ian lazes back in his chair. "Liz needed the toilet and Cress and Meggy offered to go with her."

A sigh of relief escapes me as the starters and our missing females arrive.

Yavuz makes his excuses as we are finishing our mains. He's been taking covert peeps at Allan throughout the meal. Now he pushes his chair back. "My brother texted." He flourishes his mobile. "Sorry to eat and run, but he needs me to meet him at Victoria Station."

He shrugs on JL's jacket and, with a backward wave, disappears into the night.

From behind her hand, Cress whispers, "Why do you think he's been watching Allan?"

"A Turk in London when we have high terrorist alerts. He probably knows who Allan is. So he may worry he's under surveillance, even if he has done nothing." I try for a reassuring tone.

"He makes me uncomfortable." She takes a small bite of pudding.

"You seemed okay with him the other night. Any particular reason why you're more uncomfortable now?"

She screws up her face. So cute when she's thinking. "He's too ingratiating and his teeth are too white."

"Excuse me? Did you say..."

She nods vigorously. "His clothes are poor and he looks as if he doesn't eat well. But his teeth are, well, perfect. As if they're fake."

"Interesting. I guess I didn't notice. But maybe he had to have them pulled. Bad diet and all. Used to be a commonplace in Britain."

"Implants?" Her voice betrays her disbelief.

"More likely full dentures. Dentistry isn't covered under the Turkish health care system." I study her face, seeing the traces of worry in the set of her mouth. "I know you're uncomfortable, but we're leaving for Scotland, so you're unlikely to see him again.."

My dad natters about the new Scottish Premiership, and conversation becomes heated over the merits of Hibernian and Celtic. We finish our pudding. We've pushed the remains of cheese, almond tart, and steamed marmalade pudding to the middle of the table. Dad has waved over the waiter to ask about coffee and after-dinner drinks when the noise starts.

A series of explosions cause cutlery to rattle against china. Flashes of light pulsate in from the large windows at the entrance. The building seems to rock on its foundations. Phone clicks disappear. Some diners dive for cover while the rest of us cast furtive looks, checking out everyone else's reactions. White-clad waiters come around to offer reassurance, even though the platitudes do nothing to calm down the patrons.

"Oh my God!" someone shouts. Silence becomes a cacophony as people try to find out what happened, sort out feelings, or join in the general moan. When the explosions stop and the light goes back to normal, people who had been crouching under tables or lying flat on the floor, sheepishly return to their seats.

"What's going on?" Cress whispers.

I shake my head, then reach for the phone I had silenced and shoved into my pocket when we arrived.

A string of French-Canadian curses rolls out from JL. We all stare as he wipes his forehead. In fact, the whole of the crowd in the restaurant stare at the unfamiliar words. He waves his mobile to indicate he's already got news.

Chest heaving, he chokes out, ""The police are reporting car bombs. Pain creases his face. "A coordinated attack in four places—Notting Hill, Lambeth, Clerkenwell, and Canary Wharf."

Ian and I exchange looks. One of them must have been close by, and our shared house is down the street, on the other side of St. John Square. My stomach threatens to move north, and I gag. The phone I turned on drops to the table with a clatter. Cress squeezes my hand.

"How bad is it?" I croak, my mouth so dry the words hiss out.

JL and Ian's eyes flick back and forth as they scroll on their mobiles.

"Looks like the bombs were small and mostly damaged cars and the façades of the buildings. No one reported injured. Yet." JL's comment is matter-of-fact.

I can deal with property damage. Tightness in my chest

recedes. I loosen my tie slightly and unbutton the top button of my shirt. "Any more info coming through?"

JL shakes his head no.

Ian connects to some government database. "Yeah. Half a 'mo."

We watch as he continues to listen to whoever is feeding him information,

Allan escorts his "date" out, then moves toward our table, seemingly taken aback that Yavuz has gone. "What happened to Arslan?"

Dad regards him curiously, but doesn't ask questions. "His brother texted him as we were finishing the main meal and asked him to meet at Victoria Station. We stayed on for afters."

Allan takes this in, then slowly reveals what he has learned. "Coordinated attacks, but otherwise bloody incompetent if the goal was to blow up anything in the Clerkenwell blast. There is a whacking great hole in the middle of the street in front of your house and several damaged and destroyed cars, including a Bugatti and a Smart Car. Either of them yours?"

Ian and I shake our heads no. We don't keep cars in London. Bloody nuisance with the traffic and the lack of parking. Walking and public transport are fine, along with the occasional taxi or Uber. We drive for fun, not a grind.

JL gives a sad chuckle. "Sad about the Bugatti, but the Smart Car, well, you know what I think of those tiny coffins, Max."

I let out the snort heard 'round the world, but I sober at visions of gaping holes and twisted metal. Sirens from emergency services shriek through the streets.

Ian's fist bangs against the table as he shuts down his mobile. "Bugger. Fuck. Goddamn bloody terrorists."

We sit in silence, watching my rock of a sibling break down.

My voice a harsh squeal, I say, "You said no one died."

His face twists with pain. "Not in Clerkenwell. Two pedestrians injured and taken to hospital. Several people at Canary Wharf wounded by flying pieces of metal. One dead in Notting Hill."

JL follows up. "And Lambeth?"

"Bomb didn't go off. Fortunately. The car was right outside the palace." Ian essays a smile but can only manage a rictus.

"The archbishop is visiting Canterbury, I believe." Allan's pedantic monotone informs us.

"Yes, he left this morning," Les states definitely.

"I've been there for the library."

We all swivel to stare at Cress.

Her voice holds a note of apology. "Sorry. Felt I needed to say something." After a long pause, she adds sheepishly, "but I had nothing appropriate to the situation."

After word of the bombings, the restaurant empties amid nervous chatter, and we are at one of the few occupied tables. The management brings us complimentary brandies. Cress and Mum plump for Calvados and the rest of us sip Martell XO. Allan has pushed in another chair and is sitting next to Dad.

A waiter delivers more coffee. Did we order it? Can't remember. "Would any of you like something else?"

"I'd prefer tea," I say, tapping the empty pot and pushing my fresh cup toward Cress. I'm sure she'll drink mine after hers.

"No, thank you." Ian's voice is exquisite with politesse before he gulps down a large mouthful of brandy, then coughs. I pound his back as he splutters.

"Easy, old man."

He straightens, his watery, frosty blue eyes boring into me. Then he turns his gaze away.

"Sorry, Max. All this must bring back memories."

I wave his comment away. My voice is tight. "I'm fine."

Cress weaves her fingers through mine. I'm not fine, and she knows it.

We sit, toying with our postprandial drinks for another two hours. At some point, Allan takes his leave. "Places to go, people to talk with." He disappears, not exactly in a puff of smoke, but about as close.

"Like a magician," Cress says.

"Quite right, dear." Mum's comment cuts her off. "He does come and go rather like a conjuror."

It's already midnight. Normally the restaurant closes at ten thirty, but in the circs, they have been kind enough to let us stay. "Time to check out the damage."

Dad pushes his chair back and helps Mum to her feet. He has been up and down since he's not supposed to sit for too long at a time. When he wasn't walking out and pounding the pavement, he was consoling Mum.

Now she puts on her coat. "Thank God all of you are here. No sitting and waiting for phone calls." I know she's looking at me.

"Liz and Diana will take all the children back to the Club," Les tells us. Despite loud protests from exhausted young ones, they herd the small gang out the door where a taxi is waiting.

I help Cress on with her coat. When I stand in front to button her up, I'm shocked by the state of her. Deep blue smudges under her eyes stand out like bruises. Her skin is so pale she could almost pass as a ghost. Curls tangled around her shoulders, she suppresses a yawn.

"Should have sent you back with Diana and Liz," I grumble.

"Stop fussing." She pushes her hair back out of her face, then checks her wrist, sliding off a hair tie and pulling the mess back. Then she yawns again. "Sorry. You'd think all that coffee would have kept me more alert."

I lift her chin with a finger and press a soft kiss against her lips. "The food makes you sleepy."

As we walk down St. John's Lane, I slip my arm around Cress, holding her close through the square and out the other side. Police are still everywhere, as are barriers, bright lights, and crime scene tape. As we walk into the space between the barriers, two police constables come up.

One of them shouts out in an East London accent, "Can't come through here!" He makes a push back motion.

"Our house." Ian draws Cress' attention to an enormous crater that has swallowed up the pavement and the street in front. Bits of twisted metal poke up from the cars parked there. "A Grade II listed Georgian townhouse."

I peer into the darkness. It looks as if the front door might be gone as well.

Cress whispers against my shoulder, "Looks like a war zone." A shudder runs through her and I pull her even closer.

"Come with me, sir." The cop waves Ian through, and we all stream after him.

Another constable comes over. "These people are the owners of that house over there. The one with the door blown in," the first one informs her. She takes out a small notebook and a pencil to record our information. Except for our destroyed front door, it looks as if the buildings were only slightly affected, but much of the street around the crater has turned to rubble.

"Do you have a vehicle parked here?" The constable looks up from her notebook, where she has been recording our particulars.

"No cars." Ian responds quickly. "How much damage to the properties?"

"Not sure, sir. We will notify all the owners once we assess everything."

I focused on the activities going on around us and trying to make out as much as I could about the damage. "We are supposed to leave for Scotland tomorrow," I tell her.

"Your brother gave us the details, sir. You don't have to stay in London."

We stand like statues, frozen in postures of grief and denial. We've run out of things to say. Our feelings are weighty, and words banal, expressions not able to convey the inner turmoil roiling through everyone in the crowd. To add to the distress, the first drops of rain spatter down, scattering most of the onlookers.

Loud calls for tarps echo around the area and swarms of police and fire service personnel appear out of nowhere and covering things over.

"What should we do about the house?" The gaping hole where the door used to be concerns me.

"We'll make sure it's boarded up for the moment." The police officer has already turned to help her fellows.

"Thank you," I call out to her retreating back. "We'll move out of your way, then." I look for somewhere we can shelter momentarily, but there are no large entryways to stand in. The rain has turned from drizzle to a steady shower.

"We need to go somewhere dry and talk this over." Dad waves his hand around for no particular purpose. "Your mother is freezing. And wet."

I study his face. Dad has always seemed young. Imperturbable. But now he is showing every one of his seventy-eight years as he clutches Mum to him, his eyes filmed over. It's all I can do not to rush over, hug them both, and lie to them that everything will be fine.

"We're all wet," Meggy grumps, wiping water out of her eyes.

"The Club?" Eyelashes beaded with the rain, Cress looks cold and small, huddled with mum and Meggy. A blue tinge around their mouths tells the tale.

"Somewhere closer." Mum's teeth are chattering. She is shivering after more than an hour, standing on the pavement in a short dress and high heels, with only a light coat. She started swearing softly in Russian as soon as we felt the first drops.

"Bloody hell. We're all going to be soaked. Find somewhere warm. Stat."

"Duck and Waffle," Les suggests. "It's open all night and has fabulous views of the city."

Who the fuck cares about views of the city? Or food? Getting everyone warm and dry is essential. "Fine," I hiss through clenched teeth as I grab Cress and hold her close, trying to stop the shivers running through her.

Frank already has his mobile out. "We have a couple of Ubers on the way."

～

Cress

We pull up to a private entrance to the Heron Tower, one of the tallest buildings in the City. As far as I can tell, the only reason for being here, rather than going back to the Club, is the close proximity. Exhaustion hits me. A hectic day, capped by disaster, has had my adrenaline at a record high. As we'd piled into the Ubers, I whined softly to Max. "I want to go back to the Club and crash."

"I know," he soothes, pushing wet hair out of my eyes. "No choice. Try to bear up a little longer.

I reluctantly move out of the Uber back into the chilly night. The short ride didn't dry me off or warm me up and all I want to do is thaw. From now on, I need to carry a bag big enough for an emergency set of clothing.

As the cold air hits me, I revive. Race-walking into the private elevator, I realize I am looking out through rain drops at Liverpool Station. The wall is transparent. "How high did you say this restaurant is?"

"It's the fortieth floor." Les sounds excited. "The lift zooms right up, no stops. Should be a thrill. Need to come back one of these days. Sean would love seeing the aquarium in the lobby."

Lobby? I mouth to Max. Why the hell aren't we going up from inside the building instead of in this deathtrap?

As if he can read my mind, Max strokes my arm. "The restaurant only has this private entrance. There's no egress from inside the building."

I resolutely face the doors, endeavoring to act excited rather than sick. Even in the dark, the lights of London twinkle and I don't want to take a chance of looking down. But Max folds me into his arms, holding me against his chest to keep me from seeing out.

The elevator swoops into the air and my stomach swoops too. I wish myself back at the Club. Whisked upwards at speed, acid from my stomach pushes upward. I swallow incessantly, trying to keep my dinner from re-emerging all over Max.

Two private elevator rides later, we land on the fortieth

floor. I think back to last November and dinner at Everest in Chicago, another ride in a private elevator to a fortieth-floor restaurant.

"Heights a problem?" Brian asks solicitously while Max rubs one large hand over my back. If I open my mouth, I am sure I will spew, so I give a careful, small nod. When the door opens, I totter out, a death grip on Max's arm and resolutely move forward, only to gasp at the view. Enormous windows face us. I turn my head into Max's wet coat.

"Can we sit away from the windows?" My voice is a tiny croak. "Do we have to go down the same way?"

"Brill." Meggy's enthusiastic bray jars me into a semblance of normal.

Max carefully removes my constricting fingers, moves me a bit, and rubs his arms vigorously. Then he nudges me with his elbow.

"Okay?" He strokes my hair gently. With a chuckle, he makes everything worse. "You aren't planning to lose a shoe again, are you?"

Heat creeps into my face, displacing feelings of nausea with the beginnings of acute embarrassment.

"Cress, you're bright red." Meggy makes this innocent, I hope, observation. Or did Max regale his family with our encounter at Everest last November? I wouldn't put it past him, although no one mentioned it when they visited at Christmas.

Deep crinkles form around his eyes; Max is laughing softly.

"Did you...?" My glare is fire arrows aimed at his heart.

A circle of Grants surrounds me. Their faces tell me they don't know the story. And now I'm going to have to tell it. An army of staff, bearing towels and a large basket, approach us. We take the proffered linens gratefully and try to dry off the worst of the water from our hair and faces. Not much we can do about our clothes and shoes. As we pass through to the dining room, we toss the towels into the capacious basket.

"I must look a fright," Meggy moans.

"Not important," Viktoria chides, looking around at the crowd.

The place is full, not surprising for a Friday night—uh, Saturday morning. Somehow, the Grant magic works. A smartly dressed woman joins us. "Les, glad we could find a table." Her arms full of what looks like chef's whites, she gives a dry chuckle. "I have some dry things for you to wear, and we'll pop your clothes in our industrial dryer."

She hands out the garments and shows us where we can change. I put on the jacket and pants, which are too big, and drop my sodden outfit into the provided basket. I roll up the sleeves and the pant legs and trail into the corridor. Max smirks when he sees me.

Les' friend leads us to a an eight-seat table in front of the windows I want to avoid. Stifling a yawn, I sit with my back to the view. The sound of water sluicing down the windows in competition with the electro music sets up a thrumming in my chest. I grab Max's hand, hoping his touch will calm my racing heart.

Max twists my ponytail in one fist. Good luck if he thinks he can wring out more water. "La mia stellina, it's okay. The windows are very sturdy. Nothing is going to happen."

"What if another bomb goes off?"

Max grips my hand tightly as he holds my gaze, but he is silent.

A waiter comes over, clocks my panicked expression, and offers more reassurance. "Lots of people are nervous about the heights. We had a party in a few days ago." He pauses for effect. "Well, let's say two of them got so het up that the entire party left." He shakes his head. "We offered to reseat them farther from the windows, but..."

He hands around a drinks menu. "If you want to admire the lights, make sure you focus straight ahead, and you'll be capital." His smile is reassuring.

"I'll take a photo if you like. On the terrace. Or the whole family in front of the windows. Very popular." He glances out the windows where the rain is still hammering against the panes. "If it clears out by sunrise, you can get a great photo."

He pauses, watching as we peruse the offerings. "Know what you'd like?"

Max wants cuppa and I agree to share a pot. My stomach is too acidic to allow for coffee right now. And alcohol doesn't appeal. I'm sure a few sips would knock me out completely. The rest of the group choose various special cocktails from the menu. The thought threatens to roil my stomach all over again.

An unwelcome voice pierces through the wall of sound. "So, we meet again."

Allan Mason's sibilant tones run through me like an icy wave on Lake Michigan. He looks the same as at the restaurant earlier. But unlike us, he is not wet. Either he had an enormous umbrella or shuttled around by car from wherever he's been.

Max looks up from the food menu, his face marred by a deep frown. "What are you doing here, Allan?"

"How did you find us?" Ian snarls.

"I stopped at the site and spoke to two officers. One of them remembered you and heard you planning to come to

Duck and Waffle. Had a taste for waffles myself, so here I am."

"Well, you can push off again," Ian growls.

A waiter approaches with another chair. Max goes to wave him away, but I grab his arm.

"What are you doing?" Max hisses.

"Mr. Mason." My voice is tight but steady. "I assume you have some news for us."

Allan sits down and faces us, lips pursed. "Not why I'm here."

Arms folded over his chest, Brian barks, "Why are you here then?"

With a slightly apologetic downturn to his mouth, Allan pulls a sheet of paper out of his inner jacket pocket, unfolds it, smooths out the creases. His eyes flick over the words. He holds it out to Max.

With two fingers, Max draws the paper closer. I turn my head, trying to read it, but Max is holding it away from prying eyes. I watch his eyes flick over and over. Then he sighs and goes to put it in his pocket. Allan holds out his hand. "Sorry, Max. I need that back."

Without a word, Max slides it back, face down, so the message remains hidden.

"What..." I start.

"Official secrets." Allan's retort is sharp as flint.

I'm sure it's someone taking credit for the bombing on Max's street, or another threat. Max and Allan's faces turn to stone. No more information will be forthcoming.

Fretful, Ian pushes. "What about the house?"

"No firm reports on the damage, but the investigators think it's all superficial. Fortunate the rain started before the fires could spread. Once they can access the row, they'll know more. Smoke and water damage at the very least."

Allan scratches behind his ear. "I'll make sure police keep you informed."

"I bet you will," Ian mutters, not quite sotto voce.

Allan leans toward Max and starts telling him something. Ian's icy fingers grip my bicep.

"His brother was just the same," he whispers. "We called him Stick-Up-the-Arse Mason."

I look over at Max, who is staring at us. "You were best mates," he says.

"True." Ian agrees with a grin. "I could put up with his prissy behavior. He was a wizard oarsman."

Tapping his fingers against an empty water glass, Allan reclaims everyone's attention. "I'm really here to discuss next steps. We are certain Max's house was one target of the bombings."

"Is that what was on the paper?" I ask.

Max, his face etched in stern lines, gives no sign of hearing me.

Allan turns toward Brian. But then, our waiter reappears with our drinks and food menus in hand. We all sit frozen, waiting for him to finish. The chill at the table is apparent, and he hurries in, handing everything around. "Be back in half a 'mo to take any food orders." He practically runs away.

I add milk in one cup, then pour tea for Max first, then for me, leaving him to put in his own sugar. He spoons it in, not paying proper attention.

After four spoonfuls, I touch his hand and the spoon clatters to the table. He takes a sip and winces. I push his cup aside and give him mine, adding a little milk and one spoonful of sugar. He smiles weakly. "Lifesaver," he murmurs.

Brian sips his dram of whisky. "So, Allan, you were

saying?"

Allan looks up from the menu card in front of him. "Good place to choose. The music will definitely keep other ears out of our business."

The waiter is back, and we order a plethora of small plates.

"I know. You're not hungry, la mia stellina, but maybe I can tempt you with something. The bread, if nothing else."

I give Max a weak smile, then focus on Allan, who is straightening up as if to make a pronouncement. His next words are a bit of a letdown. "I understand you were planning to go to Scotland tomorrow."

Brian leans forward to make sure Allan can hear him. He sounds angry. "Max and Ian may have to stay in London."

Allan shakes his head no. "Our office will take care of things at this end." Ian tries to interrupt, but Allan goes on. "We want Max to continue his trip."

"Mousetrap!" Meggy exclaims. "And Max is the cheese." She sounds a little too excited.

"You think something will happen up there?" The tonelessness in Max's voice is unsettling.

"No idea. But your itinerary is no secret. And we want Faez to activate his endgame. The only way to smoke him out."

Dragging myself out of my funk, I break in. "I don't get it. I can envision the other bombings as a decoy, but if Faez wants to kill Max, isn't this whole scheme inefficient?"

"The goal is to kill him, but this cat-and-mouse business heightens the tension. I'm certain Faez wants to draw you to Turkey, so he can kill you face to face."

"Why wouldn't he want a quick result?" Frank looks a bit confused.

Allan gives a short, humorless snort. "He's spent the last ten years in prison, probably thinking about how he will take revenge on his brother's killer. He can afford to be patient."

Our waiter comes back, and we fall silent. "Sunrise is in about two hours. Do you want to go to the terrace and watch?"

"We'll go out if you fetch us," Brian tells him.

"Right. I'll be back for you in"—the waiter looks at his watch—"about an hour and three-quarters. Your food will be up soon."

Brian turns his attention back to the table and does a double take. "Cressie. You're white as a sheet."

"I think I'll just sit here." My words come out in a feeble stream and Max strokes my palm reassuringly.

"We'll just sit here together, Dad. The rest of you can go watch."

JL has been quiet throughout, but now he throws Allan a pointed look. "To go back to Allan's assessment, how do you explain the attack?"

Allan tents his fingers, obviously moving into lecture mode. I give him the side-eye. He's so bloodless. This is Max's life we're talking about, not some school lesson on terrorism.

"His terrorist contacts would have been able to pull this off." His voice is dry and brittle as bone. "And, who knows, this attack could have been in the works for a while and Faez might have been able to ride the coattails of an existing terror cell."

Food arrives. After our huge dinner, I'm astounded at how quickly the plates empty. Frank and Les are quite the trenchermen and even Allan, Meggy, and Brian make inroads. Viktoria takes dainty bites of bacon-wrapped dates

243

and Max samples grilled octopus, while I ignore my favorite things and crumble some of the house bread. Food seems to be the drug of choice, but for me everything tastes like brick dust and ashes. Like the ruins on Max's street.

Chapter Twenty-Three

*S*cotland
Cress

We're standing just outside the entrance to King's Cross Station. Traveling with the Grant family reminds me of photos from the golden age of travel with heaps of luggage everywhere.

"Max! Max!" A man runs toward us, waving his arms. Yavuz, turning up like a bad penny. Out of breath, he skids to a stop as he reaches us, unfortunately colliding with the teetering mountain just as the passenger assist people turn up. A younger man comes up next to him.

He grabs Max in a hug. "I didn't expect you to be here. Sometimes I think you're following us." His joking chuckle seems strained. "What a terrible thing, last night. I had just gotten to Victoria when I heard." He puts a hand on Max's arm.

"Yes. Especially the people injured..." Max stops and regards Yavuz carefully. "And the ones who died."

By this time, JL is standing next to Max.

"Ah, JL, my friend. I suppose this is au revoir." He

reaches out a hand for JL to shake before answering Max. "A terrible shame. London is no safer than Istanbul these days."

"Why are you here, Yavuz?"

"My brother and I. Max, you remember my brother, Tanik?" Yavuz grins. "JL, this is my brother, Tanik. He went to lycée in Istanbul, so his French is very good."

"Enchanté de faire votre connaissance." JL shakes hands with Tanik as well.

"Ravi de te rencontrer également."

"Tanik." Max smiles, but it doesn't reach his eyes.

"Max. Yavuz told me you were in London." His air is casual.

"You have another brother, too, don't you, Yavuz?"

"Yes. I'm surprised you remember, Max. Emre would only have been twelve."

Max pulls me forward to Tanik. "This is my partner, Cressida Taylor."

Tanik bows over my hand. As he straightens, Yavuz gives him a little push. "We are taking the Eurostar to Paris. On business. And as we are arriving at St. Pancras, there you are, with your lovely family."

The luggage has been loaded on a cart and I look over at Brian, who stands on the station forecourt, waving frantically. Faintly, I hear him call out, "Come on. The train is already boarding."

"I hope your business in Paris goes well. We're off to Scotland for a few days." Max sounds politely distant.

"I'm sure you will enjoy being at home. Come, Tanik. We must not miss our train."

Max and JL watch until the brothers disappear into the maw of St. Pancras. JL turns to Max to ask "What are you thinking?"

Max runs his fingers through his hair, distracted. "Nothing. Wool-gathering." He leans down and picks up his bag and mine, then grabs my hand. "Let's go."

I've only been to Scotland once, for the Edinburgh festival when I was at Oxford. Hills had suggested it. Her then-boyfriend was performing. I had moved from my digs at Somerville to share a flat with Kev and he was keen to go. We were in the honeymoon phase and the trip seemed magical.

My gaze drifts to Max and I feel real magic run through me. Magic a million times stronger than anything I ever felt with Kev. An almost visible current of electricity.

My time with Kev reminds me of cheap sleight of hand ineptly performed by an amateur. Even more so after the confrontation outside the RAF Club. I shiver at the reminder.

When we planned this trip, I wanted to take the Caledonian Sleeper. Ever since I saw the series *Great Railway Journeys* on public television, I've been in love with the romance of the rails. Max, not so much. When we discussed the trip, January was in full swing. Max had moved the big armchair to face the windows so we could cuddle and watch the snow fall.

"Have you ever been on a sleeper?" He sounded incredulous.

I bristled. "Yes. Have you?"

His grimace said it all. "What was your trip like?'

"Hell," I told him.

"Then why go on another?"

247

"Romance." I stared at him, my eyes clouded with desire.

He laughed. "Tell me about the trip from hell."

"Micki, Paul, and I took a trip to Russia right after college. Part of the tour was the chance to visit not only Moscow and St. Petersburg, but also Georgia. It was an adventure, a train ride from Sochi to Tbilisi. We had these big compartments with two sets of bunk beds. Our guide drilled us to say 'Nyet komnaty' because people not in our group kept trying to push into our cabins."

Max smiled. "No room, huh?"

"It was summer, and the air conditioning wasn't work-ing. After two hours, the toilets weren't either. We had sack dinners, but I didn't eat. The tea lady came around every hour, but without working toilets, I wasn't drinking either." I scrunched up my face, thinking of the smell permeating the car from the nonfunctional but still used toilets.

"How long was the trip?" Max's query brought me back.

Reflexively I rubbed my nose. "About eighteen hours. We were on the milk train, so we stopped at every station. I remember when we pulled into Stalin's birthplace, Gori, a huge oil painting of him hung on the platform."

"And you still want to take a sleeper?" Disbelief flooded his face.

"I want to take a luxury train this time." My voice climbed to an insistent whine as I grabbed for his hand. "Tell me about your trip."

"It was unfortunate." His dismissive tone doesn't make me stop .

"Why was it unfortunate?"

"For reasons best left unexplored, I took the night train from Istanbul to Ankara."

"Secret reasons," I said sourly.

"People I was interested in were taking the train, so I took it too."

"And?"

He jumped up and started pacing. After what seemed like an hour but was probably thirty seconds, he said, "Those sleeper compartments are bloody cells. The beds are short, and I felt folded in half. In the end, I gave up and sat in the observation car drinking Gazoz—lemonade—all night."

"Did the toilets work?" My lips turned up in a mischievous grin.

"Marginally. But in those situations, there is an advantage in being male."

"Maybe the Caledonian Sleeper is more spacious," I said, looking on the bright side.

Max snorted, making the cats jump. "No chance. Sorry, la mia stellina. We'll fly into Edinburgh and Dad and Frank will pick us up."

"Max," I said in my most seductive burble, "I'd really like to take the Orient Express someday."

"That's a whole different proposition. I'll try to make a reservation from Paris to Venice." He settled back into the couch and pulled me on top of him.

"I love you," I gurgled into his neck.

"Because I'm a pushover."

"Because you're such a romantic."

Here we are, the whole family alighting from the fast train to Edinburgh. We swarm into Waverley Station in the late afternoon. After being penned up for hours, the kids are eager to hit the street. Brian has arranged for a van to transport us from Edinburgh to Grant House. In the meantime, there is dinner to eat.

Brian, Frank, and Les wrestle with the luggage while Viktoria helps Diana and Liz herd the children to the waiting modified minibus.

"These buses seat twenty-five," Brian tells me. "This one seats twenty. Five seats were taken out for a sofa-like affair in the back. Perfect for me to be able to stretch out. Otherwise we'd be stopping every half hour so I could walk."

Max and JL are standing to the side, sizing up the crowd. I wonder if they are checking whether Yavuz was on our train after all.

"Sean," Diana calls out to her teenager. "Help us set up the sprogs in the back."

"Come on, then." Brian corrals the three of us. "We're going to the Abbey."

"The Abbey?" Does he mean we're going to Holyrood? Do we have time for this? I can't imagine. "Are we going sightseeing first?"

"Nae, girl." He exaggerates his brogue. "It's one of the finest whisky bars in the city. And their food, well, can't wait for you to try it. Max said you love bangers and mash and sticky toffee pudding, and theirs are excellent."

A bang-up meal, I can hardly wait. Although I'm not sure more sticky toffee pudding is in my future. I like it but I may have had my quota, at least this trip..

Viktoria calls back from the first bench seat. "What are you planning to do with the house now?"

"Max was going to sell his share to me, but now, maybe we'll sell the whole place. I rather fancy a small flat." Ian doesn't sound too broken up.

"We'll be back, house hunting, in a few months." Max slips his hand behind my neck. "Nothing grand."

"Oh, how wonderful! When is the wedding?" Viktoria tries to turn around to grab me, but the seat belt holds her in a webbed embrace.

"No wedding." My voice wobbles like a beginner on a flute.

I've never seen a mouth make such a perfect O of disappointment.

The Abbey appears like the answer to a prayer. A prayer including bangers and mash.

Max

After our blowout meal, we eschew a leisurely drive back to Grant House. Cress seems resigned to miss the visit to Robert the Bruce's grave at Dunfermline Abbey, and the chance to tour Scone and Stirling castles.

"We'll be back and those places are going anywhere. I want to know about all those yellow flowers." she says, pressing her nose to the window glass.

"Gorse," comes from everyone.

"Really? I've seen it referred to in books, but I never knew what it looked like. It's beautiful."

"Smells like coconut and vanilla. Maybe the scent wouldn't be too much of a problem," I say.

We stop soon after for Dad to have a bit of a walk and a stretch. These long drives are murder but the train from Edinburgh would be so crowded that he wouldn't have been able to move anyway.

Cress is drawn to a huge patch of gorse.

"Careful," I call after her. "The thorns are wicked."

She starts to sneeze and, fumbling for tissues in her pocket, rushes back to the van. "It may smell like coconut and vanilla, but it still causes a reaction."

I love her enchantment with the spectacular scenery of the Cairngorms as the mountains flit past our windows. I point out the many distilleries we won't be able to try, at least not today. As we near Grant House, Castle Grant, Ballindaloch, and Muckrach Castle—all properties belonging to members of the clan—come into view.

The clan chief no longer lives at Castle Grant, which is now a tourist attraction. Muckrach is a self-catering venue built in the late sixteenth century by Patrick Grant, the son of John Grant of Freuchie. A distant cousin lives at Ballindaloch. They are planning a distillery on the grounds, yet another Grant whisky producer.

A pack of dogs greets our entrance, along with the housekeeper, Mrs. MacDonald. She tries, ineffectually, to shoo them away, finally giving up with a huff. "Come along in. I have tea laid on in the lounge."

The dogs, far more energetic than we are, gambol around our feet, tripping Cress up. I hold on to her arm to make sure she doesn't fall.

"I didn't know your parents had so many dogs," she mutters.

Dad laughs. "We only have two. The rest belong to Frank and Liz and Les and Diana."

Once seated, the dogs form a semicircle around Cress. "I think they want an introduction." Her eyes are gleaming with delight.

Mum points to her borzoi. "This is Prince. My darling boy. The gray around his muzzle shows he is no longer young." A shadow crosses her eyes, but she recovers quickly. The yellow Lab is Brian's dog, Bristol. Only two and frisky."

Sean grabs the Scottish terrier, who sports a collar in the Grant tartan. "This is our dog, Laddie. He's only two." The dog puts up with cuddling for about half a second.

The other dogs are a gaggle of cocker spaniels, excitedly jumping up and down against Cress' legs. Liz smiles indulgently. "Four puppies for four sprogs."

We tuck into high tea, more like dinner than the afternoon tea most people think of and follow up with some good whisky. Dad regales us with family stories, making each of us blush in turn as he delights Cress with our misadventures and misbehaviors, until we're all trying to hide yawns behind our hands.

"I wish I could give you a tour tonight, Cress," Mum tells her. "But we have all had a long day. Besides, it will be better to examine everything in the daylight, so I will show you around after breakfast." She gets up and stretches. "Time for bed. We will have brunch about ten. Good sleep everyone."

Dad shuffles out and I grab Mum's arm. "Is Dad doing all right?"

"Tired, and his angina waxes and wanes, but the doctor says he's still got a lot of life in him. Can't do the late nights too often any more, but he's so glad you're all home." She pecks my cheek and follows him out.

I take Cress upstairs to my old bedroom, bookshelves filled with Matchbox race cars, and models I built myself. There are rugby trophies and a few framed jerseys next to my diplomas and family pictures. The bedding is the ubiquitous Grant tartan. Two large casement windows face out onto the grounds, bathing us in moonlight.

I take Cress in my arms and kiss her over and over. Then we crawl into bed and fall asleep nestled together.

～

Our small clan has assembled for Sunday morning brunch. When Cress and I walk into the dining room, everyone but Dad has already gathered.

"Sorry we're late," I lean down to give Mum a kiss.

"You're not late, I told you to sleep in." Her scolding tone is undermined by a smile.

Ian calls out, "Or indulge in morning sex." He chortles, taking a mountain of food from the steaming chafing dishes.

Liz and Diana glare as Diana remarks tartly, "Inappropriate, Ian. Don't forget there are children here."

He puts his plate down, then sits. "Do you mean to say your children don't know about the birds and the bees?" He smirks.

"I know about birds and bees." Felicity reproves her uncle with glee. "Dad took us to visit a beekeeper. He wore a white suit and a hat with a, with a..." She screws up her face.

"A veil," Frank supplies, ever the helpful dad.

"Yeah," Felicity agrees. "A bail."

"Right you are, Lissy." Ian smiles. He raps his knuckles against the table. "I'll have to be back in town for Thursday, so I'm leaving Wednesday night. Can someone drive me down?"

"On the sleeper?" Cress' eyes are bright with envy.

"For my sins," he mumbles.

"Cress is dying to go on the Caledonian." I produce a comic shudder.

"Of course she is, She'd fit fine. Harder to manage in sleeper compartments when you're tall." Ian's lips twist in a grimace.

"You're shorter than Max," she retorts.

"Still tall, short stuff." He grins at her as he puts down a plate filled with scrambled eggs, mushrooms, bacon, sausage, tomatoes, and beans. Toast balances precariously on the side. His other hand grasps a bowl of porridge.

"What travesty is this?" Dad walks in and surveys the buffet. He glares at Mum, his face twisted in mock disgust.

Mum looks over at the huge antique oak sideboard, "What do you mean, Brian?"

"Come now, Vik, this is no proper breakfast for the family." His tone is severe, but his eyes are twinkling.

Mum surveys the buffet. "What's wrong with it? We have syrnitki, vareniki with mushrooms and with cherries, and draniki."

"Russian muck! No finnan haddie or kedgeree, no tattie scones or black pudding, and where's the whisky for the porridge?" He shakes his finger at her. "What will Cress think? Not one Scottish delicacy."

"If you want whisky, you know where it is." Mum sounds as tart as the cherries in the vareniki.

Cress brings a cup of coffee to the table and sets it next to her bowl of porridge and a heaping plate of bacon, toast, a fried egg, lots of mushrooms, and half a tomato, as well the all the Russian delicacies. No beans. "There's whisky for the porridge?" She sounds eager.

"I'll fetch you a wee dram." Dad walks off toward the library, where he keeps his collection of single malts.

"Bring the bottle," Ian yells after him. "We all want some."

Dad raises his hand over his head in an assenting finger wave.

JL frowns at the tureen of porridge. "May I drink the Scotch and skip the oatmeal?"

"Ye're missing the best part of the meal." Sean exaggerates his Scottish burr, his voice changing from treble to baritone and back uncontrollably.

Diana glares at her teenage son. "Sean, that's no way to speak to a guest. Apologize now." Then, with a sigh, she reaches to rub her back. Les leans into her and takes over as she sighs in relief. Her discomfort is palpable, making my back ache in sympathy.

Sean turns his glower to with a charming smile. "Sorry, Monsieur Martin."

"Pas de problème, mon ami. And you may call me JL if your parents do not object." Then he winks at me and whispers, "Je suis rempli de politesse."

"You're full of something," I tell him.

"We appreciate your exemplary manners, JL. Très gentil." Mum regally inclines her head.

JL smirks. "I appreciate you inviting me into your home, Madame."

"Call me Viktoria." Her face exhibits an unholy glee that sends us into gales of laughter. They've had an ongoing tug-of-war over names since they met in Chicago last year.

Dad returns, plunking a bottle of Glenfiddich on the table. Mum has put down shot glasses for the adults. We pass the bottle.

"One of the brands started by the Grant clan." Dad makes the pronouncement with pride. "Grants have been involved in the whisky trade for generations."

JL surveys the faces round the table. "You Grants are certainly ubiquitous."

"Of course. You're on the hereditary lands of the clan. And unlike other families, there were no highland clearances here." Dad bangs the table for emphasis.

Sean chances his arm. "May I have some whisky?"

Les tips a few drops in a glass, then sprinkles it into his

son's porridge. "A taste." Another hefty dram goes into his own bowl.

Sean opens his mouth to protest, but the frowns on his parents' faces makes him think twice. "Thanks, Dad," he mumbles.

Les gives his son the evil eye. Turning to JL, he grumbles, "Kids!"

"They like to push the limits at that age," says the man who has declared he will never be a parent. "I know I did."

Buttering a piece of toast, Dad remarks offhandedly, "Have you heard the joke about the butter?" Mum flashes a Medusa-like gaze, but somehow, he doesn't turn to stone. Instead, he raises his voice a bit. "I better not tell you; it might spread!"

The kids snigger.

"Yesterday, I accidentally swallowed some food coloring. The doctor says I'm okay, but I feel like I've dyed a little inside," I follow up.

Sean, who is shaping up to be a chip off the old block, comes up with, "What did the late tomato say to the other tomatoes? Don't worry, I'll ketchup."

"Good one," Les congratulates his son.

"Diana picked a good one," Brian chortles, pointing at Les.

Cress frowns. The jokes have been coming thick and fast. I lean over and kiss her as Mum comes in with a platter of cupcakes.

"The pièce de résistance," she exclaims loudly, spearing my sister and sister-in-law with a look before they can protest. "A special treat."

"So adorable, and realistic too. I love Highland Cows." Cress clasps her hands over her mouth. We're all laughing, except Ian. When I glance at him, my laid-back brother frowns.

"What's up, man? Bad news?"

"No news," he grouses, putting his mobile back in a pocket.

No one has noticed our exchange. They are all still focused on the cupcakes.

"Coos." Diana makes the correction kindly. "Fresh from Cuckoo's Nest Bakery in Edinburgh. Mrs. MacDonald picked them up for us while we were away. Although I assumed they were for dinner."

Meggy tries to snatch one off the plate before it reaches the table, but Ian slaps her hand.

"You're in for a treat, Cress. Cuckoo's makes some of the finest baked goods in the country." Dad's already reaching for one of the delectable little cakes. He breaks it in half and feeds it to Bristol.

"Dad, you know cake isn't good for him," Meggy scolds.

"A little won't hurt." He puts another piece on the palm of his hand and holds it out to the eager dog.

"Waste of good food," Meggy grumbles, and turns to Cress. "Whisky ganache center, sticky toffee pudding, topped off with a creamy vanilla buttercream to make the coo frosting." Meggy's eyes squeeze shut as she licks her lips.

The table falls silent as we stuff our faces. When Diana nods, Sean takes one while the sprogs eat a nonalcoholic version in bright pink. Little girl screams greet their arrival.

Frank and Ian had been conferring at the other end of the table. Ian, now resigned to no word about the house, has relaxed. "Frank and I thought we could all try some rock climbing later. Work off some of this meal."

Mum narrows her eyes. "Mrs. Mac is preparing a

wonderful dinner." She shakes a finger at Ian. "You say you will be back on time, but I know you all so well. I know we will eat overcooked lamb, inedible veg, and Mrs. Mac will stand in the corner, glowering. Everyone, besides you, is here for the week, so pick another day."

Frank opens his mouth, then shuts it when Ian shakes his head.

I checked with Allan when we arrived and so far there's no sign that anyone followed us here. This works out well, since my plan is to take Cress and JL to some places we weren't able to visit yesterday.

~

Cress

After our brunch, Viktoria gives me a brief tour of the house. Max's Chicago house seemed massive until Viktoria explains the layout of Grant House. The Scottish Baronial mansion, with fifty-two rooms over four floors plus a basement, covers more territory than we can possibly manage today.

"Don't linger," Max warns us. "We have to leave in the next half hour if we're to get to everything I have planned."

Viktoria gives me a carefully curated tour of the most important rooms, including two lounges and several bedrooms that have hosted famous visitors over the centuries.

"Who has visited?" I ask.

"Many people. Conan Doyle once or twice. Alexander Fleming, the man who discovered penicillin. Even Charles Dickens. He came up from Edinburgh for two nights and gave a public reading in our library."

I rhapsodize over the mishmash of antiques crowding

every room. All the mantelpieces are chock-a-block with Staffordshire pottery dogs. Several lounges, replete with Rennie Mackintosh–inspired wallpapers in the British Art Nouveau style, have furniture to match. Especially eye-catching is the Mackintosh Rose wallpaper in the family lounge.

I peek into the kitchen with its typical Aga stove, and several large refrigerators, unusual in most British houses. A butler's pantry, large storage pantry, and laundry branch off from the main room. A conservatory at the back is a wonderful indoor garden with some sort of evergreen shrubs, a few fig and lemon trees, and luxurious potted rose-mary bushes. The stained glass ceiling showers a rainbow of light over the room.

When we reach the library, I can barely believe my eyes. With row after row of rich oak shelves that climb prac-tically to the ceiling and a balcony running all the way around the room, I could be in the Duke Humfrey reading room at the Bodleian library. Centuries-old bindings vibrate with a seductive siren song. A shelf of oversized books that I guess are a collection of gazetteers and atlases calls to me. My fingers itch to move a volume to the large library table dominating the middle of the room. A long credenza in front of ceiling-to-floor windows showcases Brian's impres-sive collection of single malts. I could stay there all day on one of the comfortable-looking sofas, a drink on one of end tables.

Then Max comes in with my coat over his arm. "Time to go."

JL and I, along with Prince and Bristol, pile into the Rover. The dogs are eager for the ride and a run. They sit on either side of JL, heads poking out the windows. Although Max has two cars garaged here, both are two-seater sports cars. As we take the twelve-mile ride, Max points out Castle Grant, former home of the clan chief. "There are lots of Grants around here. We're second cousins to Sir Robert."

JL looks wistful. "Cool that you live near a town named for your family."

Max shrugs. "There's good and bad about it all. Sometimes everything is so claustrophobic. Tradition and history weigh on you. And everyone knows who you are, how you're related, and all the scandals in your family."

"I like the sense of belonging," I say.

Max reaches over and squeezes my shoulder.

"And history can still weigh on you, no matter who you are or where you live," I continue sadly.

"Vraiment. It's all woven into your identity. But even if it's part of you, it doesn't have to own you."

"It's hard to break free," I say, looking at Max.

JL stares out the window scowling. "This conversation is getting too heavy. Tell us what we are going to see."

"Should have brought Dad along," Max grumbles. "He knows all the stories." Max smooths back his hair with one hand and shifts with the other as we go up a small hill. "But I'll take a stab at it." He makes an ostentatious display of clearing his throat and humming as if to tune up before he begins.

"'Good' Sir James Grant"—he picks up a finger and crooks it for the quote, then clamps his hand back on the steering wheel—"established the town in 1765 as a center for wool and linen weaving mills. Unfortunately, those enterprises failed early on. Trade really was the driver for the growth of the town and by the mid-nineteenth century it was the second largest in the county after Inverness."

"Tell us something interesting," JL grumbles. "Scandals, murders, royal visits."

"This is interesting," I say. "You're being a pain in the ass, JL."

JL sticks out his tongue and says, "Keener."

"What?" I huff.

"It means suck up, brown noser," Max supplies. "Canadian slang."

"Well, fuck you," I tell JL, not able to come up with a clever riposte. JL snorts.

Max grimaces, then goes on. "There was a royal visit. Balmoral is only about forty miles away and Queen Victoria and Prince Albert stayed incognito at the Grant Arms Hotel on the night of 4th September 1860. They arrived by horse-drawn carriage from Balmoral Castle on their way to visit Castle Grant. They stopped at Grant House before paying their respects to the chief."

"That's it?" JL sounds disgusted.

"The queen said the visit was amusing and never to be forgotten. But we don't know what she was referring to."

"I love these little tidbits," I tell him.

"She also said the dinner was very fair, and all very clean...ending with a good tart of cranberries."

"Oh, well, clean, that's the most important," JL says teasingly.

"No other royal visitors?" I'm dying to know more.

"Prince Philip and Prince Edward stopped in on their way from Balmoral to Sandringham one Christmas season, because of Meggy's position working in the royal household."

"Enough history," JL groans.

"Because it's Sunday, we'll be enjoying the scenery. The museum is nice but closed today, as are the distilleries. We can come back if we can find a day. Aberlour isn't too far from Grant House."

I grin. Max knows Aberlour is one of my favorite single malts.

Max risks a glance at me, then refocuses on the road. "A bit of uphill walking, Cress?"

I frown. "I'm not keen unless the rise is really gentle and the path is clear." With my well-known tendency to clumsiness, spraining my ankle again is not on my wish list. Nor is looking over wide vistas from a height.

"We'll drive to some views. The scenery is spectacular, especially right around the Spey. If we have time, we can go on to Culloden and see the battlefield and their excellent visitor center. It's about an hour away. Or wander around Kinloss Abbey."

"Founded by King David I in 1150," I break in excitedly.

Max's eyes twinkle. "I thought you'd like that. Kinloss it is." He looks over at JL. "We can go salmon fishing before you leave."

"How about tomorrow, before our meeting?" JL sounds thrilled by the prospect of standing in a fast-running river in hip boots.

"Not tomorrow, mate. I'm giving Cress a driving lesson in the morning." My small frown goes unnoticed.

"When we go climbing on Tuesday, Cress, I think Mum wants visit cousin Nikolai in Grantown. He's a well-known concert pianist.

"On our last day, I thought we'd go to Ballindaloch Castle. The Macpherson-Grants live there and it's open to the public. You can go fishing then, JL, if you aren't interested in the castle. Or, if you don't want to climb on Tuesday, we can set you up with fishing instead."

Sharon Michalove

"Do you go as public or family to Ballindaloch?" I ask.

"We're related and I know them, but I don't plan to make it a family call. They built the castle in the sixteenth century and that branch of the family has lived there ever since. It's called the pearl of the north and while not well-known, it's one of the best castles in the country to visit."

We've reached Grantown and Max parks the Rover in the Highland Council car park. The dogs, gambol unleashed as we meander down to the Spey and walk along the A95, enjoying views of the river. Max keeps the leashes looped around his wrist in case we need them. We walk down to Spey Bridge. On the way back, we stroll down a lane, stopping so JL can chat with the fishermen.

"Can't wait to be up to my knees in the river with a rod in my hand," JL says as he rejoins us on the path.

"Off to a few other sights." Max corrals the dogs into the backseat.

"Remember, we need to be back in time for Mrs. MacDonald's fabulous meal," JL reminds him, licking his lips in anticipation.

~

Max

Our usual Sunday family lunch is dinner instead, and we are all stuffed. Parsnip soup, leg of lamb and mashed potatoes, buttered peas as none of us like the mushy variety, cauliflower cheese, and chocolate stout cake adorned with candied orange, caramel ganache, and orange ice cream, based on one served at Stravaigin in Glasgow. And that's when I discover Cress' guilty pleasure—skooshy cream. Mum, of course, would never serve it. We have proper whipped cream here.

264

"Have some cake," I say to Cress, who is covertly unbuttoning her jeans.

She glares. "I don't think I could eat another bite."

Ian comes back from the sideboard with a vast slab of cake, two scoops of ice cream, and globs of whipped cream.

"It looks good?" She sounds doubtful as she gazes covetously at his plate."

"You may have as much as you like." Mum's voice brims with invitation. "I fell in love with this cake the last time we were in Glasgow. Was it in 2012, Brian? The Creative Macintosh Festival?"

Choking slightly, Dad waves a hand while trying to swallow a huge bite of cake. "Yes. Lovely weekend. Max, you need to take Cress over to Glasgow when you visit again. Have tea at the Willow Rooms and finish up with dinner at Stravaigin. Where we had the cake. Your mother wheedled the recipe out of the chef."

I nod. "Cake?" I ask Cress again.

"A tiny piece. And do you have Redi Whip?"

"What's that?" Felicity, leans forward, her eyes glowing with interest.

"Whipped cream in a spray can," Cress explains.

"Oooooh, skooshy cream. We love that," Liz and Frank's littlest one bubbles. "Babushka, why don't you have skooshy cream?"

Mum rolls her eyes, then scowls. "I will only say this once. Real cream only in my house. If your parents," she glares at Frank and Liz, "want to give you disgusting aerosol cream, that is their business. You will not have it here."

Felicity, undaunted, turns back to Cress, "Why do you call it Redi Whip?"

"It's the brand name." Cress smiles. "But it's because it's already whipped and ready to eat."

"Logical," Les snickers.

"Disgusting," is Ian's rejoinder.

"Well, I like the texture. It's thicker and you can make nice designs with it." She pauses, tipping her head to the side. Then she smiles at Mum. "I'll take a dollop of whipped cream on the cake."

I hand her the plate with a sliver of cake, a smidge of ice cream, and a small spoonful of cream.

"Thank you." When our fingers touch, an electric current courses through me. Her eyes mist. Is it love, or is it cake?

Ian raps the tabletop. "I thought we'd climb tomorrow, but Max has some sort of work meeting. We'll go climbing on Tuesday."

Meggy shouts across the table, "Where are we going?"

"Huntly's Cave." Frank grins. We all know it's his favorite climb. "It's close and a pleasant climb."

"RAF Grantown developed the climbing routes." Dad's voice is full of pride when he tells Cress and JL

"Why?" Cress asks.

"Climbing is part of the training program," Dad explains. "We have a force development center here, not an airbase." He sighs, running his fingers through his short hair. "After my second crash, they assigned there me for a while. Conveniently close to home while I convalesced." He gets up, his limp noticeable, and goes to the sideboard for another cuppa, shutting down the discussion.

"Frank and I have already packed the gear into the Rover." Ian's a bit offhand, knowing Dad won't mind.

"We don't need to haul anything tomorrow and I think Max is using one of his cars for Cress' driving lesson," Dad tells him.

By now, Dad has returned to his seat. "A guide was

leading a group of people on a hike through some mountains. He pointed at a fairly majestic looking peak and said, 'This one is most popular with mountain climbers. Most days, you have a few teams doing a climb. The ascent, depending on your skill level, can take between two and five hours. The descent, again depending on your skill level, takes anywhere between four hours and thirty seconds.'"

With a sharp intake of breath, Cress looks at me, anxiety in her eyes. "Are you sure you want to go?"

Dad looks contrite when he sees her face. "Joke, Cress. Only a joke."

"It will be fine," I say. "I've been climbing all my life."

Mum comes back into the dining room, Mrs. MacDonald and the coffee service in tow. "Where doing you think you are you going on Tuesday?"

"Rock climbing." Sean burbles with enthusiasm.

"Not you." Diana frowns.

"Oh, Mum..."

"He'll be fine." Les' voice is firm. Diana gives a moue of assent.

"Oh. That should be fine." Mum smiles. "Wednesday, we have other plans. But you're leaving then, aren't you, Ian?"

"Yeah, but it shouldn't be a problem. If you'll drive me down to Edinburgh after, I'll just bring my kit with me. We can all have dinner in the city before I catch the train."

"Not your dad and me. Too long a ride, too soon after the last one. But the rest of you can go."

"What's happening Wednesday?" I quiz.

"A little birthday treat for you, Max." Mum's smile is coy. "Everyone will have to be up early if we are going to finish up in time to take Ian to Edinburgh."

Chapter Twenty-Four

C*ress*
At time for my driving lesson. Max pulls a in a fancy sports car out of the garage behind the house.

"Is this the car I'll be learning on?"

Max leans his head back against the custom leather seat with a small smile. "Definitely not. We'll use the estate Rover. If you decide you love driving, I might let you drive one of the sports cars some other time."

I stick out my tongue like a six-year-old. And he runs a finger over it.

We've turned onto a gravel road near a stone building with a long rectangular paved strip. Max tells me that the structure has been converted into a hangar where Brian houses his two WWI-era planes. The strip used to be a driveway but was lengthened into a runway.

Once we're past the makeshift airstrip, we jolt a bit farther to a large paved area of concrete are in what can only be called a parking lot on the Grant House estate, anchored by a huge corrugated iron shed. "That's where we store most of the cars and all of the maintenance equip-ment," Max tells me, pulling up next to the double doors. "The Rover's in here."

I manage to maneuver out of the low-slung vehicle and sigh, watching Max pull the big wagon out and position it facing toward the road.

"It's old but reliable. We'll start with the basics," he says. "Then you can practice driving around the lot before we take it on the road."

I get in the driver's side and wait for him to come around and sit in the passenger seat to explain how the pedals and gears work. Now, an hour later, he says, for at least the hundredth time, "Let the clutch up slowly until you feel it catch."

I push back against the frustration, check the gearshift to make sure it's in neutral, press down on the clutch, and turn the key.

"Press on the brake with your right foot and shift into first." Max's voice is soft and warm. By now, I would think he'd be screaming at me. Or giving up.

He looks down at my feet, which are pressed against the two pedals. My hand grasps the bulb of the gear shift so hard my fingers blanch. The other clings to the wheel as if it's a life preserver.

"Relax." He strokes his thumb against my neck, under my ear, and I shiver.

"Not a good idea," I snap, pulling away slightly. Can't move much when you're belted in.

He takes a deep breath. "Lift your foot off the brake." I grit my teeth as he goes on, "Now gently let up on the clutch."

We roll forward slightly, and I squeak. This has happened every time. I grunt in disgust.

"Press gently on the accelerator."

I move my foot from where it hovers over the brake and start pressing gently.

"Keep slowly letting up on the clutch until it catches."

And that's the sticking point. I never feel it catch. Frowning, I push on the accelerator and let up on the clutch, but again I stall the engine.

"I'm not meant to be a driver." I put the car back into neutral, push open the door, and scramble out. Max sits on the passenger side and smiles at me.

"You'll get the hang of it," he tells me as he gets out to stretch. Then he walks around the car and slides his arms around me. I know he's using the flurry of kisses to distract me. But I don't care. This is my idea of a glorious morning. Maybe I can persuade him to stop the lesson now. We can pull out the blanket he has in the trunk and make out for a while, although the scent of gorse...

I press my cheek against his chest, the feeling the smooth wax from his Barbour jacket slick against my skin. He smells like black cedarwood and juniper from the Jo Malone cologne combination his sisters decided was his signature scent. It's cold and windy, whipping my hair around and chapping my lips.

My heart plummets, but I know how much it means to Max that I learn to drive. And here we are, the eager teacher and the reluctant, incompetent pupil.

With a quick brush against my lips, Max releases me from his arms and gets back in the car. "Let's try again." He waves toward the driver's seat invitingly. Scowling, I slide in and refasten the belt. "Right. Put your left foot on the clutch."

I purse my lips as he repeats the now familiar instructions. And—I stall out again. Shit. Shit. Shit.

Turning on him and trying to keep my voice level, I ask, "Why am I doing this, anyway? I've gotten through forty-six years without driving."

"You never know when the need may arise." He smiles. "Be prepared, I always say."

"Were you a Boy Scout?"

"No, but I know the motto."

I rub the back of my neck to ease the tension. "Can we stop now? I think we've established I have no aptitude for driving."

"Let's give it another go." His hand snakes under mine, strong thumb kneading and releasing the knot. "If you can't do it in the next half hour, we can stop."

I pretend to bang my head against the steering wheel, whining softly.

Max peers deeply into my eyes. "You're hungry and thirsty. Let's eat the sandwiches my Mum made. They're in the back." He opens the tailgate and fishes out a basket with sandwiches and a thermos.

Instead of sitting out in the wind, we stay in the car. He hands me one in plastic wrap, which I have been told is called cling film. I eye it skeptically as I unwrap it. Thin white bread filled with something green and something yellow. "What is this?" I wave the partially unwrapped sandwich in his face.

He glances at his own sandwich. "Egg and cress on buttered bread." He wheezes with laughter. "Cress. I wonder if my dad egged her on?" He puts his sandwich on the dash as he doubles over.

I groan. Jokes on top of hardboiled eggs. I stick out my tongue. "Back to the driving," I grumble, rewrapping the sandwich and throwing into the back.

Max's eyes widen. "You don't like your namesake?"

"I don't like hard-boiled eggs. Not your mother's fault. There's no way she would have known."

He crams the rest of his sandwich in his mouth. "Do you want me to pick the egg off for you?"

I give an amused snort. "The egg contaminates the cress."

Max reaches for the thermos. "Lemon squash. Okay?" I nod and take the cup from him. After a few sips, I give it back, and he empties it. "Right. Let's try a few more times."

Ten is the charm. On the eighth try, I shift into first, but stall out when shifting to second. On the tenth try, I get into third. By that time, I'm determined to manage all the shifts. Soon I've learned to downshift and I can reverse.

"I'm proud of you, la mia stellina," Max says.

I give him a wan smile. "Can we go back now?"

When we arrive back at the house, I'm so stiff I can barely crawl out. Max grabs my hand and pulls me out and up, rubbing my back lightly before sliding into the driver's seat to park the car in the commodious garage behind the house. When he finally gets back, I say, "Your Dad wants to take me flying."

Startled, Max swallows a few times, then says, "Really? What did you say?"

"I don't want to do it, but I don't want to say no, either."

"He doesn't fly much anymore. Too painful for him."

"Physically or emotionally?"

"Both." He frowns. "Why don't you offer to let him show you the planes. You can even sit in them. But tell him you'd rather watch him than go for a ride. He may be satisfied with just sitting in the cockpit for a bit. When was he planning to take you?"

"I think he's planning on this afternoon. While you're meeting with your office."

The family pours into the hallway cheering as we push in the door. Max gives a thumbs-up and I give a tired but happy smile.

Moving over to his mother, Max puts his arm around her and whispers in her ear. She raises her eyebrows as he moves away, saying, "We could use some tea."

Viktoria turns to me. "I am so sorry, Cress. I had no idea you don't like hardboiled eggs."

"Not your fault," I mutter, my face burning. I'm sure they're all thinking I'm some kind of freak. After all, who doesn't like hardboiled eggs? Besides me.

"No beans and no eggs. You are a picky eater," Ian chaffs me as Max glowers.

"Leave her alone," he snaps.

"A little tease. You don't mind, do you Cress?"

I want to fit in, so I shake my head no as Max squeezes my hand.

"Ignore him, la mia stellina. Otherwise, you'll just encourage him."

Meggy had left the hall just after the cheering. Now she's back. "Mrs. Mac says tea will be ready in a few minutes." Then she herds us into the lounge to await the feast.

After a ridiculously lavish spread that more than makes up for my rejected lunch, Max and JL retire to the library. They are supposed to meet with Clay at ten a.m. Chicago time.

Brian has been nattering about flying and now he turns to me. "Ready for your wee flight?"

Startled, I blurt, "Max told me you didn't fly anymore."

274

"Not much, anyway. But I have two brilliant planes, and I only do quick hops to keep my hand in. No more than ten minutes in the air."

"You remember I don't like heights." Despite my best efforts, my hands are trembling, so I shove them under my thighs.

"I remember, but we won't fly very high. I promise you, it will be a fun experience."

"Can you just show me the planes? Then I can watch you do some acrobatics in the air."

"Of course. I love to show off my girls. And maybe, once you see them, you'll change your mind."

Fat chance, I think. But getting to know Max's father is good reason to go out if not up. I grab a jacket. Brian is already halfway out the door, yelling to Viktoria. "Vik, I'm taking Cress for a visit to the fleet. Be back soon."

"Have fun," drifts out faintly from somewhere.

"We'll walk over to the old barn. You probably passed it this morning. It's what I use for a hangar. Not too far from here." Brian strides off, leaving me in the dust. How does this seventy-eight-year-old man move so fast?

I run to catch up, but eventually I stop and double over, trying to catch my breath. Brian, by this time, must realize I have disappeared because he turns around, looking for me. When he spots me, he calls out. "Cressie, darling. Why didn't you say something?" He trots back in my direction.

Once I can straighten up and breathe normally, we walk at a more reasonable pace to an old stone building just visible in the distance.

Brian throws out an arm. "The barn is from the late eighteenth century. We made the conversion soon after Ian was born. Now the boys want me to sell the planes and turn it into a garage for all of their fancy cars." He pulls open the doors and I can see two planes, a biplane and a monoplane. "The biplane is a Sopwith Pup, and the monoplane is a Bristol M1."

"I take it you're not keen."

"To sell? Hate the idea, but really, I hardly fly anymore." He pats one plane as if it was a favorite dog. "Would be more practical. And Frank wants to buy this beauty off me." He pats the brightly painted Bristol again.

"I call this one Princess. One of two surviving original planes. The other is in a museum in Australia."

"Couldn't you auction it for a lot of money?"

"Probably so, lass, but I'd rather give it to Frank one of these days. Money's not everything. It's a family heirloom. My granddad flew it near the end of the war and somehow brought it home. He was a canny man and never really told the story."

I shut my gaping mouth.

"Something nefarious, I would guess. And, if you read about the few still to be found, only the Australian one is listed as an original and the others as replicas."

My mind is whirring. "Perhaps there are records in your family papers." My fingers are itching to investigate the Grant archives.

"Aye. I forgot you are planning a novel with Uncle Munro in it. Does that mean this plane might end up in your story?"

"Not if you don't want it to. But I'm still not sure whether I'll write his story. Your cousin Desmond doesn't seem too keen."

Brian strokes his chin, still gazing fondly at the machine. "Let me think about it in case you do." Then a broad smile spreads out over his face. "Don't want to court confiscation and end up behind bars at my age. Viktoria would never forgive me."

We push the Sopwith Pup out of the barn. Brian checks over everything, then hands me a helmet, goggles, and a leather jacket. Everything is slightly oversized, and I chuckle, handing Brian my phone so he can take a picture.

He takes one of me and one of the two of us together. I'd title it "The Dashing Pilot and His Beagle." My hair hangs down like Snoopy's ears and my face is hidden by the goggles. The sleeves of the jacket hang below my hands and I push them up as high as I can.

When he hands me the phone back, I text them to Max. No response. Not surprising since he's probably still meeting with his GSU colleagues.

Then we sit in the plane and he explains the controls. I don't take much in but it's fun to just sit there, watching how much he enjoys telling me about the the plane and some of his flying experiences.

"Well, at least you can say you've sat in a vintage plane." His deep, rolling laugh reverberates around the barn as we push the plane back inside.

"Cuppa?" He points to a neat area in one corner, with a cabinet holding an electric kettle.

"I'd love some," I say, gratefully.

"Go make yourself at home." He gestures to a few chairs sitting around a small table. "What do you take in it?"

"Some whisky." I'm joking, but he takes me seriously.

"Right you are." He comes back a few minutes later with two mugs redolent with the aroma of a good single malt, hands me one, and sits down heavily with the other. "Can't do that very often, lass. After a few minutes, the pain really hits."

From the way he looks at me, my face must have guilt

written all over it. "I'm glad I can do a few minutes. But I think the boys are right and it's time to pack it up. Frank's birthday is coming in June, so we'll make the Bristol his gift, and I'll donate the Pup to the National Museum of Flight. They have nothing like it in their collection."

He looks at me, his bright blue eyes clouded. "Well, enough palaver about the planes." He exhales heavily. "Now, Cressie, I want to have a little talk."

Unreasoning fear makes hot pain shoot through my chest. I take a deep breath. His family has given me no reason to think they don't like me. My mouth is as dry as the Mojave.

His brow furrows. "I'm that worried about Max."

"Why?" I gulp from the mug I've been cradling between my palms unable to suppress a yelp when I realize it's hotter than the first taste led me to believe. The liquid scalds my lips. "Is it me?" Shit. How did that slip out?

"What? No? What gave you that idea?" Brian is a perfect illustration of flabbbergasted. "Crivvens. You're the best thing to happen to him in at least ten years."

"Oh." I catch my lower lip between my teeth to keep them from trembling.

"Two things worry me. One is the toll his job takes on him. The other is this terrorist nonsense. Max may make light of the whole thing, but he's at the cracking point. And none of us want him back in that place near Cambridge."

The memory of Max telling me about the motorbike crash, the therapy, the counseling washes over me, wave after wave. "I think he's frustrated he can't do more about it. And MI6 seems to want him as a staked goat."

"Allan Mason is a bawbag."

I'm not sure exactly what that means, but it's definitely not a compliment.

"He went to school with Max, and they never got on. Looks like they still don't." He pauses for more tea. "Shame too. His brother went to school with Ian, and they were best mates. Max and Allan, though, oil and water through and through."

"I don't know what to tell you." My fingers twist. "You know how close-mouthed Max can be."

"Always good at keeping secrets. It's what made him so good at his job. Well, nothing to be done. Events are going to play out, however. I hope, when we're on the other side, Max will take some time off. The two of you need a good long holiday, or maybe a honeymoon."

"With the problems at his company I don't imagine that happening. This meeting he's in is all about getting updates on their current software problem."

Brian explodes. "That's what I mean. He's never away from it. I have a mind to talk to Clay Brandon myself."

"Max wouldn't thank you for the interference."

He runs a hand over his face. "You're right and I won't. But once a dad, always a dad." He picks up the now-empty mugs and puts them on the countertop. "Let's go back and find out what everyone's up to."

"I meant to ask about Max's birthday surprise."

Brian, now in a better mood, smiles. "Driving. We're taking everyone to the track. And now you know how to drive, you can take one of the cars."

I knew learning to drive was a bad idea.

Chapter Twenty-Five

M^{ax} When we pull up to the Lohan Beinn Hotel near Aberlour, I'm gobsmacked. Familiar with the elegant country house hotel, I can't imagine why we've made the half-hour drive here.

"Lunch?" I suppose if this is my belated birthday treat, a meal is not out of the question, although ten-thirty in the morning seems a bit early.

"We could have lunch here," Meggy throws out doubtfully.

"Racing." Mum grins at me.

Dad fills in the gaps. "The Robertsons have turned some of the land into a private racetrack, designed to be like the original Brands Hatch track in Kent."

We troop into the hotel lobby, where we're greeted by Graeme Robertson in a thick Glaswegian accent. "Nice to have you and the family here to try out our wee track, Mr. Grant."

"Good to be here, Graeme." Of course Dad is on a first-name basis. "I keep telling you to call me Brian. Unless you'd prefer Wing Commander," he jokes.

"Of course." For a moment, Robertson looks slightly uncomfortable. Maybe he feels a certain deference is due. Dad would roar at that. We all wait, as if Wing Commander might pop out at any moment.

Then Robertson comes over and claps me on the back. "You're the birthday boy?"

I wince, then force a smile. "That's me."

"We'll make this a birthday to remember."

"What made you decide to put in the track?" I ask to break the awkward pause well as pure curiosity. This area mostly brings in tourists to fish and shoot, as well as to climb. Not that motor sports aren't popular.

"Too much competition for the shooting and the salmon. Turns out there's a fair few people looking for a bit of track driving when they're on their holidays."

"Why did you choose a Brands Hatch type of design?" Frank wonders.

"Well, we lived in Kent for a while before we moved back north, and it was local to us. Familiarity, eh?" With a smile, he goes on, "Compact, so it fits well into the space where we used to offer riding. If our guests want horses, there's a good stable not too far away. We turned the barn into a garage, and the cars are all classic Mini Coopers."

"Ah, so we can pretend we're in *The Italian Job*." Ian's delighted crow resounds around the foyer.

Six cars are parked at the start. "Who wants to drive besides the birthday boy?" Robertson asks.

Meggy raises her hand, then Ian, Frank, and Les. JL nods.

"I'd rather sit with Mum," Diana declares, and Liz agrees.

"How about you, Cress? Put your new driving skills to good use."

Her eyes glaze in horror at the idea. "Forget it Max. I don't think my one driving lesson gives me the skill to go out on any kind of track."

"We have enough drivers. You can ride shotgun." I'd like her to say yes, but then again, the idea of her cheering me on from the sidelines is pretty good, too. The small grandstand will give the perfect view down the top straight.

"Perfect. Six of us and six cars." This is one of the best presents ever. "Thanks, Dad. Thanks, Mamoushka." I give them each a hug.

"I'll join you." I whirl around at the familiar voice.

"Of course you will, Allan." The man is like a yo-yo, homing in everywhere we go. "You can ride with JL." They have identical disgruntled expressions. "Do you want to ride with someone, Dad?"

"Wish I could but I'm feeling every ache today. Too many travel days are taking their toll, and those small cars..." My heart breaks at his wistful expression. Then he straightens up as only a former military man can. "Maybe I can manage one turn around before we start."

"Of course, Wing Commander," Robertson says cheerfully. And there it is. Dad grins from ear to ear as Graeme Robertson, all-mine host affability, leads us out through the lounge and out the back of the hotel.

We gape at the track. Its design almost perfectly replicates the well-known 1960s venue, with its boomerang shape. A long top straight leads into a bend that becomes a steep rise before a hairpin turn. The bottom straight is more like a curve bracketed by two bends, while the loop takes the driver back to the top. With a length of about 4.25K, it looks to be a fun, somewhat challenging ride.

"You can do five warm-up runs and then twenty circuits if that suits," Graeme tells us.

"Perfect. And lunch after?" Dad checks all the arrangements are in order.

"Yes, we've laid on a special meal for you all. Wait until you see the cake. My Lucy is a dab hand with cake."

When Mrs. Robertson arrives with a pile of cushions, her husband rushes over and grabs them before they can topple to the muddy ground. "Sorry I was so long. Guests checking out."

"Lucy, come meet the Grant family. You know Brian and Viktoria, but these are their children and grandchildren."

"And a couple of interlopers," JL interjects, exaggerating his French-Canadian accent.

She wipes her hands on her flowered pinny, face creasing into a wide smile. "Nice to meet you all. I'll go back to supervising the lunch preparations now. Enjoy the driving." She turns and walks back to the house, carefully avoiding the puddles from last night's rain.

We make sure the spectators have enough seat cushions to be comfortable, then walk over to the choose our vehicles. They are not all original colors, but we don't care. The cars on offer are dark blue, light blue, white, beige, red, and green. Ian immediately plumps for the red, edging out Meggy, who pouts.

"Not fair." She shakes her fist at Ian.

"If it had been pink, I would have let you have it," he taunts.

Meggy's frown is her only response as she moves to the powder-blue car.

"Take the green one," Cress calls out to me. I throw her a small smile and climb into the car painted her favorite color. Unexpectedly, Allan slips into the passenger seat.

"I told you to ride with JL," I snarl.

"Too bad. I'm riding with you so we can talk."

"Talk?" I can't believe he thinks I can drive on the track and talk or even listen. "Not the time nor place," I grunt. "Why don't you go sit in the grandstand and we can talk later?"

He shakes his head and folds his arms across his chest, looking straight forward.

Graeme comes over and hands us helmèts. "Safety first."

Allan puts his on and straps in with the required seat belts Robertson added to the cars. I do the same, pull down my visor, and start the motor. The noise of the supercharged engine drowns out anything he might try to say.

We start the warm ups, so we have a feel for the track and make sure the cars are ready to go. After the second time round, Dad struggles out of Meggy's car. We take three more, then line up at the start and wait for the signal.

My car has been going well and I'm neck and neck in the lead with Les, who surprises me with his skill. On the tenth circuit, we are coming down from the rise and into the hairpin when there's a sharp crack and the car starts to wobble. I grip the wheel tightly, trying to hold on course. I look around but on the side there is a deep culvert to separate the track from the woods beyond. Nowhere to pull off here. There is a roaring in my ears and a persistent stabbing in my chest as I try not to panic. Allan's mouth is open, but if he's making a sound, I can't hear it.

I wrench the wheel to avoid the culvert and we slew across to the barrier on the other side. Then I yank it back the other way to keep from crashing into the corrugated iron as I pump the brakes desperately. But there is no response. Before I have time to do anything else, my head snaps back against the seat. Pain radiates down my neck as the car slides hits the metal and bounces back toward the center of the track. It flips twice and lands upside down. We dangle, trying to release the belts.

"What the hell do we do now?" Allan yells.

Fighting to keep calm, I give him my standard flip response. "Hope your neck doesn't break when you drop."

~

Cress

A loud bang brings us to our feet. Then silence. A scream rises in my throat, but I swallow it. Everyone is frozen. All we can see is a plume of smoke from the other side of the track, which is soon displace by flames and then an explosion. A sick feeling comes over me. What if something has happened to Max? Not that I want it to be someone else, but but my thoughts are all of Max. I can almost see him, trapped in a burning car as it explodes. Tears are running down my cheeks but I can't be bothered to wipe them away. I feel a hand squeeze my shoulder. Through bleary eyes, I see that Brian has one hand on my shoulder and the other on Viktoria's. He's saying something, but the words are garbled. This is my worst nightmare come true.

I'm sitting in the middle of the row and I try to get out so I don't lose my breakfast all over Viktoria, who is sitting next to me. She grabs my wrist. "Just stay here, Cress, until we know what happened." I nod and try to will my rebellious stomach to behave.

Graeme Robertson jumps into a golf cart at the side of

the track and starts driving toward the sound, steering with one hand while clutching a cellphone in the other. The wail of sirens is nerve-shattering as several ambulances tear up the lawn toward the track and disappears around a curve.

I want to run after them, but Viktoria grasps my sleeve. "We will be in the way, I am sure, now that the medics are here. Mr. Robertson will soon tell us what happened."

Before he reappears, a few Mini Coopers come trailing toward the grandstand, none of them green. Meggy's is first. She maneuvers out of the car and runs over to the grandstand. When she reaches us, tears are running down her face

"What happened?" Brian shouts to her.

Wiping her eyes on a sleeve, Meggy says, "One of Max's tires blew at the hairpin curve. He lost control as Ian was coming up and Ian crashed right into him. Max's car flipped upside down." She's wringing her hands. "Then the petrol tank caught on fire and the car exploded." Her mouth opens and closes like a fish, but the only sounds are raspy breathing combined with stuttering wails. Brian, Viktoria, and I run out onto the track.

Someone is screaming *no, no, no*. Turns out it's me. Viktoria hugs me, our tears mingling.

Brian stands on the tarmacked track, and he enfolds his trembling daughter in his arms. Meggy is always so collected but now she is shattered.

In the grandstand, Lucy Robertson is sobbing. Diana and Liz, arms around each other, emit breathy gasps. Sean has collared the kids into a circle, eyes big with confusion, Felicity whimpering for her dad. Graeme Robertson chugs up the track in the golf cart. Ian, Frank, and Les are with him. Ian, disheveled, appears uninjured.

Frank grabs his daughter, hugging her tightly. "It's okay, Lissy." Gradually she quiets against his chest.

Max and Allan are not with them. A chill settles around my heart. Pain radiates through my chest and I feel my legs give way. Strong arms grab me. Dimly I hear Ian telling me something. I register the urgency, but not the words. I subside into noisy sobs.

Brian has slipped a pill bottle back into a pocket and rubs his chest. Then he abruptly sits down on the ground, while Ian pats my back gently.

The uneasy silence breaks as the ambulances reappear, then turn to race across the lawn the way they came, and out of sight. Their howling sound lingers in the air long after we lose sight of the vehicles. Once the noise has dissipated, Graeme yells out, "They're on the way to Dr. Gray's Hospital. You can meet them there."

"Are they alive?" Brian calls out.

Robertson jogs up, out of breath. "Your boys managed to pull them out before the car blew. Thank God."

I sag into Ian's arms, relief making me weak. Mrs. Robertson has gone back to the house, and now comes out with a bottle of whisky and glasses. "I think a drink will do us all good," she says.

Once everyone is more composed, we decide that JL and I will go to the hospital with Les. Everyone else will go to Grant House.

Brian, however, insists on going along. A tearful Viktoria remonstrates, pointing out that he's just taken his heart medication, but eventually agrees to go home and make sure there is a comfortable place for Max and Allan. She kisses Brian's cheek as he turns toward Les' vehicle.

Sean protests loudly. I'm touched by his concern for his

uncle, until he clarifies that it is all about the excitement and possible blood.

Exasperated, Diana chides him. "Really, Sean, this is too much. No matter how injured your uncle might or might not be, you wouldn't see anything. In fact, you'd be a nuisance. Get into the Rover and drive back with your grandmother and Aunt Meggy. I'll go with Uncle Frank."

Les leads the way to his SUV, and we take off north toward Elgin and Dr. Gray's Hospital. For the not-quite half hour drive, silence reigns while we are all occupied with our thoughts and fears.

As we pull up, Brian points to an impressive early nineteenth-century building topped with a short tower capped by a cupola. "I wasn't expecting anything so old," I say.

"The town built it in 1819, using a bequest from Dr. Alexander Gray. I'll tell you all about it one of these days."

Distracted by my fears for Max, I flap my hand in agreement as Les parks.

I bolt from the car and start running toward the building. JL easily outstrips me while Les stays back with Brian, who isn't moving too fast today. He seems to have aged ten years in the last hour.

When we arrive at emergency, we almost collapse in relief to hear that Allan is having a broken wrist set and Max has a minor concussion and bruises. The fact that they are still alive seems a miracle. We don't even mind sitting in the hard chairs, drinking bad coffee while we wait for them to be released. After a couple of hours, we take them home.

Max is silent during the drive in Les' SUV. Allan is uncharacteristically voluble.

"I'm pretty sure someone shot out a tire," he tells us.

JL jerks his head toward Allan. "What makes you think so?"

"I heard a ping before the tire blew, maybe two. There may have been more than one marksman."

I stare at him, puzzled. "Why not shoot into the car? Isn't that what they do in the movies?"

JL squeezes my hand. "I'm guessing the shooter wants it to be ruled an accident."

My cell ringtone goes off. Viktoria.

"Cress. How is Max?"

The phone is on speaker, so Max answers, his voice hoarse. "I'm fine, Mamoushka. A little the worse for wear."

"Thank God," Viktoria says in Russian. Her ragged breathing slows. "The police questioned everyone at Lohan Beinn. They'll come back to speak with you and your friend tomorrow."

Max grumbles. "Fine. Not that I can tell them much."

Max is settled in the library in time for Ian to say goodbye before he takes off. Liz is driving him down to Edinburgh to catch the train. A crash announces he has dropped his case in the hall and a creak announces his arrival in the darkened room. Clomping over to the couch where Max is lying, he drops to his knees and takes Max's hand.

Then he turns his head toward Allan, who perches on one of the lounge chairs, his cast resting on the arm. "Was it an accident or was this terrorist shooting at Max?"

Allan grimaces. "Probably the latter, but we won't know until the reports are in."

"How would he know where to find us?"

"If he knew Max was coming up to Scotland, then he might have been the guest staying at Lohan Beinn. Once your parents made the arrangements, I'm sure word got around in the area. Mr. Robertson may have mentioned it to one or two people. The event was only secret from Max, after all."

"So you think Nasim Faez is here?" The tremor in my voice shows how scared I am.

"Not necessarily. He may be in contact with a terror cell in the area." Allan looks at me gravely. "I still believe he is pulling the strings from somewhere in Turkey."

Ian leans down to give his brother a hug. "Take care, Max. I'm traveling back with Allan. I'll let you know what the police and the insurance say about the house."

Max touches his arm. "Lucky you." His voice is pure acid. Then he manages a smile. "Thanks, Ian. Have a safe trip."

"I'm safer than you," Ian retorts.

Max groans, and I pull Ian aside and give him a quick peck on the cheek. He and Allan walk out the door and I pull a chair over near the couch and slip Max's hand into mine.

With a sigh, Max slips into a half sleep.

On our last day in Scotland, I've escaped to the 2500-square-foot rectangular brick and glass early nineteenth-century conservatory. My condo would fit inside two and a half times. I'm not here to write. I gave that up on the first day. After I check up on Max, who is recovering well, I curl up on one of the white wicker couches with a book to read, but I haven't even tried to open it. My phone and earbuds are untouched on the glass-topped table next to me. I'm here to be alone. To hide out.

We've jettisoned our plans for visiting clan castles and

whisky tasting at Aberlour. It's raining, so no impromptu cricket or croquet for the kids.

No dolls' tea parties with Liz's girls. No neighborly cocktail parties with too many neighbors and too few drinks. If I took baths, I'd immerse myself in bubbles, knowing I'd have a modicum of privacy. Taking a shower of comparable length would have someone banging on the door. Probably Max.

I'm hit with a pang in my chest. Max is lying down in the library. I'm sure Viktoria checks up on him every few minutes. Fortunately, his injuries were slight since tomorrow we leave for Paris.

I was expecting the entire week to remind me of British golden age mysteries set in English country houses between the wars. The reality has been quite different. I want to make sense of everything—the threats to Max, what being part of his family means, whether we will spend most of our time in Chicago, or we will chunk if life up among different geographic points. I'm not used to taking other people's priorities into consideration and the learning curve is endless.

Curled up, a Grant tartan throw loosely over my legs, I luxuriate in the humid heat and the peace of my refuge. Incessant pings from large raindrops sound from the glass roof soaring thirty feet above the slate tile floor rather than a gentle plop. I wonder if the noise is from hailstones.

No little white ice pellets are visible. Water sluices down the floor-to-ceiling glass windows that nestle between brick piers. A huge eucalyptus I didn't notice before scents the air with a refreshing medicinal perfume. The fragrance is welcome in relieving my perpetually stuffy nose. They dotted a few wicker pieces around. No flowers, thank God.

I rub my nose as I imagine a massed display of histamine-inducing predators lurking in corners.

At the snick of a door latch, I assume one of kids is calling me for some meal or event. Ian's gone, but everyone else is still here. We all decamp tomorrow. Max, JL, and I are flying from Edinburgh. Everyone else is going back to London, leaving Brian and Viktoria empty nesters once more.

"How are you, la mia stellina?" Max's rich baritone holds a note of anxiety

"I'm fine," I tell him. "But you..." I pause, looking at his pinched expression. "Are you in pain?"

He echoes me. "I'm fine. It's only a minor concussion."

I stretch and unwrap myself from the throw, preparing to move. "Is it time for another meal?"

"No. You can sit back down. I want to talk, nothing else."

I scooch myself up to give him some space. He sits down awkwardly. When I focus on his face, instead of eyes frosty with pain, his are the gray of soft clouds.

"Marry me," he blurts.

My heart stutters, focusing on the silver strands that streak his blue-black hair. He's my own Lord Peter Wimsey, wooing Harriet Vane in a Scottish mansion rather than an Oxford college. My slightly wounded knight, clad not in shining armor but in a heavy gray cable-knit sweater and black jeans.

My stomach fizzes and my ears buzz. I press my fingers against the tragus in each ear, hoping to relieve the sense of blockage. With a rising sense of panic, I see his lips moving, but I can't hear anything he's saying. I lift a shaking hand and cover his mouth with my palm.

Time stretches and compresses over and over. Icy chills run through me.

The rough pads of Max's fingers stroke my cheek. Slowly, sound penetrates; soft murmuring infiltrates my returning consciousness.

"Cress?" The urgency in his voice sounds like a combination of concern and anxiety with a raw, sandpaper edge.

"I'm not sure I heard what you said after you asked me to marry you."

His eyes crinkle at the corners, and his lips bow in a small smile. "That was the important bit. The rest was persuasion and justification."

A hot flush works its way up from my chest to my ears. I try ineffectually to fan myself with one hand as I push the throw off with the other.

"Well? Are you game? I can't imagine life without you."

"Can't we have that life without getting married?"

"Maybe? I don't know. I know I'm greedy and I want it all. Official. Recognized. I want everyone to know we belong to each other." His voice catches. "Witnessed by our family and friends." Deep coughs erupt, as if they are tearing his chest open. He still has some residual effects from the car fire.

I reach out and touch his arm. The sound goes on and on. I struggle out of the couch. "I'll bring you some water."

He holds up a hand. The coughing subsides slowly and he grabs my wrist, pulling me back down. "Please, Cress. Think about it. Please." He fumbles in his pocket and pulls out a worn dark blue ring box with a gold crest. Inside is nestled what must be another family heirloom.

What! How long has he had this? When did he prepare? How did he know this was for keeps?

"Per sempre, la mia stellina."

I pull the opal friendship ring he gave me a few months ago from my left hand and slide it on my right. He replaces it with an antique opal and emerald ring, kissing my fingers one by one.

"Forever," I mutter just as Les and Sean crash into the room.

"Sunday roast is on the table," Sean trumpets, totally oblivious, while Les eyes us thoughtfully.

We smile and Max helps me up from the couch. Arm in arm, we walk to the dining room, my new ring shining on my finger.

In the dining room, the family is assembled around the table, everyone standing at their place. As we walk in, slow clapping starts. Then whistles and cheers.

"They all knew?"

"Of course they did." He slides his arm around me and pulls me close, pressing his lips to mine. "When you marry me, you get my family too."

"Package deal," Brian calls out. "Buy one, the rest come free."

Chapter Twenty-Six

P*aris*
   Max
   Micki, fresh in from Chicago, greets us with a blood-curdling yell inside the gated courtyard of the Pavillon de la Reine, our home for the next few nights. She's here to attend the awards dinner. Dr. Marten's boots hammer on the paving stones as she jumps up and down. Her blonde hair flies in all directions.

Cress smiles at her best friend, but JL lights up like a bonfire night celebration. A glow of joy surges through me as I imagine the beginnings of romance blooming.

"Ahem!" Allan taps me on the arm. He's like a glue stick. "My contact at the Sûreté, Inspector Poulliot, will be here soon to discussion security arrangements for the awards dinner. Helpful ait's down the way."

I glance around and touch Cress' arm. "I'll check us in."

She looks around, then nods before she moves toward Micki, who squirms out of JL's embrace to meet her.

I turn toward Allan. "What time, exactly? And where?"

He points to a corner of the square. "Carette, over

there." Then he glances at his watch. "About twenty minutes. Enough time to put the bags in the room."

"You're staying here?" MI6 rarely allows such luxurious digs.

"They have tasked me to stay in close contact with you. This is as close as it gets."

"Hmmm." I narrow my eyes. "Should I expect you to move into the room with Cress and me?"

His mouth purses as if he'd sucked a lemon while he delivers his one-word reprimand. "Max." The icy fog in his voice envelopes me like a shroud.

"Not my boss, Allan. Remember?" I snap, as a short, lean man approaches briskly. He looks straight ahead, focused on us. I am immediately on my guard, and I check for Cress. She stands near the entrance to the hotel with Micki and JL. They are staring at the interloper. JL moves toward me, and I shake my head no. The stranger holds out a hand with a disarming smile.

"Bonjour, Monsieur Grant." Head tilted, he studies my face. The corners of his lips curve upward.

"You're early." Allan is grumpy as hell at Poulliot's early arrival. My mood mirrors his. As if walls are closing in and time is getting short.

Allan musters a modicum of politesse. "Max, Inspector Poulliot of the General Directorate for Internal Security." He stands legs apart and braced, arms crossed against his chest, gaze swiveling back and forth from one face to another.

I hold out my hand. "Max Grant." We shake.

Clad in a distressed black leather jacket, T-shirt with obscured text, distressed jeans, and trainers, Poulliot is about thirty-five with short blond hair, fashionable stubble, and red-rimmed eyes with noticeable bags. He rolls his shoulders and crosses his arms, his gaze intent.

"I think we should move to Carette now for a coffee and a chat." He's hoarse and I wonder if he had a late night and too many smokes.

My eyes swivel toward the desk. JL has his arms folded across his chest. Cress shifts from one foot to the other. "May I?"

He nods. "Of course."

As I move toward Cress, JL intercepts me. Puts his hand on my chest. "Everything bien, Max?"

"A little business. I'm going to have a chat with Allan and his friend." I give Cress a little wave to come over.

"What's going on?" she whispers.

"What rock group has four men who don't sing?"

She puts her hands over her face and moans. "Maaaax. No. Please."

"Mount Rushmore."

JL and Micki whoop. Cress does not. I give her a peck on the lips.

"I have a short meeting. Once you're settled in the suite, go on with your plans."

JL smirks. "We're all checked in."

The corners of Cress' mouth turn down. "I thought we were all going to the Carnavelet so I could bore you for an hour or so driveling on about medieval France. Then we would eat eclairs as a reward."

"I'm sorry, darling. The three of you will have to enjoy the history of Paris and stuffing your face with eclairs without me."

"I'm going with you, Max." JL's voice is bedrock. Immovable.

I pull Cress toward me and press my lips against hers.

Hands on her shoulders, I move her slightly and drown myself in her eyes. When I caress her cheek with the pad of my thumb, she leans back in.

"I won't be long, la mia stellina. Enjoy some time with Micki."

JL grabs my arm and drags me over to the two men, who are as still as Easter Island moai. He stretches out his hand. "I'm JL Martin, Max's muscle."

"Inspector Poulliot, Directorate of Internal Security," Poulliot gives a shark-like smile.

JL's quick appraisal is shrewd. "Je comprends."

Poulliot points to a smart café. "Carette is just there, on the Place. It should be quiet at this time of day, and they know me, so we shouldn't be overheard." Underlying the hoarseness, he has the gravelly, smoky sound of Johnny Hallyday, the Elvis of France.

Our shoes scrape on the concrete under the arcaded pavement. A few steps on, we reach Carette, thread through the rattan and wood furniture out front, and claim two small, round marble-topped tables.

JL smiles his approval. "Très élégante."

"Designed by Hubert de Givenchy," Poulliot informs us. "You are French but not French?" He looks at JL, curious.

"French-Canadian. Givenchy. Isn't he a dress designer?"

Poulliot raises an eyebrow. "He designs. That's what designers do—clothes, interiors, c'est tout pareil." After a sip of coffee and a bite of canelle, he leans back and rubs his chin. "So sorry to disrupt your visit to Paris. I understand you are en vacance."

"We are here for a dinner to honor nominees for a prestigious writing award, my fiancée included. At the Victor Hugo house."

Clink. The milk jug hits the rim of Allan's teacup and drags my attention away from Poulliot. A fragment of china falls into the saucer. With a shrug, he examines the chip, then takes the cup back to the counter. When he returns with an undamaged cup, he pours more tea, then starts adding heaping spoons of turbinado sugar. The brown crystals tinkle as they fall in a never-ending cascade that makes my teeth ache as I sip my own tea and look uneasily at the piece of gateau I unwisely ordered.

"Shall we move on, gentlemen?" I can't take my eyes off the whirlpool Allan creates in his cup.

When I finally break the spell, I will him to face me. "Do you have any new intel about Nasim Faez?"

Allan contemplates the sugar that continues to pour into his cup. Poulliot responds.

"We have information there will be a series of coordinated terrorist actions in Paris over the next few days, perhaps like the London bombings. Whether these are being directed by Faez is uncertain. We think, however, one site will be in Place des Vosges."

Clink. Clink. Clink. My fork hits the side of my cup in a staccato rhythm.

JL reaches over and takes it out of my hand. "Calm down, Max."

Poulliot and Mason stare at JL as he puts the fork onto my saucer.

"What makes you think I'm not calm?"

He grins, tapping a finger against the fork. It flips onto the tile floor but we ignore it.

"Fine," I grind out. Gutted, I'm still trying to get my head round this new information, knowing that Cress will insist on going to the dinner. My desire to find a flight, take her back to Chicago right now, wars with building rage to tear this city apart, find this asshole, and end him.

I swallow convulsively. "Is this a general threat, or is there a direct threat against me?"

Poulliot lifts a shoulder. "We can't tell, but Monsieur Mason came to us about the potential threat against you, so I thought it was important to let you know." He studies my face. "I understand you and your—"

"My fiancée."

"Yes. Your fiancée. You cannot be persuaded to cancel for the dinner?"

I let out an involuntary snort. "No chance."

"Une femme tetu?"

"Stubborn? That's an understatement."

Poulliot drains his coffee and pushes his chair back. We all stand. I finish my drink before holding out my hand. "Do we need to go visit the museum now?"

Poulliot is pulling on his jacket. "No need. We will take care of it."

"Thank you for the heads up."

"We will try to circumvent the terrorists' efforts." He moves toward the doorway. "Enjoy your time in Paris, messieurs."

Allan sits back down. I follow suit, while JL gathers up the empty cups. "More?" We nod, and he moves toward the counter.

"I think we should look over the venue, anyway." My eyes move restlessly toward the windows facing out on the green square. "It's just down the walk."

"Still think you're better than the rest of us, Grant?" Allan exaggerates his London accent. "What do you think you can do? Leave it to the French police."

"We're not sixth formers anymore, Allan. Can't you let things go?"

"Why should I? I've always been in your shadow. Even now, I'm the one who has to babysit you."

"I don't need a babysitter."

"If Faez is really out to kill you, then you are our best chance of catching him."

"Cheese in the trap, then. Not exactly babysitting on your part. And if you catch him, you win the cap."

"And the sun shines on me. Finally."

"How do you envision this playing out?"

"I'll be the building, but not at the dinner, discreetly following you. So I'll be there to pick up the pieces if he comes out of the woodwork." Allan pushes back his chair and stands. "I don't think I'll bother with another cup. See you around."

Eyes glued on his back, I watch him saunter out and out of sight.

And I wonder, does he care whether the cheese is eaten if he can catch the rat?

Head in my hands, I draw a deep breath as JL puts a new pot of tea on the table along with his second cappuccino.

I finish the new pot and we head over to the Maison de Victor Hugo to check it out.

≈

Cress

Dinner at the Victor Hugo house museum is an intimate affair for eighty writers, their families, and friends. Luminaries of the literary world are here to celebrate historical fiction and its practitioners are at the perfect place for the Hugo-Dumas awards.

Goose bumps run up my arms.

Yavuz showed up not long after we arrived at the hotel, all smiles, effusive at seeing us all again so soon. I wonder who told him we were staying in the Place des Vosges. While Max went off to his meeting, Yavuz offered to accompany Micki and me on our exploration of the Marais, the old Jewish neighborhood so close to where we are standing now. He made an excellent guide, showing a surprising familiarity with the area. His youngest brother, Emre, was a student at the Sorbonne, so both Yavuz and Tanik spent a great deal of time visiting Paris.

We have extra room at our table, so I invited him to come along. His tux is sharp, his hair fashionably cut. Now, like an eager puppy, he's waiting for us at the entrance to the museum. "London is casual," he says, "but Paris calls for elegance."

Max pointed out Inspector Poulliot, dressed in Hugo Boss, sitting under the arcade at a restaurant in the Place des Vosges with Allan Mason, his shabby Harris tweed jacket, standing out like a sore thumb. I feel marginally safer with them watching out.

Then, once we have given our names in the foyer, the first-floor apartment opens to view. We have no time to admire the carefully recreated rooms as we are herded toward the the Red and Chinese rooms for the event.

Seated at a table for eight, I wish we had a party of eight, but since we don't, another finalist, Honor Ellenford, her husband, and her teenaged son sit with us. I met her a few years ago at a conference. She can't give me the cut direct when we are sharing a table. Her narrowed eyes and thinned lips tell all.

"You know, of course, they renovated the ballroom last year?" Honor drawls.

"Did a bang-up job," Max says.

"Hugh Ellenford." The stocky red-haired man sitting next to Honor rises and holds out a hand. "This is our son, James."

The sullen teenager barely looks up and mumbles, "Hi." The game on his phone is more interesting.

Hugh frowns and sips the Kir Royale set at each place. Honor shrugs.

"You must be Cress Taylor," Hugh says.

I nod. "Nice to meet you."

Max introduces the rest of our crew. "Our friends, JL Martin, Michelle Press, and Yavuz Arslan."

Much to my chagrin, I must spend the evening with Honor. I don't read Honor's books. And she's made it clear in the past that she doesn't think much of mine, even though I doubt she's ever read one.

"Maybe I can leaf through her book and then 'forget' it when we leave," I tell Max in a joking undertone.

"A bit obvious." He rolls his eyes as he contemplates the six-hundred-page book I pulled out of the red leather Longchamps goodie bag.

"Are there personal Sherpas? Or a team of weightlifters?" Micki asks.

"Fortunately, we're only a few steps to the hotel. Perfect planning." Max preens a bit.

JL roots through his bag and pulls out my book. The pages rustle as he leafs through to the end. "Four hundred pages! Why so many words? These books are enormous."

"I'm a lightweight compared to Honor." I glance over to make sure she isn't listening, but she has left the table and is talking to Henri, gesticulating toward me.

"Historical fiction is massive tomes for serious readers," Max says. "Or people needing a doorstop."

The society is giving out four "regular" categories of awards—Classical, Medieval/Renaissance, the Enlightenment through the Victorians, and Nineteenth Century. Then there are two extra categories—Regency and non-European.

My book takes place in the fifteenth century and Honor's from the seventeenth, and they are competing in the same category. Why can't we be sitting with an author who wrote about Ancient Rome?

She comes back for as the first course is served. After an interminable discourse on the mother of the future Louis XIV, rhapsodizing about furniture and the creation of Versailles, I mutter to Max, "Why doesn't she dump Louis and Anne and go straight for the Sun King?"

"Maybe she needs a warm up before she tackles the proper heat."

I swallow a giggle when Honor turns to me. "Whatever made you decide to write about Caterina Cornaro?"

Her condescension almost puts me off the oysters glistening before me. I turn to her with a smile. "I found her fascinating. Married off to the king of Cyprus, who was a Lusignan, after all. Reigning after his death, or murder. Being used as a Venetian pawn. Exiled to Asolo., where she held court. Why wouldn't you want to write about?'

Honor's smile is a narrow crescent. "Well, I suppose it was interesting enough to catch the eye of the judges, although frankly, it was a thin year. Except my book, of course."

"No one would call your book thin." Stuffed would be more like it, I think. Snark, snark.

There are six books nominated in our category. I've read

two, one on Matilda of Tuscany and another on Charles the Bold and Margaret of York. Both were very interesting. In Margaret's case, quite speculative, which is fine in a romance novel. The author made no bones about the bending of historical fact. We aren't writing biography, after all.

James grabs the last slice of bread as Yavuz reaches for it. Rather than eat it, he rolls it into ammunition. As bread pellets fly around the table, Honor slaps James' hand. "Stop it right now or I'll have your father take you outside."

I intercept a stealthy glance from James at his mother. He purses his mouth in defiance and I shiver, thinking about what he'll do next.

Honor's husband heaves a long-suffering sigh as he leaves the table to find a waiter for more wine. A long night is ahead of us.

I had thought my agent, Cal Blackburn, would sit with us, but he is a guest of honor of the president of the society, along with a few other notables in the publishing industry. Cal is a spry octogenarian who has shepherded my books ever since the first one. I wave at him. With a courtly nod, he registers where I am and gestures that he will talk to me later.

Max, Micki, JL, and Yavuz have been ignoring everyone else, comparing soccer teams, and leaving me to the not tender mercies of my colleague. Their bursts of laughter make me wish I could wriggle out of this trap.

"Americans are never true masters of literary expression," Honor says to me.

"Why do you say that?"

"Everyone knows English writers are much more skilled. I remember one of my university lecturers denigrating the skills of American study-abroad students."

My cheeks burn as my knuckles turn white. I had raised an oyster to my lips and my grasp has become deathlike. The oyster liquor slops onto my hand, droplets staining the white linen cloth as I force myself to return the shell to the plate.

Honor lightly puts two fingers on my wrist and I force myself not to flinch. Seriously? She insults me. Then she touches me. This woman doesn't know the meaning of boundaries. I pull my hand away.

"I'm not lumping you into the category of American writers, of course."

"What am I if not an American writer?"

"You're Oxford-educated. Somerville, wasn't it?"

I'm clenching my teeth so hard I'm worried they might crack.

"You went to Manchester, didn't you?" It's a great university, but I'm sure my snarky tone conveys disdain.

"Terrific school for history. Eileen Power taught there."

True, but she didn't teach you, I reflect. Many famous scholars are associated with Somerville, but I don't brag about it. I want to slap her.

"Cress, let's go to the ladies before the next course," Micki insists. She stands and her chair falls backward. A waiter appears to set it right while Micki grabs my hand to pull me up. Honor looks affronted. Are her feelings hurt that she's not included? Or is it disgust as what she decides are bad manners? Her upper lip curls, and she looks off into the distance as if the sight of us is more than she can bear.

As we walk out of the room toward the toilets, Max's impeccably British voice says, "What is it again that you write, Honor?"

Micki snickers and whispers in my ear. "What a cow. I can't imagine she could put together one interesting paragraph. Her droning is putting me to sleep. Good thing JL can be so amusing."

I push back my chair and rush out. I hadn't realized how desperately I needed the toilet. Micki follows and continues her monologue. Her voice bouncing off the tiled walls.

"You are so different from Honor. Is she typical of most historical novelists, or is she an exception?"

"I don't know," I tell her. "But I would venture to say Honor is in a class of her own."

"What's with her husband and kid? He's lounging at the bar like he owns it and James is are acting like he's seven or eight, not a teen. Except for the scowls."

I shrug. "Bored and looking for attention. I'm amazed he isn't shooting the pellets at his mother."

My oysters have been removed by the time we return to the table. Half a dozen oysters have vanished. My stomach gurgles in disappointment.

"When they insisted on taking the plate, I guzzled them down," Max tells me. "No point in letting them go to waste."

"Will you switch places with me?"

Max gets up, napkin dangling from his fingers, and changes chairs, reaching over to swap out the glasses and silverware. No need to worry about the gift totes. They are both going to the same place.

"When you were assessing the loot before, was there anything in there besides books?" I ask JL.

"Some items for the toilette. And a pocket handker-chief. Silk, I think. Perhaps there are scarves for the women. I wonder who provided such generous gifts."

"The organization is prestigious. I assume they don't have a problem attracting sponsors."

"But only for a select group. I don't think it has the cachet of Cannes, or the Oscars, or even the Booker Prize."

"Advertising." We all swivel our eyes to Honor's husband, who has now gone back to demolishing a large serving of sweetbreads. He swallows, pats his lips, and goes on. "The companies give these things because even though this isn't a big event, you will use their products and talk about them with your friends. And they can write it all off as a business expense."

Honor's smile is indulgent. "Hugh is a consultant. He knows all about advertising and product placement."

Talking through a mouthful of onion, he says, "I wish Honor wrote contemporary books. She's a big enough name that companies would pay her for product placement in her books. Same as TV. Can't really do that for the seventeenth century, unfortunately."

"If I wrote a contemporary novel and used brand names like Apple or Coke or Coach or Le Creuset, they might pay me for it?" JL cocks his head, looking like a cross between a sparrow and a vulture.

Hugh shakes his head. "You'd have to be a blockbuster bestseller. Maybe if you sell as much as Dan Brown or someone, it might work. If your publisher could guarantee sales in the millions."

"Fleeting dreams of fortune." I let out a breath.

The microphone at the front of the room crackles to life. Henri, a small Frenchman with a large mustache, stands on a small riser, tapping it. He looks remarkably like David Suchet as Hercule Poirot. "Attention, s'il vous plaît."

The room quiets as the awards ceremony begins.

Before Henri can begin, footsteps sound on the floor of the antechamber. Like boots, heavy boots crashing on the tile. Max's gaze is fixed on the corridor visible through the doorway.

"What is it?" I whisper. "Is something happening?"

My eyes rake the room, expecting Allan and Inspector Poulliot to magically appear. But they don't. JL and Max yo be on the edge of their chairs. Honor and her husband are focused on the podium and James is still obliviously playing games on his phone. Yavuz, his eyes never leaving Max's face, calmly sips wine.

Then I see a glint of metal just past the doorframe and men in fatigues, heads covered by balaclavas, swarm in to the room, automatic weapons waving, threatening us with immediate annihilation. One man strides to the podium and calmly shoots Henri in the head.

As he slumps to the floor, someone yells in French, "Police! Put down your guns!"

A hand grips my arm. But it's not Max. Lips against my ear, a voice whispers, "Time to go, Cress."

A gun presses against my side as Yavuz pulls me out of the room.

∼

Max

So far the dinner has been dull, but I'm grateful that nothing has happened—until it does. The sound of tramping feet from the hallway has me assessing the threat level, but before I can react, armed men have swarmed into the room. A shot rings out and the host of the event falls to the floor.

I jump up and reach to grab Cress, but she's not there. A French SWAT team comes and everyone dives for the floor as they start shooting at the terrorists. I try calling her name, but the noise of gunfire and screaming is deafening in the confined space. We're pinned down and I can only hope that Cress is under the table. I can't see because the table-cloth obscures everything.

Time stretches out and speeds up at the same time, but after what is probably only a few minutes at most, the shooting stops. Cautiously, people start to stand.

I pull the cloth off the table, heedless of the dishes and glassware crashing to the floor. Honor is under the table, clutching James, but Cress has vanished.

"Where is she?" I shout at the trembling figure.

She looks up. Tears streak her face and she looks human for the first time this evening? "No idea," she says, her voice dead. Then she struggles to her feet, pulling her son up. "I need to find Hugh." They stumble away.

I start to push my way through the heaving mass of people as a voice says through the microphone, "Please stay where you are, ladies and gentlemen. We must clear the room in an orderly manner. My men will come around and tell you where you may wait."

I can't wait. I need to find Cress, so I move forward.

JL grabs my sleeve. "Stop, Max," he hisses.

"Have to go find Cress," I grunt, trying to pull away.

"Yavuz took her." JL releases me and I back away—right into Inspector Poulliot.

"Come with me," he says and leads me out.

Once out under the arcaded walk, he points down toward the Seine. "We have a car on the Rue St. Paul. We must go quickly." Then he turns and runs past groups of police, down the Rue de Birague, to a waiting marked Rénault. Allan is leaning against the side, but as we near, he throws the doors open and gets in the back seat. Poulliot slips behind the wheel while I collapse into the passenger seat, quickly fastening my seatbelt.

As he guns the engine, I find my voice. "Where are we going?"

Poulliot glances at a readout on his mobile. "We are tracking your friend Yavuz and your fiancée. He is making slow progress through the traffic, but it looks like he is heading toward the airport."

"I don't understand. How did you know to track him?"

Poulliot glances at me, then takes one hand off the wheel, gesturing at Allan, who is leaning forward, elbows on knees, peering at the GPS system glowing in the dash.

"Allan realized that Arslan was wanted in Turkey as a terrorist, under an assumed name. He had escaped from a medium-security prison several months ago, along with Nasim Faez and eight other men. Evidently he then traveled to London under another identity, before resuming his real name."

He takes another look at his mobile screen. "Once we had those pieces, we started watching his brother Emre. Earlier today, Emre rented a car and left it parked on the Rue Turenne. We placed a tracking device. And now we are following Yavuz, his brothers, and Mademoiselle Taylor."

"Toward Charles de Gaulle, you said. You think they are planning to take her out of the country?"

Poulliot shrugs. "No idea what is in your friend's mind. Maybe they plan to take her to Turkey. Or maybe somewhere else. Wherever they are going, she is the bait to catch you."

"Not Turkey," Allan says. "They can't go back to Turkey. The police are on the lookout."

"You notified them?" I ask.

"Not necessary. They have been looking for him since his escape. He'll take her somewhere near here, I think, where they will have set some sort of trap or ambush."

I glance out the window and see the sign for Bagnolet.

"He's on the A1," Poulliot says. "I'll hazard a guess that they're heading for Goussainville."

"What makes you think so?" Allan asks as I say "Never heard of it."

"Goussainville is one of the ghost towns of France and conveniently close to Paris."

His mobile rings and he has a swift conversation in French. "Confirmed. Not sure why they chose the A1 rather than the A3. It's slower but that gives our guys time to get set up before they arrive. We're guessing that they will go to the chateau. Not only is it an abandoned shell, bu it is in it's own grounds so a bit private."

"I thought you said that the village is abandoned," Allan says.

"The old village is abandoned, although these days it's popular with tourists for day trips. But at night, separated by what were gardens from the other buildings, it's a perfect spot to set a trap. They will see the headlights and know you have arrived. Then we'll see how it all plays out."

"The important thing is to make sure that Cress is safe."

"Of course," Poulliot agrees, but my fists clench as I glimpse Allan's dubious expression in the rearview mirror.

My mind is sorting through all the events since that damned envelope arrived in Chicago. "This whole thing must have been planned well in advance."

"Once we knew where to look, we found evidence that Arslan knew about your trip to Paris for awards dinner."

"How?"

"There was an article in *Le Monde* about the event and

they mentioned you as accompanying Dr. Taylor. We found a message from his brother Emre telling him about it."

My head feels ready to explode thinking about Yavuz and his scheme. And how imbecilic I've been. "How much longer?" I ask.

Poulliot looks at the screen. "Not long now. They are in the Vielle-Village and it looks like they've stopped at the chateau. The team has taken up positions near the cemetary with sharpshooters in the church tower." He makes a clicking sound. "There is a wire in the glove box. Put it on, please. If you can get him to talk, we may have some evidence to help the case."

I slip on the wire and put the recorder, which already has tape attached, under my shirt.

Ten minutes later, we're parked in front of the chateau. Clouds cover the full moon so only our headlights illuminate the scene. Poulliot indicates that I should get out of the car. Almost immediately a familiar voice calls out my name.

"Max. Welcome. I hoped you would join us."

"Where are you, Yavuz? Is Cress all right?"

"Of course, Max." His voice is silky with satisfaction. "We are taking very good care of her." Then his tone hardens. "Tell your friends to be on their way. You won't need a ride home."

"Send Cress over, and she can leave with them."

He laughs so long I think he will never stop. Eventually the sound dies away. "I don't think so. She is my ace in the hole. Once we have you, we'll let her go and she can walk into the village. There is a train there to take her back to Paris."

Cress screams out, "Run, Max! Get away or they'll kill you!"

A slap sounds in the crisp air. They must be close. "Of

315

course we will kill him. If he runs, I will shoot him right now, and then shoot you too."

Cress lets out a moan and I start to move forward.

"Max," Yavuz says sharply, "first empty your pockets."

I pull out my wallet, phone, and a small handgun and put them on the ground.

"Now take off your jacket."

That goes into the pile.

And now the clouds disappear and the moon rises high into the sky, lighting us as if in a play.

Yavuz, his arms folded across his chest, still as a statue leans against a cream-colored late-model sedan. I squeeze my eyes closed for a second, then search for Cress' familiar figure. Emre and Tanik are on either side, guns at the ready.

"I'm sorry for the setting. I would have preferred the alley in Istanbul where my sister died. I always planned to get you back there, but I can't go back there now, so this will have to do."

My instinct is to charge Yavuz. Resisting the urge to pull out the gun strapped to my ankle, I keep my hands visible, fists clenched, nails digging into my palms and play dumb. "Bloody hell, Yavuz. What the fuck are you doing?"

Yavuz fixes his gaze on some distant object, or maybe he's lost in the past. Then he scratches his cheek and swings his focus back to me. In the moonlight, his face is ghostly white, his eyes slits. A chill rises from my feet up to my scalp as I fight to hold myself still. Keep him talking.

"What do you want, Yavuz? I thought we were on the same side."

Yavuz leans against the cream-colored sedan, his body relaxed. "I was never on your side, Max. Never."

I give him a puzzled look. Let him think I'm stupid. "But..." I protest.

"I told Zehra not to trust you. To stay away from you. I knew you would hurt her." He snaps his finger. "And poof, she was dead."

"I didn't kill her."

He moves forward, fists up like a boxer, his head pushed forward, angry red spots spreading on his cheeks. "You didn't set the bombs. And you didn't pull a trigger. But you are guilty." This is a rehearsed speech, prepared for this moment, coldly delivered in a menacing rumble. Then he moves back, arms folded, a malevolent glare piercing through me. Suppressed guilt rises in my gullet and I fight not to gag.

As if he can tell exactly how my body is reacting, he smiles. "Here we are, at the endgame."

A low buzz assaults my ears as I catch the last word. "Yes, the endgame, where we catch the bad guy. So where is he? Where is Faez?"

"You still don't get it, do you?" Yavuz shakes his head as if I am an imbecile. Perhaps I am. At any rate, stringing him along is keeping Cress alive. I'll have to make a move soon. The sharpshooters can't do anything with Cress positioned where she is.

I inhale a stuttering breath. "What am I supposed to get? You told me that you had contacts who knew where Faez was hiding. That he might be in Paris. The plan was to go after him once the dinner was over. Obviously you're working with him instead. So where is he?"

I watch his body shake with mirth. "The joke's on you, my friend. You're the bad guy and you fell into the pit like an unwary tiger. There was never going to be a trap for Faez." His eyes turn black and he pulls a 9 mm Turkish Canik 55 Luger from a shoulder holster under his jacket, tossing it from hand to hand, gazing at me with what looks like pity. "Faez is dead."

This is one twist I wasn't expecting. "What the fuck are you talking about?"

"He burned up in the refinery fire." Yavuz smirks again. "Identifying charred bodies is difficult. Despite what you see on TV, DNA results don't come back in a day, or even months. The government will think he got away for a little while longer."

I allow myself a small smile. "Of course we knew that," I lie. "Just like we knew that you were the one after me."

Yavuz face morphs from cold calculation to raw fury in a second. "Liar." A flock of crows that had been resting the ruins scatter in the wind. His moods are on a hair trigger and I need to make sure I don't set him off. Pitching my voice carefully, I say, "You were very clever to use the attack at the dinner to grab Cress."

Satisfaction spreads over Yavuz's face as he stares me down. "I planned to take her after the dinner, but they made it easier."

He gives a little giggle and goose bumps pop up on my arms and neck. "When Faez died during the escape, I switched my identity with his so the authorities would think I was dead, and resumed my real name. I knew everyone would search for him. The security services have been running around, chasing their tails."

I gasp, outrage roughening my voice. "You betrayed our group in 2003. Your sister died because of you, you piece of shit."

Yavuz shrugs as Tanik scratches his cheek with his gun. "What are we waiting for, Yavuz? Let's punish this murderer."

My head juts forward, the muscles in my neck bulge

and strain. Red mists over my eyes. I want to choke the life out of him.

Then I notice shadows, creeping along the ground. "I cared for your sister." I can't speak. Pain sears my chest from my sense of guilt over Zehra's death. But Yavuz's culpability is so much worse than mine. I wipe my sleeve across my cheek.

"We need to kill the murderer now, Yavuz. What are you waiting for?" Tanik's eyes, black with loathing, bore into me.

Rage builds but my voice is cold. "That was your brother's fault. He betrayed us."

I stare them down, making them focus on me, letting the shadows move unseen. "I should have suspected something when you took another assignment that day, Yavuz. Leaving your sister to die in an alley."

His mouth twists into a sneer. "I've dreamed of this day for ten years. Established my connections. Made sure Tanik and Emre never forgot Zehra." He's not looking at me now and his voice rolls on like the knell of death. "Just killing you is not enough. You need to understand, to suffer, confess."

The hair on my arms and the back of my neck rises. "I understand that you're delusional. Can't admit your own guilt."

His face reddens with fury. "Fuck you, Max. I arranged another assignment for Zehra. She should have been safe. But she refused to take it, wanted to be with you. Mend your quarrel. She cared more for you than for her own family. I tried to keep her safe. You killed her."

He snarls and bares his teeth. "I have been waiting ten years. Now I will kill you. But first, I will make you watch your whore die. The way my angel sister died."

Bile rises from my gut and chokes me. "I don't care what you do to me. But let them go." The sensation of ground glass scraping my gullet makes speech painful. I press my hand to my lips, expecting blood, but my fingers come away clean.

The shadows are now men, standing behind Tanik and Emre. Swiftly, silently, they strike, and the brothers' bodies loosen their grip on Cress and thud to the ground.

Yavus turns at the sound and uttering a sharp cry, aims at Cress. I throw myself forward, tackling him around the ankles, all while yelling, "Run, Cress! Run! Run!"

We struggle for the gun. When it goes off, I'm not sure if either of us has been hit. A is a heavy weight presses down me. Then I feel wetness against my chest and I squeeze my eyes closed, prepared to die.

"Move him off," a peremptory voice orders. Allan. Maybe I'm not dead after all.

I open my eyes as a hand reaches down. I grab on and am pulled up onto my feet. Inspector Poulliot grins.

"You did a great job, Dr. Grant. Distracted them just enough for us to get into place and take them down." He unfastens the wire and puts it in his pocket.

"Where's Cress?" I croak. I haven't seen her.

"Sitting in the car," Allan says. "Go sit with her in back. Poulliot needs to leave orders and I have to report to London. Then we can go back to Paris."

Chapter Twenty-Seven

ress
    We're finally back at the hotel, ready to decompress. I'm still trying to process all of this. Micki and JL have been sitting in the courtyard, waiting for our return. They jump up and hug us when we walk through the gate with Inspector Poulliot and Allan Mason as our escorts.

"Have to change," I groan, brushing ineffectually at my fancy gown, the same one I wore for Brian's birthday. Like the dress I wore to the consulate reception in Chicago, this one is unsalvageable. With this track record, I think I will stay away from formal affairs for a long time, maybe forever.

Poulliot bids us bonne soirée and takes off the car again parked on Rue St. Paul. The rest us pile into the elevator. "Come to our room after you change," Micki calls out as we stand in the hallway as we prepare to go into our rooms. "We'll order room service and chill."

We agree to meet in half an hour. Max pushes our door open and I collapse onto the bed, ready to sleep without even taking off the ruined dress.

Time stands stills as I watch Max stand at the windows, staring out into the evening. The square is silent in the aftermath of the earlier horror. I get up and go to him, put my arm around his waist, rest my cheek against his bicep. His fingers stroke my hair. "I thought I'd lost you, la mia stellina," he says with a sigh. "When the gun went off, I thought I'd died. But it wouldn't have mattered, as long as you were safe."

"Don't you ever say that again, Max Grant. I can't live without you. When I saw you, lying there, with Yavuz on top of you, all I could do was say, let him be all right, over and over and over again." I pinch against his waist. "So don't you tell me that everything would have been all right even if you had died. Because they wouldn't. And I would have died too."

He pulls me to him and drops kisses on the top of my head, then turns me around and unzips my dress, pulls it off, and tosses it into a corner. Then he strips off his tux and tosses it too.

"Even if these clothes were fit to wear, the memories would taint them." He frowns at the pile. "I need to find somewhere to dispose of them. Having them in the room is unacceptable."

I pick up the house phone and ask for housekeeping. When I hang up, I say, "They said to put them in the dry cleaning back and leave it outside the door and someone will come by and collect them."

Max grabs the bag out the closet and stuffs everything from our underwear out, even our shoes. Then he slings it outside the door.

He sighs. "I really wanted to cuddle with you for a bit, but we'll have to wait. Let me do a family text to set up a Skype call." He drops a gentle kiss on my lips, moving away before I can react. "Put on something comfortable. Then we need to have our debrief."

I root around in my suitcase and find a soft French terry pullover and matching pants. Before pulling my hair into a ponytail.

Max looks hot in a blue cashmere sweater that clings to his chest and softens his gray eyes. His jeans mold to his thighs. When he flips his wrist to check his watch, I'm mesmerized by the play of his biceps against the soft fabric.

He looks amused as he notices my longing gaze. "Sorry we can't linger, la mia stellina. Ready to go?"

A pang hits my chest as we walk out the door. "I'd much rather stay here," I murmur.

He threads his fingers through mine as we walk down to Micki and JL's room. Allan is already taking his ease in one of the armchairs. Micki sits on the couch, curiosity gleaming from her eyes.

JL is fixing drinks and hands a whisky to Allan. Then he turns back to the temporary bar. "Anything to drink?"

Max finds an oversized chair and pulls me into his lap.

"A glass of water, thanks." I want a clear head for the explanations. Plenty of time later to drink myself into a stupor. Max asks for a whisky.

Once we're all settled, I can't suppress an inappropriate bubble of laughter. Nothing is funny. Nerves, I guess.

Allan takes a big gulp of scotch, then coughs. "This is what we've been able to piece together.

"The terrorist cell planned their attack in London months ago. We had useful intel, but couldn't unearth the location of the organizers. Yavuz had connected with them in prison, so for him it was a simple matter to persuade them to let him join in and add your street." He runs out of steam, puts down his now-empty glass, and runs his hands through his sparse hair.

"Go on." Max's voice is quiet, his gaze is intent.

Allan nods. "When he left the restaurant, he met Tanik nearby. They used their mobiles to detonate the bombs and strolled off." He stares off into space.

"And Paris?" I ask. I have to know whether Max was the target there, or if it was me. "Did anyone die?"

"Several people," JL says. "The president of the society, but you saw that. Your agent, Cal, Cress. A few other guests. Some wounded, including Honor's husband."

I choke on my water. Poor Honor. And poor Hugh. "Is he ok?"

"Superficial," Allan says, flatly. "Poulliot called with an update a few minutes ago."

"Did Yavuz arrange the attack at the dinner?"

"The Paris attack was fortuitous. I only heard rumors about it two days ago. The target was the president of the society." Allan gets up and pours more whisky into his glass, along with a tiny splash of water.

My mouth drops open. "Why target Henri? He was a pompous snob but harmless. And poor Cal."

"They were collateral damage." Allan's dismissive comment raises the hair on the back of my neck. He is such an unfeeling bastard. I don't know what to say. In the end, I say nothing but my glare could start a forest fire.

Allan crosses his legs, leaning back in the chair. "Yavuz set up the attack so he could grab you, while making it look as if the attack was on the event. He knew Max would chase after you. I think the plan was to kill you to make Max suffer more before dispatching him. His hatred after his sister's death festered over the years."

Max frowns at Allan but instead of responding, he

maneuvers us out of the armchair. His rumbly baritone is hoarse. "Sorry all. We're Skyping with my family in a couple of minutes. Let's all meet for breakfast in the morning." He pulls me closer. Brushes his fingers against my cheek. Then we leave.

Back in our suite, we spend an hour on Skype with the Grants, reliving the past few hours. Their parents have put all the kids to bed in their respective houses, except for Sean, who sits silent, eyes enormous, between his thunderstruck parents. I don't know if Les and Diana even realize he's there. We talk until late, Max's family trying to wring out every detail.

Exhausted, we curl around each other in bed, Max's warmth lulling me to sleep.

When we show up for the breakfast buffet, JL and Micki are already chowing down. JL waves his fork and calls out, "Need to keep up our strength before all hell breaks loose."

"What does that mean?" I ask.

"The American, Canadian, and British consuls have called a meeting for us. Then Max and I have a video conference with Clay and Metin. Then I can escape, but Max has a second one with Jarvis about the cybersabotage."

With everything else going on, I totally forgot about Max's problems at GSU.

"I think I'll spend the day writing." Tomorrow we are going to a hastily planned memorial service for Henri. But, if I could, I'd leave Paris today. A city that I love has been tainted and I'm not sure I'll ever be able to come back.

Micki opts for a sightseeing tour out to Versailles. She begs me to go with her, but I just want to hole up in our room and brood.

After a room service dinner, Max and I are ready to

turn in early. But first, Max fills me in on his GSU meeting. "They think they have a bead on the saboteurs."

"Even the internal person?"

"I think they've narrowed it down, but they need more evidence. And rewriting the software and protecting the existing version is taking a lot of time." His gusty sigh is a combination of exasperation and frustration. "Then there are the clashes between Jarvis and Elizabeth Talbot. But Jarvis has all the authority now and I will just get periodic updates."

"I was thinking that maybe we should just go home after the service. I can contact the conference organizers and tell them that I can't come. I'm sure they've seen the news and won't be surprised.

Max shakes his head. "I think we should take our trip on the Orient Express and try to enjoy Venice. The break will be good for you. And you can still cancel the conference if you want."

My mouth drops open. When I recover myself, I get up, pacing and mutter, unsure about what to do.

Max clears his throat and I notice that his hands are clenched. "If you hate this, I'll book a flight to Chicago for tomorrow."

I relax slightly, having made my decision.

I throw myself into his arms and cover the parts of him I can reach with kisses. Maybe surprises aren't so bad after all.

Max

The service for Henri is low-key but attended by many literary luminaries, but Honor didn't come. I heard that she and Hugh decamped to London with James as soon as possible. I didn't blame her.

People congratulate Cress on receiving the award for the best historical novel in the pre- and early modern category and a representative of the society assures her that they will send the award, an engraved crystal plate, to Chicago.

A small woman in a vintage Chanel suit too big for her tiny frame hovers on the fringes. Cress leads me over to meet Henri's mother. When I turn away, I can feel moisture gather in the corners of my eyes.

On our final day, we take say goodbye in the hotel lobby. JL is flying to Vancouver to spend time with his mother and Micki is going with him. She is coy, however, and won't confirm whether they are actually starting a relationship.

"Too soon to know. Right now, my only goal is to have a good time." She waves a hand dismissively, then stares at her fingers. "Crap, I need to have my nails done." She calls out to JL, who is standing near the registration desk with Max. "JL, are there good nail salons in Vancouver?"

He breaks up. "It's a big city. But don't ask me for recommendations."

Micki kisses me on both cheeks, then enfolds Cress in a huge hug as JL reaches her and takes her arm. "Taxi's here. Good luck with your paper, Cress. See you both in Chicago." With a little wave, they disappear through the entryway.

Allan, a small duffle over his shoulder, walks off the elevator. Stopping a few feet away, he sweeps his gaze over us, then moves closer and shakes hands. "I suppose we may run into each other again one of these days."

I nod. "I imagine so." Allan turns and leaves for the Gare du Nord and the Eurostar back to London.

We have the day to ourselves before we board Cress'

dream train at the Gare de l'Est this evening. We spend most of our just sitting in park until dusk arrives.

"Time we're off," I tell her. "Paris and Venice await. We've come through the crossroads and we're on the right path. Ti amo, la mia stellina."

If you liked the book, think about leaving a review on Amazon or Goodreads (or both). Reviews help other readers discover new authors and few lines or even just a star rating are all you need to do. Thanks.

At First Sight, the first novel in the Global Security Unlimited series is available in ebook and paperback from Amazon.

Chapter 1
Chicago, November 2013

CRESS

I step off the private elevator on the fortieth floor of One Financial Plaza in my new shoes. New shoes—ridiculous, bright-red, three-inch stilettos. What was I thinking? Oh yeah, Everest. Maybe the best restaurant in Chicago. One of the thirty or forty best in the U.S.

As I passed the store window, the shoes lured me in. My willpower collapsed like a condemned building. This is so not me. I've only had them a minute, and they're cheese graters for feet.

A quick roll of my ankle on the slick granite floor reminds me why I don't wear high heels. My arms splay and rotate like a windmill. The shopping bag that holds my serviceable flats and my small evening bag spins off my wrist. One shoe skids away. *Crap, crap, crap.*

The brown kraft-paper bag is a missile that hurtles toward a man on his way to the restaurant entrance. My mouth opens in soundless warning as it speeds toward an invisible bullseye.

Thunk. The bag bounces off his arm.

My evening clutch pops out, wide open. Damn that broken clasp. Change rings against hard wood and granite, spraying in all directions. I drop to my knees and crawl after the quarters and pennies. Out of the corner of my eye, I see him spin. A frown twists lush lips.

"You all right?" A foot in a brogue polished within an inch of its life rests a millimeter from my fingers as I reach for more coins. A shoe, a red shoe, is in his hand.

"Lost something?" He holds it out to me. His rich

329

British accent sends a prickle down my spine. I tip my head up to give him a quick once-over.

A spark flashes through eyes that remind me of a walk on the beach in winter. A face bisected by a high-bridged aristocratic slash of a nose. My face tingles. The tips of my ears are warm. I grab the shoe, drop it on the floor, and hide my face in my hands.

"Fine. Sorry. I lost my balance and the bag escaped." My fingers muffle the sound.

He starts to bend down. His hand brushes my ear.

Zap. I scoot backward.

He straightens up and shakes his hand. "Pins and needles."

With effort, I wrench my focus back to the coins. My good luck charm, a Victorian black opal pendant I bought when my first book sold, slides back and forth against the sanded silk of my shabby chic little black dress. Streaks of fire reflect off the granite floor as it swings. I brush stray discs into the pile.

"Just trying to help."

"I can manage. Thanks, though."

A loud male voice calls out, "Hey, Max. Get in here."

"Half a mo'."

I wave him off. "Your friends want you."

"But..."

"I've got this."

"Sure?"

"Yeah. Go on."

He straightens, turns, walks into the restaurant.

I stare at his back in the perfect gray suit. The color matches his eyes.

The heap of change winks at me. I slip on my shoe and pick them up so no one else falls. Little traitors.

Purse and shoe box stuffed back into the shopping bag, I stagger through the wood-framed doorway.

The tables are all full. I have a word with the maître d' before he shows me to a center table where four people give me a standing ovation. Heat burns my cheeks. The other diners stare, some annoyed but more amused. In fact, complete strangers join in, clapping.

A group of men in elegant suits, ensconced at a round table positioned to enjoy the spectacular view, whistle loudly. My nose wrinkles. Over-aged frat boys.

With my unruly curls and my almost too-thin frame, all these people may wonder if I'm some D-list celeb. I look like a starved model, but the genes tell the story. I have the appetite of a hockey player after a game.

My best friend, Micki, leads the cheers. She is a statuesque platinum blonde, all curves, killing it in a red-sequined dress. My shoes would be perfect.

She glances toward my feet. "Nice shoes. New?"

"Yeah. Big mistake."

"About time you started to wear grown-up shoes."

We wear the same size. I'll wrap them up for Christmas. One pair of fancy shoes, light wear.

Her SO, Sam, is three inches shorter and resents it. My other best friend, Paul, is medium height with a monk's tonsure and average features that are transformed when he smiles. His wife, Ellie, is twenty years younger than the rest of us and short. I'm a giant next to her. She has long purple and pink hair with nails to match and a sharp, foxlike face.

The staff stare, wide-eyed, jaws dropped. I mouth an apology.

"Sit down already," Sam growls. He's dressed in an untucked plaid shirt and dark jeans. His gut hangs over his belt. I wonder how he even got in.

I slide into the chair pulled out by the table captain and check out the room. Enormous windows showcase the city. My best friend has done me proud.

I shoot a look at Sam.

"What? The only rule here is shirt and pants." A grin splits his face, and he pulls out an oversized clip-on bow tie. "Miche worried they might not let me in without a tie, so I brought this just in case."

He waves the red clown tie festooned with yellow, blue, and green polka dots in my face, clips the monstrosity to his shirt pocket like an obscene boutonnière, then runs his fingers through his sparse, straw-like hair.

"How many times do I have to tell you that a miche is a large loaf of bread?"

"You're tellin' me that's not a compliment? Bread is the staff of life." He smirks.

"Stop it." Micki raps his knuckles with her talons.

"Just teasin'." His fake drawl makes me cringe.

The rest of us sit down just as the sommelier comes over with a bottle of *Veuve Cliquot*, which she pours with a flourish.

Micki lifts her glass. "To Cress. Congratulations on being nominated for the most prestigious award a historical novelist can win."

"To Cress." They all lift their glasses and drink.

The server comes over. She seems slightly taken aback when she looks over our table, head slightly lowered, a glance from the corner of her eye. Her hand sweeps the air over the unopened menus. "Ready to order?"

Paul takes over. "We'll have the tasting menu with wine."

"All of you?" She picks up the menus, almost as if she wants to hide behind them.

"Yes." Paul gestures around the table. "All of us."

Sam's face twists. "Why not a bourbon tasting?"

"Wine. What a great idea." Micki squeezes Sam's hand so hard he winces.

"Okay." The woman scuttles away.

Ellie, Paul's wife, tosses her hair back and sniffs. "What got up her butt?"

"She looks familiar somehow." Micki stares after her. Paul nods.

Sam gives a dismissive wave. "Probably she's worked somewhere else we've eaten."

Micki turns and cranes her neck for another glimpse. "I eat here pretty often with clients, and I've never seen her here.

My spine tingles. The way she seemed to hide was weird.

"What is this award?" Ellie's eyes are bright with curiosity.

My apprehension drains away and excitement bubbles up. I reach for my water glass. My hand hits the stem, and it keels over. Water gushes over the table. Sam gets the brunt of the deluge.

"Christ, Cress."

"Sorry." I put my hands over my mouth.

"You're fire engine red." Paul blots his shirt.

People hover around, mop up the table, hand napkins to Sam, and pour me fresh water.

Once everything is back to a kind of normal and Ellie stops giggling, I go back to my explanation. My hand snakes out for my glass. Micki taps my wrist then moves the glass closer to my bread plate.

"About ten years ago, the *Société des Romanciers Historique*, an international organization located in Paris, decided to start an award for the best historical novel of the year. Not sure why their year is September to September, but anyway..." My voice trails off. I rub my nose.

Ellie goggles. "Do you have to be so pretentious, Cress?"

I catch my tongue between my teeth before I can stick it out at her.

"They named the award for two famous historical novelists of nineteenth-century France."

Her eyes glaze over. Why did she bother to ask if she isn't interested?

"Go on, Cress." Paul rubs his hand over his bald spot.

"Anyway, it's named for Victor Hugo, who wrote *The Hunchback of Notre Dame*, and Alexandre Dumas *père*, who wrote *The Three Musketeers*."

"Why is he called a pear?" Ellie's face looks totally innocent.

Ellie's gaze wanders around the room, but like a homing pigeon, her attention goes back to the group at the window table, lingers on the wolf-whistlers. I glance over. Four handsome men in their forties lounge in the black armchairs and sip cocktails. I peek at the man who faces our table—the guy I hit with my bag. Almost black hair, glasses, a blue Oxford cloth shirt with the top button undone and a tie, loosened. Check him out again. Squint. Can't be sure, but it looks like Balliol. A striking oval face, high cheekbones, and a chiseled, squared-off chin. Movie star good looks.

Micki checks him out. "Hey, he looks like David Tennant with glasses and dark hair."

"Who?" Ellie looks confused.

"Yeah, Dr. Who." Micki throws her a wicked grin.

"Uh..." If anything, Ellie looks more confused.

"Just some British sci-fi. Let it go," Paul advises her.

I pull my eyes away and clear my throat. "It's a really

prestigious award, and I'm one of the five finalists for this year."

"But the pear."

"P-E-R-E. French for father. Now stop being silly." Paul's voice is impatient.

Ellie's cheeks pink. Micki chortles. Sam is glazed over with indifference.

"I'll be on *Morning at 7* Friday to talk about the book and the award." The words come out in a whoosh. I slump and push back the damp curl that clings to my cheek.

Our server hovers at a nearby table. I finish my hurried explanation, and she moves off. When she realizes we've noticed her, a flush rises on the back of her neck.

Sam raps lightly on the table to get our attention and starts an interminable story about an art exhibit where he will show his "found art" installations. I'm a little ticked but not really surprised that neither he nor Ellie wants to know about the book. Micki and Paul suffered through everything while I hid in my cave to pound out words, occasionally creeping out to whine.

On and off through course after course of delectable Alsatian specialties and far too much wine, the fishbowl sensation waxes and wanes. The middle-aged businessmen glance over on and off. Maybe they expect firecrackers next. I catch glimpses of our server, who hovers around the tables near us far more than she needs to. In the end, I shake off the discomfort and celebrate with my friends.

By the time the mignardises and petit fours arrive with coffee, I can hardly move. Our server has disappeared from the room, most of the tables are empty. Paul signals to the maître d'.

"We're ready for the check." He flourishes his black AmEx card.

335

"Your meal has already been paid for." He gestures toward me.

"What?" Paul frowns.

"My celebration, my treat."

Paul and Ellie offer to drive me home to the far north side, way past their own house in Old Town. A bus home doesn't seem like a great idea. Don't want to cram into Sam's truck either.

At home, I put the new shoes in the box. *Remember, Cress, wrap them up for Micki.* I pull the dress over my head and hang it in the closet. I don't set an alarm.

Crack of dawn. My head throbs and my eyelashes glue my eyes closed. Dorothy and Thorfinn jump on my stomach. Double whammy.

"Fuck. Get off." I push them to the floor. Four green eyes glare at me. Dorothy hisses. Bad cat mom.

I stagger into the kitchen and pull a large glass out of the cabinet. A prairie oyster and a couple of ibuprofen are just the ticket with a big glass of ice water the chaser. Dig a bag of frozen peas out of the freezer then shuffle to the chair in the living room.

The pain recedes and my stomach settles. Micki shows up and suggests we go out for a hangover reviver before she drags my unwilling body downtown to pick out a suitable dress for my TV interview.

At Strings in Chinatown, I order spicy tonkatsu ramen to clear my still-fuzzy head. This is probably the third hangover I've ever had, and the worst.

"I may never drink again."

Micki rests her hand on my wrist. "You still have a

pulse. This will pass, and you'll forget all about it until the next time."

"No next time." I pull my hand out of her grasp and hold up it up to stop her. "This is the worst morning of my life."

"Three hangovers in forty-five years is nothing. You'll drink again."

I drop my head into my hands. "No way. Never."

She giggles. "Your birthday is soon—we'll get you drinking again by then."

I pick up the check. My best friend offered to take the day off from her busy law office just to help me, so it's the least I can do.

Acknowledgments

Thank you to my early readers, Kate Nodes Worrell and Pam Gennusa, and my beta readers, Brenda Clothildes and Gay Lynn Cronin. Your comments and questions made this book so much better.

And thanks to my readers and friends for all your encouragement.

.

About the Author

Sharon Michalove writes romantic suspense and traditional mystery.

She grew up in suburban Chicago. She received four degrees from the University of Illinois because she didn't have the gumption to go anywhere else, and spent most of her career at the universityIn graduate school, she met and married the love of her life. They shared a love of music, theater, travel and cats. He died in 2013.

Sharon also loves hockey, reading, cooking, writing, and various less elevated activities like eating cookies and sampling gins and single malts. After spending most of her life in a medium-sized university town she moved back to Chicago in 2017 so she could go to more Blackhawks games and spend quality time at Eataly. In 2021 she accomplished a lifetime goal by publishing her first novel. Unfortunately her other lifetime goal, to be English, is likely to remain unfulfilled.

Keep up to date—subscribe to my newsletter here.

twitter.com/sdmichalove

instagram.com/sdmichaloveauthor

facebook.com/sharonmichalove

goodreads.com/sharonmichalove

Also by Sharon Michalove

Global Security Unlimited

At First Sight

At the Crossroads

Coming in 2023

At the Ready

Coming August 10, 2022

Dead in the Alley (Mystery)

Made in the USA
Middletown, DE
27 May 2022

66180753R00210